GW00541169

FOXED

JAY HOGAN

SOUTHERN LIGHTS PUBLISHING

Trade Paperback ISBN:978-1-99-110404-5

Digital ISBN: 978-1-99-110405-2

Digital Edition Published January 2023

Trade Paperback Published January 2023

First Edition

Editing by Boho Edits

Cover Art Copyright © 2023 Reese Dante

Cover content is for illustrative purposes only and any person depicted on the cover is a model.

Proofread by Lissa Given Proofing and L. Parks

Printed in the United States of America and Australia

For my family who read everything I write and keep on saying they love it all, blushes included.

ACKNOWLEDGMENTS

As always, I thank my husband for his patience and for keeping the dog walked and out of my hair when I needed to work, and my daughter for her incredible support.

Getting a book finessed for release is a huge challenge that includes the help of beta readers, editing, proofing, cover artists and a tireless PA. It's a team effort, and includes all those author support networks and reader fans who rally around when you're ready to pull your hair out and throw away every first draft. Thanks to all of you.

BLURB

FOXED: To be thrown into a state of uncertainty—flustered, bamboozled, bewildered, puzzled, vexed.

AKA, *me*. Jed Marshall. 55-year-old successful classic car mechanic; divorced, mostly closeted, and whose wholly inexperienced bisexuality has suddenly awakened after one smouldering look and said, *'Damn, who's the hottie?'* Or words to that effect.

Cue, Nash Collingwood. 53-year-old scarily smart high school principal; out, gay, confident, and sexy as hell. He's also my daughter's boss. So, not complicated at all, right? Nash could ignite a bonfire with a single sultry look, comes fully accessorised with a charm offensive Churchill would be proud of, an easy-going flattery that thrills my heart far too effortlessly, and an impressive track record with men many decades my junior.

In short, Nash is everything I'm not, and everything I've avoided for roughly my entire life. He's the classic Mustang to my second-hand

Fiesta, that is if you like your Fiesta with a few dents, creaky suspension, unexpected backfires, and a dodgy stick.

The last thing I need is a relationship—especially with a man. I buried that pipe dream a long time ago and a little loneliness is a small price to pay. The festive season and long summer vacation are on our doorstep. I'm finally getting things right with my family who mean everything to me, and I don't want to mess that up.

But Nash doesn't care about my awkward inexperience, or clumsy excuses, or any of my insecurities. Nash only sees *me*. He wants *me*. For the first time in years, I feel alive and sexy and a whole lot more than just a good father and grandfather.

I should walk away, but the closer Nash and I become, the more he fills my grey world with colour, and the promise of a second chance at love I never thought possible.

INTRODUCTION

FOXED: To be thrown into a state of uncertainty— flustered, bamboozled, bewildered, puzzled, vexed.

CHAPTER ONE

Jed

"One more, Poppy. Pleeeeeease." Bridie hugged Tigger to her chest and gave a commendable pout, which, along with her sparkling green eyes and cascade of dark waves, was guaranteed to melt my heart and likely that of every boy or girl she aimed it at in about twelve years' time. Dear God, please let it be *at least* twelve years.

I tapped her playfully on that cute-as-a-button nose. "You're going to give your mummy and daddy conniptions when you start dating, and Poppy's gonna be there to witness every glorious second of it."

Bridie's brow bunched up. "What's a nipshun?"

"Poppy needs to hush his mouth." Abbie appeared through the bedroom's open door and crossed to give me a quick hug. "She's already got Scott wrapped around her little finger. If I left the discipline side to her daddy, she'd have to go to school with a hazardous warning label."

I snorted. "She does have a way about her."

"That she does." Abbie's green eyes danced, so much like her mother *and* her daughter. And with their dark waves, infectious smiles, and similar bubbly personalities, the likeness between the three clutched at my heart like it always did.

"She gets that cuteness overload from you," I reminded Abbie. "For the first few years of your life, you could do no wrong in my eyes. It drove your mother crazy. Then you hit adolescence and I wanted to wrap you in cotton wool covered in barbed wire and lock you away."

"Oh god, stop." Abbie slumped onto the bed and kicked off her shoes with a groan of relief. "I don't know how you and Mum did it. Scott says it only took one smile from me and he was a goner as well, but I call bullsh—oot on that." She smiled at Bridie. "I might've had some moves, but I had no clue what to do with him once I'd snagged him." She kissed a trail up Bridie's arm. "Your daddy talks rubbish sometimes."

"Silly Daddy!" Bridie bounced with unrestrained glee.

Abbie caught my eyes and tipped her head toward the door. "Your shift is officially over. I'll read this one a last story while you grab yourself a beer and relax. I don't know what we would've done without you stepping in at the last minute to mind Bridie." She leaned in and kissed my cheek. "You're always there for us."

"My pleasure." I gave Bridie a bright smile. "We had fun, didn't we, honey?"

"Yes!" Bridie wiggled under the covers and pulled the sheet over her head. "'Nother book, Poppy? Pleeeease."

I rolled my eyes Abbie's way. "She's relentless. Something else she gets from you."

"Why didn't she get the good stuff?" Abbie grumbled. "Like my winning personality and amiable charm."

"Oh, she's got plenty of that." I ruffled Bridie's dark locks and she popped her face out from under the sheet with a broad grin in place. "Your mummy is hiding from her guests," I whispered, and Bridie giggled and disappeared back under the sheet, dragging Tigger with her.

Abbie toed me in the shin. "Damn right. Lizzie Shepherd is doing tequila shots with the head of the English Department. It's bound to end in tears and likely another stain on my rug. Those two have been circling each other for six months and Lizzie is out there flirting like crazy. She'll be mortified tomorrow. Scott thinks I should just lock them in the laundry and let them get on with it. And to top things off, Lance Thoroughgood spilled his merlot down the front of my new silk blouse."

I cast an eye over the cotton tee she was wearing over a pair of slinky black evening trousers. "I didn't think you'd been wearing that at the start of the evening."

"As if," she huffed. "The shirt is totally ruined. You'd think a former national gymnast would have better balance, right?" She blew out a sigh. "If I ever mention hosting the November, pre-end-of-year slash pre-Christmas teacher's party again, please remind me of this moment."

"I promise." I got to my feet and kissed her on the cheek. "Are you sure you don't want me to tuck this little one in and let you get back to the hordes? I can hang around a bit longer until she's asleep."

Abbie shook her head. "Nah, Scott's gonna relieve me. He's the one looking to hide. The spouse's work parties are never much fun, right?"

"Tell me about it." I thought of all the years I'd been dragged along to Tamsin's law firm celebrations. "And on that note, I'll leave you to it."

"At least have a drink before you go." Abbie stretched out alongside Bridie on the bed. "There's a couple of zero and light-alcohol options in the fridge. And there's plenty of healthy food. Remember your blood sugar."

I rolled my eyes. "Like you and your mother will ever let me forget." I leaned forward to press a kiss to Abbie's head, and then to Bridie's. "My two favourite girls."

Abbie blushed prettily, reminding me so much of the teenager she'd been that it almost stole my breath. "Thanks, Dad. Bridie, thank Poppy for looking after you. You're a lucky girl."

Bridie peeked out from under the covers. "Thanks, Poppy."

"You're welcome, sweet cheeks."

Abbie shot me a hopeful look. "I hate to ask but is there any chance you're available to sit for us next Saturday? I know that's usually your day to work on the Cutlass, but it would really mean a lot. Scott and I would like to try and finish our Christmas shopping early this year and beat the December madness."

"Would that be *instead* of my usual Sunday?" I knew the answer by the endearing wince and batting of lashes that came my way.

"*Well* . . ." She added a winsome smile. "We were kind of hoping you might consider both?"

I swallowed the sigh threatening to make itself heard and schooled my expression. The new seats for the Cutlass had just arrived back from the upholsterer, and although I regularly took Bridie on a Sunday to give Abbie and Scott some quality time and me a solid few hours with my only grandchild, Saturdays were mine. Or they had been. Truth was, I could hardly remember the last time I'd got my hands dirty on my own cars. It had to be weeks.

"What about your mother?" It was worth a try, even though I guessed the answer.

"She's hosting another of those lawyer panel things again."

I quashed another eye roll. I held my ex in great affection and we remained close, but Tamsin's legal firm had undergone exponential growth in the last year, and she was increasingly unavailable. Which meant I'd been stepping up more and more.

I didn't begrudge the time—okay, so maybe that was a bit of a white lie. I hadn't at first, but I was starting to feel a little bit like the background wallpaper in my family's life. Not that I didn't deserve the role, having spent too many selfish years holed up in the workshop with my cars and business when Abbie and Ewan were growing up.

Which was all the reminder I needed. "Sure, I can do that."

Abbie leaped off the bed and crushed me in a hug. "You're the best. And just so you know, Helene Blanchet was *very* interested when I told her you were looking after Bridie tonight, so don't be surprised if she pounces on you when you go out there. Just a heads-up."

I groaned and reached for my jacket. "I hope you didn't encourage her." Helene was an attractive fifty-something French teacher at the high school where Abbie taught, and she'd made her interest in me abundantly clear the few times we'd crossed paths. But I wasn't looking for any entanglements.

"Oh, come on, Dad." Abbie lay back down and tried to tuck her daughter into the crook of her arm, but Bridie was having none of it, wriggling free so she could sift through the pile of books still waiting to be read. "You and Mum have been divorced eight years and you've barely dipped your toe into the dating pool. You have to take the plunge sometime. You're a great catch. You don't deserve a tragic love life."

"Wow, thanks for that." I threw Bridie's stuffed giraffe at Abbie's head, and she ducked, laughing. "But I *am* fifty-five, sweetheart. If I'm a catch, it's only because my hips won't let me run fast enough to get away. But *if* and *when* I'm ready to date seriously, I guarantee that you and your brother will be the last to know. I can do without the well-intentioned meddling."

Abbie snorted and kicked my leg. "You're hopeless."

"No, I'm serious." I eyeballed her. "The last woman Ewan tried to set me up with was barely thirty-two. I've got socks older than that. So, thank you for your concern but I'm quite happy with my life."

"But are you?" Abbie's expression turned unexpectedly serious. "I mean, really, Dad? You're in that big house all alone."

I sighed and bit back a sharp reply along the lines of minding their own business and told myself they were only trying to help.

"Sorry." Abbie caught my look. "I just worry. Mum too. She's really happy with Neil and she wants that for you as well."

"And when exactly did my dating life become a topic of family conversation?" I held her gaze. "I *am* happy, sweetheart. I'd be even happier if people backed off and left my love life, or lack of it, for me to handle."

Abbie's cheeks pinked. "You're right. I'm sor—"

"Eeyore, Mummy." Bridie slapped *Eeyore's Tail* onto Abbie's lap and I couldn't help but smile.

"That's a great choice." I ruffled Bridie's dark waves before turning back to Abbie. "I promise you, I'm not lonely. And I'm not pining. I'm happy your mother found Neil, but I'm not looking to be married again. So, you and everyone else can stop worrying about me." I smoothed Abbie's wrinkled brow, earning myself a smile. "I enjoy doing exactly what I want without having to consider anyone else. Your mum and I had a good marriage, and I wouldn't change anything because it brought you and Ewan into our lives. But it was over a long time before we divorced, and I'm not looking to jump into anything serious again right now. Maybe not ever."

Abbie huffed. "Eight years is hardly jumping back in . . ." She trailed off under my narrowed gaze and raised her hands in defeat. "Okay, okay. I'll back off."

I slipped my leather jacket over my arm. "Thank you, sweetheart."

"But don't forget Helene." Abbie's wicked grin reached from ear to ear. "*You* might not be interested, but I'm telling you, that woman has her sights set on you. And she's hot, right?"

I groaned softly. "She's . . . attractive, yes." Helene was, in fact, epically sizzling, especially with that damn French accent, but I wasn't about to tell my daughter that.

"Sooo . . ." Abbie pushed up on her hands and lowered her voice to a whisper. "You don't have to have a relationship to get laid, Dad. Maybe take the edge off. Get your leg over. Whatever. I'm sure those rules haven't changed since the dark ages when you last dated, although you might have to dust off your game—"

I pinched her lips between my thumb and finger to shut her up.

"Stop. From my own daughter, that's just, ugh—" I shuddered. "—wrong on so many levels. So, this is me, leaving." I turned and headed for the door.

"You're just evading the subject." Abbie somehow managed to pout and grin at the same time.

"Too right I am." I held her gaze. "And just for the record, I never said I wasn't taking the edge off on a regular basis."

Abbie's eyes widened. "But . . . who? I mean . . . you never go out . . . how would you even meet—"

"Who says I never go out? I'm a grown man. And this might come as a shock, sweetheart, but I don't answer to you or your mother." *Even if it feels like it some days.* "Bye, Bridie bird." I waved and Bridie blew me a kiss.

"Bye, Poppy."

"But . . . Dad . . .wait! You can't just say that and leave."

"Watch me." I grinned.

"Dad!"

"I'll call you tomorrow." I pulled the door closed on her gaping mouth. The small stretch of the truth regarding an implied frequency had been worth it to see the look of disbelief on my daughter's face. Hooking up a few times a year would hardly be considered taking the edge off to a thirty-year-old. Ugh. *Hooking up.* The term sounded creepier the older I got, which mattered less than the fact I couldn't even remember the last time I'd done it.

Come on. Think. A name popped up. Karen? No, Carole. Yes, Carole. A real estate agent? No, a property developer from . . . nope, no idea. We met at a mutual friend's fiftieth and went back to her hotel for what was—I sighed—completely forgettable sex. *And when was that epic occasion, dipshit?* The party was April, so that made it—I counted off on my fingers. *Shit.* Seven fucking months.

Abbie was right. My love life *was* tragic.

I headed for the conversation and laughter at the other end of the house, taking a deep breath before opening the door into the spacious kitchen and living area where the party was in full swing. With the high school year almost done and long Christmas and summer break about to start, the mood was buoyant to say the least.

Abbie's school employed about fifty teachers alone, not counting the ancillary staff or partners, and it made for a good-sized contingent, even allowing for some no-shows. Thankfully the calm and unusually warm—for Wellington—mid-November evening allowed the raucous throng to spill through the open ranch sliders and onto the patio beyond.

Abbie had made an effort with the decorations. A little early for a real tree, she'd borrowed a large fake one from the school and strung lights across the outdoor pergola to set the festive mood. There were even a few keen partygoers up and dancing, and Adele's silky voice crooning through Scott's expensive sound system brought a smile to my face.

I threaded my way through the crowd toward the kitchen in search of a light beer and some food. My regular attendance at Abbie's school events meant I knew most of the staff by sight if not by name, and quite a few greeted me as I passed, intent solely on sating my hunger before heading home. I loved my granddaughter to bits, but keeping an excited three-year-old distracted and amused while a party was going on a couple of rooms away had meant a long night for us both and I was ready to crash.

I dished a decent serving of curry and rice onto a plate, plucked a light beer from the fridge, and got out of the crowded kitchen as quickly as possible. I made a beeline for the ranch sliders and a quiet, dark place to sit and eat unobserved.

"Jed!"

I'd almost made it onto the patio when the sound of my name, bearing a decidedly French accent, struck a note of dread in my belly. *Oh, fuck no.* Tragic sex life or not, I wasn't about to get up close and personal with a teacher from Abbie's school. Like I needed that shit-show in my life.

Pretending I hadn't heard, I veered left toward the bathroom, skirted the closed door, and escaped into the laundry, exiting through the back door onto a small, paved area that was hidden away from the main part of the house by a tall pittosporum hedge. A white wrought-iron table with two matching chairs sat beside a clothesline loaded with towels and facecloths. Behind that sat Abbie's precious herb garden and a half dozen raised vegetable beds disappearing into the thick evening shadows.

A weak shaft of light from the laundry window fell across the table while the music and a myriad of conversations filtered through the pittosporum to remind me what I wasn't missing. Other than that, the space was blissfully peaceful.

I pushed the container of pegs to the side, making room on the table for my jacket and plate of food. Then I eased down into one of the uncomfortable chairs with a soft groan of relief. The barest whisper of a cool southerly breeze licked at my neck, just enough to cool my over-heated skin, and I closed my eyes to appreciate the moment. Wellington was hardly a tropical climate—read: frequent howling wind tunnel peppered by glorious days and occasional bouts of lashing rain, and you got the picture of a Wellington summer.

To be fair, on a perfect day, New Zealand's cultural hub and the world's southernmost capital city rated up there as one of the most picturesque cities in the world. Wellington was a harbour city, perched on a lake-like expanse of sheltered water surrounded by steep hills and with a narrow outlet to the sea. It could be stunning. It just wasn't often hot, and the unusual stretch of warm weather had caught everyone by surprise, making them antsy.

When I was sure Helene wasn't going to make a sudden appearance through the back door, I relaxed and took a long swallow of beer. Then I scooted down in my seat to study the starlit sky. Calm, warm, cloudless nights were another rarity in this part of the world, and it had been a long time since I'd done something as simple as take a moment to appreciate one.

Alone at last. *Thank God for that.*

CHAPTER TWO

Jed

"A FELLOW ESCAPEE, I PRESUME."

I jolted at the deep voice emerging out of the dark and promptly slopped beer all over my jeans. "Shit." I shot to my feet and almost sent my plate of food flying as well.

"Sorry." A tall rangy body appeared from the shadows of the vegetable garden, and I tried not to gawp at the face of Abbie's boss, Nash Collingwood.

Taller than me by just a smidge, with dark grey waves threaded with silver that flashed in the light. Shrewd brown eyes framed by a fine web of laughter lines. A thin scar on his right cheek close to his hairline, cheeky dimples, and a roguish smile that promised far too much fun to be safe for the likes of me. Nash had been appointed the high school principal six months before, and he was—not to put too fine a point on it—fucking gorgeous.

He was also everything I'd avoided thinking about for—oh, let me see—forty years, give or take. Not that I was counting. Or gawping . . . at him. Nope. Nothing to see here, folks.

As he wandered across, I tried not to stare, remembering with great embarrassment the first time I'd laid eyes on him at a school production. I'm pretty sure I mopped the gymnasium floor with my closeted bisexual tongue. Which came as somewhat of a surprise, considering I'd had that part of me on lockdown for so long I'd practically forgotten it even existed. And by the loud creak and shower of dust that accompanied my dick suddenly coming alive to another man, it had obviously considered I was a lost cause as well.

Which had been fine by me.

For forty years.

Had I mentioned forty years?

Until this man, the one walking toward me with a smile that I was pretty sure could drop my trousers at fifty paces.

"Here." Nash unpegged a facecloth from the line as he passed under, swapping it for the bottle in my hand as I stood there like an idiot. "I'm sorry about startling you."

"What?" I shook a few brain cells free from their persistent ogling of the way his hard, trim body fit into those dark-wash jeans and the rolled-up sleeves of his white shirt revealed smooth tanned skin with just a smattering of hair. "Oh, thanks." I made a half-arsed attempt to dry off my jeans, more than a little distracted by the way Nash's gaze dropped to watch, and then gave up and mopped the chair instead.

"I never knew Abbie had such green fingers." Nash swept his hand toward the vegetable garden.

"Then you're one of the lucky few." I lobbed the facecloth onto the back step to be washed, then turned to face him. "And unless you want to be regaled by her botanical endeavours for a good couple of hours, I wouldn't raise the subject with her. I think she got her interest from me, but she has all the enthusiasm of a late bloomer. Pardon the pun."

He grinned. "Thanks for the heads-up. I'll tuck it away for when I need to get in her good books." His eyes sparkled with warmth, his intense gaze hot on my skin as it had been that first time we'd met, and just like then, I was lost for just a second or two.

"Smart man," I finally managed.

He kept staring. "You're her dad."

"For my sins." I offered my hand. "Jed Marshall."

"Yes, I remember." Nash clasped his hand around mine. "I'm Nash Collingwood."

Like I could forget, and I'd been trying, really, really hard.

But he remembered me? *Shit.* I must really have made an idiot of myself that night.

"Abbie mentioned you were on grandkid duty tonight." Nash's deep eyes remained steady on mine—his grip warm and dry around my hand and with just enough pressure to cause my breath to catch in my throat. "We were introduced in September at the school's spring concert, but we never got a chance to talk." And still he kept hold of my hand, his forefinger gently resting on the underside of my wrist like the tip of a white-hot blade.

Something low in my belly caught fire and I was pretty damn sure it went by the name of temptation.

"Oh." I cleared my throat. "I'd forgotten all about that." A burst of heat bloomed on my cheeks. "If I remember, I had to, um, head away early that night . . . to relieve the babysitter, I think. So that Abbie and Scott could stay." *Lies. All lies.* What I'd actually been trying to do was avoid exactly *this.* Me and Abbie's hot principal . . . in close proximity . . . talking . . . or doing anything . . . or nothing. Whatever.

Nash's eyes danced with amusement like he somehow knew I was lying but wasn't going to call me on it. "Yes, I believe that was what you said."

Which told me that Nash hadn't missed my luminous scarlet face and bumbling chorus of social ineptitude as I'd made my excuses that night and fled the scene. Abbie had even asked if I was unwell.

I'd been avoiding the man ever since.

Nash finally released my hand, which hung in mid-air for a second or two before I finally reattached my brain and shoved it in my pocket. *Could I be any more of a fucking idiot?*

I glanced up at the sky to avoid him catching my look of abject humiliation. "This ridiculous run of heat is doing my head in. It's a bit like what happens in those low-budget apocalypse movies. Makes me nervous."

When Nash didn't immediately answer, I almost groaned because there were apparently deeper levels of idiocy I could aspire to, such as ham-fisted small talk. But when I finally dropped my gaze to his, instead of smiling at my social ineptitude, he was staring directly at me with a curious look on his face.

"Yes," he said stiffly, his gaze averting skyward as well. "I hear they're predicting higher-than-normal temperatures, maybe even a heatwave right up until Christmas." His brown eyes snapped down to mine. "But the night is beautiful, nonetheless."

I should've looked away, but I didn't. Couldn't.

"And getting better by the minute." He searched my face for a few seconds like he was looking for something. Then his gaze flicked to the back door, and whatever spell had removed every scrap of saliva from my mouth was suddenly broken. "So, are you out here trying to hide from everyone as well?" And that amused look was back.

It was on the tip of my tongue to vigorously deny any such thing when my French-accented name floated out into the night and stopped me in my tracks. I shot a horrified look at the slightly ajar laundry window before flattening my back against the shadowy wall of the house.

Nash watched my performance with barely suppressed laughter before whispering, "Helene?"

I nodded and rolled my eyes. "Because this isn't embarrassing, right?"

He grinned and peeked through the laundry window before turning back to me. "I think you're safe, but maybe we should move the table to the other side of the clothesline just in case. The towels should hide you."

I snorted, my cheeks a volcano.

He laughed, the deep sound of it filling the garden and pushing the shadows back just a little. "I get it. Helene can be . . ."

"Relentless?" I offered.

Another laugh. "Exactly."

I dragged the table to the other side of the clothesline while Nash held my beer and plate. "So, you're hiding too?" I asked, returning to grab the chairs as well.

"Absolutely." He grinned, popping some cute dimples in the process. Because of course he fucking did. "I get on well with most of the staff. A few keep their distance for a variety of reasons, but either way, staff parties aren't the easiest when you're the boss. You have to attend regardless of whether you want to. Conversations stop when you appear. Old issues get beaten over the head for the hundredth time. People corner you for a discussion that should be left for work." He shrugged. "Sometimes I just need to take a break."

I nodded. "And hanging out back of the laundry under a clothesline on a starlit night is just the spot to do it."

He laughed. "Exactly. And when I saw you arrive, I said to myself, Nash, there's a man who'll understand."

I chuckled, then watched helplessly as Nash claimed one of the chairs for himself, having clearly missed the part where I hadn't actually invited him to join me. I sighed and grabbed the other seat.

"Don't let me stop you." He pushed my food closer, followed by my fork. "Maybe you should give her a chance?"

I glanced up, frowning. "Who?"

He smiled like I amused him. "Helene."

"Oh, right." I studied my plate for the best attacking position as Nash continued.

"She's a nice woman. Attractive too."

"Mmm," I said noncommittally, forking a load of half-cold curry and rice into my mouth.

He frowned. "You don't think so?"

I washed the curry down with a long swallow of beer, giving me time to think how to answer. "She's definitely hot," I finally agreed.

"But I'm not looking for any kind of relationship right now, and Helene doesn't strike me as an easy woman to say no to. Seems safer to simply not open that door." I focused on my plate and another forkful of curry. "Besides, she works with Abbie, and that would just be . . . weird."

"Oh, right. Of course." I looked up to find Nash frowning down at his beer and picking at the label. "I guess I can understand that." He sounded thoughtful. "I know nothing about women, of course. I leave that to my straight friends, Lord help them." He snorted softly. "Not that men are any easier to figure out, to be honest." He looked up and I could've sworn there was a blush to his cheeks just above that meticulously groomed silver stubble. "I assume you know that I'm gay? Most everyone does."

Like it was imprinted on my fucking brain in neon capitals. "Yes. I think Abbie must've mentioned it." The mental eye roll was epic, and Nash fell quiet as I finished the remaining few mouthfuls of curry and wiped my mouth, my skin prickling under the heat of his gaze the whole damn time. It was like the man had a furnace for a brain.

When I ran out of delaying tactics and finally looked up, a small crease ran the length of Nash's forehead, his brows bunched together.

"Do I make you uncomfortable?" he asked quietly. "I can leave if you'd rather be alone."

Hell yeah, Nash made me uncomfortable, although probably not for the reasons he thought. But no, I absolutely didn't want him to go. Then again, why was he asking? Had he guessed . . . about me? I could hardly see how, although *something* had put that knowing look in his eye that I couldn't seem to fucking run from.

When I said nothing, Nash grimaced, disappointment flashing in those beautiful eyes that finally slid off mine. "I'm sorry. I never meant to make things awkward. I'm going to leave you to enjoy the peace." And with that he pushed to his feet.

"No, stay." My hand was on his arm before I knew it, my stomach swooping at the tempting warmth of his skin and the rough feel of his hair against my palm.

Nash froze, staring down at the skin-on-skin connection but saying nothing.

I immediately dropped my hand. "Sorry, that was rude of me. I'm just . . . tired. It's been a long night. Keeping a three-year-old busy with a party going on is hard work. My wi—*ex*-wife was supposed to have Bridie tonight, but Tamsin came down sick and I was a last-minute ring-in. It seemed easier to come here."

Nash nodded and retook his seat. "I don't have kids, but I'm the proud uncle of two nephews in their twenties, Jamie and Brian. I did a fair amount of child-minding back in the day, so I get it. Who knew that a classroom full of hormone-driven teens could be preferable to one tiny hyped-up toddler?"

I studied him. "You don't have children of your own?" Yep, I had subtlety down to a fine art.

A tiny smile lifted the corners of his mouth and he shrugged. "No. Never found the right guy." He hesitated, then added, "Of course, that might be because I wasn't exactly looking." He spread his hands. "Happily single."

"Huh." I emptied my beer and spun the bottle in my hands. "And yet I assume as a high school principal, you must at least like teenagers a little bit? Either that or you're a masochist?"

He laughed. "A little of both, but I wouldn't change my job for anything. I do, in fact, love teenagers. They're bizarre and curious beings who keep you on your toes. I just never saw a family in my own future. Quite possibly, I wasn't prepared to make the compromises required." His lips quirked up. "Sounds pretty damn selfish when you say it out loud, so I think that's my cue to shut up. I recall Abbie mentioning that you were into old cars. A classic car mechanic, right?"

I blinked, unsure whether to be pleased or horrified that I'd been a topic of conversation between Abbie and Nash, but I settled on being happy that she thought of me in her daily life at all.

"She was nothing but complimentary," Nash assured me. "And it was me who asked, so . . ." His broad smile once again highlighted those sexy dimples that really needed to come with a hazardous-to-your-mental-health warning.

I swallowed another groan. Why now? And why *this* man? I was too old for this crap. I'd made my peace with those questions years ago when newly divorced me had toyed with the idea of finally experimenting a little and then decided, no. Not because I wasn't curious about being with a man, but because I didn't particularly want to be with *anyone*. And if all I needed was to get laid, well, sex was sex and a woman quenched that need with way fewer complications and embarrassment. And those feelings hadn't changed, at least not until recently. Not until . . . Nash.

"Jed?"

My gaze jerked up to find Nash studying me with soft eyes that seemed to know exactly what I'd been thinking. Except, no. They weren't soft. They were just eyes. Men's eyes. Brown, mesmerising, and far-too-pretty-for-their-own-damn-good eyes. All in all, absolutely nothing special. *Dear God, kill me now.*

"Sorry." I cleared my throat. "I spaced out there for a moment." Then his words came back to me. "You said it was *you* who asked Abbie? About *me*?"

There was no imagining the flush on his cheeks that time. "Ah, yeah." He studied his hands before looking up. "I wondered if you'd caught that part." He took a breath and swallowed hard. "You . . . interest me, Jed. I just wasn't sure . . ." He trailed off.

I what? What the hell does interest mean? I frowned and shook my head. "I don't get it." Except for that part of me that really, really fucking did. *That* ridiculous part was jumping up and down on the sidelines of my life, waving a flag and shouting, *pick me, pick me. That* part made me want to push for him to say more, to say the words.

"Don't you, Jed? Don't you, really?" He regarded me warily. "If I read things wrong, I apologise."

And I suddenly needed to be anywhere else but in front of this confusing man. Desperately and unequivocally needed to be the hell out of there, right then, lickety-split. All I had to do was get up off my damn chair and leave. Go home. Put a lid on all those long-repressed feelings that Nash stirred in me. Return to a simple life I loved. To my family, my granddaughter, my business. I didn't need *this*. I'd never needed this. Fifty-five years proved that, right?

But I didn't do any of the things I needed to. I just sat there and returned Nash's stare, my heart thumping in my chest like it was about to burst through my ribs like a stupid teenager about to have his first kiss.

But Nash didn't offer anything further. He simply waited. Waited and watched me with those damn knowing eyes. He'd taken the first step, opening the door if I wanted to pass through, while leaving things vague enough that I could turn away and we could both pretend it had never happened. Whatever Nash thought he'd seen in me that night we'd first been introduced, I clearly hadn't been as discreet about my appreciation of him as I'd thought. But he'd taken a ballsy risk approaching me, nonetheless.

What happened next was up to me. Which would be absolutely nothing. No matter what I felt, what I'd fantasised about, how tempting Nash might be. *He* was a question that I'd avoided my whole life and then eventually decided *not* to answer. So why the hell was I still sitting there?

I straightened as a thought rocked me. "Did you . . . did you ask Abbie . . . if I—"

"No." Nash was clear. "I didn't ask, Jed. I wouldn't."

Of course he hadn't. I sighed and slipped down in my chair. "I'm sorry. Excuse me while I go up in a puff of embarrassed smoke."

He shot me a sweet smile. "It's okay. It's . . . complicated, right?"

I sighed and looked away. "Yeah, not as much as I make it, probably."

He nodded. "Then I think maybe it *would* be better if I leave."

And there was that opportunity again. The chance to shut this whole mess down. And so, of course I said, "Stay. I'm pretty sure Abbie would have a thing or two to say about me jettisoning her new boss from an innocent conversation, even if it's one I might need to sidestep, at least for now."

"That's not exactly a no." His eyes burned hot on my face.

I should've corrected him, but I said nothing, just held that brown-eyed gaze for a long second before lifting my face to the sky to better hide my blazing cheeks.

"It *is* an innocent conversation, Jed." His voice was reassuring in that way you might calm a frightened horse. "And it's one that I promise will stay between us. But I'm not going to apologise for giving it a shot."

I dropped my gaze once more to his. "Thank you."

He nodded. "Don't thank me for stepping away from something I'm pretty sure would've been hot as hell."

I almost choked on my tongue. *When was the last time anyone had suggested I might be . . . hot?* Years, maybe more a decade. Long before Tamsin and I had divorced. Laughter bubbled up my throat and I shook my head in disbelief. "Then you're either crazy or you need to get out more."

His laughter lines crinkled and those freaking dimples played havoc with my good intentions. Apparently, I had a thing for them . . . along with everything else about this man. He fascinated me in every possible way, including those which kept me longer in the shower some mornings than I'd care to admit. There were so many questions I wanted answers to, but I wasn't about to fish.

After a long minute of staring each other down, Nash tipped his fingers to his brow in a small salute of acceptance. "Message received." He slid down in his chair. "So, tell me about these cars?"

I arched a brow. "Nice segue. But don't feel obligated to stay and talk."

"I don't," he said bluntly. "I asked because I want to know. Are you going to answer or not?"

I shot him a look. "Bossy fucking teachers. Have some respect for your elders." *So maybe a little bit of fishing.*

He snorted like he knew exactly what I was up to. "And how old are you?"

I grimaced. "Fifty-five and counting. You?"

"Fifty-three. Which explains why I have fewer wrinkles and a lot less grey hair."

I choked on a laugh and threw a clothes peg at him. He ducked and it went sailing into the tub of rosemary behind. "Don't think I can't see that receding hairline under that stylish do of yours. My hair might be silver, sunshine, but at least it's all there."

Nash's mouth fell open and he stared for just a second. Then he laughed, and the clear sound of it sent a jolt of lust straight to my balls. "Well, I can see I'm going to be given no quarter around you, Jed Marshall. Still, you won't catch me complaining about that silver-fox thing you've got going on. It's hot."

And there was that word again, along with my scorching cheeks.

"And you're right." He lifted the messy locks from his temple to reveal a nice retreat. "All the men in my dad's family have it. I'm luckier than most. My cousin was almost completely bald by forty."

He let his dark grey mane flop like a waterfall of silk and I wanted nothing more than to feel the slide of it through my own fingers, the pull as I fisted it and—*shit*. That went nuclear fast. I cleared my throat "Well, I wouldn't worry." My eyes met his. "It's a good look on you, as well."

His mouth tipped up in a slow smile. "Thanks." Then he looked away. "Getting older isn't the easiest in any dating landscape, but vanity and youth culture can be vicious in the gay scene. There's a lot of pressure to look good. You can *get* older, but you can't *look* older, unless you can nail the whole daddy or silver-fox thing." He waved a hand my direction. "Like some I know."

I ignored the compliment. "Does that mean you mostly date younger guys?"

He said nothing for a minute, those clever brown eyes searching my face for . . . something. "To say I *date* them might be stretching things, but mostly, yes. They're less . . . complicated."

I snorted. "AKA, they're looking for sex and not much else."

"Yeah." Nash kept his gaze steady on my face, which was growing hotter by the second. "Something like that." He finally broke his stare to take a sip of his drink. "But it's hard work to stay in the game. You wanna try maintaining a set of abs past fifty. The diet sucks. The gym work is torture. And the washboard effect softens by the year no matter what you do, muscle forcibly annexed by fat in a hostile takeover. A year from now, someone will find me on the floor of my apartment, suffocated by a mushrooming BMI. It'll be like the movie *Day of the Triffids* but with fat cells."

I laughed. "Day of the lipids, then."

He threw back his head and laughed, and for a long second, all I could do was stare at him and wonder when I'd last enjoyed talking with someone as much as this.

"Well, I'm impressed you have abs at all," I finally responded. "Mine surrendered and went down with the ship about a million roast dinners back."

"I doubt you have anything to worry about." He ran an appreciative gaze over my body and I suppressed a shiver. "You look to be in good shape."

"Only because my work is pretty physical. But it doesn't produce anything close to what you're describing . . . or what's likely hiding under that shirt. Still, I can't see me putting a foot inside a gym either. It's not for me."

"And for that, I admire you." Nash nodded respectfully. "I should lighten up on it myself. I used to run until I did my Achilles in. Now I swim. I really enjoy the pool, whereas the gym has never been a sweet spot for me. I don't know why I keep going." He pulled a face. "Vanity, I suppose. I probably need to start being a bit more graceful about the whole ageing thing. Set an example for the kids or some such shit. Anyway, enough of the depressing talk. Tell me about your car business."

"We're a specialty mechanic's shop, working on hot rods and classic cars. The Custom and Classic Clinic."

Nash frowned. "I can't say I'm familiar with the name."

"I'm not surprised. It's a niche market and I don't advertise. I don't need to. We have more work than we can handle most of the time."

He smiled. "You must be good then."

I couldn't help but grin. "I like to think so. I've had a passion for old cars my whole life, and I'm damn lucky I can make a living from something I love."

Nash leaned forward, his elbows on the table, the fresh scent of bergamot and sandalwood rising off his skin. "Was it something your parents were interested in?"

I barked out a laugh. "Hell no. If Dad's car clicked over five years, both he and Mum broke out in a sweat. But my uncle had an old blue 1950s convertible Jaguar. That car was the sweetest thing I've ever seen. When I got my licence, he took me for a spin and let me drive. I never looked back. What sent you into teaching?"

Nash took a breath and blew it out slowly. "Some days I have no idea. Like today, for instance." His wince sparked my interest.

"Trouble in school?"

A frown creased his brow and his gaze lifted to the night sky. A breeze danced a lock of soft grey hair across his lips, and I had to slide my hand under my thighs to stop from reaching across to brush it aside.

"You don't have to answer," I offered, not wanting to put him on the spot.

He quickly looked back. "No, it's fine. I can't mention names, but suffice to say there are some arsehole, bigoted parents out there who leave you in no doubt as to why their kids are causing trouble at school. I spent an hour today with the father of one of my more *challenging* kids, and it was all I could do not to smack him. I was furious with myself for letting him get to me, but he insinuated, without actually saying the words, exactly what he thought of 'us lot'"—he made air quotes—"and that his son hadn't seriously meant the blast of homophobic slurs he'd directed at a young student who happened to catch him keying a teacher's car. It was a two-for-one deal. Hate speech and property damage." He shook his head, the frustration peeling off him in waves.

"I imagine that's one of the hardest parts of your job. You're not just working with kids, but whole families, right? A million ways to get messy and complicated."

Nash studied me in silence. "Exactly. And yes, it sucks. Mostly because these kids aren't *bad* kids, whatever the hell that means. They're just products of the conversations they hear at home and the way they're treated, or see others treated. It's such a fucking waste. Some you can turn around, slowly. But there are others who—" A heavy sigh broke his lips and his shoulders slumped. "Well, let's just say, it's not easy. Sometimes no matter what you do, nothing seems to work, and then suddenly these kids are on the cusp of leaving school and you feel like you've achieved nothing. All you can do is hand them over to life and hope age and experience teaches them the lessons they need before they have their own kids. Pray that it does what you failed to do."

"It must hurt."

He shot me a thoughtful look. "It does. Like so many others who don't fit the so-called norm, I had a few of my own bullies growing up, but I was definitely luckier than some. My older sister, Colleen, had my back at school, but it was a couple of teachers who really changed things for me. They stepped up and that made all the difference. It didn't always stop the name-calling and shoving, but it gave me a safe place to go."

"Did that influence your decision to train as a teacher?"

His mouth tipped into another of those winning smiles that turned my knees to jelly. "Partly. But I also love learning and research, I always have, and I thought I might be good on the other side of the classroom. I wanted . . . *want* . . . to make a difference." The smile slipped away. "But then I have days like today and I think what-the-fuck difference have I really made at all?" He shook his head and apologised. "I'm sorry. My head is not in a good place." He spread his arms wide. "Hence the reason I'm hiding out with the vegetables."

I chuckled and tightened the grip on my bottle, because if I didn't do something with my hands, I was going to reach across that table and take hold of his. *God, I wanted to touch him. To put that smile back on his face.* But I didn't. Instead, I offered the only reassurance I could.

"Don't apologise for caring. I, for one, am hugely grateful to have people like you in charge of educating my kids and grandkids. You give me hope, Nash, so don't ever think what you do isn't worth the effort. I've always considered teaching to be one of the hardest and most important jobs there is. Certainly more important than what I do. But you can't take personal responsibility for those who aren't ready to listen. That way lies endless disappointment and frustration. Take the wins where you can. Some of those kids might go on to change the world. It isn't all on your shoulders. No one is irreplaceable, an important lesson my dad taught me. To think you are smacks of delusions of grandeur if you ask me."

He snorted a laugh, then stared at me, shaking his head like I was some sort of amusing puzzle he was trying to solve, and I shifted in my seat, cursing my stupidity. What the fuck did I know about education?

"Ignore me." I waved a dismissive hand. "You know a lot more than me about—"

"No, no, no." He laid his hand on my wrist and burned right through the skin, flesh and bone, all the way down my body to my balls. A slight exaggeration perhaps, but not by much. "I wasn't laughing at you," he insisted. "I was laughing because I really needed to hear those words tonight, and of all places, I hadn't expected to hear them in a vegetable garden from you. So, thank you." His smile lit up something in my chest that I ignored. "And you know *plenty,* believe me. If all my parents thought like you, my life would be so much easier."

Oh. I didn't know what to say, and so I opted for nothing, the weight of his hand heavy on my arm, the silence growing thick between us.

It was Nash who broke it, lifting his hand before clearing his throat and changing the subject. "So, with your passion for cars on the table, what do you drive? Fair warning, I expect to be impressed."

Much safer ground, and I instantly relaxed. "A Mustang '67 fast-back, and a 1956 Ford F100. But my day-to-day run-around is a 1970 Merc." I smiled at the vacant look on his face. "You have zero idea what I'm talking about, right?"

Those dimples popped and he shook his head. "Sorry. What I know about cars you could write on the back of a postage stamp and have room left over for a summary of *War and Peace*."

I laughed. "I like your honesty. What about your chosen drive? No, let me guess. An Audi, right?"

He narrowed his eyes, a wry smile pulling at his mouth. "Close. It's actually a BMW coupe. Three years old. But I'm pretty sure your guess wasn't a compliment on my exceptional taste. It's a stereotypical car for a middle-aged guy who's trying to say I'm successful but not too flashy, right? Understated and safe."

I bit back a smile. "Nothing wrong with a nice car."

He snorted. "Very diplomatic of you."

"No, seriously. No one should be shamed for what they choose to drive. It's like fashion. You like what you like. The trick is being strong enough to ignore the haters. There's plenty of shade thrown around in the classic car business as well. Purists who hate anything done to a vehicle that isn't original. Rodders who look down their noses at classic enthusiasts. The list goes on."

"I can imagine." He sat back and stretched his long legs out, crossing them at the ankles. "You said *we* have more work than we can handle. You have employees?"

"Two. Rollo and Jemma. Rollo's been with me ten years and

could probably run the place on his own, whereas Jemma only came on board last year. They're good kids." I rolled my eyes. "Jesus, listen to me. Rollo is thirty-six, for fuck's sake. Hardly a kid. No wonder they give me so much shit about mothering them."

Nash chuckled. "My young staff say the same thing. Or they fob me off and ignore me if I happen to drop in on some conversation about social media or dating apps, like there's no way I could possibly understand. I'm tempted to remind them that I was using Grindr before most of them had even started school, except that makes me sound really fucking sad and way too creepy."

We laughed until the sound of the back door banging against the washing machine jerked both our gazes to the laundry.

"Jed?" The towels parted like the Red Sea to reveal Scott, the surprise clear on his face. "What on earth are you doing out here?" Then he caught sight of Nash and did a double take, his gaze narrowing. "Nash? I thought you'd left already?"

Nash got to his feet, his smile a little strained. "Nope. I was grabbing a bit of peace and quiet and happened to bump into Jed, and we got talking."

"Oh." Scott's brows bunched as he looked Nash over. My son-in-law would never win an award for his open-mindedness—it was the one thing I struggled with in my daughter's husband. But this was Abbie's boss and his frown finally slid into a smile. "Clever place to hide," he said before turning to me. "I saw your car was still in the driveway and so I came looking. I wanted to thank you for watching Bridie. I'm about to head in and relieve Abbie."

"Ah." I nodded knowingly. "Another party slacker, huh?"

Scott smiled. "I refuse to comment."

Nash collected our empty bottles and my plate and shot me a smile. "I'll get rid of these. I'm gonna make one more social round and then I'm off." He extended his hand. "Thanks for the chat, Jed. It was fun."

I slid my hand into his and he gripped it firmly, those wicked brown eyes meeting mine with something warm bubbling in their depths. "It was," I agreed, my voice sounding a lot calmer than I felt. "We'll bump into each other at the next school event, no doubt."

"If I'm lucky." Nash held my gaze for an extra beat, then turned to Scott. "Thanks for hosting the party, Scott. Much appreciated."

"You're welcome. Come on, Jed. I'll walk you out." Scott held the towels aside for me to pass through first, and I had the distinct impression of being herded away, but I let it go.

But when I turned at the back door to check on Nash, he was watching me with a thoughtful look on his face. He smiled and raised his hand.

I hesitated, then did the same.

And that was that.

Nash

I watched Jed leave and tried to ignore the niggle of want curling low and inconvenient in my belly. There was just something about the man. Something that hadn't left me since we'd been introduced by Abbie at that damn concert. And it wasn't just the fact that Jed was hot enough to melt the hair off my balls, if I had any. I'd met a lot of hot men in my time, but none of them usually hung around in my head for longer than it took to get their number or their arse—sometimes both if I liked them enough for another round or two.

Some might suggest it wasn't the best example a high school principal could offer to his students, and to those people I'd say fuck off. I deserved a life, and I was always discreet. None of my students frequented gay bars and clubs, or if they did, running into me there would likely scare the bejesus out of them. Same applied to the parents. The only parents I ever ran into in a gay club were people I already knew through that scene, and we all understood what was going on. I did, however, steer well clear of anything outside of those safe environments.

So, what the hell was I doing lusting after the father of one of my teachers? And not just lusting after him. All things Jed Marshall had taken up a fair amount of real estate in my brain of late. I'd tactfully grilled Abbie about her father on more than one occasion and even sneakily perved on him the two occasions he'd come into school to drop Bridie with her mother. Mortified didn't begin to cover it, and I was still trying to get my head around my idiocy.

"I thought you were heading off?" Scott poked his head back through the open laundry door and my gaze jerked up, surprised to see him back. "Is there something I can get you? Another drink?"

I blinked. "Oh, no thanks. I'm just avoiding going inside. It's much cooler out here."

Scott eyed me for a second, then nodded. He'd always been a bit awkward around me for some reason. I didn't know if it was the wife's-boss thing or the gay thing, and to be honest I didn't much care.

"Well, drive safely."

"I will." I summoned one of my patented charming smiles. "Thanks again for tonight. It was good of you and Abbie."

He stared at me again, his face a mask. "No problem. You have a good one, Nash."

I watched him go and sighed. So much for the charm offensive. I should really get my money back.

CHAPTER THREE

Nash

I CHECKED MY WATCH AND GROANED. MOST OF THE SENIOR school had finished their classes for the year, and the staff was busy organising rooms and teaching plans for their return in late January to early February. It made for a more relaxing work environment, which I enjoyed, although the school felt oddly quiet. I'd hoped to finish early, having arranged to meet up with a friend and hit a bar or two that night. But I still had another hour of informal interviews with our graduating students, followed by a staff meeting and yet another no-doubt heated phone call with the chairperson of the board's disciplinary committee, regarding a student's suspension.

I texted Gerald. ***Day going to shit. I'll have to skip dinner and meet you at the bar about nine.***

He texted back. ***I'll save one for you.*** A not-so-thinly veiled reference to the fact we were meeting up to cruise for a hookup—a phrase which felt embarrassingly inappropriate for a couple of fifty-something men. But Gerald was a big, cheerful, tatted Daddy type and rarely left without a conquest under his belt, and we'd been wingmen for each other for almost ten years. But although I considered Gerald a friend, our semi-regular monthly shared dinner and bar meetups were the only time we really got together, and I wasn't sure what that said about our relationship.

Gerald had texted that morning to see if I was interested in a night out, and although my eyes were standing out on sticks from yet another restless night's sleep, I figured I could do with the distraction. I hadn't hooked up since before the party. Since the image of Jed Marshall had wheedled its way into my brain, and into my bed, and into my shower, and my office, and any damn place it wanted to, it seemed. Enough was enough. I needed an uncomplicated palate cleanser, and a quickie with a stranger seemed just the ticket.

I checked my watch again, wondering where that familiar roll of excitement I generally felt before a night out with Gerald had suddenly disappeared to. Yet another indication that I was losing my fucking mind and needed to get a grip. The sooner I got over my little crush on the sexy mechanic, the better.

"That must be someone pretty important for you to have your nose in your phone with all this beautiful flesh on display." Gerald covered my screen with his hand and nodded to the packed bar. "You're missing half the fun, mate."

I pulled my phone free and cast a glance over the crowded room. Right Said Fred pumped through the speakers as a sea of half-naked men, mostly in their twenties, jumped up and down on the dancefloor and sang along to the lyrics proclaiming how many things they were too sexy for. It brought a wistful smile to my face.

"It's my brother." I went on to explain to Gerald how Devon's son, my nephew, had drawn names from a hat for Christmas dinner courses and I'd been given dessert.

"Riveting." Gerald rolled his eyes at me. "Can it not wait until tomorrow?"

It could, of course, but I'd been oddly out of sorts all night, had even considered calling Gerald to back out but baulked at the thought of how much crap I'd be letting myself in for.

I held my phone up. "I need to make a call." *I really didn't.* "Be back in a minute." I slid out of the booth, leaving a very unimpressed Gerald to nurse his drink alone, and ducked into the hallway for some relative quiet to call my brother.

"How can I draw dessert when I wasn't even there, arsehole?" I groused. "I smell a rat."

Devon's laugh boomed down the line. "Hey, it's the least likely thing you can fuck up. Go buy something if you're worried."

"No way. I'll accept the challenge. Tell your son I know what he's up to. Brian did the draw, right?"

Devon chuckled. "Right. Them's the rules. The course with the fewest votes cleans up, and a different person draws the names each year."

I fucking knew it. "Well, you can tell Brian he better pack his rubber gloves cos he can't cook for shit, and I won't be doing the dishes. What course did he give himself?"

"Salad."

"The fucker. You know he's just gonna do a lettuce number, don't you? What can you do wrong with that?"

"Hey, don't blame me. You haven't done dishes in five years. Everyone's out to get you. And don't ask me to pick sides between my son and my brother cos you'll lose. He has to look after me in my old age. You'll just be a drain on my patience and good temper."

I chuckled and thought of the cheeky-arse, red-haired string-bean of a nephew of mine.

"And where the hell are you?" Devon came back. "Is that Right Said Fred in the background?"

"Yes. And I'm in a club," I shouted over the chorus line, which was gaining volume.

"So why are you talking to me and not feeling up some way-too-young-for-you stockbroker or something?"

A good question and one which I ignored. "I'll get there. And you go tell that son of yours that he better be prepared, that's all I'm gonna say. Tell him I'm gonna make him suck balls at Cluedo. He's going down, my friend."

Devon snickered. "You do realise how old that makes you sound, don't you? No one plays Cluedo anymore. No. One. You ask any one of those men you chat up tonight."

"Well, I do. And board games are the only thing I have a chance at winning against your boys. I have zero thumb coordination on those damn handheld thingies. Besides—" I pictured my brother's green eyes smiling. "—I shouldn't need to remind you that you're pushing fifty now as well, sunshine."

"Maybe, but that's still a few years younger than you."

"Bye, Devon."

"Like waaaaaay younger."

I hung up and grinned at the phone. Then I pocketed it and made my way back inside and over to our booth, only to find it taken by two young men making out as if they might not survive the night. I sighed and cast my eyes around the dancefloor until I spotted a portly Gerald grinding into the arse of a slim thirty-something blond-haired beauty of a man he'd had his eyes on all night. I sidled over and whisper-shouted in his ear, "You set for the night then?"

Gerald gave me a huge grin and nodded while his partner gave me a come-hither look and ran a hand down my arm.

"There's always room for more." The young man winked.

I looked to Gerald, who shrugged. "Invitation's open, mate."

I didn't need to think, and Gerald knew what my answer would be. "No thanks. Not tonight." Or any night in the last thirty years I'd been doing this. Gerald might like to mix things up, but I'd never found threesomes to be very satisfying. I slapped my friend on the back. "Have fun. I think I'll grab another drink."

Gerald glanced over his shoulder, clocked the young man at the bar, and sent me a sly grin. "I saw you watching him earlier. Good luck. Call me tomorrow."

I promised I would and then threaded my way through the bodies packed like sardines on the dancefloor toward the equally crowded bar and a tall guy with messy blond curls and a lithe athletic body. He was dressed in a leather harness, black painted-on jeans, a silver choker, and not much else.

When he saw me coming, the young man eyed me up and down and then slid off his stool and patted the seat. "Took you long enough, gorgeous. Park yourself."

I smiled at his confidence, especially considering he had to be all of twenty-five, and as hard as I tried, I was never going to look anything even close to under forty again, even forty-five, dammit.

"Thanks." I squeezed through the tiny gap he left, which forced our groins to brush, and took a seat.

I fought back a grin. No matter how many times I'd done this dance, these early manoeuvrings were always exciting. The eyeing up. The calculating. The finding-out-if-this-is-gonna-work introductions.

He leaned in so I could hear him. "I'm James." He offered his hand.

"Nash," I answered, and we shook, his slender fingers wrapping around mine as his pretty eyes danced all over my face, blatantly checking me out.

I almost sighed in relief. James had the fun vibe I'd been looking for all evening, for days in fact, ever since the party. Ever since Jed Marshall had rattled me . . . again.

"Haven't seen you in here before," I shouted above the noisy crowd, holding up my hand to the barman who shot me a wink to let me know he'd seen.

"I've been in Australia for two years. Came back for a promotion." James followed my gaze, smiled, and said loudly, "I'll have a cosmopolitan, thanks."

I almost laughed, because of course he would. I couldn't remember the last time any guy had paid for *my* drink. Apparently, a few wrinkles came with a side order of spare money to burn. I pushed

James' half-empty glass of undoubtedly cheap rosé to the side and he had the grace to almost blush. Almost.

"I'm sure you remember the days," he explained, running his finger down the front of my chest, undoing a button or two as he went, and this time I did laugh, because I certainly did.

We chatted for a bit. The barman brought our drinks. And the music cost me another year or two of my hearing. James slipped between my knees and ran his curious hands under my shirt, popping another button in the process. Then he lifted it up and nodded in approval.

"Pretty good for—" He gave a cheeky smile and nibbled his lower lip.

I put my lips to his ear and he shivered and slid his arms around my waist. "For an old guy, you mean?"

James pulled back to look at me, a broad grin in place. "For a man of your character."

I laughed and tugged him close, pressing a kiss to those pouty lips. He groaned and shoved his tongue into my mouth, his fingers threading through my hair to hold me in place. And just like that, out of nowhere, I had a sudden and inconvenient image of Jed's laughing blue-grey eyes as he gave me stick about my haircut and receding hairline.

Jesus, fuck, the man needed to get out of my head.

"Let's go out back." James pulled off and breathed against my ear. "Or we could go to your place if you were down with that? I'm thinking we could have a lot of fun together."

I was pretty sure he was right, but the idea of waking up to James in my bed the next day wasn't as appealing as I'd expected. "Out back." I slid off the stool and took his hand, and we made our way back across the dancefloor and down the corridor to the restrooms.

"In here." James pulled me sideways into the accessible restroom and locked the door. Then he shoved me against the wall and picked up the kiss where we'd left off at the bar.

James was hot and tight and smart and confident, and everything

I loved in a hookup. He was exactly what I needed, and I should've been into him like a rat up a fucking drainpipe. Should've been. But in the mirror over his shoulder, I caught a glimpse of the two of us rutting, the distracted expression on my face and James' acres of blemish-free skin as he enthusiastically mauled my neck, and something in my brain stuttered and fizzled.

"Does that mean you mostly date . . . younger guys?"

Fuck. Fuck. Fuck.

I blinked and tried to shake Jed's voice free of my head, wrapping my arms around James instead, focusing on him, pulling him tight against me. But it didn't work, and James wasn't ignorant of the fact I wasn't as into it as I had been.

He pulled away and cocked his head, almost amused. Then he ran a finger down my cheek and said softly, "I'm not sure where that head of yours is, but it's not with me, no matter what this—" He cupped my stiff dick. "—is doing. Now, I know it's not me." He flashed a cheeky smirk that made me chuckle. "So I'm guessing there's something on your mind."

I groaned. "Would you believe me if I said I have a yoga class in the morning?"

James laughed. "Scarily, yes. You old guys are hella unpredictable."

I snorted. "Tart." Then I tipped his chin up with my fingers and kissed him softly. "You're right. It's nothing to do with you. You're pretty irresistible. And yes, I have something on my mind."

He quirked a brow. "A man?"

I shrugged. "Maybe just a hope."

James grinned and buttoned my shirt from the bottom up, then patted my chest. "He's a lucky guy."

I rolled my eyes. "He's not out."

James winced. "Then take care. It would've been fun." He kissed me again and left the bathroom.

When he was gone, I locked the door and fell against the vanity, staring at the mirror. "What the hell is wrong with you?"

My reflection stared back in an oddly mocking way.

I splashed water on my face and thought about James. I thought about how perfect he was and how I didn't regret him leaving.

And as I Ubered home, I thought about Gerald heading off with his hookup and the years we'd spent doing this, and I felt tired.

And when I was dropped at the entrance to my building, I thought about my empty, pristine apartment and the job that meant so damn much to me.

And as I curled up in my favourite armchair with a book, and a pile of school administration on the table that I did my best to ignore, I thought about the causes I'd fought for and the school programmes I'd instigated.

I downed a beer and thought about my brother and my nephews and my best friend Colin.

Not once in the thirty years since university had I ever considered my life to be less than . . . enough. Men were a garnish, never the main course, not for a long, long time.

Unable to focus on reading, I made my way to my bedroom and stripped before running a shower. Then I stared at the mirror, and instead of brown eyes, I saw crisp blue irises and short silver hair. A wide-open laugh and a nervous attraction . . . to me. That had to mean something, right?

I thought about this man I barely knew who'd gotten under my skin, and I couldn't help but wonder if all this confusion was about Jed or simply heralded a turning point in my life.

And with the groan of a convicted man, sounding suspiciously like lead dropping in the ocean, I realised there was only one way I was ever going to find out.

I eyeballed myself in the mirror and sighed. "Are you really going to fucking do this?"

The uptick in my heart at the thought was the only answer I needed.

CHAPTER FOUR

Jed

"Have the fuel pump and cylinder head for the '57 Oldsmobile Starfire arrived?" I called to Rollo who was busy in the far pit of the workshop under a 1961 Ford T-Bird.

"Not yet," he shouted back. "I phoned this morning and they said they couriered it yesterday. Should be here tomorrow or the day after, but you know what they've been like lately."

I lifted the cell phone back to my ear. "I assume you heard that, Tom?"

Tom grunted. "I heard. I know I landed you with this at the last minute, but what are my chances of getting it done before Christmas?"

I ran a finger down the job sheet on my office desk and grimaced. "We can try, but we're booked pretty solid until then, and we close on the twenty-third. What day is your daughter's wedding?"

"January twelfth."

I checked again. "I can't promise you before Christmas, but we open on the third, and I'll make sure it's first on the list. You *should* have it in plenty of time, but you know these old cars. I'd organise a backup just in case. We can only do what we can do."

He sighed. "Yeah. Yorkie's lending me his Nomad if the Starfire is a no-go. I just wanted to—"

"Drive her in your own car." I felt for him. "I get it, Tom. I did the same for Abbie, remember?" My heart squeezed at the memory of driving my little girl to her wedding in the passenger seat of my '67 Mustang. "I'll do my best. That's all I can promise."

"I know, and I don't mean to put pressure on you. Thanks." He hung up and I stared at the phone and sighed.

"Don't fret it." Jemma strolled into the office and headed to the coffee machine, her overall sleeves tied around her tiny waist, engine grease smeared across her shoulder, and her top knot riding loose in the welcome breeze channelling between the open front and back hangar doors of the workshop. "You can only do what you can do, Boss. Tom knows how busy we are. He should've got his A into G earlier. He'll understand. He could've gone somewhere else."

"As if." Rollo appeared through the door and collapsed sideways into a chair, one long leg thrown casually over the arm. At six feet five, he took up a lot of room. "Tom won't let anyone touch the Starfire except us." He looked sideways to Jemma. "Can you make me a coffee too while you're at it? Pretty please?" He batted his lashes.

She huffed and rolled her eyes. "Only because you're gonna help me with that alternator before you clock out tonight. Promise?"

"Yes." Rollo gleefully rubbed his hands together. "Absolutely."

Jemma flicked through the pods until she found Rollo's caramel mocha-mostly-sugar-with-no-coffee-achino favourite. "You want one, Boss?"

I checked the clock on the wall and nodded. "Thanks. But not his crap." I winked at a pouting Rollo. "And how the hell is it four o'clock already?"

"The caffeine withdrawal is real." Jemma shoved a strong espresso pod into the second machine and set it going. Two machines from two thankful clients. We weren't about to complain. Some days it was all that kept us going.

Rollo accepted his coffee from Jemma, took a sip, and groaned appreciatively. "Man, that's good." He looked over to me. "I can open up for you tomorrow if you want? I promised Malcolm I'd get his T-Bird finished for the weekend, and it's gonna take me all day to do it. I'm figuring on being here about six-thirty."

"On a Friday?"

"Such is my dedication."

I wasn't buying it and stared him down. "He's offering you a bonus, isn't he?"

Rollo winked and tapped the side of his nose. "But it's going in our slush fund for the Beach Hop next year. We have to get a better hotel. It took three weeks for my neck to recover last time."

Jemma handed me my coffee and I perched on the corner of my desk to drink it. "Then go ahead. Knock yourself out. I've got some bookwork to do so I might work from the house for a couple of hours before I head over—miss the worst of the commuter traffic." I grinned and they both laughed.

"Yeah, it's a bitch that hour of the morning." Rollo peered through the office window and across the lawn to my house about a hundred metres away. "You need to get that mower out, Boss. It's a jungle out there."

I winced. "Don't remind me. Abbie's been on my case as well, and Tamsin threatened to give me a six-month lawn-mowing subscription for Christmas."

Jemma laughed. "She used to mow all the lawns when you were together, right?"

"And all the DIY," Rollo added with a wink to Jemma. "Plus, the woman has mean skills on a circular saw. Better than you, eh, Boss?"

I groaned. "I refuse to engage in pointless one-upmanship regarding my ex-wife."

"So, that's a yes."

I narrowed my gaze. "My talents lie elsewhere."

Rollo chuckled. "So you say. By the way, do you need a hand to get those new seats in the Cutlass on Saturday? I can come in for a few hours."

"Nope." I took a long swallow of my coffee and then stared at the mug, avoiding Rollo's gaze. "I've got a date with my granddaughter for the day."

There was a long pause. "Again?" Rollo sounded almost pissed on my behalf. "You haven't worked on the Cutlass in weeks. I thought you were getting it ready for the Taranaki show next year?"

I shrugged and drank some more coffee. "It'll be ready." *Maybe.* "Abbie and Scott are trying to finish their Christmas shopping early before the madness starts, so . . ." I finally caught his eye. "It is what it is. You'll understand one day."

Rollo grimaced and eyed me speculatively. "If you don't mind me saying—"

I did, and my expression saw his mouth snap shut.

"Hello?" The greeting was followed by a series of knocks on the open hangar door.

I leaned forward but couldn't quite see into the workshop.

"Hello? Anyone there?"

Shit. It couldn't be. But the voice was familiar, too damn familiar, and a warmth curled low in my belly as my heart ticked up.

"Sit." Rollo waved me down. "I'll see to whoever it is." He wiggled out of his chair and headed into the workshop while I edged toward the door for a look, grateful for a little more time to get my shit together.

But when I saw Nash standing there in tight blue jeans and a black button-down, looking slightly nervous and way too fucking lickable, the warmth in my belly turned into an embarrassing flip. Rollo laughed at something Nash said, and the next thing I knew he was headed back to the office with Nash on his heels, the man's curious gaze sweeping right and left. The closer they got to where I was standing, the more my stomach clenched.

What the hell was he doing here?

"You okay, Boss?" Jemma suddenly appeared next to me, and I realised my hands were fisted and sweating. "Do you know him?"

"Yes." I rubbed my palms down the front of my coveralls and gave a half shrug. "A little."

Jemma shot me a curious look but said nothing.

Rollo walked into the office and waved a hand my direction. "Here's the man himself. Would you like a coffee, Nash?"

Nash stopped just inside the door with his back to the others and cast an apologetic half-smile my direction. "I don't want to take up your time if you're too busy. It's your call, Jed."

We both knew he wasn't talking about the workshop, and with my overall sleeves tied around my waist and only a thin black practically not-there singlet standing between me and the man's heated gaze, warmth flooded my cheeks. When he was done checking me out, his eyes returned to mine and his mouth curved up in an appreciative smile as he pointed to my cap bearing the slogan *Ford Mustangs: Better than Sex.* "Nice hat."

And—*oh my fucking god,* I was getting hard.

"Boss?" Rollo was still waiting on my answer, which had been far too long coming. "Should I make Nash a coffee or not?"

"What? Oh, um . . ." I flustered. "No, I'll do it. Maybe you guys could finish smoko outside?"

Rollo and Jemma exchanged a puzzled look, then grabbed their unfinished drinks and promptly left, with Jemma casting a final what-the-fuck look over her shoulder. I answered with a shrug and swiftly closed the door, watching through the glass as they exploded into hushed conversation and headed for the outside table and chairs to finish their coffees. When I was sure they were out of earshot, I turned to Nash, who had his palms up, and immediately apologised.

"Jed, I'm so sorry if I've fucked up. The last thing I wanted was to make things awkward for you, I . . ." He trailed off, chuckling, and shaking his head. "Well, shit, that's a damn lie. It was hardly going to be anything but awkward, was it? Crazy principal chases after his reluctant crush? Borderline stalking, at best. I think I just motored straight past undignified and crashed into abject humiliation. I have no excuse other than—" He hesitated, his gaze fixed on mine as he nibbled his bottom lip, before finally continuing. "I wanted to see you again. It's as simple as that. And if that's not okay, I'll leave right now." His words ran together, and he shook his head like he was angry with himself, his cheeks blazing, his gaze darting sideways to the window.

But I was still stuck on *reluctant crush*. My heart stuttered in my chest as I tried to wrap my head around all of what he'd just said.

I still hadn't answered when he finally groaned, "Can you just put me out of my misery? And I'll be gone."

And with those few simple words, all my noble good intentions to rise above the carnal temptation that Nash Collingwood embodied with fucking bells on flew out the window under jet-fuelled propulsion.

Martyrdom clearly wasn't what it used to be.

And also, he looked way too fucking cute standing there looking a whole lot less confident than usual. This was a Nash I could relate to.

I gave a slow blink and breathed out a sigh. "It's . . . fine. I'm not sure what good you think it will do, but take a seat." I headed for the espresso machine, feeling like a tongue-tied teenager. "How do you have your coffee?"

Nash sank into the armchair Rollo had just vacated and crossed his long legs in front, looking effortlessly cool and comfortable just like always. How the hell did he do that? The sight made me want to mess up those long grey waves of his and maybe kiss him, just to throw him off balance, of course.

"Just milk, please," he answered.

I turned my back and took a deep breath, then set about making him a coffee and topping up my own since I was going to need the extra caffeine. Nash's gaze burned hot on my skin as I worked, but he said nothing, allowing a weighty silence to fill the space between us, and I made no effort to fill it either.

I'd spent two weeks mocking myself for my ridiculous behaviour the night of the party, all but convinced I'd imagined or at least exaggerated the whole encounter with him. I was fifty-five, for fuck's sake. I had silver hair, crow's feet, a dodgy back from spending far too long under car engines, dicky knees for the same reason, a softening middle, and the beginnings of saggy jowls.

And I knew all that because a prolonged study of my naked body in the mirror when I'd gotten home that same night had reinforced the bitter truth. The idea that someone, *anyone*, but especially a guy, might think me sexy or hot or worth taking a risk for, was quite simply fucking absurd. Not that I was gonna fret about it. Until about two weeks ago, I'd been happy, or at least resigned about the state of my body. Abbie might tell me I was handsome and a catch, but then, she was my daughter and had a vested interest in buttering me up.

And yet here Nash was, calling me his crush, for fuck's sake, and telling me he wanted to see me again, and I had zero idea what to do about that. Nash certainly wasn't part of any future plan I'd mapped for my graceful swan dive into retirement, and I couldn't see that changing. I'd done my time in a long-term relationship and I wasn't looking for another. Not to mention the whole Nash-being-a-man part of the equation. A very hot man. A very hot man who seemed to want *me*. And that was a wriggling bag of unpredictable snakes too far. Way too complicated for the simple payoff of stretching my sexual wings and answering a few long-held questions.

So why am I making the man a damn coffee?

I sighed and offered Nash his steaming cup. "Here you go."

"Thanks." He took it from my hands, his fingers lightly grazing mine before wrapping around the mug, and it was all I could do not to close my eyes and moan.

And *that* was why Nash was still there. I was apparently enthralled in some B-grade period drama movie. Any minute now I'd get an attack of the vapours to the groans of the viewing audience.

Nash took a sip of his coffee, looking like he hadn't just upended my world with a single touch, and then grinned. "This is pretty good. A lot better than our staffroom version, I can tell you." He ran his fingers through his charming mess of dark grey waves, and I swallowed hard. For fuck's sake. This was getting out of hand.

"Yeah, it's not too bad." I took the chair opposite and focused on stirring in my sugar while avoiding Nash's steady scrutiny. "Then again, it's a pod and a button, hardly rocket science." I put the spoon carefully on the sideboard and took a sip from my cup, immediately grimacing at the twenty shots of sugar someone must've sneaked in while I wasn't looking. I eyed the mound of open packets by the coffee machine and winced. Okay, so maybe that was me.

"It's a pretty nice view you've got from here." Nash was looking over my shoulder and through the window to Wellington Harbour. "In all the time I've lived in Wellington, I don't think I've ever been up Hawkins Hill Road. It feels like you're in the country, and yet you're only ten minutes from the city centre. The wind turbines are at the top of the road, right?"

I followed his gaze to where Wellington city was drowning in heat and colour, the glistening harbour a sheet of glass under a spectacular cloudless blue sky, and gave an appreciative sigh. "It's pretty beautiful, all right. I regularly pinch myself that Tamsin and I were lucky enough to secure the land twenty years ago when no one wanted to live up here. Back then it was too far from the city, but it was perfect for us. The two acres of land that came with the old bungalow meant plenty of room for me to build a decent-sized workshop, and Tamsin spent ten years renovating the house."

"Two acres?" Nash nodded, impressed. "That would've been a great investment for you."

"It was. Luckily in the divorce settlement, she let me have it for way less than it was worth on the open market. The suburbs have spread to meet us, and with the views, it would've been way out of my league. But the turbines are there for a reason," I reminded him. "Wind velocities reach 160 kilometres an hour up here."

Nash gave a low whistle.

"The hills behind give us some protection from the southerly, but a good northerly can blow your brains out the back of your head and all the way to Invercargill if you're not careful."

Nash snorted. "Wellington, right? On a beautiful day there's no prettier city in the world. But when a midwinter Antarctic gale hits, and the waves are crashing over the harbour walk, the Interislander ferry is being tossed around like a rubber duck, and your inverted umbrella gets whipped off to Argentina—it's like the bowels of hell have sucked you in."

I chuckled. "But not today. Still, I wouldn't swap living here for anything. You?"

"Nope." Nash chuckled. "We must be masochists, right? I love watching the seagulls hover in a cantankerous wind, getting nowhere but just having fun. I don't even mind the frequent quakes that remind us who's really in charge."

"Nah, I'm not such a fan of those," I admitted.

"No?" Nash teased, his handsome face all dimpled-up and tempting. "Nah, I totally get it. I'm not looking forward to being here when the big one comes knocking either. But I definitely like living somewhere that has *actual* weather. I like being reminded that we're only here at nature's whim, and in a place like Wellington, some days that line is too close to call. Who builds a city right on top of a major fault line? The San Francisco of the southern hemisphere, minus the fog. Too fucking windy here for that shit to hang around." He laughed. "But it keeps you on your toes and thankful, right?"

"Right." I swallowed hard, my eyes locked on his and the way his dark brown irises bled almost to black at the edges. Conversation between us was as effortless as it had been at the party, and as a hard-core introvert who loathed social chit-chat, I had no idea what to make of that, and so I changed the subject.

"As flattering as it is to have you drop by, I'd have thought you'd have better things to do. Isn't it vacation time, or teacher-only for you lot?"

Nash's smile thinned. "Contrary to what most of the general public believe, teachers don't get the same time off as the kids. The junior school are still in class. It's only the seniors that are off with exams. And my admin doesn't seem to stop, regardless. I'm drowning in meetings, planning, budgeting, interviewing—" He stopped when he saw my smile. "Shit. You're messing with me, aren't you?"

I grinned. "Daughter who's a teacher, remember?"

Nash hummed and took a sip of his coffee. "You'd be surprised how many people think teaching is a cushy job."

"Ah, but I have Abbie to set me straight on a regular basis."

He smiled and I almost groaned when I realised what I'd said.

Thankfully, Nash let it pass. "Your daughter is definitely one of life's crusaders."

"She gets that from her mother."

He studied me and my cheeks grew hot under his gaze. "I see a lot of *you* in her as well."

"Really?"

"Yes." He lifted a finger to his face. "Here, around the eyes, and here, at the corners of your mouth. You have similar beautiful smiles. Oh, and her cheeky sense of humour."

He thinks I have a beautiful smile? What the hell did you say to something like that? Nothing, that's what. You pretended he never said it at all. And so I did, keeping my focus on the spot where Nash's finger still rested on his lips.

"Anyway—" Nash shot me a playful grin, breaking the spell. "— believe it or not, I hadn't exactly intended to lead with the whole crush scenario. It must be that spell you've woven over me."

I wasn't sure my cheeks could get any hotter, but apparently, I was wrong. "I'm gonna pretend you didn't just say that."

"I can repeat it if you like?" And he was back to staring again.

And I was back to seeing how much coffee I could swallow in a single gulp without choking, while simultaneously ignoring my heart leapfrogging in my chest.

"But maybe we'll save that for another day." His lips twitched. "I actually had what I thought was a pretty legitimate plan."

He was so damn open and . . . fun. I couldn't help but smile. "Go on then, spill."

"Well . . ." He stretched those long legs again. "I was going to ask for your expert opinion. I still am."

"My expert opinion? This should be good. On what, exactly?"

He held my gaze. "About getting some work done on my car."

My brows soared and I almost laughed outright because I knew damn well what he drove. "Your car, huh?" I levered myself up on the arms of the chair and squinted into the car park just to check I hadn't got things wrong. I hadn't. I snorted and slid back into my seat. "As in the *three*-year-old BMW parked outside? And you really thought I'd go for that?"

Nash's lips twitched. "Yeah, great idea, right? I knew you'd be impressed."

I laughed. "It's not exactly in the wheelhouse of a *classic* car mechanic."

"Ah." His brown eyes filled with humour, and he leaned forward. "But that's where I think you're missing an opportunity."

"Is that so?" I grinned. The man was really hard not to like. "Then please, enlighten me."

Nash sat back. "Well, first of all, said vehicle *will* be a classic one day, and so getting the best mechanic onto the job early has to be a no-brainer, right?"

The man was way too charming for his own good. "I'm listening."

"Good. And so, imagine my surprise when I googled your name—sorry if that's creepy—only to find that *you*, my friend, appear to be *the best* mechanic. You're pretty big in your world, it seems."

"You googled me?" I stared, ignoring the creepy part of the comment, as valid as it was, because I too might also have googled Nash Collingwood, several times, images included . . . So sue me.

And what I'd discovered was . . . sobering. *Dr* Nash Collingwood had a not-at-all-intimidating PhD in education and was a highly thought of and progressive educator and a champion of diversity in the classroom and syllabus. He was an LGBTQ+

spokesman and activist and had taken a lot of media heat and push-back from parents upset with his liberal views on gender and sexuality. He'd made principal by the age of thirty-eight and had keynoted more conferences than I bothered to read about. His zero tolerance for bullying had gotten him offside with a number of parents who'd made their opinion of him crystal clear on social media.

Nash Collingwood was, without doubt, a highly skilled and successful educational trailblazer. All the man needed was a super-hero cape and a Lycra onesie, and I was pretty sure his caped-crusader invitation was in the mail.

Five minutes of reading was all it took to realise Nash inhabited that rarefied world of worthy and successful men way beyond the reach of humble car mechanics like me. It should've been good news. It meant I could let go of those silly fantasies that were crowding my bed and simply get on with life. But instead, I'd felt an ache of disappointment that shocked me.

"I did indeed google you." He gave a cheeky smile. "Are you creeped out?"

"I should be," I admitted. "But then you haven't done so badly yourself, *Dr* Collingwood."

Nash gave a laugh of genuine surprise. "You googled me too?" His hand went to his chest. "I'm touched."

My smile came unbidden. "Yeah, well, don't let it go to your head. I wanted to know more about the man who is my *daughter's boss.*" I emphasised the last two words and watched them register in Nash's eyes.

But instead of backtracking, he simply gave a lazy smile and said, "*Her* boss, yes. *Not* yours. Is that a problem?"

Was it? And how had we gotten back here again? I shrugged. "I don't know what it is. I'm not even sure it should be a question for a harmless conversation. Because that's all this is, right? A *conversation.*" We locked eyes, and at length, he reluctantly nodded.

"If that's what you want," he offered. "But harking back to our *conversation* from the other night, that's still not a no." He shot me a cheeky grin. "Just saying."

Riiiight. Like he was *just* fucking with my head. His eyes. His voice. His undivided attention. His . . . appreciation.

Oh god. Nash genuinely wanted me. This wasn't a game. It wasn't my imagination. The understanding hit me like a punch to the chest and I almost couldn't breathe. And what's more, I wanted him back.

The office shrank until all that was left was this tiny space between us that I ached to cover.

And do what? What the hell am I going to do?

Finish my coffee and change the subject, that's what. "Well, Nash." I slid the empty cup next to the spoon. "First of all, regarding your BMW's classic-car aspirations." I pulled a face and wiggled a hand between us. "Debatable. Only time will tell."

Nash feigned outrage. "Such callousness in one so young. You own a 1956 Ford F100 pickup right?"

I nodded, somewhat taken aback. "So you *were* paying attention."

His lips curved up in a slow, sexy smile. "I always do if the subject interests me enough. And I might've possibly googled it as well." He grinned unashamedly and continued, "That's it parked next to the old white Merc, which, if I remember right, is also yours?" He nodded to where my bright red baby sat in the car park just outside the window. "She's gorgeous."

"She is." I admired the pickup's fluid curves while noting that Rollo and Jemma must've finished their coffees and headed back inside. "But that *old Merc,* as you put it"—I tried to sound as offended as I could—"happens to be an iconic collector piece. A 1970 300 SEL 6.3 sedan that launched a legend. A cross between a luxury sedan and a muscle car."

Nash looked suitably impressed. "Thank you for the education."

I couldn't tell if he was serious or not, so I flipped him off.

He laughed. "What about the pickup? Did you do her up?" He seemed genuinely interested, and I might have preened just a little.

"Yes, it's mostly my work. A friend did the panel job for me. Took me ten years to get her finished. My ex-wife called her the other woman." I shrugged. "Maybe she was right. There were certainly weeks I spent more time with my car than I did with my family." And how the fuck did we get onto this train wreck of a conversation? "I doubt it helped our relationship." I held up my left hand sans ring. "Divorced, remember?"

"Oh, right." But then Nash grinned, big and wide. "Still, I'm thinking that's lucky for me."

I rolled my eyes at his ridiculousness. "Anyway, back to your . . . project." I tipped my head to the window. "You should know that I don't take on any *project* much under fifty years old."

"Fifty, huh?" He shot me a sly grin. "Lucky me . . . again. I just sneaked in."

Heat bloomed in my cheeks. "The age of the *car*."

"Oh, right. Sorry." He bit back a smile, looking anything but. "So, are you saying my BMW doesn't fit your ageist criteria?"

The man was impossible. "What do you think?"

He chuckled. "I *think* you want me out of here so you can get back to work." He stood and put his cup next to mine. "Am I right?"

I stood, putting us almost eye to eye, bar the couple of centimetres he had on me. Which would've been fine if he'd done the socially acceptable thing and actually fucking stepped back. But he didn't. Which left his body right there, heat rolling off him in waves to break over my bare skin with that fresh, tempting scent. This was in stark contrast to my own less-than-appealing blend of grease, sweat and brake fluid which suddenly seemed to choke the very air from the room, and I instantly stepped sideways out of sniffing distance.

"You're right. I should get back." I waved helplessly toward the door. "And please excuse the state of me. The workshop is an oven."

Nash's mouth curved up in a slow sexy smile and his gaze trailed fire over my bare shoulders and arms. "Never apologise about smelling like a hardworking man, Jed. It's sexy as hell." And with that bombshell, he winked and headed for the door.

Which left me standing like an idiot, still processing the wink and the man part and the whole sexy-as-hell-stink surprise because, damn, was that really a thing between men?

"Yes." Nash turned, a wicked smile spreading over his face. "It's very definitely a *thing*."

And, oh fuck, I'd said that out loud.

He chuckled at whatever mortified expression played over my face. "Goodbye, Jed. Thanks for the coffee."

And he was gone before I could answer, the bunch and swell of his arse in those tight blue jeans as he strode across the workshop floor a siren song to my rallying libido—and holy shit, I was checking out a guy's butt.

Nash almost made it to the hangar doors before Rollo called out from the pit under the T-Bird. "Hey, Nash, if you're interested in classic cars, you should check out the car show a week from Sunday in the Hutt Valley. Did Jed tell you about it?"

Nash shot me a look, laughter dancing in his eyes. "Why no, he didn't. He must've forgotten."

I rolled my eyes, but Nash's poker face remained unperturbed.

"Perhaps you could text me the details, Jed?" Nash deadpanned. "We should exchange numbers."

"His number's on the business card." Rollo pointed to a stack of cards on the work bench just inside the hangar doors, and I briefly wondered if killing your employee for dropping you in the shit was a punishable offence.

"Awesome." Nash all but laughed as he reached for a card and waved it with altogether far too much satisfaction. "I'll be sure to get in touch."

"Our shop's got a trade stand there," Rollo pressed on, completely oblivious to the killer look I fired his way. "Come and find us if you have any questions."

Nash pocketed the card and shot me a gleeful look. "You know, I might just do that. See you later, Jed. It's been . . . enjoyable." And with that, he headed out of the workshop humming "You Can Leave Your Hat On."

It was all I could do not to laugh. *Cheeky fucker.* And he'd only got a dozen metres into the car park when I found myself inexplicably following. "Nash, wait up."

He turned and there was that damned smile again. "Something wrong, Jed?"

I narrowed my gaze and aimed for stern. "Look, I'm sorry you came all this way for nothing. Am I attracted to you? Yes."

His eyes lit up.

"*But* I'm not interested in anything happening between us."

He stared at me without blinking. "Are you sure about that?"

Yes. No. Fucking fuck, no. O, Jesus. "I . . . can't . . . I don't . . . I'm just . . . not interested." *So many lies.*

Nash held my gaze for so long, I almost changed my mind. But then he gave a resigned sigh. "I *really* like you, Jed."

Oh god.

"And believe it or not, I don't normally chase men. I don't usually have to. But I also don't go where I'm not invited." He winced. "At least not usually. But I suppose I hoped . . ." He closed his eyes and took a deep breath, then blew it out slowly before meeting my gaze once again. "It doesn't matter. Here." He placed the workshop's business card in my palm and closed my fingers around it. "I'm sorry I made you uncomfortable. I hope the show goes well for you. I won't be going to the show, and I won't disturb you again." And gone was the bright smile, replaced by one that missed his eyes by a mile as he turned and headed for his BMW.

I stared at the card in my hand, then Nash's back, then back at the card. *Oh fuck.* "Nash?"

With his car door open, he turned, but he didn't say anything, his expression carefully neutral.

I crossed to stand on the other side of the door and clicked my fingers. "Give me your phone."

He eyed me for a couple of seconds, then slid his cell phone from his pocket, unlocked it and handed it over. "Jed?"

"Be quiet." I added my number into his contacts and then looked up. "The business card doesn't have my personal number." As if that explained my obvious brain explosion.

His mouth twitched. "Okaaaay. So, am I to take it—"

"Nope." I shook my head. "You are to take nothing from this at all. But if you send me a text, I'll send you the show details."

"Is that all?" he asked carefully, and for a few long seconds, we simply stared at each other.

"I . . . I don't know," I admitted, glancing back to the workshop where Jemma was surreptitiously watching us from under the hood of her car.

Nash lowered his voice and leaned closer. "That's not a no."

I huffed softly. "And it's not a yes."

He gave a solemn nod and tucked an errant lock of hair behind his ear. "Point taken. I'll behave."

I rolled my eyes. "Why do I not believe you?"

He grinned. "Because I'm cute?"

I snorted. "Find me at the show and I'll give you a tour."

His eyes lit up. "You're on."

I held his gaze a moment longer, then headed for the workshop.

"Hey, Jed?"

I stopped and spun to face him.

"Thank you."

And that was not my heart doing a little Riverdance in my chest. Not one bit.

CHAPTER FIVE

Jed

I THREW THE HAND TOWEL AT THE MIRROR AND WALKED AWAY in disgust. No matter how long I stood there, how much I sucked in my stomach, or how many positions I tried to get a better angle, nothing was going to miraculously tighten my soft belly into a six-pack or reduce the lines around my eyes and mouth in the thirty minutes I had to spare before I left for the car show. I was fifty-five and I had the body to match. It could be a lot worse.

Get over it.

I crossed to the sash window on the other side of the ensuite and wiped the fog from the glass before opening it. A warm breeze curled around my bare chest, promising a hot day to come. The cicadas were already doing their thing out in the backyard and the happily-coupled blackbirds who lived in my garden were jauntily digging up my sprouting carrots.

"Oi." I waved an arm out the window to scare them away. "Get your own breakfast." They startled, hopped a couple of metres, and then turned to consider their options as they scoped out the threat.

Seeing it was only me, they immediately returned to their carrots and got on with it. It seemed an apt metaphor for the way my day was going. A bunch of carrot fronds was infinitely more interesting than me standing naked. Go figure.

I hadn't given a damn about my appearance in too long to remember. Tamsin had always said I was hot, but then, wives were supposed to say that, and I'd spent the eight years since we'd divorced looking for nothing more than the occasional hookup. For that, a haircut, a shower, and a pair of decent jeans seemed to work well enough. So why the hell was I suddenly angsting in front of a mirror, especially when the reason for all that concern was a problem I could well do without?

Was it because Nash was a guy?

I returned to the mirror and stared at my reflection as I considered the question.

Yeah, maybe.

That and the fact I hadn't been able to get the man out of my head in a week. Nash was smooth, accomplished, out, gorgeous, and had considerable game. I, on the other hand, was none of those on a good day, even with a tailwind. Not to mention, I'd never been with *any* guy other than a few secretive kisses with Beuden Butler behind the school gymnasium when we were both fifteen. Secretive, because there'd been no way I was ever going to endure what Beuden had been put through when he'd come out. But since he *was* actually out, in my year, and an all-around nice guy, he'd been a safe bet to test my theory.

The whole test idea wasn't something I was particularly proud of in retrospect, but it wasn't like I'd taken advantage of Beuden, either. He'd been surprised at first, sure, but then he'd been keen as mustard. I'd simply wanted to know, and pretty Beuden had answered that question for me with bells on. I still liked girls, no question, but my little tryst with Beuden confirmed that I had an equally interested string to my sexual bow, albeit one that didn't get a lot of airtime. Back then, I'd lacked the courage to take things further.

I grimaced at the mirror. I still did.

I sighed and lifted my razor to my face as I contemplated the vexing question of what *did* guys look for in other guys? I'd noticed Nash's arse . . . on more than one occasion . . . so that was obviously a good place to start. I glanced down in the mirror, turned a little, and sighed. Pretty damn bony—

"Ow! Shit." I tore a piece of Kleenex and dabbed at the trickle of blood running down my chin. Jesus fucking Christ. This wasn't a date or anything like it. I simply said I'd show the guy around the cars. Perfectly innoc—

"Goddammit!" I glared at another trickle of blood, this one on my neck. I stemmed it with more Kleenex, then rested my hands on the vanity to take a couple of deep breaths and calm the fuck down.

"What the hell is wrong with you?" I posed the question to my unhappy reflection. "You're a grown man. This whole shebang could be nothing. Nash could be nothing. He probably doesn't even see you as anything more than a . . . challenge. Is that really all you want?"

Was it? My reflection remained silent.

Maybe Nash got off on closeted guys. He'd already admitted he'd never wanted a serious relationship, and did I really want to pop my bisexual cherry on a passing hookup? Hell, did I want to pop it at all? And why was I even angsting over the question? I wasn't looking for anything, either. I *wasn't*. I loved my work, my business, my cars, my friends, my life. I didn't need any . . . complications. What I needed to do was walk away. It would be so much fucking easier.

Silver fox, my arse. And what the hell was that anyway?

I was simply a grown-arse man with age-appropriate wrinkles and the ability to say no, dammit. So why the fuck was I tied up in knots over a man who'd done nothing more than flirt a little? Because I was a fucking idiot, that's why. And because there was a part of me that ached at the thought of Nash Collingwood's hands on me . . . Yeah okay, and maybe a lot more of him as well.

"Ugh!" I flicked my razor at the mirror, sending a spray of shaving foam across its shiny surface, and then stared at the Rorschach-like pattern for a few seconds like it might offer some kind of explanation for the muddled state of my mind. All I saw was . . . Nash's arse in those tight jeans.

"You're an embarrassment to yourself," I complained as I wiped the mirror clean. Luckily, before I could answer myself and confirm the theory, my phone buzzed with a text.

Good luck with the show. Tamsin always had her finger on the pulse of her family's lives, including me, and divorce hadn't changed that one little bit, which probably was a little bit creepy if I thought about it too hard.

I texted back, *Thanks.*

We might drop by and see you. Neil wants to check out the cars and there's a new garden centre close to the stadium.

Drop by? My stomach lurched. It was the last thing I needed if in fact Nash did show up. I quickly texted back. *It's going to be a busy one.*

Text bubbles came and went. *Then we'll just wave from a distance. Neil wants to look at some 77 Firebirds.*

Best thing about Tamsin's new husband was his burgeoning interest in classic cars, except I could've done without it right then. Nothing left but to pray the universe had a soft spot for me, because I could do without the grief of my loveable but nosy ex-wife and her husband running into Nash and me.

I groaned and somehow finished the remainder of my shave without slitting an artery, a miracle in itself. Then I mussed my short grey hair with a small sample container of gel I found covered in dust at the back of the vanity and went on to spend an embarrassing amount of time deciding what to wear.

I eventually settled on dark jeans, which hid that bony arse, and a brown-and-cream check shirt that Abbie had bought for my birthday, saying it made my eyes pop, whatever the hell that meant. But when I found myself agonising over which cologne might better hide the stress sweat I was brewing, I mentally slapped myself, grabbed the keys to my shiny red F100, and headed out.

Nash said he liked the smell of a man, right? He had no one to blame but himself.

A couple of hours later, the stadium interior heaved with hundreds of people escaping the sizzling heat beyond. Jemma was away at a family wedding, and so Rollo and I had set up our stand the day before, leaving nothing to do but turn up on Sunday and talk to people. Rollo was already there by the time I arrived, and two giant coffees sat on the table waiting. I could've kissed him.

"Take your time." He handed me one of the monster cups. "We're all set."

"Thanks." I drank half the coffee before coming up for air. "I really needed that."

Rollo gave me a keen once-over. "I have to say, you're looking particularly sharp today, Boss." Then he leaned closer and pulled at my hair. "Oh my god. You've used product."

"Shut up." I batted his hand away. "I found some in the drawer and figured why not? No need to make a big deal out of it. And I'll have you know, I've worn this shirt before, plenty of times." All lies.

"Nope." He shook his head. "I would've remembered. Unless it was on a date?" His eyes lit up gleefully. "Oh my god. Are you going on a date after the show?"

I choked on my coffee and held my cup out from my shirt so I didn't ruin it five minutes in. "Wh-what?"

"Are. You. Meeting. A. Woman. Today?" He grinned and plucked a wad of Kleenex from my neck, waving it aloft like a piece of evidence, and my cheeks blazed hot. "It's been a while, right?" He flicked the wad away and I watched it sail through the air, along with my dignity.

"Don't be ridiculous," I huffed. "And for your information, it *hasn't* been that long."

He gave me a sideways look and I caved.

"Okay, so maybe it's been a *few* months."

He pointedly cleared his throat, and I sighed. "All right, lots and lots of months. Are you happy now? Jesus, you'd think I never dressed in anything but coveralls."

Rollo arched a brow.

"Don't." I eyeballed him. "Now, I'm going to stand over there and finish my coffee in peace." I headed five metres away to check out the neighbouring stand with Rollo's chuckle ringing in my ears.

The morning sped by. Two hundred spectacular vehicles—a mix of street rods, classics, and a good contingent of motorbikes—drew a large crowd to the Upper Hutt Event Centre. The trade show and a few of the rarer cars were housed inside the stadium while the rest lined the sports ground and car park outside.

Rollo and I were kept busy on the stand all morning, chatting with car owners, offering advice and handing out cards. We were pretty well known in the industry, so it wasn't that we were particularly touting for business, but it never paid to drop your profile. We had a few working engine systems mounted on displays and they always attracted interest. People, especially teenagers, crowded to see exactly how various engine parts worked, and we fielded questions about fuel-injected versus turbocharged, rebuilds versus new, and all the modifications in between that you could imagine. Exhausting but fun.

I'd just finished explaining the difference between an inline and a V engine to a teenage girl and her moderately interested boyfriend, when the hair prickled on the back of my neck and I turned to find Nash watching intently from a couple of metres away, a half-smile playing on his lips.

"Hey there." His words fell like a soft whisper of silk, his brown eyes running over me in approval before crinkling at the corners in a heart-stopping smile.

Oh god. I swallowed the beaming grin threatening to jump onto my lips and took a sobering breath because, Jesus fucking Christ, I was in trouble. Big-arse, drool-worthy trouble because, holy shit, Nash looked good enough to spread on my bed with a hot knife and lick clean . . . slowly . . . one glorious centimetre at a time.

My resolve to play things cool and nonchalant evaporated like the last few millimetres of boiling water in an empty pot before the thing caught fire and burned the whole fucking kitchen down.

The teenage couple I'd been speaking with murmured their thanks, and all I could do was grunt in reply and keep staring at Nash. Nash, who was wearing an anxiety-inducing crisp white Huffer T-shirt with so few wrinkles it had to be illegal, or the owner of it worthy of at least some prolonged therapy, and buttery light-blue jeans that hugged the swell of his arse and looked thin enough for any stray finger to poke a hole in with zero effort. Not *my* finger, of course, but you know, it was possible . . . by accident . . . in a leap year or lunar eclipse . . . just saying. *Oh god.*

I dragged my eyes up from his—nope, not even gonna say it—cleared my throat, and made an attempt to look like maybe I'd forgotten he was coming, but the heat radiating from my face no doubt blew that entire big-arse lie asunder.

"Oh, hi," I practically croaked. Yep, I had all the best lines. But Nash's interest confounded me. He was everything I wasn't. Sophisticated, educated, hot, sexy, effortlessly cool, and . . . sexually experienced. Yeah, maybe mostly that last one. He was just so damn comfortable with who he was, it highlighted everything that I wasn't. Nothing seemed to ruffle him. And suddenly I was right back following Beuden behind that gym all those years ago and feeling nervous as hell, mostly because I knew exactly what I'd find. That I liked boys.

Some things didn't change.

But Nash's wicked smile promised things Beuden's had yet to even dream of back then. Things that curled my toes and had my breath catching in my throat. Things I'd spent forty years trying not to think about.

"I brought lunch. Thought you might need a break." Nash smiled brightly and held aloft a brown paper shopping bag. Either he was oblivious to my near-catatonic state or he was being kind. The way his brown eyes danced in merriment, I figured it was the latter. "Your partner in crime"—he nodded Rollo's way—"said you could have a hall pass for an hour."

Nash glanced to where Rollo's gaze flicked between the two of us like a metronome, his bewildered frown saying everything there was to say about my oddball behaviour. It only took a few seconds for my way-too-perceptive employee to come to some kind of decision and a huge grin replaced the frown. "Go on, Boss. I can handle things here. You two have fun."

I almost groaned, rolling my eyes at his pointed comment. Not much got past Rollo's shrewd instinct for people, and I knew I'd face questions later. I ignored the obvious tease and held up my phone. "Call if you need me."

"I'll be fine." Rollo waved us off and I fell into step alongside Nash like I'd been doing it for years.

Outside the building, the sweltering midday heat hit like a furnace. "What is it with this weather?" I grumbled, glancing up at the sky where a lazy breeze shuffled a few clouds west over a cobalt-blue sky. On the ground, people meandered through the rows of parked cars in slow motion, sunhats and caps forming a sea of bright colours undulating like an incoming harbour swell.

"It's crazy, right?" Nash's elbow brushed mine and I suddenly realised how close we'd drifted as we walked.

I was about to sidle sideways a little more when—

"Jed." The all-too-familiar voice called from somewhere to my right. Tamsin.

I mentally cringed, then turned and squinted into the bright sun before pulling my cap out of my back pocket and jamming it onto my head like it was personally responsible for all my poor life choices.

"Hey, Tamsin." Nash sounded delighted to see my ex-wife, and it suddenly occurred to me that of course they'd bloody know each other. Before Tamsin's job had become insanely busy, she'd often helped with school productions. She was a whizz with a sewing machine and the drama department's best-kept secret. She looked stunning as usual, wearing a yellow strappy sundress with white sandals and earrings, her olive complexion glowing, her dark hair pulled back in a messy French knot.

"Nash?" Tamsin's eyes widened comically as she dragged Neil toward us. "What on earth are you doing here? You've met my husband, Neil, right?"

The jolt of surprise I usually felt every time Tamsin introduced her new husband was absent and my gaze flicked to Nash as the two men shook hands.

"Hi, Jed." Neil offered his hand, and I shook it. A tall, lanky guy with green eyes, a mop of long brown disobedient curls, and a twinkle in his eye, Neil was a solid, kind man and completely besotted with Tamsin. He made her very happy and that made him more than okay with me.

"So, have you seen anything you like today?" I asked him.

Neil beamed. "Yeah, that green '63 Corvette is pretty sexy."

I couldn't help my grin. "I thought you were looking at the Firebirds?"

He shrugged. "Keeping my options open."

"Then you should talk to the owner. I've heard he's looking for a buyer."

"Really?" Neil's eyes popped. "Thanks for the heads-up."

"Yeah, *thanks*, Jed." Tamsin narrowed her gaze. "Just what I need —another car in the garage." Her gaze flitted between Nash and me, and her expression turned sly. "I didn't know you liked classic cars, Nash. Quite a coincidence."

"I'm trying to learn," Nash answered smoothly. "And Jed was kind enough to offer to show me around. I like the F100s." He never even blinked.

I, on the other hand, almost choked on my tongue while shooting him a glare of total disbelief. What Nash knew about F100s would fit inside a four-word sentence. Not a fucking clue. And it would take Tamsin precisely two seconds to ferret that lie out.

"Oh, really?" Tamsin's gaze slid to me and narrowed. "My, my. What a coincidence. Lucky for you, Jed happens to own one of those."

"Right? What are the chances?" Nash deserved a gold medal for ballsy staredowns. "And when he mentioned it at Abbie's party, I twisted the poor guy's arm until he agreed to show me the ropes."

Oh, he was good. But he had no idea the hornets' nest he was stirring. I shot him another warning glare, but he simply grinned and ignored it.

"Oh, he did, did he?" Tamsin's gaze slid craftily to mine. "I shouldn't be surprised, I guess. Jed's a good egg like that. Always wanting to help a mate out."

I was in so much fucking trouble.

"What year did you say you were looking for?" Tamsin's mouth twitched with barely suppressed humour and I almost groaned. She totally fucking knew something was up.

"Oh, I didn't," Nash refused to be thrown. "And to be honest, I'm still a total greenhorn when it comes to cars. Don't know my thruster from my stick shift."

The choking noise was the sound of my tongue heading south down my throat.

"But Jed's helping me to straighten things out."

And that was it popping out my arse. "Yes, that's me." I somehow got the words out without adding a fist to Nash's face. "Generous to a T. Now if you'll excuse us, Rollo's looking after the stand while I show Nash a few cars, and I don't want to abandon him for too long."

"Of course," Tamsin said, then promptly ignored me in favour of turning back to Nash. "I see you're a fan of one of my favourite delis." She indicated the logo on Nash's shopping bag.

Nash's gaze shot to mine, slightly panicked this time, and I gave him an I-told-you-so stare. "Ah, yes. I um . . . I thought it was the least I could do to thank Jed for his time."

"Mmm." Tamsin's eyes twinkled with mischief. "Very kind of you, I'm sure. Well, we won't hold you up any longer. Enjoy your . . . picnic. Come on, Neil, let's leave these guys to their day." Her gaze lingered on mine for just a few seconds too long, but I somehow managed to hold it. "Talk to you later, Jed."

Not if I don't answer, you won't. It was definitely more threat than promise.

When they were gone, Nash shot me a look. "Sorry, I didn't really think that through, did I? Is it going to be a problem for you?"

"No, it's fine." And surprisingly, it was. "It's just that . . . Tamsin knows . . . about me. She's the only one who does. And she wasn't buying any of that excellent bullshit you were offering, just so you know. Plus, I can't lie for shit, so . . ."

Nash blew out a sigh. "We haven't *done* anything, Jed. There's nothing to hide. And we can keep it that way. If you really want, I can leave now. No harm, no foul."

"No." I took a breath and met his level gaze. "I meant what I said. I'm fine. And I'm looking forward to whatever smells so good in that bag."

His slow-spreading smile warmed my heart in a way I didn't want to think about too hard.

"All right then. Let's find some shade to eat, and then you can give me a personal tour of your favourite cars." Nash cupped my elbow and steered me through the crowd full of people, chugging back water and fanning themselves with their catalogues, toward a large copper beech at the edge of the rugby field.

And I let him do it, as intimate as it must've looked to anyone who bothered to pay attention, too fixated on the searing heat of his palm cupping the bare skin of my elbow and the clean, freshly show-ered scent of him. Every few steps, his body brushed mine. Delib-erate or not, I couldn't tell. All I knew was the surge of want that simmered in my blood at the feel of his body so close to mine.

I was a living example of an embarrassing midlife crisis and I really, really needed to get over myself.

CHAPTER SIX

Jed

"This looks perfect." Nash let go of my elbow and I almost chased his hand to slap it back where it belonged. He settled gracefully onto a patch of grass on the opposite side to a young couple picnicking on a blanket and began to unpack his paper bag. A couple of hefty sandwiches, two water bottles dripping with condensation, and a cardboard carton carrying two large slices of carrot cake and two forks all made their way onto the grass.

My stomach growled.

"Sit." Nash patted the ground close to him and I raised a brow at the invitation. He snorted. "I promise I won't bite." Then he winked and added, "Not unless you want me to."

I rolled my eyes, and unlike Nash, I sank awkwardly to the dry, crunchy grass, my knees creaking and protesting every inch of the way. I was careful to put a *lot* more room between us than Nash had indicated, but if he noticed, he didn't say anything.

Which was just as well, as I had just spotted an important detail I'd previously overlooked. To complete his effortlessly hip outfit,

Nash wore a pair of leather jandals. *Jandals.* One look and I was pretty sure I groaned. For some reason, Nash's long naked toes staring back at me with their faint tufts of dark hair and cute little wrinkles framing each joint sent a wobble through my belly. It shouldn't have been as sexy as it was but . . . damn.

"You want the Reuben or the ham and salad?" Nash held two sandwiches aloft and I dragged my gaze northwards.

Both looked delicious. "Ah, Reuben, thanks." I managed a smile.

He returned a broad grin. "Ah, there it is. I was beginning to wonder if I'd made a mistake coming today." He handed me the Reuben and one of the bottles of ice-cold water.

"I'm sorry." I ran the plastic bottle over my hot cheeks to hide my blush. "I wasn't being rude. I just . . . you caught me off guard with the whole lunch thing. You didn't have to do this, you know." I put the bottle down and unwrapped my sandwich.

"I know I didn't," he answered simply. "And yet here I am. Now eat. And get that water into you. It's hot as hell today and the air conditioning in that stadium sucked. You must be dehydrated."

I couldn't argue with him, and so I did as he said and sculled half the water bottle before starting on my sandwich. "Oh wow, this *is* good." I spoke around a mouthful of Reuben.

"Right?" Nash looked pleased. "The deli owner is a chef who ditched his restaurant in search of more family-friendly hours. He's a genius with sauces, and his baker wife makes all the bread. Glad you approve."

"I do," I mumbled around another mouthful, groaning in appreciation, and then looked up to find Nash watching me intently.

"If I didn't know better, I'd swear you were torturing me deliberately." He took a large bite of his ham and salad sandwich.

I swallowed and wagged a finger at him. "And you were doing so well, too."

He smirked. "Don't blame me. You're the one making all the sexy noises."

The very idea jolted me and fired my curiosity. And so while

Nash returned to enjoying his sandwich and studying the crowd and the cars, I returned to devouring mine and discreetly studying *him*, and okay . . . maybe doing a little of my own listening as well.

He was just so fucking comfortable in his own skin. So very, very different to how *uncomfortable* I felt trying to really own and allow myself to *feel* my sexuality for the first time. To feel that attraction, that . . . lust. Feelings that hungered for weighty muscle holding me down, coarse palms tracing the length of my body, the scratch of scruff between my legs, and the low growl of want in my ear.

"Let me know when you're done checking me out and we can eat that cake." Nash glanced sideways with a smirk and my cheeks lit up.

Shit. That's what you got for letting yourself *feel*. "Sorry." I screwed my sandwich wrapper into a ball and attempted to three-point it into the open paper bag. I missed.

Nash scooped it in. "Crosswinds are a bitch." He nibbled his lower lip and studied me for a second. "Can I ask if you like what you see?"

I rolled my eyes at his blatant fishing. "You know damn well I do."

He grinned. "It's nice to hear the words, though, because the feeling is very mutual."

"So, you keep saying." My gaze slid sideways to the increasing number of picnicking folks seeking shade under the line of beeches. "But I don't see it myself. I don't get why someone like you is interested in me. I'm a middle-aged divorced mechanic grandfather, who's ten years away from a pension. Hardly in the prime of my life."

"Neither am I."

I shook my head. "But you're—" I waved a hand over his body. "—you. I mean, just look at you. You're hot and accomplished and sexy. You could have anyone you wanted. I'm sure there's a ton of *young* eager men who'd give anything to get you in their bed."

"And yet here I am." Nash lowered his voice and leaned closer. "I won't lie and say I haven't walked that road a fair bit, although possibly for expedience more than anything." He shrugged at my frown and explained. "Less chance of unwanted entanglements."

Oh. "Of course. I guess that makes sense."

"I'm not apologising for it, Jed."

I held his gaze. "I wouldn't expect you to."

His eyes softened. "But right now, the man who has grabbed my attention is you, Jed. *You.*" His obvious sincerity was . . . unexpected. "Can you honestly say you don't feel the same?"

I stared at him, wanting to say exactly that. Tell him he was wrong about me. That he may as well pack up and go home. But the words crumbled to dust on my tongue and all I could manage was a shake of my head. "That's just lust. You're an attractive guy and I'm . . . I'm . . ."

"Bisexual?" he offered with a soft smile, and I rolled my eyes, something I seemed to be doing a lot of.

"Yes." I admitted in almost a whisper. "I'm bi. Are you happy now I've said the word?"

"Ecstatic." He beamed, raising his water bottle in a toast.

"You're ridiculous," I softly scolded, but touched my bottle to his anyway.

"Maybe you could do with some ridiculous in your life."

He wasn't wrong. "Maybe. Maybe not." But it was time to flip the conversation. "How old were you when you came out?"

Nash flashed those dimples. "I saw what you did there, but I guess it's only fair. I knew I was gay pretty much from the get-go. I was always drawn to boys, the way they looked, smelled, moved, talked." Another sweep of his gaze fired across my skin. "It was a no-brainer. I told my sister Colleen first. I was thirteen and all she did was shrug and say, of course I was. My younger brother Devon was much the same, not that I think he really understood at the time. Then again, my bedroom walls were plastered with posters of Elton John and George Michael, so I don't know who I thought I was kidding."

I laughed. "That probably did it. I stuck to movie posters like The

Blue Lagoon. A much safer bet. Plus, I got a two-for-one deal with Christopher Atkins and Brooke Shields."

He frowned. "Would your parents have minded? Is that why you never came out?"

I thought about that. "To be honest, I have no idea, and they're both dead now so I'll never know. I'd like to think they wouldn't have been too upset, but maybe that question mark was why I never said anything. They were . . . quiet people. Hard to read, if you know what I mean. I don't think I heard the word gay, or even sex, mentioned once in my house. My birds-and-bees talk amounted to a no-picture book left on my bed when I was thirteen with a note that said we're here if you want to talk."

Nash's eyes popped. "Really?"

I shrugged, thinking back to how I'd laughed about it at the time but how determined it had made me never to do that with Abbie or Ewan. "I think they were simply uncomfortable with the whole subject, regardless of the sexuality involved. And since I liked girls, it was easier . . . and yes, *safer* . . . not to say anything. Then I met Tamsin, and I didn't see the point."

"Did you have any teenage boy-crushes?"

I nodded. "Richard Gere, as mentioned. And then there was Harrison Ford. Gotta love a man with eyes like that."

Nash grinned. "*Star Wars* fan, huh?"

I faked a look of horror. "Hell no. *Raiders of the Lost Ark* all the way. None of that sci-fi shit. And with Karen Allen as the co-lead, that was another two-for-one deal. I watched that movie till my eyes bled. But getting back to when you came out. Your siblings were okay, but what about your parents?"

Nash sighed and leaned back on his hands. "I was nervous, especially about my dad. *His* dad was very conservative, always calling gay men fairies. Shit like that. And even though I hadn't heard any of that from my own dad, I was still worried. Turned out for no reason. They were both great. And after I told them, I think Dad must've laid the law down to his own father, because from that day forward, my grandad never said another bigoted word in my presence."

"Do they live close by?"

He shook his head. "They moved to Sydney for Dad's work just after I headed to university, and my older sister, Colleen, went with them while Devon and I stayed in New Zealand. Then Dad died about ten years ago from bowel cancer, but Mum stayed over there. She'd made good friends, and Colleen had her own family and was living close by." He studied me for a moment. "Have you *ever* been with a man?"

And there it was.

No beating around the gay-virginity bush any longer. Not to mention how to look an inexperienced fool in a single word. "No." Heat flashed in my cheeks. "At least nothing more than a couple of hot and heavy make-out sessions as a young teen, clothes intact." My gaze skittered away to the lines of cars, their colourful paintwork baking in the sun. "And meeting Tamsin by the time I was fifteen meant I didn't exactly have the time or the inclination for any further . . . exploration."

Nash went quiet and my belly churned, but when I finally got the courage to look back at him again, the kind warmth in his eyes lacked any of the pity I expected to see there. "You said Tamsin knows you're bi?"

I nodded.

Nash waited, saying nothing but watching me closely, leaving it to me to decide. I'd never talked about my sexuality with anyone other than Tamsin, and the idea of finally being able to open up after all these years to someone who really understood was too damn tempting. But it also opened a door that I knew I couldn't and maybe wouldn't close. To Nash. To my kids. Like the decisions were interlinked.

Was I really going to do this? God, help me, apparently I was.

Then again, maybe it was time.

"I never hid it, not from Tamsin," I finally answered. "She doesn't have a bigoted bone in her body and not much gets past her. She . . . worked it out." I took a deep breath and continued. "We were high school sweethearts, stupid in love as only teenagers can be. We were married by twenty and had two kids in the back pocket by the time we were twenty-five."

Nash's eyes widened. "Wow."

I chuckled. "I know it sounds fast, but at the time it didn't feel it. Abbie wasn't exactly planned, arriving in Tamsin's final year at university, but we managed, as you do when you're young and think you're bulletproof. I thought she was it for me and so I never came out to anyone else, not even my parents. Tamsin wanted me to, especially as Abbie and Ewan grew older, but at the time I didn't see the point. Or maybe I was still too chicken."

Nash said nothing. His quiet manner, gentle expression, and total focus coaxed far more from me than I intended.

"We had a good marriage for a long time. And then suddenly we were forty-five, the kids were gone, and we were looking at each other like strangers." I winced. "That sounds embarrassingly clichéd and a whole lot worse than I meant. It was more like we'd lost something of ourselves over the years and something of us as a couple. We hadn't protected and cared for it enough, and we weren't in love anymore. We both knew it, something I'll always be grateful for. It would've been much harder if only one of us had called time on what we had. We decided to call it quits while we were still good friends."

Nash frowned. "I still can't imagine. After all those years and a family between you. It must've been hard."

I blew out a heavy sigh. He was right. "I don't know if it's ever easy, regardless of circumstances. For me, telling the kids was the worst part. They had this idea that Tamsin and I had this perfect marriage. But by that stage, neither was living at home, and eventually their adult brains kicked in, helped by the fact that Tamsin and I remained friends throughout. I won't say I enjoyed seeing Tamsin with Neil when he first appeared in her life, but I got over myself. They married three years ago, and I actually gave her away on the day." I shook my head. "That was some weird shit, I can tell you."

Nash laughed and the sound of it lightened the heaviness in my heart. "I still miss her. Or rather, I miss what we had when it was all bright and shiny. But we're both in a better place."

"And what about you?" Nash shot me a quick smile. "Not tempted to tie the knot again?"

"Hell no." I laughed. "In fact, when I ran into you at the party, Abbie had just finished chewing me out for not being willing to even date seriously. She and Tamsin are always trying to set me up."

Nash's eyes widened. "You haven't dated? In eight years?"

"Don't you start." I stabbed a finger his way. "It's like you said that night. For once in my life, I'm able to enjoy doing what I want, when I want, and how I want, without feeling guilty. Having kids early in life means you don't get the opportunity to seize enough wild and reckless."

Nash's eyes crinkled at the corners, and he huffed softly. "If I'm totally honest, you don't strike me as the wild and reckless kind, regardless. Or selfish, for that matter."

I grimaced. "You might be right about the first two, but I definitely aced the third. When the kids were young, I spent way too much time with my cars and my business and not near enough with my family. I could've done a lot better. I'm not saying Tamsin didn't contribute to our marriage going south, but me not being there as much as I should've been certainly didn't help. To her credit, Tamsin never slagged me off to the kids, and I'll always be grateful to her for that. But you only get one chance to be there for your kids when they're growing up, and I'll always regret not making the most of that time." I fought the guilt and emotion rising in my chest. "As a teacher, I imagine you know the importance of that more than most."

He studied me for a moment. "Sure, but as a teacher, I also know that it's not that simple. Lots of families are time-poor these days. It's endemic to our way of life. The majority of kids and parents muddle through regardless and come out the other side miraculously well-adjusted and thriving. Yes, quantity is as important as quality, but I don't see you as ever being a neglectful parent, Jed. The fact you worry so much about how much time you spent at work gives you a leg-up on half the population who never even question it. Do you think Abbie and Scott are good parents?"

My mouth dropped open, horrified at the question. "Yes, of course they are. They're great. A lot better than I was at their age."

"But they both work, and Abbie told me she uses the day care close to the school and that you and Tamsin help them out a lot, right?"

I nodded, seeing where this was going.

"So getting enough time with Bridie is equally hard for them."

"But they make sure that what they do get counts."

He raised a brow.

"Okay. Okay." I blew out a sigh. "I admit I tried to do that as well. But it never seemed to be enough. At least according to Tamsin."

Another brow raise. "People say a lot of things when relationships are breaking apart, not all of it justified. I bet you said some stuff you'd rather take back."

I had, but loyalty to Tamsin had me swallowing any agreement.

When the silence stretched out, Nash sighed. "I'm sorry. That's absolutely none of my business. Occupational hazard. I play witness to a lot of heated parental discussions in my office, and who spends how much time with the kids is right up there."

"I don't doubt it, and it's okay. Tamsin and I have moved well past that now."

"It's clear to see there's still a lot of affection between you." His gaze softened and his mouth tipped into a smile. "But getting back to the roots of this discussion, none of that explains the fact of you not dating for eight long, dry years. Do you even remember how?"

I chuckled. "It's really not that bad."

"Nope. I'm not buying it." Nash stared at me, brown eyes lit with humour and something a lot less innocent. "I'd think most single women of *any* age would be gagging to get their hands on you. Self-made, successful, and hot." He rested back on one hand and looked me over. "There's an awful lot to like."

Heat raced up my neck and into my cheeks, and I hastily looked away. "Even if they were—" I turned back to find Nash watching me with that familiar amused glint in his eye. "—I'm not sure I want to marry again. For all that the divorce was mutual, it still hurt. I still feel like I . . . failed."

Nash's hand covered mine. "You're not required to marry everyone you date. You *can* just have some fun. You *are* allowed to do that."

I side-eyed him. "Are you sure you haven't been talking to Tamsin and Abbie?"

He pulled a horrified face. "Oops. Sorry."

I rubbed the back of my neck, but not with the hand that was still wrapped in his. "And I'll tell you what I told them. I do . . . have fun, I mean. I just keep it . . . simple." *Albeit too damn infrequent.*

Nash held my gaze, his hand gently squeezing mine. "So, here we are. Two men keeping it simple. There might be a story in that, yet."

I turned my hand in his and squeezed back because . . . because I fucking wanted to. "Yeah, well, don't go getting ahead of yourself. Just because I said the B-word doesn't mean I'm going to let you . . . let us . . . ." Just the thought of all the things I wanted Nash Collingwood to do to me had me stumbling for words.

"Let me what?" He shot me a wicked smile. "Kiss you, maybe?" He leaned closer, putting his lips right next to my ear, the wash of his hot breath on my skin sending a shiver down my spine. "Because I'd like to do that very much. And there's a lot more we could do together. I could make you feel so good, Jed, if you'd let me."

And oh, Jesus fuck. My heart jumped in my throat, heat pooled low in my belly, my breath quickened to soft thunder in my ears, and my cock plumped uncomfortably behind my zip. *Christ, the man was potent.*

Nash sat back, taking his hand with him, and all I could do was mourn the loss, the hair on the nape of my neck still standing at attention. I couldn't look at him, focusing instead on a couple laying down their picnic blanket about ten metres away, too terrified Nash would read in my eyes how very, very much I wanted him to do every single thing his teasing words promised.

"Don't look so worried." He tapped my knee, making me jump. "I'm not about to ravish you in public outside the Upper Hutt Event Centre." He shot me a salacious look. "Well, not unless you ask me *very* nicely."

I glared in response. "You're a high school principal. Aren't you supposed to set some kind of moral example?"

"I'm also a man." He unpacked the cake slices onto napkins, sat one in front of me with a fork jammed into its icing, and looked up. "A gay man."

Like I needed the reminder. I said nothing, mostly because I was still stuck on all the things he wanted to do to me.

Nash caught my eye and softly snorted. "Eat your cake, Jed." He pulled the fork from my slice and handed it to me. "Sometimes you *can* have your cake and eat it too."

I snorted an awkward laugh, pretty sure Nash was wrong about that, but I wasn't about to go there. So I did as he suggested and shovelled some carrot cake into my mouth, which afforded a distraction, at least. A burst of creamy sweetness exploded over my tongue so delicious that I quickly returned for another. "Oh yeah, that's good." I stole a sideways glance at Nash who was pulling his fork from between his lips, his eyes closed in obvious pleasure. And yep, that had been a mistake.

"Damn, this is good." He opened his eyes, his tongue darting out to lick at a smidge of cream cheese icing caught on his lips in a move that I was pretty sure was deliberate.

Don't look. Don't give him the satisfaction. Fuck it. Too late.

He caught me staring and smirked but said nothing. *Bastard.* Then he swivelled to face me, crossing his legs beneath him with an ease that I could only dream about.

"How the hell do you do that?" I pointed to his offending legs with my fork and tried not to stare at the way the soft denim hugged his package, which was tucked just behind those tempting bare toes. "I can barely kneel without needing a shoehorn and a dozen ibuprofen to get me back up again."

"Yoga."

I almost laughed until I realised he was serious. "You do yoga?"

Nash nodded. "After my Achilles repair, the surgeon recommended it to increase my flexibility and core strength. That and swimming. I used to run, but those days are long gone. And I go to the gym, but only under sufferance to appease my vanity."

"Well, I'm impressed. I thank God every day that I had the foresight to put good work pits in the shop. I can mostly stay on my feet and hand the awkward stuff to Rollo and Jemma these days. There's no way I'm as bendy as you." And there I was, back staring at his groin. I reached for the bottle of water standing between us as cover.

"You should come with me to a class. You might like it."

My eyes bugged. "Me? Do yoga? Abbie and Tamsin would piss themselves laughing."

"Do they know everything you get up to?" Nash's brown eyes remained steady on mine, and I had the distinct impression we weren't only talking about yoga anymore.

But his question still threw me, because yes, they pretty much did know all about my life, every excruciating detail. And for the first time, I stopped to think if that was a good thing. Even my occasional hookup had clearly become fodder for discussion, and since when was I okay with that?

I didn't know a lot of what went on in my kids' relationships, and even less about Tamsin and her new husband, and that was how it should be. So why was mine open for everyone's perusal and opinion? And with that thought, I felt suddenly . . . exposed.

"It's a good question," I acknowledged with a frown. "They do know most things. Maybe too much. I take your not-so-subtle point on that."

Nash regarded me sombrely. "You have a right to a private life, Jed. A *full* private life."

I bristled at the comment for no good reason other than my sudden sense of transparent shallowness. "I'm perfectly aware of that, *Nash*."

He blinked. "Sorry. That was rude. I didn't mean to imply anything."

I eyeballed him. "Didn't you?"

He winced. "Okay, maybe a little."

I emptied the dregs of my water bottle onto the parched ground. "How about we ditch the rubbish and I show you around?"

He held my gaze. "I'd like that."

And so, for the next forty minutes I did precisely that, introducing Nash to my world and some of my favourite cars: a black 1963 Lincoln Continental convertible owned by a close friend, a black-and-gold striped 1966 Ford Shelby Mustang, a white 1954 Cadillac Eldorado Coupe convertible, a blown 1934 Chevy hot rod in mandarin orange, and a cherry-red 1960 Chrysler LeBaron Imperial sedan with an engine I'd laboured over for six months.

Nash asked a lot of questions, seemingly genuinely interested. Why did I like the cars I did? Which ones had I worked on? How much time and money did it take to restore a car? How did some of the cars get to New Zealand in the first place? Did I show my own cars? How did I get into the business? A lot more questions than mere politeness or flattery might demand, and I couldn't deny the buzz of having his attention locked solely on me.

The tour took longer than expected because I kept bumping into people I knew who wanted to chat about their cars, and Nash observed each interaction with an expression caught halfway between admiration and amusement.

"You've garnered a lot of respect around here," he observed as we left the crowd behind and made our way into the car park at the back of the stadium. We'd only managed a decent look at about a dozen cars, but I'd been gone too long from Rollo as it was.

"Yeah well, New Zealand is a small place," I brushed his compliment aside. "Classic car mechanics aren't exactly thick on the ground. You can't afford to piss any of us off."

Nash took my arm and turned me to face him, those intense brown eyes drilling into mine. "You're good at what you do, Jed. An expert by the sounds of it. Those guys weren't just being polite. They practically revered you."

A bubble of pride swelled in my chest. It had been a long time since I'd been handed a compliment about the work I was so passionate about from someone *not* in the industry. Most pats on the back these days came from being a good grandad and dad. Not that there was anything wrong with that, but I almost didn't know what to do with the other.

"Thanks." My gaze slid away, and an awkward silence filled the space between us. "I should go," I said. "Rollo will be stressing by now. This is a much bigger crowd than usual. Are you going to stick around and look at some more?"

Nash shook his head and nodded to the entrance gate where a tall, good-looking man in his forties stood watching us. "My friend's taking me to some local brewery for a beer and a catch-up. I figured an Uber was better than risking driving after a couple of drinks. I have a moral example to set, remember?" He shot me a wink and I blushed . . . again.

I glanced to where Nash's handsome friend waited, and just like Nash, the man oozed unruffled self-confidence. I immediately disliked him and then hated myself for it. "An old friend?"

Nash smirked. "Why, Mister Marshall, you wouldn't be fishing, would you?"

I blushed furiously and stepped away. "Of course not."

Nash dropped the smirk and put a hand on my forearm. "I'm sorry." He glanced over to his friend and gave him a wave. "And yes, Colin's my best friend, although I have to say, the older you get the more ridiculous that term sounds, but we went to university together. He's the principal of Upper Hutt High School now."

"You mean he's our age?" I shot the guy a look of disbelief and disliked him just a little bit more.

Nash laughed. "Yeah, the bastard. Don't know how he does it, but I'm watching carefully and taking notes." He turned his attention back to me. "And he's as straight as they come, in case you were wondering."

I shrugged. "It's none of my business."

Nash stared at me for a long minute like he was choosing his words carefully. "Maybe I'd like for it to be."

My heart leaped in my throat, and I swallowed hard as Nash continued, "I had a good time today, Jed. A *really* good time."

Oh. I hesitated, wondering how to answer and settled for, "Me too. Thanks for lunch. It was thoughtful of you."

He grinned. "Thanks for the company. I'm pretty sure I got the better end of that deal. Can I text you?"

And there it was, my opportunity to shut down whatever this was that was happening between us before I made a hopeless fool of myself or worse. "Sure." And then because I was a complete idiot, I added, "I could, um, give you a lift home later if the timing works out?"

Nash's eyes widened as I stumbled on. "I mean, I'm going back into town anyway, and the show finishes at three-thirty . . . I could text you when I'm ready to leave . . . if you like?"

"You don't even know where I live," he pointed out, those brown eyes dancing with amusement again.

I was such a loser. "Then maybe you should tell me," I shot back.

He studied me carefully. "My apartment is in Kelburn."

I nodded. "Then you're on my way."

He said nothing and I wondered if I'd read everything wrong, after all. "You don't have to agree now. You might decide to stay, or take that Uber, or the train, or——"

"No . . . shit . . . I mean, yes," Nash tripped over his words. "I'd, um, like that . . . very much . . . thanks."

I blinked at the unexpected pink stain rising on his cheeks.

"Right. That's settled then. Text me the brewery name and I'll text when I'm on my way."

"I'll do that." He was still staring at me. "And thanks, again."

"No problem." I glanced to the stadium and back. "I should be going. I'll, um, see you later, I guess."

"Yeah." Nash finally smiled, broad and beaming. "See you later."

CHAPTER SEVEN

Nash

"So are you heading to Devon and Fiona's for Christmas again?" Colin emptied his glass of old dark malt and caught the eye of our waiter, who was finishing up at another table.

I nodded, admiring the server's pert young body and the way he couldn't seem to take his eyes off my best friend. "Jamie and Brian will be back from university, and Brian's bringing his new girlfriend. Should make for an interesting family dynamic. Apparently, Fiona's not too sure about this new girl, but we'll see. I'll be the safe option if any debriefing needs to happen."

Colin chuckled. "Amen to that. I love being the uncle. All the fun. None of the expense."

"Right? I don't know how they manage financing two kids at university. It's a big drain even with the help of eye-watering student loans and part-time jobs."

"Is your mum coming from Sydney?"

"Not this year. My sister has booked a beach house on the Gold

Coast for Christmas with my brother-in-law's family. Mum's going to that."

The young server arrived at our table with a Christmas tree earring dangling from one lobe, a swish to his hips, and hungry eyes. He cleared and wiped the table, making sure to lean as close as possible to Colin as he took his order for two more of the same.

The minute he left, I broke into a laugh. "You do realise he thinks you're on the menu?" I watched the young guy make his way back to the bar, no doubt hoping Colin was watching.

"Oh god, really?" Colin's head whipped around in time to catch the young man looking over his shoulder. The kid winked and Colin groaned and slid lower in his seat. "Fucking hell. How do I not know this shit? I've seen you flirt often enough to give me heartburn. You'd think I'd recognise the signs."

I laughed and downed the last of my beer. "Because you're totally unaware of how sexy you are to men *and* women. It's a damn shame you're straight."

"No, it's not." Colin scowled. "I have enough trouble under-standing women. The last thing I need is to fail dismally at door number two as well. Marcia says I'm a chronic romantic under-achiever."

I snort-chuckled. Marcia was Colin's girlfriend of just over two years—God bless her patient cotton socks. Colin needed to get that gem of a woman moved into his life permanently before she blew him off in frustration. "She does have a way with words," I pointed out.

"That she does." He sat back, his expression suddenly serious. "I heard you've got yourself a problem with the board."

My gaze shot to his. "Wow, that got around quick."

"You know how it is."

I did. I played with my coaster, rolling it over and over on its side. "One of our delightful year twelve students was caught keying the car of a teacher who'd put him on detention. He then verbally laid into the poor year ten witness who also happens to be gay. There was a bit of shoving and some pretty disgusting commentary, according to the year ten's friend who was also present, and this particular year twelve student already has two formal warnings in his file in the last twelve months and a host of informal complaints that go back years. Am I just supposed to let him start his final year thirteen with just a slap on the wrist? What message would that be sending?"

Colin winced. "How's the year ten boy?"

I blew out a heavy sigh. "Getting there. His parents pulled him from school the day exams were done, and I've kept in touch. He's quiet and a bit fearful of retribution, but he's talking and they're getting him help. I don't think there's much chance of him coming back next year if we can't do something about this other one, though."

"I take it you suspended the older bully?"

I nodded. "Right off the bat. But the problem is his dad is some big-name ex-professional rugby alumnus who everyone adores and who has connections on the school board. The kid is following in his dad's footsteps, showing lots of promise on the field, and his dad wrote a letter protesting my decision. The board are fighting me on it, claiming it could affect his professional rugby career opportunities. Apparently, recruiters frown upon homophobic outbursts. Go figure."

"Oh, for fuck's sake." Colin shook his head in disgust.

"Exactly. I want this kid to be on suspension until he and his parents agree to restitution for the damage to the car, sign a behaviour contract, and engage in some counselling and commit to attending our anti-bullying programme which he should've been required to do a long time ago. Having said that, my predecessor probably faced the same pushback I am. But this student has had numerous chances and it's gone on long enough."

Colin shook his head angrily. "The board is supposed to be there to support *us* and to follow best practices."

"I know, right? I almost had to get the dad escorted from the school grounds last week. He turned up in my office to tell me what he thought of the suspension and stopped just shy of calling me the F-word."

"Fucking hell."

"I know. I was this close—" I sighed and opted not to finish the sentence. "Anyway, I'm trying to get the board to agree to undergoing some mediation around this issue in the new year. I'm not folding without a fight, but I'd also rather forget about it for a few hours if you don't mind."

"Sure." Colin gave my hand a squeeze. "But I'm here if you need to talk or strategize."

"Thanks."

"You're welcome. And now that we've got the preliminaries under our belts, you can explain what was with you and the silver-fox hottie at the car show?"

I groaned.

"In *fact*—" He eyeballed me in clear amusement. "You really need to explain the whole being-at-the-car-show thing *At. All.* Hardly your style, I'd have thought." He slid down in his seat to dodge the afternoon sun painting hot golden stripes across his face.

"I can appreciate a nice car." My gaze slid to the window where the outdoor tables were packed with people, listening to a surprisingly good bluegrass band who'd set up under a wilting liquid amber strung with Christmas lights and Chinese lanterns. Along with a half-deflated Santa on the bar, Merry Christmas coasters, and passable if incongruous eggnog and mulled wine options on the menu, the brewery was doing its best to show a little early December festive spirit. "And Jed is just the father of one of my teachers who happens to know a bit about old cars and offered to show me around."

Colin reached across and turned my face back around. "Don't lie to me, Nash Collingwood. And you've pretty much answered my question already. You like this guy, whoever he is, and you're on the prowl."

"Pfft. I am *not* on the prowl, whatever the hell you think that means. I haven't *prowled* since I was thirty. These days I'm lucky if I can manage a decent saunter. These days I have to rely on my good looks and charm and the fact I usually pay for the drinks."

He laughed. "Bullshit. I recognise the signs. Your headlights are on full beam and your satnav is locked and loaded." He stroked his chin thoughtfully. "Did you crash and burn perchance?"

"Shut up. And no, I didn't. We're just in the . . . delicate negotiation phase."

He grinned. "Interesting. He's not your usual style."

I narrowed my gaze. "You mean he's older than I usually go for?" It came out sharper than I'd intended, and Colin's hands shot up.

"Hey, calm down. That's not what I meant. But it's interesting that it's the first thing *you* thought of." He smirked and I couldn't help but smile back.

"Fucker."

"Bastard."

We laughed, then sat back as the young waiter arrived with our beers.

"Anything else I can get you gents?" His gaze lingered on Colin who turned an interesting shade of scarlet.

"No, thanks. This is fine," I answered while Colin did his very best to look anywhere but at the young man who left looking more than a little disappointed. "You're safe. He's gone," I whispered.

"Shut up." Colin reached for his beer, then shuddered as the gritty strains of "Fairytale of New York" filled the bar for the second time in two hours. "Don't get me wrong, I love Christmas, but whoever decided this was a festive song needs their head read. Right, tell me more about this car hottie."

"Will you stop calling him a hottie?" I took a swallow of my pale ale. "His name is Jed Marshall, and yes, I like him."

Colin quirked a brow.

"Okay, I really like him."

"Wow." He bit back a smile. "*Really*, huh?"

I scowled and held up a finger. "Just one really. Singular. Nothing serious."

He laughed and held up both hands. "I refuse to comment."

"Fuck." I groaned and slid down in my seat. "Okay, so I admit the door is open on a potential second really at some point, although I'm not committing. You know I only spoke to him properly for the first time at the staff's early Christmas party, and then I completely embarrassed myself by just turning up at his workshop unannounced a week later and practically invited myself to the car show."

Colin's mouth dropped open for a few seconds. "Holy shit."

I pulled a face. "I know, right? The worst part is how damn nervous I am around him. Me? Nervous about a guy? I don't know what the fuck's got into me. He just makes me feel . . . I don't know . . . soft. Fuck, it sounds so stupid."

"Soft?" Colin slapped a hand on my forehead. "You sure you're okay?"

"Fuck off." I shoved his arm away.

"Aw, you've got a crush," he declared, like it was some kind of royal pronouncement. "And also, you swear too fucking much for a school principal."

I huffed. "I'm fifty-three, and as to the other, fuck you."

He laughed. "There's no age limit on having a crush, you know."

I groaned. "I know. I know. And you're right. I *am* crushing. And yes, he *is* slightly older than me by a couple of years."

Colin shot me a look filled with mirth but said nothing.

My scowl deepened. "I don't know why you're so surprised. You know damn well I've dated guys my age before. I'm not sure what you're implying."

Colin's eyebrows shot up. "Whoa, back the Freudian truck up. You just used the word *date,* my friend." He leaned across the table and shoved my head to the side. "Just saving you from that bolt of lightning because you have *not* dated anyone, young or old*er,* in a long, long time. At least not in the way most of the rest of the world use that term, as in more than a couple of weeks."

I shoved him off again, ignoring the curious looks being sent our way from the table next door. "It's not funny," I grumped.

He chuckled. "I happen to disagree. It's hilarious. But where the fuck did all this spring from?"

"I don't know, all right?" I reached for my beer, but Colin got there first and set it out of reach.

"Not so quick. Yes, you've been with a range of guys, I admit. Although to be fair, the majority weren't overly conversant with the word mature."

I flipped him off and made another lunge for my beer. He beat me to it for a second time and I flashed him a warning glare. "You're beginning to piss me off."

He bit back a smile and pushed the glass my way. "There. Don't say I never do anything for you. But getting back to the topic, based on what you've told me in the past, any older guys you've been with have always been firmly in the hookup column of your life with a side order of maybe brunch the next day if they behaved themselves. *Never* have you actually *dated* a mature guy, more's the pity. It could've saved you a ton in waxing and Botox and whatever the hell else you do to try and keep your youthful glow for the younger crowd. You could've added another investment property to your portfolio instead. But the more important fact is that you haven't dated *at all, in years*. Not since Jeremy of the achy-breaky-heart fiasco took your offer of love and shoved it into the next sugar daddy he laid eyes on."

I hissed and held my fingers up in a cross. "Shut up. You'll summon the ungrateful little bitch from the depths of twink hell and I'm too old to fuck with the sorcery required to send him back."

Colin snorted a laugh. "Amen to that. But he wasn't a twink, Nash. He was thirty-five years old, for fuck's sake. A man-child who never gave a shit about you. I told you not—"

"To trust him. I know." I rolled my eyes. "You've said it often enough and I learned my lesson."

He gave a put-upon sigh. "The *lesson* was to listen to your best friend and half the planet if they warn you off the guy, *not* to give up on relationships altogether."

"So *you* say," I grumped and turned my glass in a slow circle as a not-too-terrible rendition of "Nine Pound Hammer" leaked through the open window. "But it's not like you have a leg to stand on, is it?" I eyeballed him. "When are you going to get your shit together and tell Marcia you love her? She's not gonna wait around forever."

Colin pursed his lips. "We're not talking about me. We all know I'm a loser when it comes to relationships and taking risks. You, on the other hand, have proved you have the balls."

"Yeah, and look where that got me. I had them handed right back to me on a platter," I grumbled. "Besides, I didn't give up on relationships. I just got busy with work and my causes, and then it just didn't seem important anymore. I'm good at what I do, Colin. I'm where I want to be. I love my life."

He reached out a hand to cover mine. "I know you do. And there's no one better than you to lead a band of creative stubborn high school teachers and push them to their potential. As long as you're happy."

"I am. Thank you."

"So . . ." Colin leaned back in his seat and eyed me meaningfully. "Tell me more about this guy who's got you all tied up in knots, because it seems this wonderful happiness of yours has room for something more."

I shot him a glare. "I'm *not* tied up in knots."

He smiled but said nothing, and a groan slipped between my lips.

"Okay, maybe just a few teeny tiny slip knots that are easily undone," I hastened to add. "It's more that he . . . intrigues me. He's different. I don't know what it is, but I can't seem to stop thinking about him and it's driving me nuts."

"Oh?" Colin leaned forward on his elbows. "Even better. Tell me more."

"No. You'll only take the piss."

"Of course I will. Jesus, Nash. I'm fifty-three years old with a girl-friend of two years that I can't find the balls to ask to move in with me. Revelling in the disasters of your love life or hookup life is the closest thing I get to living dangerously. Don't deprive an old man of his amusements."

I lobbed my coaster at him, and he ducked and let it sail over his shoulder to land in the booth behind. One of the men at that table stood to hand it back. Colin accepted and offered an apology. Then he leaned in and said something I couldn't quite hear and the man glanced at me in sympathy.

When the guy sat down again, I kicked Colin under the table. "What did you tell him?"

Colin smirked and took a long swallow of his beer. "I just said you were having relationship problems. It wasn't a lie."

I groaned and slunk down in my seat. "For fuck's sake. They could be a parent, arsehole."

Colin's hand went to his chest. "Really? I never thought of that. So, what does he do, this Jed person you're mooning over?"

"I am *not* mooning over him."

Colin said nothing.

I groaned and dropped my forehead to the table. "Okay, so maybe I am, just a little." And with that I caved and told him everything. How I'd met Jed, our conversation at the staff Christmas party and the workshop, and how I'd taken lunch to him at the car show and talked some more. By the end, my cheeks were blazing, and Colin was staring at me like I'd lost my fucking mind. He didn't even have to open his mouth for me to know what he was thinking.

"I know, right?" I slumped against the back of the booth. "I barely recognise myself? I'm such an idiot."

"You're *not* an idiot." Colin regarded me seriously. "For some reason, this guy does it for you, and that's nothing to be embarrassed about."

"You're only saying that because it's not you."

His lip twitched. "True."

I booted him under the table. "I haven't behaved like this since I was fifteen and watched Matty Ormsby swim anchor for the school relay team in a pair of barely there speedos. He was a year ahead and had an arse you could bounce a penny off."

"Ah, to be young and horny."

"It was enough to confirm I was indeed happily gay, and from that point on, I set about discovering everything there was to know about dick, starting with young Matty, who was luckily fully on board with the idea. I came up for air around seventeen when Matty left for university, and I was ready to expand my horizons."

Colin snorted. "You always did love your research."

I shot him a grin. "Matty was epic. Nothing fazed that boy. I heard he made it big in corporate finance. Married some hotshot lawyer dude. Still looks hot too."

Colin finished his beer and pushed the bottle aside. "Well, your Jed isn't exactly short on good looks, so they have that in common."

"He's not my Jed, but he *is* hot," I agreed with a smile. "Not that he has any idea. He's totally clueless about his effect on me."

"Maybe because he's not like most of the men who dangle from your coattails, hoping for a little attention. Jed's making you work for it, and I for one couldn't be happier."

I cocked a brow. "You make me sound like a callous man-whore."

Apology flashed in his eyes. "I don't mean to. You're just . . ." He trailed off, clearly evaluating his ball-retaining options.

"Shallow?" I offered with an amused smile.

"Detached," Colin corrected, pretty much nailing it.

"Probably true," I admitted. "Although I did actually walk away from a guaranteed hookup the other night when I was out with Gerald. So, you see, I *can* say no."

Colin gaped. "You what? Was it anything to do with this other guy?"

Fuck. Backtrack. "Of course not. I just wasn't . . . feeling it."

Colin gave me his total-bullshit look, and I sighed. "Okay, maybe a teensy bit. But I don't even know if Jed's interested. Or rather, I know he likes the idea of *sex* with me." I couldn't stop the smile.

"He's pretty easy to read that way, and he did offer me a ride home, so that's something."

Colin nodded. "True, but then most men who lean your way want sex with you. Doesn't mean diddly-squat."

I snorted a laugh. "Wow. Way to support a guy, *friend*. But then there's also the small matter of him not being out, except to his ex-wife, and this whole family-man thing he's got going on that he doesn't want to upset. That shit is nowhere near my wheelhouse, and I don't wanna hurt the guy."

"Why would you hurt him?"

"Because I don't . . ." I stopped and sighed. "Because I'm not looking for something long-term, you know that. And nothing about Jed screams casual."

"There's nothing wrong with long-term."

"Says the king of non-committal."

"You might eat your words one day."

I blinked and stared at him. "Really?"

He shrugged. "You never know. But we're not talking about me. I don't know this Jed guy from Adam, but from the glimpse I caught today and from what you've told me, his clothes don't shout designer, he doesn't stand like he's waiting for a camera to appear at any moment or with his phone clutched to his chest, and I doubt he knows a single gay anthem. Every ounce of him screams solid, God-given natural, take it or leave it, wrinkles-and-all man. Kind of refreshing, to be honest. Although, Lord knows how you'll cope with a man who doesn't give a shit about whether you wax your pubes or when you last had a haircut. And you do understand it's more than likely he won't be doing any of that shit either, right? I thought you preferred your guys well-groomed and stylish?"

I couldn't argue because he was right, at least until recently, and Colin didn't press, leaving me to think while he sat back and ordered another round of beers. There was a sad, bald truth to his pithy summary of me. There was nothing faked or remotely unnatural about Jed Marshall, right down to the man's complete ignorance about how attractive he was in all senses of the word.

I'd spent most of my life pursuing meaningless encounters with confident, sophisticated guys, groomed to within an inch of their lives, who knew their appeal to the last waxed follicle on their body. Jed was a breath of fresh and unpretentious air that I had no idea what to do with. He was just as clever and funny and successful as any of those guys, but he was also unassuming and so . . . real. Things I'd never even considered sexy before, and yet they so fucking were.

"What's going on in that big brain of yours?" Colin's question jolted me from my musing, and I looked up to find him studying me with an expression somewhere between hope and outright amusement.

"Nothing," I lied, something I seemed to be doing a lot of.

"Bullshit," he called me on it. "You want to know what I think?"

I rolled my eyes. "Do I have a choice?"

He grinned. "I think you're tired of the whole damn circus."

"Jesus, Colin." I spread my hands in frustration. "A little clarity would be appreciated."

He waggled his brows and gave a sly smile. "You know exactly what I'm talking about. You're fifty-three years old and you've grown tired of the endless, shitty, whack-a-mole hookup dating scene that you've lived thirty-odd years celebrating. And then along comes Jed, whoever he is, and you take one look and see something very, very different, and you think to yourself, hmm, I'd like me some of that."

I choked out a laugh. "I'd like me some of that? Really, Colin? You're a fucking English major. Have some respect." I paused to digest what he said, and my phone buzzed in my pocket. I took one look at the screen and smiled. Jesus George, I had it bad.

We're all done. Do you still want a lift? No problem if you've changed your mind.

"That him?" Colin's gaze flicked to my phone.

I groaned and handed it over, but when he grinned delightedly, I scowled and snatched it back. "I'm so glad I have you to support me," I snapped, rereading Jed's message.

"Always happy to help out a friend." Colin chuckled. "So, what are you going to do?"

I texted my reply, then fell back in my seat and slid the phone back to him in disgust.

Would love a ride if it's no bother.

Colin read the text, laughed, and raised his glass in a toast. "Fucking A. This is going to be awesome."

CHAPTER EIGHT

Nash

Fifteen minutes later, when Jed texted to say he was outside the brewery, I glared at my still-laughing best friend, flipped him off, and headed out. So much for professional dignity.

In the parking lot, Jed's cherry-red F100 with its gleaming chrome had drawn a lot of attention from the patrons crowding the outdoor tables. A few had even wandered over for a closer look and Jed was chatting to them through his open window. I might not have known much about cars, but the throaty rumble of the big engine was sexy as shit, and I couldn't deny it felt good to open the door and slide onto the bench seat alongside the driver.

Jed waved off his admirers and turned to greet me with a nervous smile that did nothing to make me feel any better about crashing his life uninvited.

"Hey there." A welcome warmth crept into his eyes and some of the tension left my body. He did seem genuinely pleased to see me.

"Hey." I returned his smile. "Thanks again for the lift. I'll make sure to give you a five-star review."

His smile turned into a full-wattage chuckle. "I'd hold back on that for now. You puke in my baby from too many beers and you might not even make it home."

I laughed. "I've had three beers in as many hours. I think you're safe."

He nodded and threw the car into gear. "Good to know. Now buckle up. She's a beauty, but there's none of the safety features of that fancy BMW of yours."

"Aye, aye, Captain." I belted up, and while Jed drove, I set about admiring the interior of the car—red-painted dash, a black leather bench seat with two wide red vertical stripes, black carpet, a thick black racing-style steering wheel, and a set of impressive chrome gauges. Every inch was pristine and reeked of the owner's pride and passion. "How come you showed me all those other cars but not this one today? She's gotta be your favourite."

Jed fidgeted in his seat. "She is, but I wanted you to see a selection."

"Well, she's beautiful, and I think she might be my favourite too. And I'm not just saying that because she's yours." I ran my hand along the gleaming red dash and caught Jed's sideways glance of approval.

"She took me ten years from rust bucket to this."

"Do you mind my hands on her like this?" The question was innocent enough, but Jed blushed to his hairline. He really was cute as hell.

"Not at all." He kept his eyes on the road. "I'm not precious about her in that way, although you're right to ask. Some owners can be like that. But my baby likes the attention."

"Don't we all?" I muttered, catching Jed's soft snort in reply. And yeah, I might've been messing with him just a bit. "Does she have a name?"

His cheeks brightened again. "Lola."

I took a second to think. "As in The Kinks, L-O-L-A 'Lola'?"

"Mhm." He kept facing forward and I guessed there was a story there.

"It's a cool name," I offered. "Any particular reason for choosing it?"

His grip on the steering wheel tightened, and then he sighed and shot me a glance. "I'm betting you can guess."

This was about to get interesting. "Are you telling me you're a drag queen in your spare time?"

He turned and gawped. "What? No! I mean, there's nothing wrong with that, but . . . no."

"Is there a kink I should know about? Excuse the pun."

He snorted at that. "No, I am exceedingly boring in that respect."

I highly doubted that, but I let it go. "Hmm. Then it has to be a nod to your bisexuality? To what is assumed on the outside versus what is underneath? That's what the song was about in general terms, right?"

He flicked me a startled glance. "You're good at this. It was actually Tamsin who came up with the name. She got a perverse kick out of it. Most people thought I was simply a fan of The Kinks. And most people also think I'm a straight, pedestrian guy."

Not me. I tapped his arm and he turned again to face me. "I think it's kind of great."

His mouth tipped up in a slow smile. "I think so too."

We stared at each other for a long second before Jed returned his gaze to the road.

"Well, it's nice to meet you, Lola." I stroked the dash a couple more times, and when I noticed Jed watching, I did it again.

The ensuing silence sat comfortably between us, as if we'd passed some kind of unspoken test and were taking a breather before the next one came along. To that end, I sat back and enjoyed the scenery as the F100 rumbled south down the Hutt Valley expressway—an impossibly narrow ribbon of road carved directly on top of the fault line. Being early December, the road was jammed with Christmas shoppers and day trippers, the blistering heat and bumper-to-bumper traffic snapping many already short fuses.

I glanced across to Jed, but he seemed immune to the madness, humming softly to Ry Cooder's "The Prodigal Son", his fingers lightly tapping on the steering wheel. A smile crept over my face. "You're very calm for a guy driving his baby through this nightmare. Aren't you worried someone will clip her?"

He turned with a huge grin in place. "Any day I get to drive her is a good day. Besides, we're in no hurry." He paused for a beat. "The company's good and dents can always be fixed." He went back to humming and watching the road and I stared at him, wondering who the hell this man was.

The company's good and dents can always be fixed. I almost laughed. It would make a great, cheesy self-help title. I shook my head and tried to focus on the Somes Island Ferry slicing through the flat harbour water on its journey back to the city, but my attention was quickly distracted. The bench seat we shared acted as some kind of pleasure conduit that carried every ripple of his movement straight over to my side of the car. I fought the urge to slither across and feel the heat of his leg alongside mine, the rub as he shifted to change gear, the warmth of his hand on my thigh, the nudge of his body . . .

I lowered the window to get some oxygen to my brain and to stop myself from simply sliding over and fucking kissing the guy. "You weren't tempted to keep her original?" I asked, more as a distraction than anything else, as I ran my hand once again along the dash. "I read something about the tension between restoration purists and those who like to mix things up."

Jed glanced sideways. "You've done your research."

Colin's earlier comment came to mind and I almost laughed. "Yeah, I can be a bit obsessive."

Jed laughed. "Well, as much as I love the original lines, I also like the idea of putting my own stamp on a car, making it one of a kind. The mechanic in me wanted to up spec the engine, install better gauges, and make it a right-hand drive so it was easier to travel long distances on my own. The original had little more than a speedo, headlights, ignition, and wipers. That was never going to satisfy this grease monkey."

I couldn't help but laugh. When you got him talking about his car, quiet, nervous Jed took a back seat to this smart, funny, confident guy that I wanted to see a whole lot more of. And since cars seemed to be the key—

"So tell me more about Lola. Where you got her. How you decided what you wanted to do to her and what it felt like to finally finish and drive her."

Jed shot me a look of disbelief. But the smile that followed exploded somewhere in my chest and left my blood singing. "You are so gonna regret asking me that."

No, I absolutely wasn't. "Humour me."

And so he did, filling the remaining fifteen-minute drive with a fascinating summary of Lola's restoration that continued under the shade outside my apartment building for another twenty—engine off, windows down, the two of us facing-off across the bench seat with our backs to the doors and sharing his stash of boiled lollies. I asked a ton of questions and Jed did his best to make his answers as idiot-proof as possible.

And through every second, his blue-grey eyes held tight to mine, his passion for the subject clear in every word, his animated hands flying around the car. He was so alive and so fucking captivating, I couldn't have dragged myself away if my life depended on it. But the minute he was done and the car fell quiet, he shrank back into his seat and that wariness returned.

"Jesus, listen to me." He rubbed his palms down his thighs and shook his head like he'd disappointed himself. "I warned you about getting me started. Abbie and Tamsin skedaddle as soon as the word *carburettor* gets mentioned, saying everyone in a radius of twenty metres is at imminent threat of narcolepsy."

"Wow." I blinked. "And they say family are supposed to be your greatest fans." I paused and slid him a grin. "Well, I'm not Abbie *or* Tamsin. Not even close."

A small smile tugged at his lips. "Yeah, I'd noticed."

"Good." I chanced laying my hand on top of his and his eyes widened. "Also, I *asked* because I *wanted* to know. And it was worth every second. Do you have any idea how sexy you are when you talk about your cars?"

He snorted. "You've got a great line in flirting, I'll give you that."

"Stop," I snapped in frustration. "It's not a *line*. And as of now, I'm instituting a personal no-fly zone on any more self-deprecation. When you're with me, you don't put yourself down, got it?"

"A no-fly zone?" He raised an amused brow. "And how exactly do you see that working?"

I studied him for a few seconds, wondering how far I could push things. "How about, every time you diminish yourself in front of me, I'll have to kiss you?"

His blue eyes widened, but he didn't look away. Instead, he licked his lips and gave a soft nervous huff. "And that's supposed to dissuade me exactly how?"

Oh boy. I gave him a slow look up and down and those pretty cheeks brightened on cue. "Well, I haven't kissed you *yet*, so you can't really be sure that I don't completely suck at it. You might hate every second of my tongue sweeping through your mouth as I press you up against the nearest flat surface."

His gaze dipped to my mouth and I swore he shuddered. Then he dragged a hand down his face and over those plush lips. "Jesus, Nash. What are we doing?"

"Nothing you don't want to. Just say the word." I slid toward him, thanking every deity I could think of for the convenience of a bench seat until finally, finally, I slipped my knee between his thighs and the heat of his trembling body washed through me for the first time.

"Nash, I . . ."

I paused but when he didn't finish, I took both his hands and lifted the back of them to my lips one at a time as he watched with wide, wary eyes, his breath coming in short shaky gasps, his back pressed hard against the door pillar like he was trying to merge into the metal.

I kept my eyes steady on his, alert for any sign he wasn't totally on board, but for all the tight-muscled tension rolling off his body, Jed's eyes were hungry, wanting. But I needed to be sure, so I leaned forward until my lips brushed his ear and there was no mistaking the tremor that ran through him. "Do you want me to stop, baby?"

He went still, no breath, no sound. Then he gave the smallest shake of his head. "No."

"That's good." I pressed my lips just once to the shell of his ear, drawing a low rumbling growl from his mouth. "Because you are so fucking sexy, and I've been wanting to do this since the first time I laid eyes on you." I pressed another kiss to his ear, flicking my tongue in and out of the canal and smiling when he jumped.

"Oh fuck." He panted and craned his neck sideways to give me more room.

Well, all righty then. I took the hint and suckled on his lobe, tugging gently before letting go to lick a stripe up behind his ear.

"Oh shit, shit." He moaned and shuffled in his seat. "I need to touch you. Tell me I can touch you."

Like there was ever going to be anything other than one answer to that. "Yes, please. Anything you like."

His hands found my waist, his fingers slipping under my shirt to trail fire across my back as they roamed shamelessly up and down my spine, over my shoulders, and down again to cup my arse. "Fuck, how come you feel so good?"

I snorted and kept kissing. If I'd thought Jed's lack of experience might make him shy and nervous, I clearly needed to think again. He turned his face to bring our lips closer and I wanted to taste him so fucking much. But all I did was press mine to the corner of his, close-lipped, on and off, a tease and nothing more.

"Bastard," he hissed as I moved away.

"Just taking my time." I smiled against his jaw, then kissed down his neck to the dip between his collarbones where I lingered, sucking at his skin, shaken by just how fucking turned on I was at the knowledge he'd wear the mark for days.

"I know what you're doing," he muttered against my hair.

"You want me to stop?" I nipped and he groaned.

"No." He gave a low rumbling growl that vibrated against my lips, and fuck, he was sexy.

I didn't need to guess what he liked or didn't; the sounds he made were crystal clear. He was so vocal, so responsive—I don't know why it surprised me, but it did. I kissed my way up the other side of his throat and paid attention to the other ear—licking and nipping and darting my tongue inside until he was arching beneath me, desperate for friction.

He widened his thighs, the invitation clear, but I hesitated, wanting to relish the moment, these first tentative touches between us. I wanted slow. And I really, really wanted him in my bed, or his, before we went further. He tugged on my hips, but still I resisted, and just like that the spell was broken.

He leaned away with a confused frown. "Nash?"

"Shhh." I hooked a finger under his chin and pulled him toward me, covering his soft lips with mine, the brush of his stubble sending a bolt of delight down the length of my spine. He opened to let me in, groaning at the first sweep of my tongue over his, the first taste, the first thrill of exploration. That moment you could never have again.

My heart hammered in my throat as the flavour of him roared in my head—sweet from the candy, salt from the day's heat on his skin, and I couldn't get enough. I wanted to shove him down on the seat and devour him. I wanted to hold back and savour every second. I wanted it now. I wanted to wait. I wanted—

"Come here." Jed's hands wrapped hard around my face, angling my head until he had me exactly where he wanted, his tongue fucking deep into my mouth as he groaned with each thrust. Then he pulled away and shoved me back along the seat to my side of the car, until I was caged against the door, his blue-grey eyes dancing over my face from just centimetres away.

And then his lips lowered to mine once again, but softer this time. "Jesus Christ, you taste good." His hands slid around my neck as he peppered my face with kisses and then nipped the length of my jaw. "Mmm, stubble. I haven't kissed a man in forty fucking years."

I snorted. "Well, I'm glad . . . to be . . . of service," I managed between another onslaught of kisses, marvelling at the fact that, unlike Jed, I'd done a whole lot more to a man just a month before, but nothing that felt as electrifying as what was happening in that car in that moment, and I still had all my fucking clothes on.

"Ah, shit." Jed jerked back with a groan. "Bloody hip." He shifted his weight to his other knee.

I snorted. "Just as well we have two of them."

"Shut up." He kissed me again and I tunnelled my fingers through his short hair, loving the way he moaned his approval into my open mouth and took the kiss deeper.

He tasted so good, I didn't want to stop, but making out in my apartment car park wasn't going to cut it, and so the next time Jed came up for air, I used the opening to wriggle my hands free and onto his shoulders, bringing things to a reluctant end.

"As much as I love where this is going—" I reached up to kiss him softly. "—any minute now, someone in my apartment building is going to report us for lewd conduct. I have my good principal example to consider, you know."

"*Now* you decide to get all moral on me." Jed slid back over to his side of the car where he sat and watched me tug my shirt back into place over my jeans.

"I feel like a teenager after a make-out session," I grumbled, smoothing the wrinkles.

"The last time I did that, I *was* a teenager," Jed pointed out.

"Wow. Way to make a guy feel old."

He laughed. "We *are* old."

We stared at each other for a long minute, and I wondered what was going on behind those beautiful blue eyes. "Are you okay?" I broke the silence, half-dreading his answer.

Jed smiled and reached for my hand. "I don't think I know yet."

My stomach dropped. "I'm sorry if I overstepped."

"You didn't." He squeezed my hand. "It was me who shoved you back against that door, remember?"

"How could I forget?"

He nudged my leg with his foot. "I loved every minute of what just happened. But I don't know what it means for me yet, or maybe what I want it to mean, if anything." He mustered a smile that didn't quite reach his eyes. "Today has been a good day, Nash. Really good. Thank you."

Figuring that was as much as I was going to get, I nodded. "You're welcome." I grabbed my jacket and slid out of the car, then crossed to his door and leaned beside the open window. "It doesn't have to be complicated, Jed. You get that, right?"

His gaze searched my face. "It already is." He leaned forward and pressed a kiss to my lips. "I'll call you."

And I watched him leave . . . again. It seemed I was always watching Jed leave. But this time my belly flopped with the troubling realisation that if he decided to simply leave things between us at that, I was going to find it almost impossible to walk away.

I was hooked.

That first sweet taste of Jed, as new and awkward to the whole man-kissing-man thing as he'd been, was everything I'd fantasised. It also confirmed every suspicion I'd ever had that I was in trouble with this man. My tongue in his mouth had been like setting a match to a fuse and he'd surprised the hell out of me—everything I imagined but also nothing like it. Confident when I thought he'd be reticent. Bossy when I thought he'd be submissive. Enthusiastic and uninhibited and so fucking sexy.

I wanted a whole lot more of where that came from.

I wanted Jed.

But I wasn't at all sure he'd decide he wanted me.

CHAPTER NINE

Jed

I DIDN'T CALL NASH THAT NIGHT. OR THE NEXT DAY. OR THE one after that. And by the time Thursday came along, I was still avoiding my phone. I was also running out of high-neck T-shirts to hide the damn bruise Nash had left at the base of my throat. The bruise that I stared at in the mirror every morning, my fingers tracing the line of his teeth, and no closer to any decision about what to do about him.

Fuck him. Literally. My dick's unsolicited opinion was helpful like that. It had been on that loop ever since I'd left Nash standing in my rearview mirror looking like he could fulfil every fantasy I'd ever had over the last forty years. But while my dick might've been very down with any scenario that saw Nash naked in my bed, my mind was taking a bit longer to come around to the idea.

And Nash wasn't exactly making it easy—texting funny car memes and titbits about his day, like I wasn't the rudest arsehole in the world for not replying to a single one. Was I being a dick?

Fucking oath. But how could I answer when I didn't have a clue what I wanted to say?

A few things sprang to mind such as—

Changed out a muffler and started the Chev for the first time, and by the way, how about you drop by after school so I can swallow your cock down my throat and spill my load all over your sexy face?

Hardly good manners.

Or maybe—

Thanks for the offer of popping my bisexual cherry with world-shattering sex, but I'm a bit busy at the moment being a grandad and making sure I keep my blood sugar out of type two diabetes range.

Or my personal favourite—

I've thought long and hard and I've come to the conclusion that the last thing my life needs right now is a smart, interesting, sexy man who makes me laugh and has the potential to fuck me into oblivion.

I mean, pfft, who wants that, right?

God, I was ridiculous. But no matter what I did, I couldn't stop the hamster wheel spinning in my head, teetering on this precipice, and feeling fucking fifteen, for fuck's sake. And I hated alliteration.

What happens if I come out? What will Abbie and Ewan think? And what about Scott? And Rollo? Jemma? And how would I explain Nash to Bridie? What about my car mates? My friends? My business clients? There was a thick band of red on the necks of some of those guys, and the thought of losing that part of my life, losing their respect was—fuck—I couldn't even think about it.

And all for what? To satisfy my curiosity about being with a guy? For sex? For a few minutes of fun?

I groaned and dropped my head, knowing I was lying to myself. If this thing with Nash was just about sex, it wouldn't be the problem it was. But it wasn't just about that, at least not for me, no matter what Nash said about keeping things simple. I wasn't that guy. I never had been.

But that led to another question. What if uncomplicated and simple was all Nash really wanted? What if I was just another tick box for him? He'd said it himself—he mostly went for younger guys. And why was I even thinking about wanting more than just sex with him? What did *more* even mean? If I risked something like that, everything would change.

Everything.

Where would Nash or *anyone* fit into the life I'd worked so damned hard to build, which had cost me so much? Being a good poppy to Bridie meant everything and I was finally getting things right with my family. I wasn't good at putting a partner first; I'd proven that. So what if my personal life had taken a bit of a hit? I could live with that.

And last but by no means least, I'd been out of the game for so long I wasn't even sure how reliable things were . . . down there . . . at least not on a regular basis. I was out of practice and . . . it happened, right? When men reached fifty? Things didn't necessarily work . . . consistently. And then there were those beta blockers I'd been taking for my blood pressure the last year. They could cause problems with . . . things. What if I took a chance with Nash and then—

Oh god, I wasn't ready for that level of embarrassment. I hadn't had a problem yet, but—

"You gonna drink that beer or save it for New Year?" Tamsin slid into the chair next to me and took a sip of her gin.

I lifted the bottle to my lips, then winced at the warm rush of ale that filled my mouth.

"Here." Tamsin held out a fresh one, dripping condensation.

I narrowed my gaze and took the beer. "You could've led with that."

"No fun in that." She fell back in her chair and studied me. "So, what's up with you? We're about ready to decorate the tree and Bridie wants her poppy."

"Shit." I pushed to my feet.

"Sit down . . . please." Tamsin's lawyerly tone brooked no argument and I sighed and did as she said. "I said I'd deliver you soon."

I glanced over my shoulder to find Abbie watching from the

kitchen window. "In case you've forgotten, we're not married anymore, Tamsin. I'm not required to talk to you. Don't you have a new husband to annoy?"

"You didn't talk back then either, and look where that got us," she sniped. I made to leave and her cheeks brightened. "Shit, sorry. Don't go. That was uncalled for . . . and untrue."

"It was." I dropped back into my seat and took a long swallow of the ice-cold brew. "I don't answer to you anymore, Tamsin."

"I know. You've just been quiet, that's all. Too quiet. Do you wanna share?" She did her best to sound casual, but I'd known Tamsin for far too long. She was busting to ask about Nash, and I'd been half-expecting a call all week.

"Not particularly." I stared over the sea of houses clinging precariously to the steep hillside that led down toward Cook Strait.

"Jemma mentioned you'd been out of sorts all week."

My gaze jerked back to hers. "Jemma? When did you two talk—"

"Don't get upset," she soothed. "I called in yesterday, but you'd left to pick up a delivery of car parts. She didn't tell you?"

Goddammit. This was getting past a joke. "No, she didn't. What was so important that it couldn't wait until tonight?"

"I was hoping to talk to you alone," she explained, glancing back toward the house.

Here we go.

"You and Nash looked . . . *cosy* last weekend." Tamsin pitched her voice evenly. "I'm not prying, but he's a nice guy, Jed. Did he put that there?" She indicated the mark on my throat, and I immediately tugged the collar of my shirt together.

Not prying, my arse. "It's none of your business, Tamsin. And yes, he's a nice guy."

She followed another of my glances inside and patted my arm. "If Abbie noticed the mark, she's more than likely just happy that you're putting yourself out there." Tamsin waited, but I wasn't playing her game, and eventually she sighed and sat back. "Okay, I'll keep out of it."

"Thank you."

"I just want you to know that I support you one hundred percent if you decide to do something . . . with Nash . . . or any man . . . in case you were thinking of spreading your wings."

I rolled my eyes. "Nash is just looking to buy a car."

"Don't lie to me, Jed Marshall." She huffed. "I saw the way he looked at you. Like he wanted to eat you alive."

He did?

"And you looked nervous enough to have stepped right out of a Charlotte Brontë novel, if poor Charlotte had ever written about man-on-man love. The mind boggles. Oh, the scandal of it all."

I couldn't help but laugh. Tamsin knew me as well as I knew her, and the thought sat softly in my heart. I blinked and locked eyes. "Nothing big has happened between Nash and me."

She held my gaze. "But you want it to." Statement, not question.

"I don't know," I replied honestly.

Tamsin studied me for a long minute. "Maybe it's time, Jed. Do you like him?"

I couldn't stop from smiling as an image of Nash flashed front and centre in my brain. "What do you think?"

Tamsin studied me for a minute. "I think you like him a lot or you wouldn't have spent the week worrying."

"I didn't spend—"

She arched a brow.

"Okay, maybe an hour here and there. But there's a lot at stake, Tammy."

Her eyes crinkled at the corners in delight. "You haven't called me that in years."

"Shut up. I'm being serious."

She sighed. "I know you are, and I agree. What's at stake is your happiness, Jed. I know you're worried about what people will say, but maybe it's time for you to be you and to hell with everyone else. You get one life, Jed. Don't clip its wings just because you're scared."

"I'm *not* scared."

"Yes, you are."

I gritted my teeth while she took a deep breath and studied me.

"Look," she finally began. "Maybe you like Nash; maybe you don't. Maybe it'll go nowhere. But that's not the point. The point is, you won't know if you don't take a chance. Since we divorced, it's like you mothballed your personal life. You're a great ex-husband, a great dad, a great poppy, a great mechanic. But you're only fifty-five, Jed. You're not fucking dead. You have so much more to offer than that, and I should know. I was in love with you."

"I was in love with you too." My voice broke a little. "But that didn't save our relationship, did it?"

She shrugged. "Didn't it? I'm not so sure. Look at us now. I think we did all right in the end, and not everyone can say that. Maybe we're not in love anymore, but we're still good friends. When we divorced, I thought that was it for me. No more men. Then I met Neil. I didn't think it was possible to fall in love a second time, but somehow, I did. Take a chance, Jed. Fuck everyone else. I guarantee our kids will be fine with whoever you date. We did a damn good job raising them."

I finally smiled. "We did, didn't we?"

And then it hit me. The echo of Nash's throwaway comment in Tamsin's words. *You have a right to a private life. You mothballed your personal life.*

And fuck, if I wasn't doing it again. Talking with my ex-wife about my love life or lack of it while ignoring the one person I should've been talking to—the man who'd turned my world upside down and the only one who could answer my questions.

Tamsin was right about needing to have a life, but Nash was right too. If that life was going to mean anything, I had to make it mine. My choices. My decisions. And some damn privacy.

"Who did what?" Scott poked his head through the open door. "No, on second thought, I don't want to know. Are you guys ready to eat?"

"Poppy!" Bridie squeezed around her father's legs and launched herself at me. I caught her mid-flight and whirled her around before lowering her back to her feet. She kept hold of one of my hands and grabbed Tamsin with the other. "Come on, sillies." She tugged us both inside.

In the warmth of the lounge, I shot Tamsin a look and mouthed the words "thank you." She nodded in reply and then crossed to the couch and plonked herself on Neil's lap, planting a kiss on his surprised lips.

Before long, we were all laughing and eating pizza. I got the vegetarian option thanks to Abbie's concern for my blood sugar and overall cardiac health—cue one epic eye roll and a sneaky slice of meat lover pizza while she wasn't watching. After dinner, we each chose our favourite decorations to hang first. Following that, it was pretty much a free-for-all, with Abbie trying and failing to enforce some overall design strategy whilst everyone ignored her. Bridie and I worked as a team. She chose the decorations, and I hung them wherever she pointed. She lasted until about eight-thirty, when her eyes started to droop, her fists balled at her sides, and tired tears trailed down her angry cheeks.

I bundled her onto my lap, swaddled her in a blanket along with Tigger, and held her close while we watched the others make a mess of the tree. By the time they were done, Bridie was asleep on my shoulder and the tree had enough tinsel and feather boas to pass muster for a drag queen ball. I carried Bridie to bed and sang a little Ry Cooder to her as she slept. You can never start too young. And when I was sure she was out for the night, I tucked the blankets around her shoulders, pressed a soft kiss to her sweet cheek, and turned to find Abbie smiling at me from the bedroom door.

"She's done for the night," I whispered as I reached past Abbie to dim the light.

"Thanks, Dad. I can't believe this is our fourth Christmas with her." Abbie kissed my cheek and I pulled her in for a quick hug.

"I remember when you were about that age and your mother had to leave the bottom half of the tree empty to stop you eating the damn bread ornaments."

Abbie huffed a soft laugh. "Scott's rearranging it as we speak. Bridie won't even notice."

I shot her a look. "Good luck with that. Our girl doesn't miss much. But it's time I headed home." I made to step past, but she grabbed my arm.

"Are you okay, Dad? What were you and Mum talking about outside?"

"I'm fine." I squeezed her hand. "Just a little tired. And true fact, your mother's way too invested in my life for someone who's not married to me anymore."

Abbie chuckled. "Yeah, well, good luck changing that."

I was sure as hell going to try. "Goodnight, sweetheart." I pressed another kiss to her forehead and headed for the door.

CHAPTER TEN

Jed

I sat in my car like the total creep I was, my gaze fixed on the soft light shining from Nash's apartment on the top floor. I'd been parked outside almost thirty minutes already. Any second now, someone was going to report me as a peeping Tom, and I wouldn't have a leg to stand on. What the hell had I been thinking, getting almost to my own driveway before turning around and heading here, only to chicken out when I finally arrived?

What am I so damn scared of?

I didn't have to look far because the reason was sitting up in that apartment just a short walk that may as well have been a million miles away from me. Nash. He'd been dismantling my world from the first time I'd laid eyes on him, like he had a set of personalised blueprints to work by. Like someone had conjured him up just to fuck with me.

Four days obsessing over that kiss, replaying every tiny second. Wondering what it would be like to watch Nash lose all that irritating cool-arsed composure of his and come undone at *my* hands. To have him writhing under me, begging for release. But more shockingly, I'd found myself wanting to know what it might feel like to be full of *him*, so full that my body was lost to his, guided by his, overwhelmed by his, one with his.

I didn't get it. The idea of anal had always been quite frankly . . . terrifying, and all the googling I'd done hadn't allayed those fears one iota. I'd played around, sure. Tamsin was pretty fearless in bed, and I'd been fingered and rimmed and loved all of it. But I'd stopped short of ever thinking of experimenting with a dildo or anything like that. Until Nash. Until I'd started having these thoughts about what it would be like with him. Until I'd found myself scrolling adult shops and porn on my laptop.

"Could you be any more ridiculous?" I chided, then figured I may as well answer myself as well while I was at it. "Yes. Yes, you could. You could, for instance, be talking to yourself at night in your car, watching the windows of a guy you're crushing on at fifty-five embarrassing years of age while wondering what it would feel like to have his dick in your arse, or yours in his. How's them apples, you pervert?"

I groaned and dropped my forehead to the steering wheel, banging it a couple of times for good measure before a soft knock had me spinning to find an all-too-familiar face smiling at me through my window.

Nash.

Oh. My. Fucking. God.

I fired a silent complaint to an uninterested universe, then took a deep breath and waggled my fingers in some kind of hello as if this was a perfectly normal situation to find myself in.

His deep brown eyes shone black in the low light emanating from my dash, but there was no missing the crinkles of amusement in the corners. He waggled his fingers in reply and then signalled for me to wind the window down and I complied, my cheeks flushing with a heat just south of incendiary.

"You gonna sit there all night or are you gonna come inside?" His lips twitched, clearly fighting an outright laugh.

I groaned. "How did you know I was here?"

The laugh broke free. "I happened to look out my window, you dipshit." He shook his head. "You're hardly flying under the radar in this thing." He cast an appreciative eye over my old Mercedes. "You told me about this car, remember? The day I came to your workshop? What are the odds the one parked outside my building would belong to anyone but you?"

Fuck. "I guess I should pull my CIA application." I groaned, earning myself another laugh.

"Come on, Mata Hari." He opened my door for me to get out. "I've got a beer with your name on it. You can drink it while you explain why you've been ghosting me since Sunday."

I shot him an imploring look. "Can't I just go home?"

He snorted. "Get inside, before I have to kiss you for being so fucking adorable."

"I'm too old to be adorable," I grumbled, slinking out of the car.

Nash swatted my arse as I passed. "And that's for being such an idiot."

It wasn't like I could argue with that.

Nash chose the stairs rather than the elevator, no doubt to avoid being caught in a confined space with a total screwhead. On the positive side, the climb provided an outstanding view of his impeccable arse, those low-slung sweats and worn T-shirt doing a bang-up job of not hiding a single one of those delicious curves, and I wasn't above admiring the captivating landscape all the way to the third floor.

"I could make it easier for you and just ditch the sweats right here." Nash glanced over his shoulder with a broad grin in place.

Busted.

I groaned and gave him a shove to keep him moving. "Funny guy."

He laughed, and when we finally reached the top of the stairs, he led me through another door to an outside landing and stopped beside a door flanked by a mass of potted geraniums.

I raised a brow. "Didn't take you for a flower guy?"

He shrugged. "There's a lot you don't know about me. Starting with the fact my mother was a florist and my father a grower. Pretty sure I could name more flowers by their genus than you could list cars from the 1950s."

I followed Nash up the short hallway of his apartment and into the living area, which boasted an entire wall of glass sliding doors with a spectacular night-time view over the city. The doors led out onto a comfortable balcony holding a couple of loungers, some more of those potted geraniums and a small table and chairs.

Inside, the décor oozed modern minimalist in black, white, and grey with warm rose for contrast, and the room was immaculate, everything in its place. All except for one corner where an oversized armchair was parked next to an enormous shelving unit chocka with books and magazines stacked in higgledy-piggledy piles. Alongside the inviting chaos sat a coffee table strewn with papers and pens and two pair of glasses. I smiled. The teacher revealed.

But as my gaze continued around the room, the lack of a single Christmas decoration became obvious. "I take it you're not a fan of festive cheer then?" I teased. "Or is it too early in the season for you?"

Nash screwed up his nose. "My brother, Devon, waves the festive flag on the family's behalf. He has enough decorations to start his own shop, and although I enjoy it when I visit, the thought of decorating and then *un*-decorating on my own seems kind of tragic. I imagine your place is dripping with seasonal spirit?"

I shrugged. "I have a three-year-old granddaughter whom I babysit on a regular basis. It kind of goes with the territory." I made my way across to the wall of glass and blew a low whistle. "This is really something."

"It is, isn't it?" Nash slid alongside, close enough for the heat of his body to itch on my skin, which was already jumping from just being in the same postcode. Not to mention, those ridiculous sweats looked a whisper away from falling off his hips, and my dick was tying itself in knots, trying to preserve some sense of decency. Then he turned and brought his mouth alongside my ear, his hot breath raising goosebumps in its wake and scrambling my thoughts. "Outside appearances can be deceiving, don't you think?"

And I wondered if we were still talking about the apartment. He turned back to the window again and I managed to suck some air into my lungs.

"I signed on the dotted line the same day I viewed it," he continued. "Crazy when I think about it, but I just fell in love with the place. Sometimes you just know, right?" He let the words hang between us for a moment and then nudged me gently with his elbow. "The view from your place is just as good."

I risked a sideways glance to find his eyes locked on mine, that constant pull between us stretched tight to the breaking point. "But there's a fairy-tale quality to city lights, don't you think?" I swallowed hard, my gaze dipping to his mouth and those lips I'd been thinking about for days. "They can make even the dullest metropolitan sprawl appear somehow . . . magical."

His lips turned up in a slow, soft smile. "Why Jed, I do believe you're a romantic."

I huffed out a laugh. "Just because I spend my days with my head stuck inside car engines doesn't mean I don't appreciate beauty."

His gaze turned intense. "No, it doesn't." He hesitated, then reached up and brushed the back of his knuckles slowly across my cheek, and I had to fight the urge to lean into his touch. "You're just full of surprises, Jed Marshall." His brown eyes glittered gold in the city lights and my breath caught in my chest. I almost leaned in, so sure he was about to kiss me, but then he cleared his throat and the moment passed. "How about that beer?" He headed for the gleaming black and stainless-steel kitchen situated along the back wall of the apartment, and I followed.

"No, but thanks. I've actually had a couple already."

Nash turned and raised a brow. "Dutch courage?"

I chuckled, although the comment was warranted, and we both knew it. "No. I came from pizza and Christmas-tree-decorating night at Abbie and Scott's. I was on my way home when I thought . . ." I hesitated, my cheeks heating as I remembered exactly what had been running through my mind at the time. That I wanted to taste Nash again. That I wanted his hands on me. That I wanted his tongue down my throat and a whole lot more.

"You thought what?" he pressed. "That you'd stop by and apologise for ignoring me all week?" The laughter in his eyes went some way toward easing the niggle of guilt in my belly.

"Yes, that," I admitted, taking in the gleaming kitchen. "Wow, this is nice." I ran a hand along the sleek black marble island. One end functioned as a work area, while the other end was lowered to form a table large enough to hold six chairs. I took a seat at the latter while Nash made his way to the refrigerator.

"I have juice and pop, or a low-alcohol beer if you'd like to try that?"

"A pop will be good, thanks. Anything you've got."

He passed me a can of Lemon & Paeroa and took a pale ale for himself. Then he leaned against the fridge and held my gaze. "Well, I'm glad you came, regardless of the reason."

I cracked the tab on the can but left it sitting. "I . . . I got . . . scared . . . I guess." I looked up to find his brown eyes locked on mine. "I had all these excellent reasons why I just needed to shut the door on you and throw away the key, including the fact you likely only want me for a quick-and-empty . . . *encounter*."

I waited for him to deny it, but although his lips twitched, he simply raised his bottle to his lips and said nothing and so I continued. "I convinced myself I wasn't your style based on your usual demographic and the history you gave. Young, short-lived, meaningless, and with zero commitment."

Nash spluttered and wiped the back of his hand across his mouth. "Wow. I'll have to check, but I think I'm offended."

I chuckled. "I highly doubt that, but to be honest, that part still worries me. As old-fashioned as it sounds, I'm not a one-and-done guy. Maybe it's that *romantic* side you so astutely pointed out. Maybe it's my age. Maybe it's the fact I have no experience with men at all. But . . ." I sighed and took a sip of my soda before setting the can back on the marble. "It sounds stupid when I hear myself say it out loud, but I guess I don't want to come out for nothing more than empty sex with some random guy."

Nash looked two seconds away from pissing himself with laughter. "Now I *know* I've been insulted."

My cheeks burned hot. "Jesus, I'm sorry. I am so screwing this up."

"Hey." And he was suddenly there next to me, his hand covering mine. "I'm only kidding, Jed. But just so you know, I'm not looking for one and done either. At least not with you. And no one said you had to come out."

"But I would." I wanted to make that clear. "Maybe not right away and maybe not about *you* if . . . well, if there's nothing to tell." I looked away. "I've used a lot of excuses in my life to avoid exactly what's happening here, and I'm tired, Nash. I'm tired of not being me. And I'm tired of my kids not knowing that man either. And I want Bridie to have a chance for those conversations as she gets older, maybe even with me."

"She's a lucky girl." Nash squeezed my hand and then let it go and took a step back.

I looked up to find nothing but kindness in his eyes, and it gave me the courage to continue. "Since the divorce, I've gone eight years feeling nothing more for *anyone* except a bit of easily satisfied lust." My breath left me in a rush. "And I was okay with that. It was actually kind of reassuring, and I convinced myself I didn't need more. And then you came along and . . ." I couldn't finish.

"And?" he pressed.

I drew a sharp breath and stared at him, hoping to find some reassurance that he didn't see me as the total joke I felt, sitting there baring my soul in front of him.

"Hey." Worry lines creased his brow. "I want to know what you're thinking, Jed. I want to hear the words. And if it makes you feel any better, I don't know what the fuck I'm doing here, either."

His words stunned me, but when I took a second to really look, I could see it. All that intoxicating and intimidating easy confidence Nash oozed was nowhere to be seen. *I'm not looking for one and done, either. Not with you.* His earlier words came back to me.

Not with me.

My heart stuttered and I shoved off the chair to stand directly in front of him. His eyes went wide as I slid my hands around his neck and pulled him down for a soft, chaste kiss. "You're gonna be so much fucking trouble." I nuzzled his nose, and in seconds his arms were around my waist, his mouth greedy on mine, the smooth slide of his tongue sending ripples of lust through my body as it swept into my mouth like he owned it.

The force of his possession rocked me just as it had the first time —so . . . different, so demanding, so hungry, and so fucking hot. Every niggly thought in my hamster brain evaporated. All the questions, the doubt, the endless second-guessing. Only Nash and his mouth and the heat of his body pressed hard against mine remained. And oh god, I was gonna come if he kept that up any longer.

"Jesus Christ, what you do to me," he huffed, disengaging long enough to slide his hands under my arse and hoist me up onto the marble table section. The move put us almost eye to eye, something I could definitely get on board with.

"You taste just as good as I remember," I gasped, shuffling to find my balance on the slippery surface. "Kind of a relief, to be honest. Rules out the whole senior moment thing."

He snorted. "Speak for yourself, old man."

"Fuck you." I opened my legs and dragged him between them for another kiss, letting him know he wasn't running the show uncontested. I might be a slow starter, but I knew what I liked, and I liked his lips on mine. I liked it a whole lot.

"Oh yeah." He handed himself over and let me explore, my

tongue in his mouth, his lips between my teeth, the taste of him exploding in my senses just like it had in the car on Sunday, my dick straining against the confines of my jeans.

"You marked me, you fucker," I muttered, running my nose up the side of Nash's cheek and into his damp hair. The scent of coconut and citrus washed over my face, and the image of Nash under a spray of hot water, naked and wet, shot my cock to full attention. "I had to wear high-necked shirts all week in this damn heat. Rollo and Jemma thought I was crazy." I kissed him hard, his fine stubble brushing my cheeks and drawing a groan from my throat.

"Sorry, not sorry." He mumbled into my open mouth, ramming his tongue down my throat to shut me up, his grip on my waist verging on painful. I wasn't sure I'd ever been kissed like that, but I sure as hell wasn't complaining.

He pressed a line of kisses up my jaw, the heat of his breath and the gasp of delight as my fingers slid under his shirt, almost tipping me over. "Tell me I can taste you." The words sounded desperate against my ear. "Tell me I can suck you off."

I froze, and Nash pulled back to look at me. "I'm sorry. You don't have—"

"Yes." I cradled his face and pulled him so close my lashes brushed his. "Yes. Do it."

"Have you ever—"

I slapped a hand over his mouth and grinned. "In a few minutes the answer to that will be yes, so just shut up and do it."

He laughed and patted the black marble. "Then lie down."

I glanced down at the cold, hard surface and arched my brow. "Really?"

He shrugged. "I'd offer to go down on my knees on the floor, but that's not as easy as it used to be. And I kind of like the idea of you laid out like a feast for me."

I snorted. "They have these crazy things called beds these days."

"We'll get there," he said. "Let's live a little first." He pushed me flat across the table, spun me side-on to him, and pulled my jandals from my feet. Then he began unbuttoning my jeans.

"I can live a little on a comfortable mattress," I pointed out. "Just saying." I lifted my hips and then my feet so he could finish removing my jeans and briefs. And just like that, I was almost naked in front of a man, in front of Nash, for the very first time.

He ran his hungry gaze over me from head to foot and I fought the urge to tug my shirt down over my slender, bobbing cock. I didn't wax. Hell, I didn't trim or groom or whatever it was everyone seemed to do these days. I didn't have piercings or tattoos or fancy under-wear. There was nothing remotely exciting to see, just me atop the table of a man I barely knew—every stretch of skin, every crease, every soft inch of flesh on display. Helluva way to spend a Thursday night.

"You waiting for salt and pepper?"

Nash's gaze shot up to mine and he barked out a laugh. But just when I thought he'd take the hint and be on me in a flash so I could escape that intense scrutiny, he slowed everything the fuck down.

"You are so beautiful." He trailed a hand up my leg from my foot to my hip, taking in every inch and I shivered under his touch, barely suppressing a groan.

"Save the flattery," I chided softly. "In case it's not obvious with me spreadeagled on your very expensive marble table, I'm a sure thing. And I'm not twenty anymore. You get what you see."

Nash shot me a strange look and then stepped up to my shoulder and stared down at me. "And *I'm* not one for lying." He cupped my cheek in his palm and I leaned into it before I could stop myself. "*You* are a beautiful man, Jed. A *man*. Mature, fascinating, and sexy as hell, and I am very fucking thankful for the privilege. Don't you dare dismiss yourself. Remember my rule? No putting yourself down."

Heat bloomed in my cheeks. "I didn't mean—"

"I know exactly what you meant." He lowered his lips to mine for a long, thorough kiss that curled my toes on the cool marble. "And that's your punishment."

I held his gaze, biting back a smile. "I'm a horrible person."

"So very bad." He grinned and kissed me once on each cheek.

I stretched my neck to the side. "My arse has an alarming droop."

"Wicked man." He tongued his way down my throat to my clavicle and oh god, that felt good.

"I might get reflux when I deep throat and be deeply disappointing."

He snorted and ran his tongue over my nipple. I almost vaulted off the table. "I'll cope."

"My balls hang a centimetre or two lower than they used to and I'm not sure they're done."

"Easier to roll in my mouth." Nash ran his tongue down my quivering belly, stopping just shy of my aching dick, and it was all I could do not to shove him right on top of it.

"I forgot which car I was driving at the supermarket and had to look at my keys to remember."

He laughed and took my mouth in a hard kiss. "Really?"

I shrugged. "It is what it is."

He nuzzled his nose against mine and then kissed me sweetly, softly, like it meant something, like *I* meant something. "I forgot the code to the school alarm last month," he confessed. "I failed three attempts and then set it off."

I blinked. "Wow. That's tough to beat."

He chuckled. "Tell me about it. So, can we please stop with all this shit about how old we are? There's a very pretty cock with my name on it bobbing right in front of me. It's kind of distracting." He ran a finger up my length. "If you're still interested, that is?"

I slid a hand around his neck and pulled his lips down to mine. "I am." I kissed him hard. "*Very, very* interested."

"That's good news." He slid his hand down my leg, raising goosebumps in his wake. "I'm recently tested, and negative, by the way."

Oh, right. I'd forgotten. "Me too. Not so *recently*. It's . . . been a while," I admitted. "But there's been no one since."

His mouth curved up in a pleased smile. "Then this should feel extra good. Now, don't move a muscle."

Like I was going *anywhere*. My heart slammed in my chest as I practically vibrated in anticipation. Forty years I'd waited to know the touch of a man's hands on my body. To be kissed with the graze of stubble on my cheek. To be sucked off with the low growl of a man's voice rumbling through my cock. You couldn't have fucking pried me off that marble.

Nash shoved my shirt up and out of the way, reached for the olive oil from alongside the cooktop, ignored my raised brow, and wrapped a slick hand around my hard, flushed dick. Two seconds later the back of my head slammed into the unforgiving marble.

"Oh god." I wasn't going to last. My cock jumped in Nash's hand and I arched up. Forty years of waiting, and I'd be lucky if this wasn't over in forty fucking seconds.

"Not yet, baby." Nash sank his mouth over mine and set up an excruciatingly slow stroke with his hand. "I'm not gonna miss a second of this." His lips moved to my belly and my hips, skirting my cock as he kissed down my thighs to wring a series of frustrated moans from my throat. Then he kissed back up to my tight balls before licking a hot damp stripe along the side of my cock and then swallowing me down to my balls in a single long slide.

"Oh Jesus, fuck!" My hands clenched at my sides, but I couldn't keep them there. Next thing they were around Nash's head, fisting his hair as he bobbed up and down, sucking me deep into his throat, saliva pouring from his mouth to pool in my groin. He scooped some up and slid a finger into my crease, pressing against my hole and . . .

Oh shit. "Yes," I hissed, and the tip slipped past the ring of muscle, lighting me up from the inside.

Nash groaned around my cock, his shoulder jerking in rhythm with his mouth.

Jesus, was he . . . ? I glanced sideways to find Nash's sweats nowhere to be seen as he worked his own dick, and fucking hell, it was hot. I couldn't look away.

"I'm close," I gasped, trying to push him off, but he just grunted and worked me harder. His mouth on my dick, his hand stroking his own, his finger in my arse, up and down, wet and hot and tight and—

"Fuck!" A wave of pleasure roared through my body as I arched and gave a strangled cry, spilling down Nash's throat and watching as he sucked and swallowed every drop. And when I was done, he rested his cheek on my thigh and kept working himself.

Well, fuck that. "Hey." I nudged his head aside. "Let me."

"You don't have—"

"Please." I slid less than gracefully to the tiles, registered I was standing all but naked in another man's kitchen about to suck dick for the first time in my life, experienced a moment of unbridled panic, and then thought, fuck it. If Nash thought I was sexy, who was I to argue?

I looked up to find him watching me like he knew what I was thinking. "Just don't expect too much," I warned. "And I'll try not to bite."

"I'd appreciate that." He shot me a grin and we both laughed. Then he pulled off his shirt and stepped out of his sweats, and without a trace of self-consciousness, he took my hand and led me over to his roomy, black leather couch.

"What? No buffet for me?" I teased. "You get cushions and everything."

He sat, still holding my hand. "I'm telling you right now, this isn't gonna take long and I want to cuddle after."

Oh. I swallowed a smile. I wasn't about to argue with that. It sure beat being shown the door with a thank you and see you later. Nash was so comfortable in his own skin, and so . . . gorgeous. I desperately wanted time to appreciate his body just as he'd done with mine, but I wasn't about to keep him waiting.

He dropped a cushion onto the floor by his feet, and as I sank down, I took a moment to eye the first cock I'd ever been up close and personal with. It was . . . intense.

"Jed?" He tipped my chin up to look at him. "You don't have to—"

"Shhh." I slapped my hand over his mouth. "I just want to remember this."

He smiled and fell quiet, and I dropped my hand to trail a fingertip over the broad head of his dick, dark red and twitching. I dipped into the wet slit and lifted it to my lips, revelling in the tangy burst of bitter salt that exploded over my tongue.

My eyes fluttered closed. Jesus, this was it.

"So, what do you think?" he teased, and I looked up to find him watching me with a half-smile.

I lifted up to press a kiss to his mouth, sliding my tongue across his lips to share the taste. "What I think is that I want more."

"Mmm." Nash pressed his thumb between my lips and I circled it with my tongue, watching his pupils darken. "That makes me very happy."

"Good. Now sit back and let me give this a go."

He cupped my cheek and held my gaze. "Just so you know, there's no way this is going to be anything but spectacular."

I nodded, grateful that at least one of us was confident. Then I slipped free of his hold and leaned in to run my lips across that hint of stubble on his chest that had been calling my name, marvelling at the rough novelty of it on my tongue, sucking at each taut dark nipple, lapping at the firm nubs until he moaned and squirmed with every pass. Then up to the dip at the base of his throat and along his jaw as he growled his frustration, his fingers finding my hair and fisting it gently.

And then down over the hard ridges of his belly, so different from my own soft lines, watching as the muscle twitched and jerked for attention. Then lower still, low enough to take his gorgeous cock into my mouth. Thick, hard, huge between my lips as I stretched around it to try to swallow it down. Satin on my tongue. Rolling pulsing veins, hot and salty, demanding, and so fucking sexy.

I wasn't practiced, or smooth, or anywhere near as skilled as

Nash, managing only half his length before gagging and needing to make the difference up with my hand. None of which seemed to matter to Nash, judging by the wanton moans and desperate curses that kept falling from his lips.

It was heady and intoxicating, bringing a man like Nash to his knees. Having him beg to be finished off. And he'd been right. It didn't take him long. Not nearly long enough for me to finish cataloguing which kind of touch drew the loudest sounds and which ones made him wiggle and thrust and dig his fingers into my scalp.

"I'm close," he groaned, bucking into my mouth. "If you don't want—"

Like hell. I swallowed him as deep as I could manage, and he arched and cried out.

"Jesus . . . fuck . . . yesssss." Nash's cock pulsed and hot come spurted over my tongue, tangy and salty and everything I'd been waiting for.

I swallowed it down and the next burst as well, sucking him through each rolling wave until he jerked free, too sensitive for more.

"Fucking hell. Come here." He lay flat and yanked me on top of him, ravaging my mouth and fucking me with his tongue until my bruised lips protested and he pulled off to crush me in his arms instead. "That was amazing." He chuckled against my head. "Are you sure that was your first time?"

I crossed my arms over his smooth chest and smiled down at him. "Now you're just fucking with me. You and I both know that was amateur hour. But I'm a quick learner, given a bit of practise."

His mouth curved up in a slow, sexy smile. "I'm not sure I'll cope with any new and improved version, but I'm more than willing to be your guinea pig. I haven't come that hard in a long time."

I brushed a sweaty lock of hair out of his eyes. "If that was all you wanted, I won't hold you to anything more."

Nash grabbed my wrist and pressed a kiss to the back of my knuckles. "But I *want* more. I told you I wasn't looking for one and done, not with you. That hasn't changed."

"So, what *do* you want?" I slid off his body and stretched along-side, flinging a leg over his thighs and smiling at the thrill of soft hair brushing my skin.

He blinked slowly, keeping his eyes on mine. "Would it scare you if I said I don't really know?"

Did it? I thought about that for a moment. "A little." May as well be honest. "But since I don't know what I want either, other than more of what we just did, then I guess it's a fair comment. That was the best sex I've had in a very, very long time."

His expression brightened, brown eyes gleaming. "Me too." He kissed me on the nose as I puzzled his answer.

"But we didn't . . ." I hesitated. "I mean, I have no idea what the normal is . . . but . . . I guess I just assumed you'd be used to . . . more?" The last word might've come out more of a squeak, and Nash laughed out loud.

"Sure, I like . . . *more*." He smiled and kissed my nose again, which was kind of fucking awesome and not something I'd ever imag-ined guys doing to each other. "Both sides of the . . . *more*, as it happens." He winked and I had to think about that for a second before it twigged.

"Oh." I was pretty sure I blushed . . . again.

Nash ran a finger down my cheek and over my lips. "But I like what we did just as much. Anal can be on or off the table. It doesn't matter to me. Some men do, some don't. I can work with either. There are a lot of ways to get off, baby."

Baby? That shouldn't have felt as good as it did.

Nash turned on his side and kissed me long and slow, his tongue sliding sexily through my mouth and over my swollen lips. "We can find out together." He kissed my chin. "What we want." He kissed my eyelids. "What we like." He kissed along my jaw. "And how far we want to go." He found my mouth again and took his time before pulling off and whispering in my ear. "We can take it as slow as you want. What do you think?"

Think? Hell, I could barely breathe when he ran his mouth over my skin like that, my cock twitching with an interest I wasn't sure it had any ability to follow through with. I blew out a shaky breath and laid my cheek on Nash's chest, my tongue darting over his nipple, just because it was there.

"Hey." He jolted and I smiled up at him.

And just like that, the answer was easy. "Yeah, I think I like the sound of that."

"You *think?*" He gave a slight frown. "Hardly the ringing endorsement I was hoping for."

I pulled him down for a kiss. "Sorry, it should've been. I was thinking about Abbie and Ewan, not us. When to have that talk with them. Ewan's coming for Christmas, so it makes sense to tell them together, but then . . . it's Christmas. Doesn't seem the best time."

Nash relaxed and ran his hand over my short crop of hair, something he seemed wont to do. "The timing is totally up to you. Go with what feels right, and you can include a mention of me in the conversation. Or not. That's up to you. Just give me a heads-up if you do. I'd like to be ready for any incoming interrogation from your daughter."

I shot him a look. "Does that worry you?"

He huffed. "You know Abbie better than I do."

I grimaced. "Yeah, point taken. She'll want to read you the riot act."

He brushed his nose against my cheek. "I'll be ready for her. Now, how about we go get cleaned up?"

I blinked. "Oh. Um, thanks, but you don't have to do that. I can shower at home." I made to stand but Nash grabbed my hand.

"Now you're just hurting my feelings. I'd love for you to stay. I'd love to have you in my bed tonight, *all* night. But first—" He waggled his eyebrows. "—I'd love to see you in my shower. You're responsible for a number of fantasies in there of late. I'm not about to pass on the opportunity to get the real deal, wet and soapy, in my arms. What do you say?"

Oh. I couldn't stop the smile spreading over my face. "I say I'd be an idiot to turn that down, so yes, I'll stay. But I don't have my meds with me."

"Are they important?"

I shrugged. "Blood pressure. Lipids. The usual suspects. So no, as long as I get home at a reasonable time."

"Then we'll make sure you are. So, does that mean we're good?"

I hesitated and Nash frowned.

"Jed?"

I groaned. "It's just that I . . . well . . . I'm not sure I can—" I sucked in a breath. "I don't know if I can *go* . . . again, if that's what you were hoping. If you thought we might . . . argh, god, this is so embarrassing." I circled his nipple with my finger. "It's just that it's been a while . . . since I tried . . . *that*."

Nash snorted and tugged me close for a kiss. "Well, to be honest, without some help, I'm not sure I could either. Although it might be fun finding out, right? Maybe we should make it number one on our list."

I cocked my head, running his words through my brain. "You use . . . help?"

He shrugged. "Sometimes. Younger guys. Enough said."

I guessed it was. "And we have a list?"

Nash flashed those dimples. "We do now. I'm calling it my 'all the things I want to try with Jed' list. Refractory periods are now officially included."

I chuckled. "I hope you're a patient man."

He nailed me with a look. "I'm a determined one. And I'm not without a trick or two if you're up for it." He snorted at his own joke, and I might've gulped.

"I'll, um, need to check with my doctor?"

He laughed. "You do that." He grabbed my hand and wriggled to his feet, taking me with him. "Come on." He leaned in and whispered in my ear, "We should get started. It's gonna take me a lot of time to wash all your creases and crevices clean."

I opened my mouth to laugh at the idea, but nothing came. *He's gonna wash me?* That never happened in any of the porn I'd ever watched.

Nash pulled back to look at me, his expression deadly serious. "Are you okay with that?"

More stunned silence. I had nothing.

Nash laughed. "I thought so." He tugged me down the hall. "Come on. That list just got longer."

"So what's number two on this list?" I followed him into the sleek, modern bathroom, which sported a large soaking tub and a spacious shower with two heads. "I have a feeling I should be prepared."

He caged me against the vanity and pressed his face into the side of my neck, inhaling deeply. "Damn, you smell good. Oil and grease mixed with fresh grass and fucking sunshine. How the hell do you do that? It's so fucking sexy."

I swallowed hard, gobsmacked, because what did you say to something like that? I settled on, "How very poetic of you. Although I'm trying not to take the oil and grease thing as a commentary on my social class. Maybe with a few 'Uptown Girl' vibes thrown in for good measure."

"What?" He sprang back, looking horrified. "That's not . . . I never meant . . ."

I grinned and pulled him back in. "I was just teasing. Although if we're talking fetishes, I wouldn't say no to some thick-rimmed glasses and a bit of chalk dust." I looked him over and a sly grin played at the corners of his mouth.

"I can do that. The list?"

I summoned my best coy look and nodded. "The list."

Nash shook his head. "As I said, full of surprises." He ran his nose through my hair and groaned appreciatively. "The first time we were introduced, I wanted to do just that, and then follow it with this." He kissed the slope of my shoulder, then nipped it none too softly, and a bolt of heat slammed into my balls. "I bet you didn't know that."

"Ah, no," I said in a thick voice, angling my neck and praying he didn't stop. The flattery, the sex, the teasing, the tenderness—maybe especially the tenderness—it was . . . unexpected and . . . overwhelming. *Nash* was overwhelming.

"Well, I did." He kept kissing and nipping, and I kept waiting for the other shoe to drop, for him to step back and tell me it was all a mistake, that this was it. But he didn't. "And don't think it didn't shock the hell out of me as well, cos it did." He took a step back and slowly ran his gaze over me. "Oh yeah. Fucking Christmas come early."

Jesus Christ. The man was insane. But it felt good to be appreciated. Powerful. To be the centre of someone's attention. To feel . . . sexy. To feel wanted. God, I hadn't felt that in so long.

Nash reached a hand toward me. "Are you coming?"

My skin warmed at his words and the memory of what we'd just done—my dick rallying for a few hopeful seconds before opting for a graceful retreat. So much for getting that item ticked off the list. I glanced over at Nash's equally soft cock and sighed. "Not any time soon, I don't think."

Our eyes met and we burst out laughing.

"And I'm more than okay with that." Nash flipped both the shower heads on and then enfolded me in his arms while we waited for the water to heat. "And to answer your earlier question, number two on the list was simply you asleep in my bed. Not very exciting, I know, but it's pretty much a novelty for me."

His tone was serious enough to make me wonder if maybe this thing between us was as unsettling for Nash as it was for me. I slipped my arms around his waist and rested my chin on his shoulder, rocking us in place like we had all the time in the world. "Well, from a guy whose experience of men has just gone from fantasy hopeful to stratospheric in the course of an hour, I feel oddly at peace with that."

Nash chuckled in my ear. "It has to be said that most of the things on our list so far are mine. You want to add a few more of your own from those fantasies of yours over the last few decades?"

Oh boy. Yep. Yep. Yep. There were about a million, including but not beginning with Nash's dick in my arse, although that one had definitely leapfrogged up the research agenda. "Let me think on it." Much safer.

"Take your time." He tested the water and added some heat. "But just so you know, nothing is off the table. I'm pretty open." He eyed me pointedly. "And if you want to fuck me, I'll be there with bells on."

My heart jumped in my chest as an image of my dick shuttling in and out of Nash's tight arse slammed front and centre in my head. "Right . . ." I blinked. "I'll, um . . . yeah . . . I might need . . . Jesus, Nash," I finally groaned. "You have to stop saying shit like that. My brain just short-circuited."

He laughed and the clear sound of it rallied my heart.

I cupped his cheek and he fell quiet. "I'm not sure my head has moved much past more of those epic blowjobs, but thanks, I'll definitely keep that in mind. And colour me surprised, by the way."

He frowned. "That I want you to fuck me?"

"That you want *me*, full stop." I ran my thumb over his lips and he sucked it into his mouth, making my balls ache. "I'm a middle-aged, inexperienced bisexual mess." I pulled my thumb free and replaced it with my tongue, delving deep to let him know how very much I wanted to be there—in his bathroom, in his apartment, in his arms, and later, in his bed. I might be insecure. I might not know what the hell I was doing. But I was very, very on board with him and where this was going.

"Mmm," he hummed as he pulled away. "But you're *my* middle-aged, inexperienced bisexual *delight*. So don't knock it. I'm not sure how much more I can do to convince you that I want you, I want this."

There was no censure in his eyes, just concern, and I knew I had to get off this fucking pity train I was riding before I screwed everything up. For whatever reason, Nash really did want me, and I needed to stop questioning the why of that and just fucking enjoy it.

"You've done more than enough and I'm sorry. I think it's just that I'm not used to being told I'm sexy." I snorted. "Especially by another guy. But it's nice." I stepped into the shower and turned to face him, letting the water cascade over my shoulders and down my chest. "It's really nice."

I held out my hand, expecting him to take it and follow me under the water, but he stayed where he was, watching me with darkening eyes, and his appreciation fuelled a courage I didn't know I had. I straightened and ran my hands—seductively I hoped—down my chest and over my soft belly to give my cock a firm tug. When Nash's eyes tracked the movement and he cupped his dick in response, pride flared in my chest.

"Like what you see?" Hardly original, but Nash didn't seem to care. His gaze jerked up and I crooked my finger at him. "Get in here."

His pupils flared and he had me pressed up against the cold tile wall in two seconds flat. "Fuck me, but I like that bossy side of yours way too much." He licked up my neck and then held me in place, his hand firm but not tight around my throat while he tongue fucked my mouth.

Damn, it was hot to be manhandled like that, and when Nash finally released his hold, I leaned in and suckled on his earlobe while he rutted softly against my hip. "This isn't very principal-like behaviour, just so you know," I huffed into his ear. "Not sure what your right-wing parent moralists would say."

Nash grunted. "Principal Handbook 101 on how to deal with homophobic arseholes." He kissed up my throat. "Fuck 'em."

I laughed and made sure to grab two handfuls of his naked arse as he turned to capture my mouth. "Closer." I yanked us groin to groin, neither of us fully hard, and maybe we weren't going to get there, but it felt so fucking good. And as Nash ground into me, telling me how beautiful I was, how much he wanted me, how much he was looking forward to spending time together, I felt fifteen all over again, lost in the thrill of pleasure coursing through my veins and willing to imagine a future that for the first time was maybe big enough for two.

CHAPTER ELEVEN

Jed

My eyelids fluttered open to find my body dripping in sweat and a hot band of sun slicing across my naked chest. *Huh.* My bedroom faced west, ergo no morning sun, so what the hell? Creams and muted greens slowly inched their way into my focus, and I slow-blinked twice before memories of the previous night crashed into my brain along with the sudden realisation of a heavy arm wrapped loosely around my waist and a single snore arising from somewhere at my back. *Holy shit.* Nash.

And Nash's bed.

I was *in* Nash's bed.

I took a second to digest that not insignificant fact, along with the accompanying details that I'd had sex with a guy for the first time in my life and also slept with him. Yep, that taking-it-slow train had barrelled right on through the station, and all I'd done was blow it a kiss as it passed on its merry way. *"When you go in, you go all in,"* my mother's somewhat disconcerting voice rattled in my brain. I wasn't sure what the hell she'd make of her son right in that moment, but maybe she'd have been happy for me if she were still alive. I was gonna go with that.

But she really, really needed to get out of my bed—ah, *Nash's* bed.

Oh god.

I turned and took a sneaky peek, and some of that tension instantly dissolved at the sight of Nash's loose grey waves resting on my shoulder, his body plastered against my back like he was making sure I didn't go anywhere. I waited for the panic that never came. He felt so relaxed, so peaceful, so . . . content, and a smile tugged at my lips as I figured I might've had something to do with that.

I left him sleeping and turned back to face the window, letting the memories of the night before wash through my mind.

We'd fooled around a little more in the shower, but neither of us had pushed for more and I was grateful for that. As much as I loved what we'd done, it had still been a total mindfuck, and it was going to take some adjusting to.

After the shower, we'd dried off and fallen into bed, chatting until the wee hours about our families, Nash's activism projects, and my latest passion, the Oldsmobile Cutlass. Nash kept me wrapped in his arms the entire time, pressing kisses to my head, my cheeks, my shoulders, anywhere he could reach.

I could still hardly get my head around it, expecting the director would call "cut" any minute and I'd be told to pack up and go home and the check was in the mail. It had been surreal. Glancing once more back at Nash, I sighed, because it still fucking was. Being held as I would've once held Tamsin had been a first. *Another* first. Protected . . . coveted. Alice down the fucking rabbit hole.

Regrets?

I thought about that for all of a second, maybe less. Nope. Zero. None whatsoever. It had been one of the hottest nights of my life and that was saying something. Tamsin and I were no slouches in bed—sex had never been the problem. She was adventurous and uninhibited, and I'd loved every minute of it. Maybe that's why I'd never imagined sex with a guy would even come close. How fucking bigoted was that? But it had, or at least it had with Nash. I hadn't felt that satisfied in too long to remember.

My phone vibrated on the nightstand, and Nash snuffled and tightened his hold but didn't wake. I tipped it up, noting a text from Abbie, and the fact it was already seven o'clock. I needed to leave before Rollo arrived at the workshop and wandered over to the house to check on me.

Nash murmured something and rolled to his back, his arm falling from around my waist, the rush of cool air not the relief I'd expected. I'd have much rather had Nash and a dripping back.

I opened Abbie's text, surprised at the complete absence of any guilt.

Hope you had fun last night. Just checking cos you seemed a bit off when you left.

I stared at the text, then grinned as I replied. ***Just tired. Feeling a new man this morning***. I rolled my eyes at the inside joke. **What are you up to today?**

Not much. Might take Bridie to the beach later. Any chance you can have her tomorrow afternoon?

Another Saturday? I stamped down the irritation bubbling in my chest and typed, ***Of course.*** But my finger hovered over the send button, and when Nash snuffled and rolled to smoosh his face against my back once again, I deleted the reply and instead sent, ***I'll let you know. Gotta go.***

Sliding carefully out of bed so as not to disturb Nash, I tiptoed to the bathroom for a much-needed piss, then made my way across the dark hardwood floors to a promising bundle of clothes thrown over the back of the bedroom armchair. I fished out my shirt quickly enough—somewhat worse for wear but passable—but as for the rest of my clothes . . .

I replayed the night in my head, grinned like a ridiculous teenager, and headed to the kitchen. In less than twenty-four hours,

I'd somehow become the kind of man who left his underwear on another man's kitchen floor. The kind of man who had sex with another man on their freaking kitchen table.

That list of firsts was growing.

My jeans were exactly where Nash had dropped them, along with my briefs and jandals, in a pile on the kitchen floor. I got myself dressed, downed a glass of water, and then rustled up a pen and paper to leave a note. But that's as far as I got. What the hell did you say to the first guy you'd ever slept with? Thanks for popping my cherry? For giving me some of the best sex of my life? For putting up with my fumbling inexperience? For bringing my fantasies to life? For not kicking me out? For turning my whole fucking world upside down?

Hallmark really needed to get with the programme. *Thanks for the epic BJ. I'll think of you every time I see black marble.*

In the end, I opted for the basics, figuring I'd call him later.

"Going somewhere?"

"Jesus Christ!" I spun to find Nash leaning casually against the kitchen door in nothing but a pair of skimpy red briefs, arms folded. "You scared the living daylights out of me." I ignored the wariness in his brown eyes and walked straight across to muscle my way into his reluctant arms. "I wasn't running, so you can wipe that look off your face and hold me. I simply didn't want to wake you. And I did leave a note." I pointed to the kitchen island.

He kept hold of my hand as he wandered over and read the note aloud. "Thank you. It was amazing. I'll call you later." He raised an unimpressed eyebrow, and heat raced into my cheeks.

"Okay, I admit when you read it like that, it doesn't sound the best." I raised my hands in defence. "But I swear it wasn't meant that way. I had every intention of calling you the minute I got home."

"Uh-huh."

"I'm sorry." I slid my arms around his waist and soaked up all that hot bare skin. "I'm not very good at this. I had no freaking idea what to say."

"You should've woken me." He tipped my chin up and pressed his lips softly to mine. "When I saw you'd gone, I . . . I was worried you were upset . . . about last night . . . and that's the last thing I wanted."

"No." I kissed him back, slowly, thoroughly, feeling his body relax inch by inch. "Nothing is further from the truth. Last night was so much better than I'd imagined. *You* were better than I'd imagined. And believe me, I've imagined *a lot* these past couple of months since we first met. You have no idea."

"Is that so?" His eyes danced in a way that made me want to drag him back to bed and fuck him senseless and . . . okay, that was new. "Tell me more."

"Not a chance. Your ego's big enough as it is, and I have to go. I still can't believe we did that." I tipped my head to the table-end of the marble island.

He chuckled and ran his nose through my hair . . . again. "Neither can I."

I pushed back and stared at him. "Are you telling me you don't make a habit of fraternising on kitchen work surfaces?"

"Not usually. If I had to count, then you'd be my—" He ticked off his fingers. "—first." He grinned. "And that includes breakfast bars, butchers' blocks, and all rolling prep tables. I may never be able to look at a string of sausages again without sporting wood."

I swallowed a laugh. "Or spotted dick."

He snorted. "Toad in the hole?"

"Boston Cream pie."

"Head cheese."

"Dry rub."

"Sloppy Joes."

"Ew." That one threw me for a second, but I rallied. "Pulled pork?"

Nash snorted. "Oh. My. God." Then he narrowed his gaze. "Strip loin."

Oh, he was good. I drummed my fingers on my lips for a few seconds and then smirked. "Horlicks."

"Hor—licks?" He hooted and hauled me into his arms. "Jesus Christ, I can't beat that. You win. And your prize, should you decide to accept it, is number three on our list . . . or is it four, or five . . . to be honest, I've lost count."

He seemed flustered and I leaned back and eyed him quizzically. "I'm listening."

He blew out a sigh. "Okay, here goes. I'd, um—" He took a deep breath. "I'd really like it if you'd have dinner with me Saturday . . . tomorrow."

I blinked, my heart thumping in my chest. "Dinner? As in a *date*, dinner?"

"Yes." He watched me carefully. "If that works for you? Unequivocally, a *date*."

"But you don't do dating," I reminded him.

"I don't do a lot of things that I suddenly seem very interested in doing with *you*." He flushed, suddenly so different from the cool, collected guy I'd come to know that it was all I could do not to laugh. "I mean, I know we're keeping this quiet for now. Taking it slow and all that. But a dinner date is slow, right? We eat, we drink, we talk . . . and maybe we can make out a little?" He eyed me hopefully. "So, are you going to bust my balls about this or tell me what you think?"

I bit back a smile. "Then yes. I'd love to have dinner with you." I watched as his eyes lit up. "But I'd rather not go anywhere public, just for now. How about we make it my place? I should be done working on my car by about four. Steaks on the barbecue?"

"Sounds great." He hesitated. "Would I be able to see this new car of yours? Unless it's a secret, of course?"

My heart tripped. "No secret. Come around three and I'll introduce you."

His mouth curved up in that sexy way he had that turned my knees to jelly. "I'm already looking forward to it."

A few lingering kisses later, I left Nash standing in his red briefs in the open doorway of his apartment and headed for my car, marvelling at how my world had been turned on its head in the space of a few short hours from when I'd parked it there the night before. I slid into the Merc's leather seat and pulled up Abbie's text.

I deserve a personal life, a love life. It's what everyone kept telling me on repeat. But I had no chance of having either of those if I kept giving my time away. They couldn't have it both ways. *I couldn't.*

I took a deep breath and glanced up to where Nash was still watching. Then I looked back at the phone, my stomach knotting as I typed the words.

Sorry sweetheart. Can't do tomorrow afternoon. I'm meeting someone. Next time.

I sent it before I could change my mind, before I could think about the frown on Abbie's face when she read it. Then I threw the phone on the passenger seat and headed home.

CHAPTER TWELVE

Nash

"Hand me the feeler gauge, will you?" Jed stretched his arm behind him and flipped his fingers open and shut.

I rolled my eyes. "Now you're just fucking with me. I might know zip about engines, but you can't tell me there's a thing called a feeler gauge." I stepped up behind him in the pit. "Unless, of course, you mean *this* feeler gauge?" I slid my hand around his hip and down the front of his coveralls, the sleeves once again tied loosely around his waist. In the heat of the workshop, Jed was bare-chested and . . . commando.

I knew that little morsel because our first kiss, only seconds after I showed my face in Jed's workshop, had pretty much gone nuclear. The rest was history. According to Jed, he'd added *make out in the workshop pit* to our growing to-do list, and I was happy to oblige. An armful of greased-up and seriously-determined Jed was a gift from the car gods, and you don't fuck with those.

With his junk in hand, I squeezed firmly and smiled at his answering groan.

"Mmm." He wriggled his arse back into my groin. "As good as that feels and as much as I'd like to see the look on the faces of my petrolhead friends when I try to explain *that* particular interpretation, I actually do need that gauge. Find the thing that looks like a metal fan."

"Spoilsport." I grabbed a handful of his arse and kissed the nape of his neck just because I could. "You sure you don't want to play mechanics and dashing men in automobile distress?"

He choked out a laugh. "As oddly arousing as that sounds, once you find me that gauge, I'm done for the day, and a beer sounds mighty good about now, certainly before any potential role-play shenanigans."

I laughed. "We really need to talk about your priorities." I went in search of the damn gauge and slapped it in his hand.

"Yeah, well, you try deep throating with a mouth like sandpaper." He popped a kiss on my lips and disappeared back under the engine, and I had to admit, he had a point.

I leaned against the edge of the pit and watched him finish whatever he was doing. As much as I wasn't a car guy in the slightest, through Jed I was learning to appreciate the classics, and even I could see his Cutlass was going to be a beauty. Watching him work had been a surprisingly erotic way to pass the time, but an hour down the track, I was keen to get him out from under that car and into a shower . . . preferably with me.

Unfortunately, my luck was out, and I was banished to the kitchen while Jed cleaned himself up. I tried not to read too much into that, figuring we'd moved pretty damn fast the night before for a guy who'd done no more than kiss another man sometime back in the Stone Age. He laughed at my grumpy disapproval, and twenty minutes later when a pair of arms snaked around my waist and a line of kisses was pressed to the back of my neck, all was forgiven.

"Mmm, I like seeing you in my kitchen." Jed's chin rested on my shoulder and the clean scent of freshly showered man and not much else folded like a cloak around us both. Jed rarely wore cologne, something I was appreciating more and more.

"You've done a good job there." He gave me a squeeze and then slid alongside with his back to the counter, watching as I transferred the last of the scuffed-up, parboiled potatoes into the roasting dish and checked the oven temperature.

Jed had assigned me the task, undoubtedly to keep me busy and out of his bathroom after my first incursion, and I'd obliged . . . mostly. Who could blame me for sneaking a few kisses from the wet and soapy man once I knew he was under the water. He grumbled at the intrusion, of course, but couldn't hide his amusement and indulged my thorough groping with a smile on his face before sending me packing.

"No thanks to you," I complained. "The thought of you naked in that bathroom almost put a knife through my finger, and a trip to the ER would've definitely put a dampener on the evening. Here." I passed him the beer I'd opened when I'd heard the shower turn off.

He smiled and kissed me softly. "This just gets better and better. A sexy man in my kitchen, cooking dinner, *and* handing me a beer."

"That's not all that's on the menu," I suggested, ogling him shamelessly. "There are always daily specials, *if* you're interested."

He laughed and nudged me playfully back to work. "Focus. I skipped lunch, so I'm hungry."

I turned and slowly ran my gaze over him from head to toe. "So am I."

He shook his head and tugged open the cutlery drawer. "You're incorrigible. But I take it you're okay with an early dinner, then?"

I nodded. "More than. I missed lunch too."

"Good, then let's eat and then you can tell me more about these so-called daily specials of yours." His smile turned wicked. "But fair warning, I make it a rule not to put out on the first date."

I blinked. "Pretty sure that horse has already bolted. Even making allowances for your advanced age, you can't have forgotten Thursday night. Best blowjob of your life, I think you said."

Jed huffed out a laugh. "Really? Can't say I remember using those *particular* words."

I threw a potato at him, and he caught it mid-air. "As I said, advanced age."

His eyes narrowed. "Your chances of getting lucky are dropping by the second. Anyway, *Thursday* wasn't a date, so it doesn't count." He leaned in to kiss me on the corner of my mouth while his hand tracked down to squeeze my arse, making me jump. "But then again, I'm open to persuasion."

I turned to capture his lips and slipped my tongue inside for a quick taste. "That's very good to know. But I feel so dirty now." I batted my eyelids at him, and he laughed.

"Get back to work, Cinders." He patted my arse and began collecting the requisite barbecue and eating equipment, while I returned to my potatoes, revelling in his easy-going nature and the relaxed surrounds of his country-style kitchen with its impressive gas range, butcher's block countertops, slate floors, and cream wood cabinetry.

When the potatoes were safely in the oven, Jed gave me an in-depth tour of the rest of the bungalow, which had much the same feel as the homely kitchen. Restored wooden sash windows bathed the rooms in light and worked beautifully with the polished original rimu flooring and large earth-toned mats. Deep couches and armchairs in soft pastels blended with neutral curtains and some carefully chosen pieces of aged wooden furniture. A ton of family photos mixed with the occasional coastal print completed the look.

"Tamsin was responsible for the decorating," Jed explained, catching me studying the photos lining the wall. "It's hardly my forte and I like what she did, so I didn't see the need to change anything when she moved out other than replace some of the things she wanted to take with her. Is that weird?"

I shook my head. "She has a good eye. The place suits you, and it wasn't like you two had an acrimonious divorce, right?" I nodded to the photo I'd been staring at. "You both look pretty happy in these." Was I jealous? Maybe a little.

Jed moved alongside and slid an arm around my waist. "We *were* happy, for a long time. Then we had the kids and I stopped paying attention and we both got lazy."

"It happens to a lot of couples." I kissed his forehead and he leaned into me.

"Yeah, but I could've done better. I missed out on a lot of time with the kids that I can't get back, and I guess I've tried to make up for that with Bridie." He pulled back to look at me, his expression serious. "I said no to babysitting Bridie today, after you asked me to have dinner with you. I can't remember the last time I did that, if ever."

We both knew what he was saying, and I kissed him softly for it. "Then I'm honoured, and even more grateful that you agreed. But just so we're clear, you could've said no, Jed. I would've understood. I'm not going to pout or sulk or demand to be number one in your priorities. We're not kids and I get that you have a family and commitments. We could've done this another time."

His jaw ticced. "I know and I wouldn't be here if I thought otherwise. My family will always be my number one. But I wanted to be with you tonight and I don't regret my decision."

I wanted to believe him. "How was Abbie about it?"

He shrugged and looked away. "I don't know. She didn't get back to me." Concern flashed in his eyes. "I'll call her tomorrow."

I let it lie, not wanting to press, torn between feeling thrilled that Jed had prioritised dinner with me and worried about the singular way such a small decision seemed to gnaw at his guilt.

Jed quickly changed the topic of conversation and bundled me outside to the covered deck where I watched him fire up the barbecue. While it was heating, he pulled a second Adirondack chair alongside mine, and we chatted about our plans for Christmas Day while finishing our beers and watching the lazy heat of the afternoon sun burn what was left of Jed's back lawn.

Being with Jed, talking and laughing and even arguing about my BMW (not a favourite brand of his) and his favourite horror movies (not a favourite genre of mine) was almost too easy. We simply clicked, and I wasn't naïve enough to dismiss that out of hand. I'd been with a ton of men, and I knew that kind of easy connection was rare, especially in a more limited LGBTQ community. Jed, on the other hand, had pretty much been with one woman his entire adult life and I couldn't help but wonder what *he* thought. Did he have any idea how special this was? Or maybe he didn't feel it the same way I did. It was a sobering thought.

When Jed finally deemed the barbecue hot enough, he looked after the steaks while I took the potatoes out of the oven. I then transported everything to the picnic table parked under the shade of an old magnolia whose gnarly roots threaded through the lawn like varicose veins. It sat alongside a large vegetable garden that caught me by surprise. The rest of the gardens needed a fair amount of TLC, but the vegetable beds were immaculate.

As we talked and ate an outstanding dinner, Jed caught me looking around the yard and shrugged. "You'll get no apologies from me. Tamsin was the gardener. She did all the work. But the vegetable patch is my happy place. It's where I de-stress."

His answer surprised me, as so many things about Jed did. "Not working on your car then?"

He snorted. "Hell no. I'm too much of a perfectionist for that to ever be truly relaxing. But vegetables are very forgiving and pretty difficult to get too serious about." He chuckled. "I give away most of what I grow. How about you?"

I pushed my empty plate aside and shook my head. "Sorry. By the time I left home, I was well and truly over anything to do with gardening or the whole outdoorsy thing per se, if I'm honest. My pots are as far as I go. But I have to admit, the idea of watching you work shirtless amongst the peas and basil has me re-evaluating those life choices right about now."

He laughed but I was deadly serious. And when I told him that, those beautiful blue eyes pooled black in the centre and he leaned across the picnic table and kissed me. "I'll be sure to arrange a private viewing."

I held his gaze. "You do that."

Jed finished his meal. And then we chatted about the state of his runner beans, the failure of his corn, whether the New Zealand cricket team had a chance against Pakistan in the upcoming Boxing Day Cricket test, what present you bought for a three-year-old granddaughter when her parents and grandmother had stolen all the good ideas, what I could take for my contribution to Christmas Day lunch with my brother when I didn't have a sweet tooth, and finally, when might the two of us be free to grab a few hours to ourselves over that time?

A couple of persistent mosquitos had me punctuating the conversation with the odd grumble and occasional slap until Jed finally headed inside for the repellent and set about spraying me head to foot with enough repellent to catch anything flying under the jet stream. And all the while, I had to mentally pinch myself that this was actually happening. I was sitting under a tree having dinner in the backyard of a guy I'd been obsessing over, getting eaten alive by mosquitos and planning when we could meet up for Christmas.

There was so much in that one frightening sentence to unpack, I didn't know where to start.

Firstly, I didn't do Christmas with *any* man I was involved with, no matter how much I liked them. Not since Jeremy.

Secondly, thirdly, fourthly and the rest—see above note. I was hardly what you'd call outdoorsy. An annual stroll in the botanical gardens was about it. The last thing I'd ever wanted was a garden, vegetable or otherwise. Or a lawn. Or an outdoor barbecue area. Or the need for damn insect repellent on a regular basis.

Jed's place was so far removed from my pristine glass-and-brick home with its enclosed mosquito-free balcony, black-and-white aesthetic, and gleaming, mostly empty kitchen, that my head hadn't stopped spinning. Not because I was uncomfortable in his environment, but because I . . . actually liked it. I liked him. And most of all, I liked him *in* it.

I was ridiculously charmed. Enthralled by his whingeing about how fast his recent crop of coriander had gone to seed and how the heritage tomatoes weren't doing well in the heat. And all the while his hands never stopped moving, his bright blue eyes dancing as he pointed to all the things he was talking about. If you'd asked me, I couldn't have told you half of what he said, I was purely and simply captive to *him*.

"You're not really listening, are you?" He shot me an amused look. "It's okay. Next to cars, vegetables are the second most dangerous topic to get me started on."

"Who'd have guessed? Not me." I reached across and took his hand. "And I am listening."

"Liar."

"Okay, I might've lost one or two threads along the way, but that's only because I was too busy watching you being so passionate about it all. It's kind of a turn-on."

"Oh." His cheeks pinked but he looked pleased. "Then I guess I can forgive you. But I've talked long enough." He sat back, sliding his hand from my grip. "I want to hear more about you. You've asked a lot about my workshop, but you haven't told me much about *your* job."

And so I offloaded what I could about the challenges of my new position, the schools I'd worked at in the past, and where I saw my career going in the future—possibly back to university to teach.

"What happened with that bullying incident you told me about the night of the party? The one that had you so worried." Jed waited on my reply, which was a long while coming since I'd been carefully avoiding the subject. Eventually he reached across to squeeze my hand. "You don't have to answer."

But I wanted to. It seemed important somehow. "Well, put it this way . . ." I watched as he traced a finger in a circle on the back of my hand. "I'm not exactly hopeful the board is going to support my decisions. The disciplinary subcommittee has their heads up their arses and seem reluctant to draw a line in the sand with this kid. Three of its members have asked to talk with me on Tuesday, and I'm thinking that's not exactly a good sign. I'm steeling myself for bad news."

Jed flipped my hand and threaded our fingers together. Just the sight of it made me smile. "Well, that sucks. What options do you have left if they decide against you?"

I blew out a long sigh. "To be honest, not many. Short of threatening to resign, there's not much I can do. They're my employer, and I can't effect much change if I'm not there, can I?"

His eyes never left mine as he thought about that for a minute. "Aren't the board obligated to provide a safe environment, both for the staff *and* the students?"

"Yes, but—"

"So, wouldn't bullying and then you actually being threatened by the bully's parent be counter to that?"

"Of course."

"And you said the kid keyed a teacher's car, for fuck's sake? That's property damage. Vandalism, surely, regardless of what the school thinks."

"Yes, you're right. But in most cases like this, the police get behind what the school decides is the best solution since we know the kids involved, and we often have a more overarching view. Slapping a kid with an unnecessarily harsh penalty without a multifaceted approach more often than not simply leads to a worse problem in the future."

"But from what you told me, letting the bullying student off lightly in this instance *isn't* the best solution for either of the kids, or the school, correct?"

"Correct." There was nothing to argue with there.

"And the penalty you instituted was appropriate considering the kid's history, right?"

"Yes. Absolutely. But that doesn't mean the board will listen to me."

"So, what can you do?"

"Try and change the policy so it doesn't happen again." I didn't have to be a mind reader to know what Jed was thinking as he stoically held my gaze.

"And what about the victim? What happens to that poor kid while the policy is being changed?" He uncoupled our hands. "And I'm sorry, but I can't help thinking, what if it was Bridie?" And there it was.

"I know. I know," I flustered, because there was no fucking good answer to his question and so I fell back on my perennial response, hating how much of a cop-out it sounded. "But I can't help kids like him in the future if I lose my job." But even as I said the words, they felt wrong in my mouth. Sour. A tired excuse. Wrong in front of this straightforward man who was quietly calling me on my bullshit.

What if it was Bridie?

How in the hell did anyone answer that?

I couldn't even hold his gaze.

"Hey." Jed dipped his head to catch my eye and I reluctantly looked up, wondering what I'd find. But rather than the judgement and disappointment I expected, I only saw concern and a genuine desire to help. "I'm sorry. I didn't mean to put you on the spot."

"Don't be sorry." I cupped his face. "It's a valid question. I just don't have an easy answer. And I have no idea what I'd do if it were my child or grandkid. Rage at all the bureaucrats like me making excuses, I suppose."

He smiled and took my hand from his cheek, wrapping it in both of his on the table. "I don't know much about your job, but I'm guessing there are many ways to effect change and to challenge policy and that you'd know most of them better than me, Mister LGBTQ Activist. I read about what you've done for trans rights and school bathroom policies." Jed eyeballed me, his thumb tracing circles on the underside of my wrist. "I'm sure you'll think of something. After all, how many kids hurt are too many? Where is the line in the sand?

When does it hurt enough for us to risk experiencing some of our own pain in order to change it?"

I couldn't keep the smile from my face. "That sounds way too familiar."

He grinned. "Does it? Oh yes, I believe you said something like that in a speech at the Wellington Rainbow Community fundraiser last year. Smart man."

I groaned and fell back in my chair. "Hung by my own words. You've been googling again, haven't you?"

Jed laughed. "I refuse to answer that on the grounds of looking pathetically infatuated."

"I'll have you know, pathetically infatuated is one of my favourite looks on you—just as long as it's about me," I qualified.

He smiled. "I think you're safe."

I leaned across the table and pressed a kiss to his lips. "Then that makes two of us. And thank you."

His brows bunched. "What for?"

"For reminding me why I got into this job—to make a difference— and that I've done this before. For making it personal with Bridie. I needed that jolt. And also, for giving me a much-needed kick up the butt, because you're right, there are many ways to bring about change." Jed's words had sparked the threads of an idea that was busy circling my brain. "Some take a little more courage than others, and somewhere along the way I got scared."

He huffed. "I'm pretty sure I didn't do any of that, at least not on purpose, but I'll take the compliment, along with another kiss." It was his turn to lean across, and I cupped his cheek and dipped inside his mouth, revelling in the blunt refreshing candour that washed over my tongue like a palate cleanser.

I'd worked hard to get where I had in life—respected in my job and in the community that was so important to me. These days, few people challenged me like Jed had just done, and with no agenda other than to try and help. Challenged me to do better, to be better. I'd gotten pride-fat and lazy.

What if it was Bridie?

Yeah, things needed to change.

I brushed Jed's lips one last time and then sat back with a ridiculous smile spilling over my face.

Jed gave my hand a squeeze and stared at me. "You look drunk, like those monkeys on that documentary after eating overripe fruit."

I snorted. "I'm gonna try not to take offence at the analogy, but you are kind of intoxicating and a little bit . . . fruity?"

His cheeks brightened. "Shut up. Anyway, getting back to the bullying thing—"

"Do we have to?" There was a distinct whine to my voice that made Jed chuckle.

"Yes," he said flatly. "I was wondering if . . . well, maybe you'd be up for a visit . . . from me . . . after this so-called meeting of doom on Tuesday? We could order in, something really unhealthy, since my family won't find the containers in my recycling."

My eyebrows shot to my hairline. "Your family goes through your recycling?"

He shrugged. "You have no idea. Then we could watch a crap action movie, *or*—" He waggled his brows comically. "—we *could* find something more . . . adventurous to fill the time."

I laughed and lifted his hand to my lips. "Will you promise to bring those damn coveralls?"

His eyes grew sultry, those icy blue irises bleeding almost black at the edges. "Yeah, I can do that."

My breath quickened at the memory of our make-out session in his workshop pit, but when I thought of the meeting, I slumped in my seat. "As enticing as that sounds, there's no bigger buzzkill than talking with a bunch of arse-saving bureaucrats, so I can't guarantee exactly how I'll be feeling by the time I get home. I'd hate to disappoint you."

Jed's eyes softened. "Then let's play it by ear." He stood and perched on the edge of the table then pulled me up to stand between his legs, his arms around my waist. "No coveralls . . . this time. And if all you're up for is a beer and a cuddle on the couch, I'm down for that too." He huffed in amusement. "Not that I ever thought I'd be saying those words to another guy."

I brushed my nose against his. "In that case, I'll give you a key to let yourself in if the meeting runs late."

"A key?" He looked startled.

"Yes, a key. Is there a problem with that?"

Jed stared at me a moment. "No. I guess not."

I kissed him firmly. "Good. And you can keep it for any future . . . surprises."

His eyes danced. "You like surprises?"

"I love surprises." I cradled his face. "Are you sure you're okay with all this?"

"Surprisingly, yes. If I'd known what I was missing, I might not have waited this long."

"Well—" I rolled his hand in mine and traced the lifeline on his palm as he watched. "I, for one, think you waited the perfect amount of time." I glanced up and our eyes met.

"Because?"

He was going to make me say it. "*Because* any sooner and someone else would've taken you off the market." My eyes stayed steady on his. "You're far too good to pass on, Jed, and this way, you're all mine."

He blushed prettily, clearly pleased with my answer, but then a small line formed between his brows, and he dropped his forehead to mine. "Am I, Nash? Is that what we're doing here? Am I yours?"

Shit. I hesitated, cursing my stupidity, unsure whether the only answer I could give him might send Jed running. Too late now. I steeled my heart and took a breath.

"Well now, I think that's up to you." I blinked and our lashes tangled. "Two days ago, we both said we didn't know what we wanted and agreed to take things slow. But this conversation *doesn't* qualify as slow, so I shouldn't have said what I did and I'm sorry. But if you're asking, am I serious about you? Then yes, without a doubt."

His eyes widened but he said nothing.

"I'm serious about dating, and yes, the whole boyfriend thing as well." I rolled my eyes. "Whatever that means for a couple of fifty-something grown men, right?"

He snorted. "Boyfriend, huh? Fuck me. It's been a long time since I've been called that."

I brushed my thumb across his lips and he kissed it in passing. "I like you Jed, more than I've liked a guy in a long, long time. And so yes, I really do want to see where this goes. I think I already knew that on Thursday, I just didn't want to admit it. I'm not looking for friends with benefits or a casual lay, and I don't share. I would want us to be exclusive. I should probably have mentioned that last part earlier." He winced. "So, if that's something you don't think you can—"

"I've no intention of sharing either," Jed quickly added. "And yes, I'd like to try something serious with you, as well, although to be fair, I don't really have a clue what that means these days. I figure it can't have changed that much in forty years."

This man. I cradled his face in my hands and kissed him tenderly, swallowing the soft moan that escaped his lips at my touch. Then I brushed our noses together and sighed contentedly. "How about we discover what it means *together*? It's not like I know anything about dating these days, either."

"Okay. Then we find out together." He quirked a brow. "But what about the school? Will Abbie be a problem for you?"

I didn't hesitate. "Not unless she makes herself one. There's no policy discouraging a principal from dating the father of a teacher. Will either of your kids be a concern?"

He blew out a long breath and shrugged. "I'm not expecting problems, but you never know."

Based on conversations in the staffroom, I doubted Abbie would have any problem with her dad being bi. And although I didn't know Ewan, Jed described him as a very laid-back kid with a live-and-let-live attitude, so that also boded well.

"Scott is another question entirely." Jed took the words right out of my mouth, and I tried not to wince, having wondered if Jed was aware that his son-in-law wasn't likely to be waving a rainbow flag anytime soon.

But of course, Jed hadn't missed a thing.

"Yeah, I know," was all he said about my reaction to Scott's name. "And just to be careful, I'm not going to tell anyone until after Christmas. If things go pear-shaped, I don't want that memory hovering in the background year after year."

"Fair enough. So we keep things between us until you're ready." And if Jed still wasn't ready in the new year, I'd back him all the way. This was one hundred percent his call.

"Thanks. But full disclosure, I'll need to keep Tamsin in the loop. She won't spill anything to the kids, but if I don't tell her, she'll make my life hell and I can do without the grief."

"No problem. And Colin is wise to us as well. But just like Tamsin, he's trustworthy."

"I'm not going to tell you what to do with your friends, Nash. That's your decision. But I'm fine with Colin knowing and anyone else you trust to keep it quiet. This isn't all about me." He gave a cheeky grin. "Although, from a purely academic standpoint, I'm pretty chuffed that I can think of you as mine, as adolescent as that sounds."

"Oh, I'm yours, any way you want me." I kissed him hard, swallowing his grunt of satisfaction. "We might not be kids, Jed, but I'm pretty damn chuffed as well, and I don't give a fuck how that sounds." I ran my hands over his back, the heat of his skin burning through his thin shirt. "And so it begins."

He slid his arms around my waist and rested his cheek against my shoulder. "And so it begins."

CHAPTER THIRTEEN

Nash

"So, LET ME GET THIS RIGHT." I LEANED BACK IN MY CHAIR AND
steepled my hands on my chest, glaring at the trio of board members
wasting space on the other side of my desk. "You want to keep
Garrett Poulsen, a thrice-warned bully *in* school, with almost zero
consequences, while the target of his hateful abuse will likely not
return in the new year because he's too damn terrified?"

Chelsea Burbank, the spokesperson for the committee, pulled a
sour face. "You're twisting our—"

Fuck that. "And this is all because Garrett's father is some star
alumnus who played professional rugby about a million years ago and
whose son, apparently, has similar potential, along with a similar
genetic coding for arseholery. What is it with rugby and this country?
Have you even talked with Rick Poulson? He's a bigoted jerk, pro
rugby player or not. I almost had him thrown off the school grounds a
few weeks ago for attempting to intimidate *me*."

"Calm down." Chelsea pumped her hands slowly up and down.

"Of course we talked with Ricky. And Garrett isn't getting off without consequences."

Ricky? Jesus Christ. That said it all. I tried and failed to stop the eye roll and added a huff of disgust for good measure. "A formal caution in his file regarding the keying, which gets expunged if Garrett keeps his nose clean for the rest of next year, but with no mention of the bullying incident and the fact he laid hands on another student? Plus, the suspension I'd given him is retracted. I hardly call those adequate consequences, Chelsea."

"The board disagrees."

"I'm a member of that board," I pointed out acidly, "and I *don't* agree. If it was a first offence, I'd be fully on board with a more engaging attitude, but Garrett has blown every chance he's been given. This is the third serious complaint in a year, and there were others when he first came to the school. Who are we protecting here?"

"Garrett claims Tane taunted him."

I blinked. "You've got to be kidding me. Are we victim blaming now? Tane's friend was present. He didn't see the keying, but he was there for everything else."

"But as you just said, the boy is a *friend* of Tane."

I turned slowly to meet Chelsea's gaze. "And so he's lying?"

"No," she flustered. "I'm just saying there are mitigating circumstances."

I threw my hands up in disgust. "This is such bullshit. I won't have kids getting away with unacceptable behaviour in my school regardless of who their parents are."

"Nash." Chelsea's tone brooked caution. "I don't need to remind you that this is not *your* school. You're here at the pleasure of the board who *hired* you. *We* employ *you*."

The threat was pretty explicit, and I took a deep breath and shuffled my ducks into a passable row, give or take a kink. "And exactly what am I supposed to tell Tane and his parents, because I presume *that's* still part of my job? You lot aren't going to suddenly grow some balls and do it for me, are you?"

"Crudity is unnecessary," Chelsea said haughtily. "And quite frankly, I'm surprised. But you can tell Tane and his parents that Garrett will steer well clear of him. Garrett's father will make sure of that."

You have to be fucking kidding me.

Chelsea continued in a patient tone. "You could've avoided all of this if you'd run your initial decision past us first before suspending Garrett."

I couldn't believe what I was hearing. "It's my role as principal to make those decisions," I fumed. "That's what you employ me for." My hands fisted and unfisted under the cover of my desk, and I bit back a dozen unhelpful but no-doubt satisfying responses, such as telling the trio of pandering arseholes to go fuck themselves while I wrote Garrett's letter of expulsion.

"It wasn't a straightforward case, which you should have realised at the time."

Code for notable school favourites and influential persons involved.

What if it was Bridie? A thought which had been running through my brain since Saturday, along with a plan.

I took a deep breath and steeled myself.

"Well, here's something very straightforward for you to understand. Garrett Poulson is a proven, recidivist bully who verbally and physically attacked another student *and* vandalised a teacher's property, and who is therefore a threat to the emotional and personal safety of vulnerable and marginalised students at this school and the staff."

I let that sink in for just a second, drinking in the stunned faces and then continued.

"Therefore, I cannot, in good conscience stand back and condone the board's response to this latest incident. According to our mandate, every board member is equally accountable for every board action and decision, and I cannot morally do that in this instance. To that end, I will, *as my role demands*, be counselling Tane's family in their options moving forward. This will include the option of filing a formal police complaint against Garrett, which will no doubt include a summary of the board's inaction on their behalf. *And* in addition, *I* will be filing my own concerns with the Ministry of Education regarding the board's decision and the safety of students in this school."

You could've heard a pin drop as my words were met with wide-eyed stares and utter silence.

Chelsea's gaze shot to the other two members who looked shell-shocked to say the least, but they remained tight-lipped, leaving it to her to respond. I knew at least one of them, Robert, most likely didn't agree with the committee's decision but had gone along because it was easier and because he lacked a spine. Chelsea shot them both a look of disgust, cleared her throat, and then turned back to me. But her expression held none of her earlier confidence. "Then you'll leave the board with little alternative but to recommend suspending you while the matter is investigated."

I met her glare with a steely one of my own. "I'd like to hear you justify that in the court of public and parental opinion."

She said nothing for a moment, her jaw working hard as she digested the bald truth of what I'd said. "You're willing to risk your job over this, Nash? For one student?"

"I am." Without question. *How many hurt kids are too many?* "And I'm not without authority in this arena, Chelsea. You know that. People *will* listen to me."

But Chelsea wasn't giving in so easily. "The school will suffer, Nash. It can't function healthily or meet its well-being objectives if you alienate the other board members you're supposed to work with. It's a partnership."

I almost smiled. "You need to be careful you don't drown in all those buzzwords of yours. And I won't alienate *all* of them. When this leaks out, as it inevitably will, each member of the board is going to have to justify their decision." I knew that from a little canvassing I'd done the previous day, and to make my point, I glanced at Robert who promptly turned a bright scarlet.

Jed's words rang in my ear. *"There are many ways to effect change."*

Chelsea chewed on her lip and glanced again at her colleagues, and I pressed a little harder. "I don't know about you lot, but I'm pretty sure bullying is a hot enough political topic to bring considerable media interest into any school board feud surrounding it."

Chelsea's gaze hardened. "That sounds awfully like a threat, Nash."

I didn't even blink. "The *board's* inaction is threatening the safety of my students in this school."

More silence that I made no attempt to break, and eventually Chelsea got to her feet. "I'll pass your comments on to the Chairman, along with my recommendation that the board postpone its decision until the next full meeting in January, following further discussion."

Relief coursed through me, but I kept a straight face. "So, until then, my decision stands? Garrett remains suspended?"

Chelsea sighed. "Yes, until then."

Yes! I barely suppressed a fist pump and decided to press a little further. "And I assume, as part of that discussion, the board will be open to expert opinion on the matter?"

Chelsea hesitated, then nodded, the fight seemingly draining out of her. "Send us the full details of anyone you're considering so we can vet their credentials prior to approval. And bear in mind the board will likely call its own experts."

Yeah, good luck finding any who will back you.

I nodded. "Understood. Feel free to show yourselves out. I'm sure you know the way."

Chelsea gave me one last look. "I hope you know what you're

doing, Nash. You've just made life very difficult for yourself in this job."

"I'm trying to keep my students safe, Chelsea. What are you doing?"

She held my gaze but said nothing, and they finally left about five and huddled in the parking lot, no doubt complaining about me in private.

"So, what happened?" Colin asked the minute he picked up my call.

"They're . . . reconsidering."

"Yes! Tell me everything."

And so I summarised the meeting with the three board members, and at the end of it, Colin actually laughed. "Wow, I'm impressed. That was pretty damn ballsy of you. Kind of reminds me of the old protest-leader version of Nash from university. No mountain too high, right?"

"Maybe." I breathed slowly in and out, the adrenaline starting to crash. "To be honest, I don't know if it was the smartest career move, but I feel good about it. Ask me again in January when I'm looking for another job."

He grunted. "It might never happen. You just need to scare them a little in January. What about that educational psychology lecturer at Auckland University who specialises in bully behaviour? We went to that workshop of his, remember? He'd set the cat amongst the pigeons with your board. Miles . . . someone."

"I know who you mean. Good idea."

"I'm really pleased for you." Colin sounded almost as relieved as I was. "I was getting a bit worried. I haven't heard much from you lately. I'd say my feelings were hurt, but we both know that's a lie."

It might've been said in jest, but I got the message. I'd neglected a lot of things since Jed had appeared in my life, and I had some grovel-ling to do, including with Gerald. He'd been blowing up my phone wanting a boy's night out, but I didn't know how to explain Jed to a previously fellow confirmed bachelor, so I'd just avoided saying anything. "I'm sorry. I've been a shit friend. I've been a bit . . . busy."

Colin huffed. "Is that what they're calling it these days? And how is our handsome classic car mechanic?"

I smiled at the memory of Jed padding around his kitchen in bare feet while I chopped potatoes. "He's—" *Shit.* What did I say about the man who had slowly taken over most of my waking thoughts? "I . . . I think I'm in trouble, Colin. I like this guy way too much. I might even be red-lining the *really, really* scenario."

An ear shattering silence greeted my words.

"Earth to Colin?"

He breathed a sigh down the line. "Just hang on a minute while I piece together my mind which you just blew to fucking smithereens. I knew you liked him, Nash, but really? You've only known this guy a couple of weeks."

"I know, I know." I groaned and spun to stare out the window at the mostly vacant staff car park. The school always felt strange when it was void of students, like it was somehow holding its breath, like an empty bottle of pop, all the fizz and excitement gone. I threw my feet up on the sill and leaned back in my chair. "It's crazy thinking, but I can't help it. He's just really . . . great. He's solid and funny and smart and easy to be around."

"And the fact he's hot doesn't hurt, I imagine," Colin pointed out.

An image of Jed's blue-grey eyes, lazy smile, and laughter lines put a grin on my face. Not classically handsome but very definitely hot. "Yeah, that too," I muttered. "But it's more that I *feel* so different around him compared to other guys I've been with. More . . . me, I guess. More . . . relaxed. Jesus, I even cancelled my next waxing appointment," I exclaimed, like I'd pulled out of peace negotiations in the Middle East. "And don't piss yourself laughing, but last Saturday he invited me to his place for a barbeque—"

Colin interrupted with a gasp. "He cooked for you? Jesus, I might marry this guy myself."

"Anywaaaay." I ignored him. "We ate outside next to his vegetable garden, drenched in insect repellent and chatting about his runner beans, for fuck's sake. It was the best time I've had in years. *Years*, Colin. Have I totally lost my mind?"

Colin barked out a laugh and I had to wait a good few seconds until he got his shit together enough to talk. "*You*, Nash Collingwood, of the 'I don't want to sit on the sand cos it gets everywhere' varietal, ate in a vegetable garden . . . in the actual outdoors . . . with clouds and insects and humidity and everything? I thought the picnic thing was bad enough, but at least then I simply figured you were trying to get into his pants."

"Shut up."

He laughed. "It must be love."

My heart jumped in my throat, because no, it wasn't love, at least not yet. I didn't think. But for only the second time in my life, I thought maybe it was headed that way.

"Nash?"

"Sorry. I just . . . ugh. I feel happy when I'm with him, okay? And I haven't been this way since . . . well, you know since when."

Colin said nothing for a few long seconds, and I wished I could see his face to tell just how much of an idiot he thought I was. But then he surprised me. "I get that you're concerned," he began, "but I personally think this is a good thing. To actually, really and truly like a guy after so long? It's a start, right? Don't fuck it up just because you're scared."

God, I didn't want to. "Jed's never been with a man before," I admitted bluntly. "He's not out, not yet, although he says he's planning to if we get serious."

"Okay, so wow." Colin went quiet for a few seconds. "That's . . . big. I feel like I'm playing catch-up here. This isn't just a start, is it? You guys are genuinely trying this."

I sighed. "Yeah, we are. And I know it's all kinds of stupid having only talked properly for the first time a month ago, and I'm Jed's first . . . in lots of things, so I don't want to get ahead of myself and scare him off."

"Then don't," Colin answered simply. "Give him time and room to move. What's the rush? Stop worrying and just enjoy being with someone you genuinely like for once. You deserve this, my friend. Stop catastrophising the finish line when you're barely out of the blocks."

It was good advice. "You're right. Thanks."

"You're welcome. And I definitely want to meet the man who can tie my avowed bachelor best friend in such complicated knots."

I grinned at the thought, pretty sure the two men would get on well. "I'd like that too. And to be honest, Jed's the reason behind what I did today with the board. We were talking about it the other night and he brought up Bridie, his three-year-old granddaughter, and what if she was the one being bullied? It's too easy to forget when you're at a distance, and it reminded me of why I'd wanted to teach in the first place. It was also an uncomfortable wake-up call that maybe I'd got a little complacent and political along the way."

I could almost see Colin's wide grin as he said, "I'm liking this guy more and more."

I smiled. "Me too. Anyway, enough about me. How's Marcia?"

"Well." Colin hesitated. "Funny you should ask that, because I was wondering if you might be free to help me pick out a necklace for her this week? I'm . . . I'm . . . fucking hell, I'm gonna ask her to marry me on Boxing Day." His words ran together in a jumble that I had to decipher, and then my brain fell out of my head.

"What? Um—" I blinked but . . . nope, nothing came.

"Oh fuck, you think it's a bad idea, don't you?" Colin almost squeaked. "But I thought you wanted me to—"

"No!" I flapped my hands even though he couldn't see them. "I think it's a great idea. The best. Yes, do it. Absolutely. But . . . a necklace?" I shook my head. "Colin, bro, have you maybe thought about a ring? Traditional, I know, but I've heard people really like them."

"Yeah, yeah, funny guy. I want her to choose her own ring," he explained. "I just need to have *something* for the occasion. Something . . . special."

"Then of course I'll help. Text me where and when and I'll be there." I finished the call with a huge smile on my face, and just in time to hear a soft knock and find Abbie and Scott standing in my doorway with Bridie between them, bouncing on her toes.

My cheeks grew a mind of their own, instantly flaring at the knowledge of what Jed and I were up to behind Abbie's back. I felt like a kid caught with his hand in the lolly jar, and Scott's scowl didn't make me feel any better. "Abbie, Scott. Come in and take a seat." I waved them inside.

"Hey, Nash." Abbie settled in the chair recently vacated by Chelsea, and Scott sat alongside. "We happened to be passing your office, and I couldn't help but overhear a little of the conversation."

I froze, remembering with horror that Colin and I had just been talking about Jed. My concern must've been obvious because Abbie quickly added, "We were on our way to my classroom. I promise we weren't eavesdropping, but just so you know, I think the board has their head up their collective arse over this bullying thing."

Oh, thank God. The breath I'd been holding whooshed out of my lungs. It was my conversation with Chelsea they'd overheard, not the one with Colin. "No." I flustered a little, straightening the pens on my desk. "I'm the one who should be sorry. I should've held my temper better." I turned my attention to their cute-as-hell daughter. "Well, hello there, Miss Bridie. It's so lovely to see you today."

"Hello, Mister Collingwood." Bridie held on to her father's hand, her gaze scanning the room.

"Do you see that drawer over there with an elephant sticker on it?" I pointed to the bottom drawer under my bookcase.

Bridie nodded.

"I think there might be some new books in there. Would you like to take a look?"

Bridie's eyes lit up. "Really?"

I nodded. "Go on."

Abbie looked to Scott, who held my gaze and hesitated for just a second before letting go of his daughter's hand, and Bridie raced over to the drawer, shouting, "Thank you, Mister Collingwood."

I couldn't help but smile.

"So, I gather they aren't going to expel our young friend?"

I shot a glance to Scott, but Abbie waved a hand. "He knows all about it. Someone with a bit too much to drink was talking about it at the party."

I sighed and watched Bridie pull an alphabet book from the drawer and start flicking through the colourful pages. "If we were that loud, then you no doubt heard me accuse them of why they're letting it ride as well."

Abbie bit back a smile. "I'm pretty sure half the street heard that part. Not that we didn't already know."

"Oh god." I fell back in my chair with a groan. "That wasn't very smart of me."

Abbie shrugged. "Everyone knows who Rick Poulson is."

Scott nodded. "Yeah, he was a good player in his day."

I couldn't help the eye roll, and Scott looked away with a shrug. "It's true."

Abbie frowned at her husband for a few seconds, then turned back to me. "It sounds like you might've won the battle."

"Maybe. But the war is definitely not over."

She nodded in understanding. "Well, you've got my backing and that of most of the rational teachers and parents, even if you're unlikely to convince the ill-informed diehard Rick Poulson fans." She tipped her head, indicating her husband.

"What?" Scott scowled. "I'm entitled to an opinion."

Abbie blinked. "Rick is an arsehole." She stared at her husband until he eventually flushed pink and looked away.

Time for a subject change. "So, what brings you guys here during rush-hour traffic?"

Abbie pulled a face. "Tell me about it, but my new textbooks arrived yesterday, and since we had to collect Bridie from Dad's, I decided to call in and pick up a copy on the way back."

I blinked. Bridie had been with Jed? News to me. Last I'd heard, Jed was switching out the muffler on a Dodge Charger and expected it to take most of the day. "Does your dad often take her on a week-day?" *Yeah, I know, so sue me.*

Abbie shrugged. "Not usually, but Scott had an orthopaedic appointment about his ACL, and I wanted to be there. Specialist's rooms aren't exactly the best place for a three-year-old."

I grimaced in sympathy. "Yeah, I can see that."

"Plus, Dad loves having Bridie. To be honest, I don't know what we'd do without him."

I was about to comment how that must be nice when my phone vibrated on the desk, and like I'd conjured him from thin air, Jed's name flashed on the screen. *Shit.* I grabbed it before Abbie or Scott had a chance to see and shoved it in my pocket.

Abbie took that as their cue to leave and quickly got to her feet. "We've held you up long enough. Don't take the dickheads too seri-ously, Nash. You're a great principal. We all love you." She hesitated, then grinned. "Well, all the best teachers do, anyway."

I laughed. "Which lets me know I'm doing my job. Thanks for the support. Scott, nice to see you again." I offered Scott my hand, but he already had his arms full with Bridie, so I picked up the book Bridie had been reading and handed it to Abbie. "Bring it back when she's done."

The minute the office was clear, I updated the Nelson family on the postponement of the board's decision, and then pulled out my phone and grinned at the dozen messages waiting for me from Jed.

Three days since the barbecue and the man had taken up resi-dence in my brain. I thought about him constantly, wondered what he was up to and how his day was going. We texted back and forth during the day and talked late into the night. Nothing world-shatter-ing. Just little things. Stupid heart-skipping nothings that made me want to barf at my own ridiculousness. And as I scrolled through his texts, the frustrating weight of the day eased with each one I read. Such was the power he had to improve my mood.

Workday was a washout.

Figured I knew the answer as to the why of that.

Heading in to clean up ;)

I grinned at the winky face.

In the car and on my way to yours.

Gave Rollo a heart attack by closing up early.

Stopped to pick up Thai with a side order of fries. Fusion cuisine.

Oops. A cheesecake just fell into my trolley . . .

. . . and a very nice Pinot Gris

. . . plus a new IPA from that Marlborough brewery you like.

Almost at your place.

Hope things went okay

Don't let the arseholes get you down.

Call me when you can.

PS. I bought more lube . . .

. . . just saying.

I lingered over that one and might have read it twice. And after the shit afternoon I'd had, I would never have believed I'd be driving back to my apartment with a lift in my heart and a smile on my face. But I was, and wasn't that a fucking miracle?

A miracle who went by the name of Jed Marshall.

A miracle I was beginning to care about far more than was safe for my heart. A miracle who was waiting in my apartment just for me. *Me.* Not simply for sex. Not just as a swipe-right hookup. Not simply for a free meal with an older date—and yeah, there'd been a few of those over the years.

No. Jed was there waiting Just. For. Me.

To talk. To find out how my day had been. To share a beer. To eat. To sleep. And maybe to make out, if I was lucky.

Two months ago, I'd have laughed at the very idea that I'd be looking forward to this as much as I was. That I might want nothing more. But then this was Jed. And there wasn't anyone else I'd rather be going home to after the day I'd had than him.

It should've been a warning, but it felt way more like a promise.

CHAPTER FOURTEEN

Nash

WHEN I WALKED INTO THE APARTMENT, JED GREETED ME WITH a sizzling kiss that curled my toes in my socks and went a long way toward soothing the frustrations of the day. I had to remind myself this was all still very new to him and not to get carried away, because you wouldn't have guessed it from the way he plastered himself to my body.

But true to Jed's first-date pronouncement at the barbecue, we'd done nothing more than make out a little that night, and my hands itched to peel his clothes from his freshly showered body and be reintroduced to all that creamy skin. It was a sharp turnaround from how I'd felt just an hour or so beforehand when sex had been the last thing on my mind.

I ran my nose up the side of his face and smiled at the familiar scent of my coconut and sandalwood body wash. "You've been in my bathroom." The thought thrilled me. Both that Jed felt comfortable enough to just go ahead and use it and that he smelled of me and my things.

"Guilty." He nuzzled his lips along my jaw and nibbled the lobe of my ear.

"Damn, that feels nice." I groaned and ran my hands the length of his back, smiling at the feel of seersucker under my fingertips. "And I do believe you're wearing my shirt."

"Also guilty." He kissed my neck, my shoulder, and my chin. "I hope you don't mind. I only freshened up at home, thinking maybe I could shower here. I . . . I wanted to see you."

Five little words that somehow meant everything curled into a warm ball in my chest and stretched their tiny fingers deep into my heart. "I missed you too," I murmured against his cheek, and for a few seconds we simply stood there, rocking gently, the warm northerly from the open door licking at our backs. "You have no idea how much I was looking forward to seeing you tonight."

He pulled back with a frown. "Bad day?"

"Not as bad as it could've been." I kissed him on the nose. "Thanks to you."

"Me?" His brows knotted.

"Yes, you. What you said the other night really helped clarify a lot for me."

His smile was electric. "Well, you better come in and tell me all about it so I know how great I am." He kicked the door shut and tugged me into the lounge like it was his apartment not mine and I arched an amused brow at the sound of the Pet Shop Boys singing "It's a Sin."

He chuckled. "Pure chance. Sucked to be Catholic, not straight, and living in Ireland in the '80s, right?"

I tugged him close for another kiss, needing to refresh the taste of him on my tongue, and he opened for me immediately, deepening the kiss and melting against me like he needed the intimacy just as much. And just like that, I remembered Bridie and how Jed's day had gone to shit as well.

I pulled back so I could see his face. "I ran into Abbie and Scott at school, and Abbie mentioned you had Bridie today?"

He shrugged. "It was fine."

It didn't look fine. Jed looked . . . tired. "Hey." I cupped his cheek. "Are you okay?"

He pressed his lips into my palm. "I am now. Come on." He tugged me toward the black leather couch and shoved an open beer into my hand. Then he grabbed a spot for himself at the other end and hauled my feet onto his lap. "I want to know everything." His no-nonsense tone made me smile.

"Okay, but you first." I pulled *his* feet onto *my* lap and began kneading. "I want to hear all about your day before I unpack the shit-show of mine."

And so we spent the next hour massaging each other's feet and discussing the highs and lows of the three days since we'd seen each other. It felt weirdly normal, disturbingly domestic, and . . . nice. So damn nice. Slobbing on the couch with a beer and talking with Jed seemed somehow infinitely better than my usual solution to a hard day, which relied on finding a willing partner to fuck the frustration from my weary bones. Not that I'd entirely given up on the second part of that scenario. It just happened to involve Jed as well. Go figure.

For his part, Jed didn't say much more about babysitting Bridie, other than he'd needed to delay the muffler job and about how Bridie had found a cicada in the workshop bathroom and spent an ear-piercing half-hour running in and out, squealing and sending them all into fits of laughter. It wasn't hard to see he was torn, and so I didn't push.

Jed had to work that one out for himself. Not that it stopped a niggle of worry at what might happen if and when Jed came out and if we were still together. There was no question that Jed's family had to come first. They were Jed's world. There *was* no choice, and I had zero issue with that. Jed and I didn't need to live in each other's pock-ets. My concern wasn't for me but for Jed. He was already struggling to draw a line regarding the time he needed for himself and his own interests. The last thing I wanted was to add to that guilt in any way.

When it came time to talk about the meeting with the board members, I did my best to keep it brief, although I couldn't keep from smiling when I remembered Chelsea's sour-lipped expression at the end.

"I am so fucking proud of you." Jed shimmied down the couch, fisted my shirt, and planted a blistering kiss on my lips that all but fried the newly growing hair right off my balls. And with his tongue halfway down my throat, I came to the sudden realisation that I was damn proud of myself as well, maybe for the first time in far too long.

When he was done licking my tonsils, Jed scrambled to his feet and headed for the kitchen. "That family have no idea how lucky they are to have you on their side." He continued talking over his shoulder about how amazing I was and how he wished he'd been there to see it as he gathered the takeout from the warming drawer, delivered it to the coffee table, and then went back to get something to eat it with.

"How did you even know where that stuff lives?" I nodded to the chopsticks and bowls he'd magicked up from somewhere and which he was busy filling with an assortment of goodies. I couldn't remember even buying them. "You've only been in my kitchen once."

He laughed at my confusion. "How is it that you *don't* know? I opened a few cupboards and drawers, that's all. Although to be fair, I did disturb a number of moths and bats in the process." He arched a brow. "Rick Stein, you're clearly not."

"It's not that bad," I lied. "I can cook perfectly well, thank you very much. I just . . . don't . . . very often." I dragged Jed in for a kiss just to stop him laughing. "I'll have you know, I have other . . . skills."

Another laugh. "Promises, promises. Now eat." Jed handed me a mouth-watering plate of khao pad, pad thai, gaeng daeng, som tam, and a selection of steamed dumplings.

I shovelled my fully-loaded chopsticks into my mouth and groaned with pleasure. "Damn, that's good."

"Mmm." Jed nudged my thigh with his toes and circled his chopsticks in the air as he chewed to tell me to keep going.

And so I told him of my plan for tightening up the school policy on bullying, about using experts at the next meeting to pave the way for that change, and about garnering more board support from those members I knew weren't happy with the way things had gone but who felt intimidated. And when I was done, he nodded enthusiastically.

"Well, if anyone can do it, you can. But be careful. As much as I was all for you drawing a line in the sand, I'd hate to see you fired."

He had a point. "I'll try. I just don't want to let Tane's family down."

Jed's chopsticks paused halfway to his lips before he set them back on his plate. "If this doesn't work out, Nash, it won't be because of anything you did or didn't do. You're putting yourself out on a limb here, and that takes a whole lot of courage. And if you lose your job, we'll just have to figure out the next step."

We. The idea of someone having my back, of wanting to be part of my life in that way had me blinking hard.

Jed frowned at my silence. "Did I say something wrong?"

"No." I leaned forward to share a greasy kiss. "Not at all. You just constantly amaze me."

He flushed and dropped his eyes to his bowl, pushing the food around with his chopsticks. "Yeah, likewise," he said without looking up, and for a few seconds the room fell quiet as we both ignored what was so very clearly happening between us.

To that end, I shovelled a dumpling into my mouth and waggled my chopsticks at him. "So, tell me more about this lube you bought."

Jed choked on a mouthful of rice, sending a spray of it tumbling down the front of his shirt. "Jesus, Nash, y—" He choked again and had to cough to clear his throat. "You can't say shit like that." He slid his almost empty bowl to the coffee table, and while I was pissing myself with laughter, he held out the bottom of his shirt all the way across to the kitchen.

"It's not funny," he scolded, shaking it over the sink.

I snort-laughed. "Yeah, it kind of is."

He threw a damp cloth my way and I used it to wipe the remaining rice off the polished floor. "Besides—" Jed shot me a smug look as he returned to the couch. "—you did say you might not be up for anything. Perhaps we should leave it for another time."

"Mmm, I did say that, didn't I?" I looked him up and down. "What can I say? It's a miracle."

He laughed and took my unfinished bowl from my hand. Then he pushed me flat and proceeded to crawl up my body until he was staring down at me.

"My, my, what do we have here?" I cradled his face and pulled him down for a thorough kissing, the zing of lime and ginger and chilli darting across my tongue like a skipping stone. "You feel good on me, Mister Mechanic Man."

Jed chuckled and sank down on top of me. "You say the weirdest things. Ask me again."

"About what?"

"You know what."

"Oooh, thaaaat."

Jed jabbed me in the ribs.

"Okay, okay," I huffed. "You mean the part where I asked if you had particular plans for that lube?"

"Exactly. *That* bit." Jed rolled off my stomach—in all honesty, a blessing—and I scooted back against the cushions so he had room to stretch out alongside. The change of position brought us within easy kissing distance, and I drank in the soft crinkles at the corners of his smiling eyes and that short silver hair tipped with rose-gold in the setting sun. I pressed my nose against his and inhaled the scent of coconut and everything I'd come to associate with this man who was filling my heart as easily as he filled my arms. And then I kissed him until he finally pulled away, and we were both half-hard and hungry for air.

He sank into the crook of my arm and ran a finger down my nose. "I've been thinking about that list of ours."

I nipped the end of his finger. "Oh, you have, have you?"

He stroked my nose again. "Yes, I have. And it occurred to me that I should really get a lesson in hand jobs . . . between men . . . just to make sure I've got the gist of things right in this brave new world I find myself in. After all, I would hate to make a mistake."

I sniggered. "Heaven forbid. And I take it you have a plan to remedy this terrible situation?"

He nodded sagely. "I do. When this gaping hole in my experience revealed itself to me, I said to myself, *Jed, who do you know who might be able to recommend a good teacher in said subject?*" He shot me a wicked grin.

It was all I could do not to bundle him into my arms and kiss him silly. "Ah." I stroked my chin thoughtfully. "I can see how that might pose a conundrum for you, seeing as how you're not out and all."

He beamed. "See, I knew you'd get it. So, Mister Principal, any . . . recommendations?"

"Well, now." I cupped his arse and pulled him tight against me. "That's a *hard* one all right." I ground into him, and fire ignited in my belly.

"Oh, fucking hell." He buried his face in my shoulder and whimpered softly.

"But as it so happens, by pure luck—" I circled again, and he groaned and hooked a leg over my hip. "—it appears I have a space in my diary right this very minute, if you're interested? I can even show you my credentials." I slid a hand between us, unzipped my trousers, and pulled my briefs out of the way, freeing my cock. "Would you like to check?" I breathed the question against Jed's ear just as a tube of lube landed on my cheek. "Ow."

"Sorry, not sorry." Jed groaned and turned to kiss me, his hand wrapping around my solid dick. "Yep, credentials all hunky-dory. We're good to go. And we're going to do this without a damn bed again, aren't we?" he grumbled into my open mouth as he ran his thumb over my slit.

I nodded. "Unless you wanna press pause and—"

"Like hell." He shoved his tongue into my mouth to shut me up and then started to stroke.

I grunted and my hips shot forward. "I'm gonna take that as a no." I gasped and worked the button on his jeans until I managed to pop it open, a surprise to all concerned. Then as my hand slipped inside his briefs to cup his dick and balls, Jed bit down on the side of my neck and . . . *Damn, that felt good.*

"Lube, remember?" He huffed against *my* neck.

Shit. Somehow, I found the lube and squeezed some into our hands—a fucking miracle, considering Jed refused to let go of my dick —then chucked the tube over his shoulder without bothering to find the cap. That done, we got down to business, shoving our shirts out of the way and jerking each other like teenagers. Snorting with laughter. Our faces buried in each other's shoulder. Grunting and moaning and gasping for breath in the cloying heat of the room. The patio doors flung open to carry the sounds of our lovemaking out across the still evening to whoever wanted to listen.

Like I could give a fuck. I had a pissy day to forget, and there was no better way to do it than with an eager, half-naked Jed in my arms.

"Jesus, I'm close," he groaned, still working me hard, my cock shuttling in and out of his grip, bringing me closer and closer to the edge.

"Likewise. Watch and learn, Padawan." I nudged his hand out of the way so I could wrap mine around the both of us.

Jed's eyes went wide, but after the first couple of slides, a huge smile broke over his face. "Fuck, yeah." He pulled away and peeked between us for a look. "Now, that's a first." He crushed his mouth over mine in a fierce kiss and then added his hand to my endeavours.

It wasn't going to take long.

A few strokes later, Jed tensed and threw his head back, neck corded, his hand stuttering over mine as he shuddered and came undone with a strangled cry just a few seconds before my own orgasm hit, and all thought exploded from my brain. I jerked in his arms, once, twice, and then we clung to each other, our stomachs slick with sweat and come, waiting for the rush of pleasure to fall away and our hearts to tick down.

"So . . ." I finally panted into his ear. "How was the lesson?"

He chuckled and kissed the side of my neck. "I think the teacher has a thing for me."

I laughed.

"But seriously. How the fuck is that so damn good? Two cocks together? Wow."

I nuzzled into his neck, breathing him in. "One of life's small miracles."

"Mmm. Well, we're definitely going to be glued together *and* to this eye-wateringly expensive leather couch of yours if we stay here much longer. In ten years, someone will find our desiccated bodies still wrapped around each other and we'll become one of those cold cases. Death by hand jobs and dehydration. I hope you have leather cleaner."

I cracked an eyelid open and stared at him. "You watch too many horror movies."

He chuckled and slowly peeled his arm from the skin of my waist. "I wish this heatwave would break." He tried to roll onto his back, his arms flailing when he hit the edge and almost went over.

"Whoa there." I managed to haul him back. "Come on, we'll get cleaned up, and then you can roast me alive in my bed . . . again. I've never known anyone to put out heat like you do. Last time, I woke up looking like a leg of pork, complete with crackling."

Jed patted my cheek. "Aw, you loved it, or you wouldn't have run after me when you thought I was leaving." He scrambled to his feet and then pulled me up into his arms.

"You think you're so smart, don't you?"

His smile wavered. "Not next to you, I don't."

His throwaway words gave me pause, and I held his gaze. "You are *so* fucking smart, Jed. It's not about diplomas."

"I like that you think that." He licked his way back into my mouth. And not for the first time, I marvelled at how comfortable Jed seemed to be with what we were doing.

I ended the kiss and took both of his hands in mine.

"What's wrong?"

"Nothing." I brought his hands up to my chest. "I just keep waiting for the other shoe to drop, you know?"

His mouth quirked up. "You mean for me to suddenly realise what I'm doing and freak the hell out and run?"

"Yeah, I guess."

He pulled free of my hands and cradled my face. "I'm not running. Am I worried about my kids' reactions? Absolutely. But as for you and me?" He shrugged. "The mechanics might be new, but I'm more than good with the feelings. The fact you're a man doesn't scare me, Nash. Not anymore. *You* don't scare me. I had a great marriage for a long time. I know what to look for, what to trust, what to hope for. You're a good man. Smart, sexy, talented, and with a big heart—even if your taste in cars leaves a lot to be desired."

I rolled my eyes.

"But the rest of it, the sex, the making out, just being with you is kind of fucking exciting."

Jesus, this man. I slid my hands around his waist, and he wrapped his around my neck, and we leaned into each other. "As someone once said to me, I knew you'd be trouble," I whispered against his ear.

"I think you could use a little trouble in your life," Jed whispered back.

"I'm not sure you classify as a *little*," I answered honestly.

He pulled back to frown at me. "Is that a bad thing?"

"No." I brushed our noses together. "That's the only thing I am absolutely sure about. You and me are a very, very good thing."

"Then I think we're safe, right?"

No, I wasn't at all sure we were.

I stripped my clothes to the floor, waited for Jed to do the same, and then threw the lot into the washer. Then I led him into my shower, and after that into my bed, curling around his furnace of a body to sleep while desperately fooling myself that I hadn't also led him right into my heart.

This had hurt written all over it.

CHAPTER FIFTEEN

Nash

I ROLLED MY SHOULDER TO EASE THE CRAMP THAT WAS RUNNING up my neck and pressed the tiniest of soft kisses to Jed's temple. He never moved. He hadn't done so much as twitch an eyebrow in the fifteen minutes I'd been watching, ever since daybreak had slipped through the opening in the curtains to stripe a weak grey light over every dip and curve of his pale legs, which he'd thrown free of the sheets at some point in the steamy night.

I brushed my hand lightly up the rough hair on his thigh, over all that creamy skin with its soft sheen of humid heat, my palm coming to rest over his sheet-covered hip. Jed was no gym-bunny. No granite abs or chiselled thighs for him. But every curve and lean slope of muscle was real, earned, and all of it Jed. And two weeks after our barbecue, I still couldn't stop staring. My palm ran around his waist to cup his belly, and I smiled at the soft give in the flesh, so different from the hard, cut muscle of youth that was so often wrapped in envy and sharp-edged angst. Jed was none of those things, and by consequence, when I was with him, neither was I.

Which, in a partially related side matter, meant I hadn't gone to the gym in a week and, dear God, I hadn't missed it. I needed to stay fit, but as I ran my gaze over the swell of Jed's arse and the long run of his back, noting the soft touches of age around the edges, I realised there was nothing about him that didn't stir my blood or was anything less than sexy.

I'd been tilting at damn windmills for years, fighting to look thirty again. Hell, forty would've done, even forty-five. Worthless goals, desperate and exhausting. I trailed my fingers once again up his back and then leaned down to press a soft kiss to the nape of his neck. He twitched but settled quickly enough, and I smiled against his warm skin, feeling the length of my cock thicken. It was time to take another look at those life goals of mine. Up the swimming and yoga and down the rest.

I almost laughed. And Jed thought *he* was the inexperienced one. That he was learning from *me*. If only he knew. I'd have traded a hundred men in my bed for a decent fuck-you to growing old. Not saying Jed didn't have his own insecurities about his body, because he did. But he wasn't rushing to the gym, or booking Botox, or waxing his follicles to death to subscribe to some ill-advised youth culture that weighed your value alongside your BMI. He wasn't trying to change who he was. I, on the other hand, had never done anything *but* cave to those pressures. Until recently.

Until Jed.

Jed snuffled and rolled to his back, looking so damn at home in my bed, so . . . content. I was even more content to have him there—a novel thought, which not too long ago would've sent me scurrying to the hills. And yet, there I was, blissfully satisfied and not at all sure I'd ever grow tired of waking up and finding him next to me. A few weeks and I was putty in Jed Marshall's hands.

Not that I'd tell him that.

He was still as skittish as a rabbit with his eyes locked on the horizon when it came to his coming out. All I could do was hope we didn't get rumbled beforehand, which was increasingly likely with the amount of time we were spending together. Our few nights apart were owed mostly to Jed having Bridie or visiting with his family.

More often than not, Jed had ended up in my apartment and in my bed, with or without sex leading us there. In the morning, we'd kiss each other goodbye early enough for Jed to open his workshop before Rollo arrived, and I'd head into school. Sometime in the afternoon, one would check in on the other, and more often than not we'd meet back at my place after work, drink a beer and eat dinner on the couch or out on the balcony, talking and laughing like we'd been doing it for years.

I ran a finger down the side of Jed's cheek, making him snuffle, and then continued along the dense silver thicket of stubble that seemed to spring from nowhere overnight and cover his jaw by morning. I still bore the whisker burn on my inner thighs from when he'd woken me with an epic blowjob just two days before. He'd taken me almost to the root for the first time—a quick learner for a guy who'd swallowed his first cock not that long ago. Another thing I wasn't complaining about.

And we'd also managed to tick a few things off the list along the way. We'd christened the bed with mutual knee-wobbling rim jobs. There'd been an experiment with thigh fucking, which had us both howling in laughter until Jed finally cottoned on to the mechanics and a fuckton more lube. And there was the occasion I'd ground into him alongside the refrigerator while we danced, badly, to Jethro Tull, until we both came. He'd then returned the favour up against my front door, our bags of Christmas shopping lying forgotten on the floor, and to an apt and festive rendition of "It's Beginning to Look A Lot Like Christmas." I'd offered him my arse on numerous occasions, but he still hadn't taken me up on it . . . yet.

Not that it mattered. I'd love to fuck Jed and be fucked by him, but it wasn't a dealbreaker, not even close. We were having a ton of fun and if that was all there was ever going to be, I was more than okay with that. I'd fucked a lot of men in my life. Enough to know it didn't make a jot of difference, not in the ways that truly counted. Sex with Jed, however we did it, eclipsed anything I'd done with a man before, and I knew exactly why, even if I wasn't prepared to verbalise it just yet. For only the second time in my life, I was with a man who could really hurt me.

So much for taking things slow. I was already in way, way over my head.

"You're creeping me out." Jed's eyelids fluttered open, a soft smile breaking through the pillow wrinkles on his cheeks. "How long have you been watching me?"

I brushed my lips over his, our morning breath mingling. "A while. You're cute when you sleep."

His gaze narrowed. "I'm *not* cute. Ask anyone." He breathed into his palm and winced. "Jesus, I stink. Save the kisses until I don't need a toxic gas sign on my forehead, yeah?"

"Nope." I squished his cheeks in my hands until he made a kissy face. "My breath is no better and I wanna kiss you." I tried to take his mouth, but he laughed and wriggled away.

"Not on your life, and actually, now that I've had a whiff, yours is a hell of a lot worse." He dived for the side of the bed, but I grabbed him and hauled him back into my arms, silencing his laughter with a long, slow kiss.

"Mmm." He pulled away, smiling. "I'm still alive, so I suppose it wasn't too terrible."

"Cheeky fucker." I tucked him into my side. "Did you sleep well?"

"Not bad." He rested his cheek against my chest, then quickly lifted his head and stared at my nipple. "You're getting *very* bristly." He eyed me with interest. "Is this an ongoing trend that I should be aware of?"

I snorted. "Well, that depends on what you think about it."

"Mmm. Let me see." He ran his cheek lightly over the silver-threaded regrowth. "I *think* it has definite potential."

"Potential for what?"

He licked a swathe across my nipple, and I jolted up the bed.

"For that." He gave a wicked grin. "I like the feel of it on my tongue. I like the fact that I know I'm with a guy, a *man*." He reached up a hand and stroked my cheek. "But don't fret about what I think. To be honest, I don't give a shit whether your chest is silky smooth or long enough to backcomb into a beehive. I like *you*, and any version of you that *you're* happy with is just fine with me."

Huh. "Is that so? Then what about . . . ?" I lifted the sheet and nodded toward my straggly, untidy pubes, a sight which generally made me cringe the few times I'd ever let them get that far.

Jed yanked the sheet right off, got down at eye level with the offending tresses, and took a long thoughtful look. "Personally, I'd like to see more of these too. It's like having lettuce in your ham and salad sandwich. It gets in your teeth and you think it's unnecessary, but then you miss it when it's not there."

I swatted him and he fell on his back, laughing. "Idiot." I primly smoothed the sheet over my stomach. "I barely even remember their colour; it's been that many years."

"Try grey," he mocked and then jerked back, clutching his chest and scowling at the long grey hair I held aloft.

"You were saying?" I waved it in the air like a trophy and his mouth tipped into a grin.

"You're only jealous because my chest hair is way more manly and impressi—no!" He ducked sideways to avoid me plucking another and slid off the mattress onto the floor.

I leaned over the edge and peered down at him. "I'll have jam on my toast, since you're up."

He narrowed his gaze and scrambled to his feet, which put his naked cock right in front of my face. "Well, look at that." I gave it a tap and watched it jiggle, then start to fill.

"Like hell." He covered it with his hand and sauntered haughtily toward the bathroom. "You don't deserve the pleasure of sucking my dick."

I laughed and crossed my arms behind my head, enjoying the

unobstructed view of his naked arse. "That's not what you said last night."

"You caught me in a weak moment." Jed disappeared into the bathroom, and I smiled at the sound of his early morning waterfall. The man's bladder capacity was the eighth wonder of the world.

"Just so we're clear," I called out. "Would that *weak* moment happen to be the one when you strolled buck naked through my kitchen for a bottle of water and told me I had thirty seconds to be similarly attired and in my bed, or you were going home to jerk off to some porn where at least the guys did as they were told?"

His face appeared around the open door. "Hey, I'm not getting any younger, and an erection can come and go in the amount of time it takes you to obsess over the correct alignment of the coffee mug handles in the dishwasher."

I snorted and shook my head, mostly because he was right. "These things are important."

Jed's laugh bounced off the tiles, and a few seconds later he wandered back into the bedroom and threw a pair of boxers my way. "Are you hitting the gym today or the pool?"

"The pool. I'll stop off on the way to school. I've got a ton of work still sitting on my desk."

"Then you better get moving. I'll take the shower first and get the toast cooking, but I'm not touching that space-station of a coffee maker again. Last time, it spat the dummy and shut itself down for *scheduled maintenance.*"

Also true. The man was epically cursed when it came to kitchen appliances.

Fifteen minutes later, we were moving around the kitchen in the easy domestic dance we'd quickly become practiced at while watching the news on the morning programme and occasionally exchanging sappy kisses. I refused to think about how much I liked it and just smiled and snagged another kiss as Jed passed.

"So, tomorrow is Christmas Eve." He raised his eyes from his bowl of sliced banana and muesli, his cheeks pink.

I smirked. "Brains as well as a pretty face. I hit the jackpot."

He kicked me under the table. "I'm serious. Tomorrow's a washout for me. I've got some last-minute shopping to finish. Then I'm having lunch with Ewan, and you're seeing Colin, right?"

I nodded.

Jed hesitated then added, "How would you feel about trying to carve out a bit of time on Christmas Day itself? I'll understand if you can't—"

"Yes." I pushed aside the tiny fake Christmas tree that had mysteriously appeared on my table one afternoon, so I could better see him. At the time, I'd grumbled and whinged about having to find somewhere to store it for eleven months of the year, but I'd left it exactly where he put it and tried to ignore the way it made me smile every time I passed. Tiny classic cars hung from its branches and I kind of fucking loved it.

"Let's make it happen." I threaded my fingers with his. "You guys eat mid-afternoon, right? About two?"

He nodded and drank the last of the milk directly from his bowl. "Give or take."

I took a small bite of my toast and chewed thoughtfully. "Devon and Fiona usually have us sitting down about noon, but the boys aren't kids anymore, so there's no fuss. We drink a glass of champagne in the morning while we open presents. Then Devon sets up the barbecue and we add our contributions to the table and pitch in to get things ready. After lunch there's the requisite food coma and catch-up for a couple of hours before I can legitimately make my escape. And your passionfruit parfait idea was brilliant, thanks. I made it yesterday and put it in the freezer after demolishing a bowl. It's delicious. Fiona is going to be super impressed, and Brian is gonna be washing dishes again."

"Thank Tamsin." Jed kissed the back of my hand, then let it go to butter a slice of toast. "It's her recipe. She was so damn excited that the two of us were giving things a go, she would've made the dessert for you as well if you'd asked."

I frowned. "And you're sure she won't let anything slip over Christmas?"

Jed shook his head. "I was crystal clear about that. Besides, Tamsin's a lawyer. Nothing breaches those lips without legal representation."

"So, what's your Christmas Day look like? I take it Tamsin and Neil will be there. Neil's family are all in Oz, right?"

"That's right. Ewan is staying with Abbie and Scott until the twenty-eighth, and after that, he's heading north to his girlfriend's parents' holiday home at Hot Water Beach for New Year. We think he figures that staying with Abbie avoids pissing Tamsin or me off." Jed laughed. "Honestly, we couldn't give a shit as long as we each get to spend some time with him." He shifted closer, tangling his legs with mine before reaching for his coffee. "After Christmas lunch, we lounge around and play board games or outdoor cricket, and Tamsin and Neil usually head home around sevenish."

So that was most of the day gone. "When do you usually leave?" I tried to remain hopeful.

He grimaced. "That's where it gets a bit sticky. Since Bridie arrived, I've sort of made a habit of staying with them Christmas night, so I can put Bridie to bed with a story. It's kind of become our Christmas . . . thing."

Shit. And there was no way I would take that from either of them. "Then you should definitely stay." I tried not to show my disappointment.

"No." Jed reached for my hand. "I said I want to see you and I meant it. So just shut up and let me finish."

"Bossy little shit." I leaned forward and kissed him, dipping my tongue in for a quick taste. Bananas with the sour creamy edge of yoghurt and bitter coffee.

He grinned, then scowled. "Dammit. You made me forget what I was going to say." He blinked twice. "Oh, right. I'm going to call Abbie today and suggest I stay with them Christmas Eve instead of Christmas night. That way Bridie can crawl into bed with me

Christmas morning, and everyone can sleep in a little longer. I'm sure Abbie will be thrilled, and I'll simply tell her I'm too whacked at the end of Christmas Day and I want my own bed. Which is also true."

"Very sneaky." I gathered his plate on top of mine and walked them both to the dishwasher. "So how about we meet back here whenever you can get away?"

Jed's arms slid around my waist from behind, and he pulled me against him. "I was kind of hoping you might want to stay with me instead."

I froze, my heart hammering against my ribs. We'd tangled a little on Jed's couch for a few delightful make-out sessions, but I'd never stayed the night or even made it into his bed. It felt like a big step. Like he was telling me something important. "Are you sure?" I turned and slid my hands around his neck. "We don't have to."

"I want to." He pressed his lips softly to mine. "I've been thinking about it all week. Having you in my bed? That's the best Christmas present I could wish for."

My heart filled just a little more. "Well, I'm sure I can do better than just that." I pressed my groin into his.

"Promises, promises." He returned the favour. "But at the end of a long day and with a ton of food in our bellies, if we only manage a couple of kisses and make it to the bed without falling asleep on the way, I'll call it a win."

I groaned. "You might be right. But then there's always the morning."

He brightened. "Very true, and I'll be holding you to that. But for now, I have to go. If Rollo asks one more time what's up with me, I'm gonna spill everything, I swear. The two of them are like bloodhounds. Jemma went up to the house yesterday to grab some extra milk for morning tea and came back brandishing the two-litre container I'd bought the week before, which she'd found still sitting on my countertop. She waved it in front of my nose, adding that the house barely looked lived in, like it was evidence of foul play. I almost choked on my caramel Mallow Puff."

"You left milk on your kitchen counter for a week?"

"Don't give me that face, Mister Clean and Spotless." He smoothed my brow and patted my horrified cheeks. "I just forgot, all right? I mean, I've hardly fucking been there. Besides, it happens. No one got hurt. We can't all have CDC-approved kitchen surfaces, you know."

"So, I might have a small obsession with hygiene?" I admitted. "There are worse things."

Jed pulled his lower lip between his teeth and fired me a saucy look. "Didn't seem to stop you eating me out like a champ the other night."

My cheeks flamed, and okay, fair point.

"And my work here is done." Jed grabbed his duffel from the barstool and his keys from the drawer where they'd found a home with mine—yet another small thing that made me far too happy. "So, this is it until Christmas, then." He slid his arms around my waist. "I'll miss you."

I kissed him softly. "I'll miss you too. Have a lovely time with your family. They don't know how lucky they are to have you with them."

He huffed. "I'll be sure to remind them. And you too."

I nodded. "Until Christmas night, then."

Jed's smile was tender. "Until Christmas night."

I tipped his chin up and lost myself in his taste, in the feel of his body hard against mine, in the way he fit so perfectly in my arms with that familiar scent of coconut and everything uniquely Jed, and in the effortless way he filled the hole in my heart that seemed curiously shaped just for him.

CHAPTER SIXTEEN

Jed

MERRY CHRISTMAS, GORGEOUS.

I'd read the text from Nash a million times since he'd sent it at the arse-crack of dawn, and I still couldn't wipe the sappy smile from my face. I'd replied in kind, and he'd sent two lines of emojis, most of which I had no idea about other than the eggplant one, which sent my cheeks flaming and my mind to places unbecoming for a Christmas morning in my daughter's house.

I settled for returning hearts and kisses rather than invite a fatal emoji faux pas, and then I returned to mulling over the upcoming evening's possibilities. Nash in my bed and me in his arse. Seemed a fair exchange. Merry Christmas, indeed.

"Who's that, Poppy?" Bridie glanced at my phone, which I quickly slid face-down onto the bedside table before wrestling her into a hug. "A friend." It wasn't a lie, and even though Bridie couldn't identify more than a few words at her age, it was a timely reminder that I needed to be careful. The night before, I'd had to stop my lock screen text notifications, never more thankful that I'd given Nash the handle of BMW in my contacts.

Bridie wriggled free of my hold and continued on her Christmas-morning mission to get me to read all of her favourite books in between emptying her Christmas stocking, one little gift at a time.

"There's one more, Poppy." She shoved her hand deep into the enormous bright red woollen stocking, a determined expression on her face. "Got it." Her eyes lit up as she pulled out a marshmallow Santa and waved it in the air. "We can share," she announced, snuggling close as she ripped the foil covering off and twisted the poor Santa into two squished pieces. "Here." She held one out for me, and I stared at the crumpled chocolate mess, then sighed and popped it in my mouth.

"Mmm." I waggled my eyebrows while doing my best to look delighted at the dubious offering. "Yummy. My blood sugar is indebted to you. Type 2 diabetes for Christmas. Who'd have guessed?"

Bridie frowned. "What's dibees, Poppy?"

I chuckled. "It's what you get when you're older and life sucks the fun right out of your food."

"Not if you eat right." Abbie pushed the door wide, looking warm and sleep-rumpled in a pair of reindeer pyjamas. "Man, it's hot in here." She threw open the window and joined us on the bed.

"Mummy!" Bridie launched herself onto Abbie's lap, flinging her tiny arms around her mother's neck. "Poppy's reading me lots of stories and we ate a chocolate Santa."

"Oh, you did, did you?" Abbie gave me the stink eye.

"It's Christmas," I said loftily. "There are *no* rules. And you wouldn't be so hot if you ditched the fluffy festive pjs for some more appropriate summer shorties."

"Where would be the fun in that?" Abbie grinned and smothered her daughter with kisses. "Merry Christmas, Angel. And thanks, Dad." She shot me a grateful look. "I hope she didn't wake you too early."

I stifled a yawn. "Five on the button. If I remember, even you slept longer."

"Oh god." Abbie looked horrified. "Still, you did say you'd take the early shift."

"I did and I loved it. We had a lot of fun, didn't we, munchkin?" I pulled Bridie's dark waves back from her eyes and spun them into a messy side bun.

"Morning all." Ewan practically fell into the room, brown curls asunder, and matching brown eyes bleeding red at the margins after having stayed up far too late playing Halo and drinking beer with Scott. "Merry Christmas, everyone, especially you, little chicky." Ewan crept across and grabbed a giggling Bridie from Abbie's lap, spinning her around before collapsing on the bed beside Abbie.

"If she throws up that marshmallow Santa, you're on clean-up duty." I stabbed a finger at Ewan.

"Ew." He stretched his lean frame across the bed and snagged the spare pillow from under my head. "Merry Christmas, Pops." He winked and I gave him a playful shove.

"What's wrong with your own beds?" I grumbled, unable to keep the smile off my face. Surrounded by my kids and my only grand-child, I was pretty damn happy. "Come on. Christmas selfie time." I reached for my phone, and everyone groaned. On the third attempt to fit us all in, I texted the one and only reasonable shot off to Tamsin, who immediately returned one of her and Neil in the car on their way over for present time.

I lingered over the photo of us all on the bed for a few seconds longer, my heart going to the one person missing. Maybe next year. I allowed myself a moment of hope and then returned my phone to the bedside cabinet and gave Ewan a closer once-over. "Good God, you look like something the cat threw up. What time did you two finally get to bed?"

He pulled a pained face. "Around two, I think? Something like that. But it wasn't in vain." He polished his knuckles on his chest. "I whipped Scott's ars—oops, butt." He grinned sheepishly.

"Well, thanks to you pouring beer down his throat, Scott snored all night," Abbie grumbled. "He's not twenty anymore, and neither are you."

Ewan raised his hands. "Hey, don't blame me. He's a grown man, not to mention a sucker for punishment."

"Hey, I won a game." Scott poked his head into the room, blinking furiously at the bright dawn sun.

"The operative word being one. Singular." Ewan gave a smug grin. "And were you eavesdropping?"

Scott waggled his brows.

"Don't you even think about getting on this bed," I warned my son-in-law. "One more body and it'll collapse."

Scott chuckled and pushed back his messy red locks. "I wouldn't dream of it. I'm heading for the coffee machine, and since it's Christmas and I'm such a kind and generous person, I'm open for orders."

"Oh god, yes," I almost whined. "Have I told you you're my favourite son-in-law?"

"Yeah, yeah." Scott waved me away. "Just get your butts into the kitchen. I'm not doing delivery."

"That's it. Everyone out," I ordered.

The demand was met by a tide of grumbles and groans and Bridie-sized giggles, but no one moved.

I narrowed my gaze at my favourite people in the world. "If you lot aren't out of my bedroom in ten seconds flat, I will personally take back every present I put under the tree."

The room was clear in five, and I grinned to myself. "And that's how you do it."

I slid out of bed and smoothed the Poppa Claus pyjamas Abbie had bought for me the year before and which had sent Nash into hysterics, and headed for the bathroom.

The morning passed in a blur of wrapping paper and bacon and egg butties, ear-piercing shrieks of delight from Bridie, and groans of embarrassment from the adults as they unwrapped their secret Santa gifts.

Mine was a jar full of lollies labelled *Take a Chill Pill*, which was going to be put to good use in the workshop. Scott got a small plastic container of *Bits of Coin*, which was literally what was in it and a great gift for a financial planner. Tamsin got a woman's stand-to-pee chute for her tramping expeditions, which Bridie immediately stole for a bathtub toy. Neil got a rude barbecue apron, and Ewan a set of plastic cactuses since his real one had died on the windowsill of his university flat—he was just that hopeless. And we all laughed at Abbie's, which could only have been bought by her brother—a book on how to swear your way around the world in twenty different languages. And we all lied through our teeth when Bridie wanted to know what it was about.

Nine hours later, we'd managed a few cringeworthy carols and a hysterical attempt by six adults to assemble and fill Bridie's massive two-foot-deep paddling pool. We'd put a good dent in a protein and carbohydrate tsunami feast, had a million laughs, and witnessed two impressive toddler tantrums.

As for the paddling pool, when it was finally ready, Bridie barely got five minutes alone to splash around before the aforementioned six adults took one look at the inviting water and decided it was the perfect place to have dessert. Sunblock and wide-brimmed hats were dished out and we ate while sitting chest-deep in water with the sun sizzling overhead and the festive streamers on the lemon tree hanging still and wistful in the sultry air.

Typical Wellington crazy-arse weather. Where was a freezing southerly when you needed it? A white Christmas never sounded so good.

Nash

"Go on, move over." I nudged Brian sideways and grabbed a spare tea towel to help out. "Let today's humiliation be a lesson to you. Never try to bullshit a bullshitter."

He laughed and flicked water at me and I noogied his head.

"Get off." He wriggled free, grumbling, "I don't know how you pulled that off." He nodded to the last melted remains of the passionfruit parfait. "You *never* make desserts. I was sure you'd fuck it up, and instead, you get freaking dish of the day. And no one ever told me you had to squeeze lemon over avocado to stop it turning all brown and nasty. I smell a big hairy rat. You had help, didn't you? And that's against the rules."

"So is rigging the draw." I eyeballed him, then tapped the side of my nose. "And you'll never get it out of me."

"Never get what?" Devon appeared in the kitchen, looking so much like our father, it stole the breath from my lungs. Disobedient red waves cascaded to his shoulders, highlighting crystal green eyes and a spray of freckles that fanned over his nose and across to the fine web of lines at the corners of his eyes.

"I was just saying, Uncle Nash had to have help," Brian complained. "He sucks at desserts."

Devon threw me a roguish grin and spooned the last of the parfait into his mouth. "It's probably this new boyfriend he's been hiding from us."

I schooled my expression. "Pfft. What new boyfriend?"

Brian's gaze darted between his father and me, his mouth hanging open. "Uncle Nash has a boyfriend? An actual *boyfriend*?"

Jamie appeared in the kitchen like a demon summoned, wide-eyed and slack-jawed. "What the hell, Uncle Nash?" He peered through the window up at the sky. "Nope, no airborne porcine to be seen."

I huffed. "Shut up. Your father might be talking complete rubbish, but I am capable of dating, you know?"

Jamie snorted. "Since when? You've never had a boyfriend, *ever*, at least that I can remember."

I threw a helpless look to Devon. "They're your kids. Tell them that I've actually had a serious boyfriend."

Devon raised his hands. "Don't drag me into this. Your nephews know you as well as I do. What was that name they had for you in their teens?" He tapped a thoughtful finger to his lips while Brian and Jamie answered together.

"Nash, pash, flash, and dash."

"Oh, yeah, that's right." Devon laughed.

I growled and swept a glare over all three of them. "Stop picking on me."

Devon laughed. "So, who is he then?"

"Don't just stand there, help." I threw a tea towel at Jamie. "And I have no idea what you're talking about." I gave Devon my best zip-it-right-now look.

Which he totally ignored because . . . annoying brother. "Don't lie to me." He grinned unapologetically. "You've been way too cagey of late, and you blew off our pub night with some lame excuse about needing to work."

"Oooooh, what have I missed?" Fiona joined the circling pack, no doubt smelling blood in the water.

I threw up my hands. "What is this? The Spanish Inquisition?" But my defensiveness only served to make everyone even more curious, and I was pummelled with questions until I blew a shrill whistle and cut a hand through the air. "Enough! Methinks it's time I headed home where there's no one to bug me. Merry Christmas, dearest one and all."

Everyone gave a collective, "Aw," and then laughed.

"You're just pissed because I beat you at Cluedo," Brian said loftily.

"Am not." I flicked him with the tea towel, but he jumped out of the way just in time.

"You are too, old man." Brian twirled his own tea towel, and I ducked behind the breakfast bar as a shield.

"I only let you win because it's Christmas," I explained, then jumped sideways as he performed a nice round-the-corner shot and nipped me on the calf. "Ow." I grabbed Devon and pushed him in front of me. "If you accidentally get your father, he won't pay for your tuition."

Brian froze. "Good point."

"Whereas I have a clear shot." Jamie got me with a solid whip to my butt.

"Goddammit." I ran from the kitchen, laughing. "That's it, I'm going home." I grabbed my satchel from the sideboard. "Come and hug your old uncle and thank him for clearing his bank accounts to give you ungrateful Gen Zs some spending money over the holidays."

"Thank you, Uncle Nash," Brian and Jamie sing-songed in unison and then landed on me in a group hug that almost crushed the air from my lungs.

When they finally let me up for air, I pulled Brian aside while the others headed back into the kitchen. "She's lovely." I nodded to where Brian's girlfriend, Hannah, was watching our antics with wide eyes. "Hang on to her."

"I will," Brian said with obvious gratitude, since his mother was still being a little standoffish. "Thanks, Uncle Nash."

"Devon loves her, and your mother will come around." I flicked my gaze to Fiona. "She's just worried you're too young for something serious."

"But—"

"Give her time," I cautioned, and he nodded.

"Come on. I'll walk you out." Devon slapped my car keys into my hand and I followed him down the hall. At the front door, he paused and turned to face me. "I was right, wasn't I? About a guy. To be honest, it was just a stab in the dark based on how oddly you've been behaving, but there *is* someone, isn't there?"

I glanced back up the empty hall and sighed. "Yes, but I can't talk about it. Not yet."

Devon frowned. "Jesus, he's not married, is he?"

I rolled my eyes. "No. What the fuck do you think of me? He's divorced. But he's also not out."

Devon sucked in a breath through clenched teeth. "Nash—"

I held up a hand. "But it's not like that. He's just waiting for Christmas to be over before he talks with his family. His ex-wife knows and she's supportive."

Devon studied me for a second. "Wow. This guy must be something special." He didn't try to hide his concern. "You haven't shown any interest in a man since . . . well, since he who shall remain nameless. Oh god, this one's not two decades younger than you or worse, is he?"

I snorted and leaned back against the wall. "No, he's not. And your ageism is showing."

He huffed. "I'm not ageist. I'd just rather you were with someone who doesn't think The Doobie Brothers are a craft beer supplier."

I barked out a laugh. "You've got nothing to worry about. He's actually a couple of years older."

Devon blinked. "Jesus." He frowned and put his palm on my forehead. "No fever that I can tell."

I shoved his hand away. "Why does everyone do that? I'm quite capable of a relationship, you know?"

"I know you are," he said simply. "I just wasn't sure that *you* knew it, or were willing to risk it again."

He had a point. "I like him, Devon. I like him a lot. And I do really want you to meet him. We're just not at that point yet."

Devon hesitated like he was about to say something, then shook his head. "Fair enough. Just . . . be careful, yeah?"

"I think it's a bit late for that." I held his gaze, hoping to convey what I couldn't quite get out in words yet.

He read my eyes and let out a resigned sigh. "Fucking hell. Well then, if you can't be careful, be smart. And if things go tits up, you come and talk to us, okay? Don't fucking disappear on us like you did last time. We were so damn worried. I know you've got Colin, but we're brothers, Nash. We're family. We do this kind of thing together, right? No more fucking lone ranger shit."

I grabbed him in a hug. "I won't. I promise."

He held on tight, his fist pounding against my back a few times just to drum the point home. "You damn well better not." He let me go and stepped away. "And I hope it works out for you. I really do. You deserve someone special in your life, Nash. We all get hurt, brother. Even when you're with the one you love, you still get fucking hurt. Life's a bitch like that."

I chuckled and patted his cheek. "And people wonder why you're not a therapist. Catch you later, brother."

When I was safe in my car, I sat for a few seconds to digest what had just happened. Was I that bloody transparent? I wasn't sure what I was most pissed about. That my family could read me like a cheap novel. That the kids thought the idea of me having a boyfriend was so damn preposterous. Or that I'd been made to face how very, very much I was going to hurt if this thing with Jed fell apart.

Not that thinking about it was going to change anything. I'd already sailed over the safety barriers and was floundering at the bottom of the cliff. All I could do was wait to see if Jed followed me over, not that my history in that department was very encouraging.

I pulled out my phone, smiled at the Mustang pic I'd swapped in place of Jed's name, and fired him a text to say I'd meet him at home.

Home?

Jesus. Refer to aforementioned cliff.

CHAPTER SEVENTEEN

Jed

By six in the evening, I was hot, exhausted, and doing my best to edge toward the front door so I could go pick up Nash. He'd texted to say he was headed back to his apartment to put a sling on his stomach and to ask if I had any Gaviscon in my medicine cabinet? I'd laughed and sneaked outside to call him, my knees almost buckling at the obvious pleasure in his voice when he picked up.

I could only hope that it meant he felt it too—this stupid, adolescent, head-over-heels galloping in my stomach. I knew what it meant. How much I liked him. How much I wanted him. And I wanted to date him . . . seriously. Like, out-and-about and no-sneaking-around seriously.

"Don't make me hurt you." Tamsin caught me slinking back inside, wearing a hapless grin from ear to ear. "You've been talking to him, haven't you?"

There was no point denying it, and her eyes softened. "Are you two going to see each other today? Is that why you stayed last night and not tonight? You know Abbie wondered about the change."

"Yes, and yes. I'm heading to his place now."

She folded her arms. "Good. Don't you lose that man because you're too scared to talk to our kids." Never one to mince words was Tamsin.

"And this is your business, how?" I snapped, then instantly regretted it. Tamsin was on my side.

She sighed and chewed on her lip. "Point taken, and I'm sorry. But you should really trust our kids. I've been feeling Abbie out about the whole LGBT thing—"

"What?" Panic gripped my chest. "Tamsin, please stay out of it." It came out louder than I'd intended, and my gaze flicked to the lounge to find Abbie looking our way with a frown on her face.

"It's fine." Tamsin lowered her voice and steered me toward the edge of the patio. "It was just general chit-chat about that basketballer who came out recently. Abbie was horrified at some of the public pushback. She'll be fine. Anyway, I finally got Bridie to sleep, and Neil and I are going to stay here for a bit, so that means you can skedaddle. Merry Christmas, Jed." She waggled her eyebrows. "Go have some fun."

"Thanks." I squeezed her hand and headed inside to make my escape.

"You going already, Dad?" Abbie looked up from pouring a huge jug of iced lemonade into glasses. "I saw you and Mum talking. Is everything okay?"

"Everything's fine." I wandered across to kiss her cheek. "I'm just a bit tired is all. Your daughter gave me a pretty early wake-up call this morning."

Abbie grinned and offered me one of the glasses. "Sorry about that. But you're still coming for Boxing Day brunch tomorrow, right? Scott's promised to make his world famous taquitos this year."

I took my time swallowing a mouthful of lemonade before I answered. "Not this year, sweetheart."

Abbie tabled the jug and frowned. "You're not coming? But we always do the brunch thing on Boxing Day, even before Bridie came along. Something's up with you, Dad? You've been acting really off lately."

"Nothing's wrong," I hedged, setting my glass down. In many ways, nothing had ever been more right. "And what do you mean, off?"

She pulled her lower lip between her teeth, and just like that, she was seventeen all over again and asking to borrow the car. "I can't put my finger on it. Distracted, maybe? And you hardly ever don't take Bridie when we need it, but it's been twice in the last two weeks."

Guilt washed through me.

"And then you switch staying Christmas night for Christmas Eve, and now you're pulling out of Boxing Day brunch." Then her voice grew small. "You're not sick, are you?"

Shit. "No, sweetheart." I took her hands. "I promise you, I'm not sick. But you're right. I have been a bit distracted lately, although it's nothing bad." Far from it. I bit back the smile wanting to break over my face. "I'll talk to you soon, but for now I'd just like a quiet day tomorrow. I might even work on my car. I haven't done that in a while." I held her gaze and she had the grace to blush.

"Sorry. I guess we *have* been monopolising a lot of your time off lately, with it being Christmas and all."

"Hey." I cupped her cheek. "You know I love having Bridie. She means the world to me. But tomorrow I'm gonna take things slow. Maybe even sleep in—" It wasn't a lie. "—and then just hang around at home—" Also not a lie. "I might even eat really, really bad food with no one around to see and tell me off."

She laughed and threw her arms around my neck. "Okay then. Message received. You take it easy and we'll eat a taquito in your honour. But come around the day after, promise?"

"I promise."

Twenty minutes later, I pulled into Nash's car park and tooted the horn on the '67 Mustang. Nash appeared in seconds, his duffel thrown over his shoulder and wearing the biggest smile as he took in my wheels. I met him by the passenger door, took his bag from him, and slung it into the back seat. Then I handed him the keys.

"What?" He stared down at them, then up at me, eyes dancing in delight. "You're actually gonna let me drive?"

"Are you sober?" I raised an eyebrow.

"One champagne and two mid-strength beers over the course of the day."

"Excellent." I slid a hand around his neck and pulled him in for a long, thorough kissing. "Mmm. I've been waiting to do that all day." I ran my thumb over his damp lips. "Merry Christmas, Mister Collingwood."

He grinned and pulled me back in for an equally thorough mauling. "Merry Christmas to you too, Mister Marshall. And just so you know, today my brother asked if I was seeing someone. Said I was behaving *oddly*."

Well, shit. I rolled my eyes and waved him around to the driver's side. "Abbie said exactly the same. She even thought I might be sick and wasn't telling her." I blew out a breath. "I'm not exactly sure what it says about the sad state of my social life that my kid thinks I'm dying just because I say no to babysitting a couple of times?"

Nash leaned across the leather seats and pressed a soft kiss to my lips. "*Previously* sad state. There is nothing whatsoever sad about your social life now. And if Abbie knew what you were really up to, she'd be gobsmacked."

I gave a soft chuckle. "I guess we'll find out soon enough. But you're right. My *social* life has never been better." I leaned in and kissed him again. "In fact, I've been so damn *social*, my dick is one hand job away from chafing and throwing in the towel."

He looked horrified. "Say it isn't so." Then his eyes kindled fire. "Would it help if I kissed it better?"

I met his smirk with one of my own. "Maybe later."

"I'm holding you to that. Now—" He looked around the dials and flexed his fingers. "—exactly how fast am I allowed to go?" He laughed at the panic that must've shown on my face. "Just kidding. Come on, fill me with your wisdom. I'm an excellent student."

Well, I certainly wanted to fill him with *something* before the night was over, but wisdom wasn't it. "You are not a good student. You're a bossy fucking teacher who always thinks he's right."

"This is true." He waggled his eyebrows. "But only because I usually am, ninety percent of the time."

I groaned and looked up at the bluebird sky. "Give me strength."

He snorted. "Okay, I'm listening, I promise." He blew out a breath and settled himself, all except for the adorably excited smile on his face that just made me want to do a whole lot of dirty things to him.

"What are you staring at?" The corners of his eyes crinkled in amusement.

"Jesus Christ, come here." I grabbed his shirt and pulled him across the gap between the seats so I could kiss him, fierce enough to make him wobble in his seat when I let him go. "You look so fucking sexy behind that wheel, I almost can't stand it."

He fired me a wicked grin. "You wanna shift my stick?"

I rolled my eyes and slapped away his hand, which was creeping up my thigh. "It's an automatic, idiot."

He glanced down and smiled. "So it is. But on the basis of that look in your eye, I'm gonna add something to that list."

I arched a brow. "Such as?"

"Anything to do with me spread naked across the hood of this sexy bit of machinery and you doing whatever the hell you want to me should about cover it."

I might've swallowed my tongue because, fuck me, that sounded epic. I took a deep breath, dragged my gaze from his, and gave the bonnet a thoughtful look. Then shook my head. "It's an expensive paint job—"

Nash clamped a hand over my mouth, and just like that, he was right up in my face, brown eyes laughing. "We're so fucking doing it. I'll throw a damn rug over the thing if I have to."

I peeled his hand away and frowned. "It would have to be a very clean rug, freshly washed, no grit—"

His mouth crushed over mine, shutting me up with a tongue down my throat in a kiss that left me gasping for breath. "We. Are. Doing. It." He held my face in his hands, enough heat in his gaze to set my fucking clothes on fire.

All I could do was grin. "I have to admit, it's an interesting proposal." I cleared my throat and tapped the steering wheel. "But for now, seatbelt on, face the front, and pay attention."

A smile tugged at his pouty lips. "You're so hot when you get all bossy and shit."

I pushed his head around to the front. "Shut up or I'll take the keys back."

He zipped his lips and waited for instructions.

I couldn't resist. "You're so hot when you're all submissive and shit. Maybe that's another one for the list."

He snorted but never moved.

I walked him through the basics of driving my baby, and a few false starts later—no such thing as automatic chokes or power steering on my girls—and we were off . . . slowly. You didn't just get in and drive a big block Mustang as if it was any other car. It was a raw power with none of the modern modifications to temper it. And all classic cars had idiosyncrasies. Driving them was a relationship, not a dictatorship, but after a couple of circuits of the car park, I figured Nash had enough of a feel for her to let him out on the road.

Not that he agreed, judging by the flash of panic in his eyes when I directed him toward the gate. He was clearly nervous as hell. It was actually pretty endearing. And when he finally hit the road, he drove like a damn nana, and it was all I could do not to laugh.

With a deep crease between his brows, he leaned forward and put his full attention into the task at hand, almost like he could get the Mustang to do his bidding by sheer force of will. It was so like him, so like the born teacher that he was.

When we came to a stop at the first intersection, I rested my hand lightly on his jiggling thigh and he almost jumped through the roof. "Loosen up a little, sweetheart," I reassured him. "You're doing fine. If you relax, she'll be good to you. It's just like sex. You give a little. You take a little."

He snorted and shot me a look. "I'm gay, remember? There's never been any *she* in my sex life." But his shoulders relaxed a little nonetheless and his lips turned up in a bright smile. "And don't think I didn't hear you call me sweetheart."

I cupped his cheek. "You were meant to hear."

He turned his lips into my palm and pressed a kiss there. "And I love it."

My heart stuttered in my chest and my gaze slid to the side mirror to hide the sheen in my eyes. "You better pick things up to the speed limit before the guy following decides to try and go around," I alerted him. "Who knows just how merry he's feeling today."

"Damn." Nash accelerated a little and the other driver slid back where he belonged.

"Let's take the long way via Scorching Bay," I suggested, indicating the far exit off the roundabout. "The roads are pretty empty."

Nash followed my instructions, his eyes glued to the bitumen, that frown of concentration growing deeper. "I'm surprised you trust me to drive all that way first time."

I ran my hand down his thigh. "I trust you with a lot more than that."

He shot a glance my way and I could feel the question in his eyes.

I kept mine carefully on the road ahead and simply said, "You heard me." Then I stole a sneaky look to find him staring through the windscreen with a soft smile in place.

As Nash's confidence grew, so did the smoothness of his driving until eventually we were cruising smoothly at the speed limit, the deep rumbling growl of the engine vibrating through my body like a familiar lullaby. I sighed and leaned back, determined to simply enjoy the view and the car and the man driving it.

Nash sailed through yet another set of green traffic lights on an almost empty street. Soon after, we turned onto the narrow coastal road with the grandiose name of Great Harbour Way and wound our way past an endless run of rocky bays toward the narrow entrance to Wellington Harbour itself.

Families braved the lingering heat to splash through shallows in search of crabs or to throw Frisbees on the slim grassy banks that lined the rocky shore. There were even a few large family Christmas picnics still in full swing, replete bodies sprawled under colourful beach umbrellas or hogging the limited shade. The entire city had a curious sleepy vibe that mirrored the food-coma state of most of its residents, and I half-expected the flat harbour waters to be drawn back and released in a resounding burp.

The thought made me smile.

The Mustang's deep-throated growl was hard to miss in all that sluggish quiet, and we drew more than a few appreciative eyes and whistles and thumbs up as we passed. I bit back a smile as Nash sat straighter in his seat, his elbow lifting to rest on the ledge of his open window. He looked as cool as a sexy cucumber, and I wanted to lick him all over. Instead, I laughed and gave him a gentle poke in the ribs. "You're looking very *American Graffiti* there, sunshine."

He smirked. "It's pretty damn cool, I have to admit. You might be winning me over to the dark side, just saying."

My hand went to my chest. "Be still my heart."

"Well, I'm not sure I'd drive this particular beauty to school every day," he qualified. "But on a scale of sheer coolness, compared to my little BMW, this wins every time."

I slid my hand up his thigh to cup his dick and lightly squeezed. "You just got yourself lucky, Mister Principal."

He flashed me a grin. "Oh yeah? Are we talking over the bonnet?"

I snorted and squeezed again. "In your fucking dreams. But maybe you should take me home."

And while the idea of getting Nash into my own bed for the very first time was good in theory and front and centre in my brain, the minute we walked into the bungalow, the steam left both of us in a sputtering puff of carbohydrate hangover and sheer exhaustion, and we collapsed onto the shaded outdoor sofa with a beer instead, snuggling and holding hands as we caught up on each other's Christmas Day. Then we fell into bed at a ridiculous nine-thirty in the evening with the sun barely setting in the sky, and a few minutes of unhurried making out before the sleep bunnies finally took over.

How to know you're over fifty without breaking a sweat.

CHAPTER EIGHTEEN

Nash

"CAN I FUCK YOU?"

The words slid into my sleep-addled brain, jerking me awake as effectively as a bucket of cold water to the face, and I spun so fast in Jed's arms that my feet caught in the sheets, effectively hobbling me.

"Shit. Dammit!" I tried to kick them free, only to end up in more of a tangle, and Jed fell back laughing.

"Hell, if I'd known it would have that effect, I might've asked sooner." He helped get me free and then threw the sheet onto the floor, leaving us both naked on the bed.

"Say it again." I cradled his face and slid closer. "I want to hear the words when I'm fully awake."

Those blue-grey eyes glinted silver in the shaft of early morning sun breaking across the bed and locked onto mine without a flicker of doubt. "I. Want. To. Fuck. You." He brushed his nose against mine and ran his tongue along the seam of my lips, sending a bolt of lust deep into my belly. "If that's okay?" He cocked his head, a smile tugging at his lips.

"Over the bonnet of the Mustang?" It was worth a try.

"Like hell." He grinned. "I want to fuck you. In my bed. Right here. Smelling of my sheets, and Boxing Day morning, and the first cool breeze we've had in weeks."

Jesus, this man.

"Can you feel it?" He stilled, and the hair on my body tingled with the welcome lick of a cool southerly riding lightly over my fiery skin.

I groaned in relief, my gaze lighting on the pale linen curtains drifting in and out of the patio door, which we'd left open in the heat of the previous night.

His gaze roamed over my face, a soft affection welling in its depths. "You are so beautiful."

I'd have been lying if I'd said no one had ever called me that before, but never had those words caused such a rolling tide of warm pleasure over my skin.

"And I love how you do this." He ran his finger over my flushed cheeks. "I love the way the cool, calm, and collected guy I first met runs only skin-deep. And this warm, funny, and sometimes uncertain and awkward man lies just beneath the surface. The man not many people get to see."

I swallowed hard, lost for words. All I could do was kiss him. "*You* do that to me, Jed." I stared into those crisp-blue morning eyes and the dark lashes that beat a slow pulse under my gaze. "You make it so damn easy to be real. You make it safe to show that part of me. It's a gift I can never repay."

He tilted my head and pressed his lips to each of my eyelids and then took my mouth in a long, slow kiss, his hands stroking up and down my back before crushing me against him. And when he pulled away, a light glistened in his eyes that hadn't been there before, and my heart caught in my chest. "I . . . I don't know what to say. Except I'm falling for you, Nash. Hook, line, and fucking sinker." The words tumbled from his mouth and his eyes sprang wide as if he'd shocked himself with the admission. He instantly buried his face against my chest. "Feel free to call an Uber."

I laughed and cupped the nape of his neck, holding him close as I ran my cheek across his hair. "I'm not going anywhere."

He said nothing for a few seconds then finally sat back and stumbled on. "I know it's too soon and that it's crazy and that you probably think I'm out of my mind—" He hesitated, then took my hand. "But all I can say is that it's the truth. I get that you might not—"

"Shhh." I pressed a finger to his lips, took a breath and steeled myself. "I'm falling for you as well. Fallen, if I'm honest."

"But . . ." He stared at me, a single tear forming in the corner of one eye. "You never . . . I wasn't sure . . . I thought it might be just me . . . I didn't want to . . ." His head fell back with a groan. "Ugh, listen to me. I'm fifty-five and I can't use my fucking words." He huffed a sigh of disgust, then tipped forward to meet my gaze. "You never said anything."

I ran my fingers through the soft bristles of his hair. "Neither did you, until now."

He grinned sheepishly. "Fair point."

I swallowed hard. "I was, *am*, a little scared," I admitted. "And I'm guessing you're the same, even if our reasons might be different. I'm your first real experience with a guy, Jed. A part of me is worried that you're still testing the waters. That you don't know what you want. And maybe you should—" *Dammit*. "—look around a bit first. But you had my attention from the first day we were introduced. You were different right from the start. You still are. I've only ever felt this deeply for someone once before."

"Jeremy, right?" Jed's gaze softened. "The guy who broke your heart."

I nodded. "Well, I thought he had at the time. Now—" I stroked Jed's cheek. "Now I'm not sure that what I felt for Jeremy was ever really love. Infatuation, maybe? But whatever it was is eclipsed a thousand times by what I feel for *you*. What I feel every moment that I'm with you. I'm falling in love with you, Jed."

Jed blinked and his face paled. "Oh, thank fucking god. I'm falling in love with you too." He fell against me and I held him tight as his breathing slowly steadied, our confessions settling over us like a soft blanket. And as the cooler air lapped at our bare skin and the cicadas rose in cadence in the garden outside the window, we held on to each other and let the bright morning light slowly fill the room.

A few minutes, an hour, or even two—who the hell knew how much time later—Jed started to hum, and his fingertip lightly grazed my nipple, making me jump. "So." His tongue flicked out to catch the nub.

I groaned and murmured, "Yes?" Or maybe it was the other way around.

"I woke like this." He took my hand and placed it over his very interested cock.

I ran my nose up the side of his face and nibbled on his ear. "How very uncomfortable for you. Perhaps I could help with that. It would be the neighbourly thing to do."

He snorted. "The thought did occur to me. *Jed,* I said to myself, *this is an excellent opportunity to cross another thing off that list.*"

"Oh, you did, did you?" I ran a lazy hand down his spine to cup his arse, and he wriggled closer. "You seem to have a habit of talking to yourself." With a good grip on his body, I levered myself up and rolled him under me, grinding down hard enough to send his eyeballs to the back of his head.

"Fucking hell," he muttered, arching up to increase the friction.

I obliged, changing the angle until I got—

"Oh, god."

—*that* response. "And did you answer yourself?" I ran my tongue over his nipple, keeping our cocks aligned as I worked my hips against his.

"Fuuuuuck . . . What? Oh, right. I, um . . . yes. I answered, *Jed, you have a great guy sleeping right*—oh god, right there." He wrapped his leg around the back of my thighs, and everything ramped up another notch. "Oh Jesus, Nash . . . *and I want to . . .* ahhhhh shit . . . *I want to fuck you.*"

"Mmm. That's what I thought I heard." I flipped our positions again and clamped both my legs around Jed's waist, positioning the head of his hard cock right behind my balls. "And I can't wait. I'm all yours, baby."

He pushed up on his hands and stared down at me, a deep frown in place. "Are you sure?"

I grabbed his face between my hands. "One hundred percent."

He sucked in a shaky breath. "But I've never . . . We just played a little, Tamsin and I. Shit, what do I do?"

I laughed and fell back on the bed. "You have a very nice dick. I have a very welcoming hole. And I'm assuming you have lube and have done a little bit of research." I winked. "I'm sure you'll figure it out."

"But—"

I pulled him down for a hard kiss. "I'm not made of glass, Jed. And this isn't my first rodeo. Plus, I'm quite capable of using my words if I need to redirect or nudge things along. So tell me what you want."

He stared a few seconds longer, then gave a hesitant nod. But there was excitement in those blue-grey eyes and his hands were shaking. "Turn over." His steely tone sent a jolt of lust straight to my balls, and I was on my stomach in a flash, lifting up to my hands and knees.

A condom and lube appeared next to my pillow and then Jed was pushing my thighs apart to kneel between them, his hands trailing the length of my back and over the swell of my arse. "So beautiful." He pressed a kiss to the base of my spine, just above my crease, and then one to each of the dimples that sat either side. Then he ran his chest lightly up and down my back, the soft hair of his chest brushing over my skin to sprout goosebumps in its wake while his hand reached around to stroke my thickening cock.

"Oh god." I wriggled to position myself better, desperate to get his cock closer to my arse. "You feel so damn good."

But Jed was having none of it, sliding over my calf to kneel at my side, his erection digging into my hip.

"Not yet." He stretched up to kiss the shell of my ear, his breath hot and teasing, while somewhere in the distance I heard the snick of a cap. "Soon, baby. I've been thinking about this moment from the first time I saw you, all buttoned up in your principal's suit and tie. So correct. So perfect. So fucking hot. But never in a million years did I ever believe I could actually have you."

"Jesus Christ, Jed," I groaned into the pillow. "You can have me any fucking way you want. Just do it already."

"Nope." He leaned close and sucked the lobe of my ear into his mouth, his dick jabbing at my side, his slick fingers finding their way into my crease to press against my hole.

"Oh fuck, yes." I rocked back and managed to draw the tip of one inside.

"Jesus, you're like a furnace." He breathed the words against the nape of my neck, shuttling his finger gently in and out as he groaned and nibbled his way down the slope of my shoulder. "And so fucking tight."

I snickered. "Yeah, well, it might've been a while."

He hesitated.

"Don't you fucking dare," I warned him. "I'm just getting going here."

He huffed out a laugh and pressed that finger deeper, curling it until—

"Oh, Jesus fuck, right there," I cried out. "More. A lot more."

But instead, he slipped his finger free, and I rained curses down on him. He laughed and slid off the bed, pulling me back by the hips until my knees were almost on the edge of the mattress with my naked arse up in the air.

So much for the nervous first-timer.

"Does this work for you?" He ran a hand over my arse, and I grunted something that sounded like, yes, because at that point I wasn't exactly particular. But nothing happened, and I was about to repeat myself when a hot, wet tongue licked a long, slow path up from behind my balls, through my crease to circle my hole, and then pressed inside.

Oh shit. Oh fucking shit. I moaned and fisted the sheets, thrusting back to drag him further inside, all the way, as far as I could take him.

"Behave," he grumbled with a light slap to my rump, and okay . . . that was hot as fuck.

I stilled and Jed lowered his head and went back to work, a cool draught of air from the open door colliding with that wicked tongue in a seductive one-two punch of sensation that had me fisting the sheets with a loud groan. Then Jed's finger slid alongside his tongue and into my arse, pumping back and forth to send jolts of white heat through all those sparkling nerve endings. And when his other hand slipped between my thighs to wrap around my dick, I almost lost it.

"Too close . . . too . . . ugh . . . stop." I collapsed on the mattress, popping his mouth and finger free of my arse. Then I flipped onto my back and scooted up the bed until my head found the pillow.

"Is there a problem?" Jed eyed me with a self-satisfied smirk and reached for the condom and lube.

"Yeah, yeah, laugh it up, you smug bastard," I grumbled. "You might have one or two rimming skills, I'll admit, but I want to see your face when you fuck a guy, fuck *me*, for the first time." I waggled my brows. "I want the full Jed Marshall experience, so cut the small talk and get the hell up here. Your dick, my hole, got it?"

"Got it." But when he'd finished getting ready and looked up to find me with my legs drawn up, waiting, doubt crept into those glittering eyes, and I wanted none of that.

"Hey." I held out a hand and he took it, letting me draw him down between my legs and up my body until we were face to face. Then I cupped his jaw in my hands and ran a thumb over his lips. "There is *nothing* that you can do wrong here, not a single thing. I'm gonna love every goddamn second. Understand?"

He sighed and pressed his lips gently to mine, breathing the words "thank you," into my open mouth. Then his cock nudged against my taint and his cheek rested against mine, a hum of pleasure rising deep within his throat. Then he whispered, "Tell me if I do anything you don't want."

I circled my legs around his waist and answered, "I will, but I won't need to. Fuck me, sweetheart. Make me yours."

He lifted on one hand and locked eyes, repositioning just a little before slowly, slowly pressing inside. And—

"Oh, dear God." I groaned and stilled with the initial sting and fierce burn of the stretch around his solid cock—so . . . full, so . . . impossible, so . . . fucking much. My breath caught in my lungs as I bore down, opening, taking him in a centimetre at a time until a gasp broke my lips.

Jed froze, a wrinkle forming between his brows. "Nash?"

"I'm good. Really good." I grunted the words between clenched teeth, my body trembling. "Just keep going."

The wrinkle flattened and he brushed my mouth with his, that thick morning scruff blazing a trail over my sensitive lips. "This is amazing," he huffed, nuzzling his nose against mine as he kept pressing in. "*You're* . . . amazing. So damn tight. I'm not gonna last, sweetheart. You're too good. Almost . . . there." He bottomed out and I panted through the biting ache.

"Mmm-mmm," was all I could manage. My head slammed back into the pillow until the burn passed over the edge into pleasure and breath returned to my lungs. Then I looked up and smiled. "Good, right?"

He snorted and kissed the end of my nose. "There are no fucking words. You ready?"

I nodded. "Don't hold back. I'll let you know."

Another flash of uncertainty crossed those grey eyes, but it was quickly lost to a gleam of anticipation as Jed slowly drew back and I grabbed purchase on the sheets.

Then he slid back inside, and his expression erupted in pleasure.

"Holy shit." He kept going, still tentative and cautious, but as soon as I clasped my ankles around his back and dragged him deeper, Jed finally took me at my word and slammed into me, just how I liked it.

He filled my body, over and over, the pleasure etched into every line on his face. He never once took his eyes from mine, measuring every expression, every reaction to whatever he was doing. I wanted to lose myself in the feeling, to close my eyes and disappear inside my body like I always did, but with Jed, I couldn't look away, not wanting to miss a second of what was happening between us.

Jed was fucking me, yes, but it was more than that. We'd crossed a line and we both knew where this was headed if we let it. And we both wanted it. *I* wanted it. More than anything. More than I thought was possible. I wanted this. I wanted Jed.

"I'm close," Jed huffed, his rhythm stuttering.

"Me too." I cupped the back of his neck and buried my face against his throat, working my hand between us to fist my cock, the relief instantaneous. "Any time now would be good," I warned.

"Yeah . . . okay . . ." He lifted one of my hips to adjust the angle, and whatever he did was enough to send a wave of pleasure crashing through my body.

"Oh fuck. Oh fuck." My head slammed back into the pillow and I shot between us, while above me, Jed came with a sharp cry and a final couple of thrusts that sent another lash of fire crashing through me.

"Holy fucking shit." He slowly thrust again, once, twice, and then collapsed on top of me, a quivering heap of boneless flesh.

"Jesus George and Merry Christmas to all." I wrapped my arms around him, holding him tight.

Jed grunted something that sounded like a laugh but didn't move, and that's how we stayed, covered in sweat and come and gasping for air, until my brain came back into orbit and I rolled Jed off to the side and onto his back before I perished from the sheer heat of being sandwiched between his furnace of a body and the mattress.

Jed didn't open his eyes, didn't make a sound, didn't even try to remove the condom, just lay there and so I did it for him, nervously wondering what was going through his head. Then I curled into his side and ran my fingertip down his ribs. "Hey."

His hand encircled mine, bringing the fingertip to his lips. "Hey yourself." Then he smiled, and my worry eased a little.

"So . . . ?" I waited.

He rolled on his side to face me, his gaze soft, still edged in pleasure, and he stroked my cheek. "I think you broke me."

I laughed and stretched up for a kiss. "I'm gonna take that as a good sign."

He pulled me on top of him and smothered my face in kisses. "Was I okay? For you? Did I—"

I shut him up with another kiss. "Yes, you were great. I loved it. You were . . . perfect." I held his gaze and my voice dropped to a whisper. "You *are* perfect . . . for me."

A tender smile tugged at the corners of his mouth, and he blew out a long soft breath that washed over my damp skin to settle in my heart. "You're pretty damn perfect for me, as well." He tucked a stray lock of sweat-soaked hair behind my ear. "I never in a million years saw this coming. Never thought I'd ever love again. Never thought I wanted to. And then you come along and dust my heart off for another ride."

"Likewise." I pressed a line of kisses between his nipples. "Except for the bit where I think this is my first time, but I'm so glad I waited."

"Me too." His gaze travelled my face. "Do you think we have what it takes? This thing between us? I mean, I didn't do so well last time."

I made sure to lock eyes with him. "This isn't a competition, Jed. You're not the same young man who married Tamsin. You've changed, grown, and so has she. And I'm not the same frightened idiot I was, either. So yes, I think we have everything we need, if we want it badly enough."

He stared for a few seconds, then nodded. "But that's the worrying part."

"It is?" I didn't get it.

He sighed. "Because that makes this thing we have precious and too damn easy to fuck up."

Oh. I smiled and kissed him. "Well, my take on that is, if it's too easy to fuck up, then maybe it wasn't real to start with, and I don't believe that about us. I'm not going anywhere, Jed. I'm all in."

"Me too." He swallowed hard and rested our foreheads together. "I just don't want to disappoint you."

I wasn't about to ask how he could do that because we both knew the answer and I didn't want the words said out loud. Instead, I pulled him into my arms and tried to tell him with my body exactly what he meant to me. That I believed in him. That I understood how new and complicated things were. That I would wait as long as it took for him to feel comfortable coming out. And that regardless of whatever he was struggling with . . . I already loved him.

Yeah, mostly that last one.

CHAPTER NINETEEN

Jed

Nash and I talked until the cooler air grew thick and sultry and dense grey clouds gathered in the mid-morning sky outside the bedroom, promising much-needed rain. No serious topics—there had been enough of those already. We talked about cars and school and family and how I'd freaked out at the idea of being a grandad until the first time I held Bridie in my arms and melted under her spell like a cheap tart.

Nash talked about his nephews and how they'd filled that place in his life that he'd never looked to fill himself. How he didn't regret his decision not to have his own family, but that he understood it had come at a cost and how incredibly grateful he was for the chance to share in his brother's family.

As he talked, it struck me that Nash might get another opportunity through *my* family. The idea of sharing that with him squeezed at my heart, but I kept my mouth shut. The very thought that I might have someone to talk with, laugh with, and whinge to about how our grandkids were being raised, blunted those sharp edges of loneliness I worked hard to ignore.

Our grandkids.

Holy shit. If this thing between us actually worked out, we would be grandparents . . . *together.* And the more I thought about it, the more the notion settled around my soul like a warm blanket, and I fell silent, snuggling into Nash's side to let it gently enfold me.

And like he could read my mind, Nash didn't press for any explanation for my silence. He just held me, humming against my hair as his fingers traced small circles on my back. It left me feeling somehow shielded—safe to dream.

Then later, in the shower, he ignored all of my weak protesting and proceeded to wash and dry me, before wrapping me in a towel and sending me out onto the shaded deck to muse at the brewing storm gathering over the Cook Strait while he organised breakfast and coffee.

I grizzled all the way, but the minute he left me on my own, my smile broke free and I curled up in an outside chair to listen to him talking to himself and pottering around my kitchen like he'd been doing it for years. The last person to have done that was Tamsin, about a million light years before. It should've freaked me out, but I felt strangely at peace.

"I need to learn where things are myself," he shouted back to yet another of my insincere offers of help. "Go check on your beans and zucchinis. I can hear them calling."

I chuckled. "It's gonna rain."

"Maybe, maybe not. Forecast says it might pass up the East Coast before it lets loose."

Bugger. Two minutes later, I was standing in my vegetable garden wearing nothing but a towel, holding a hose, and humming to Fleetwood Mac, which Nash had blasting through the house speakers loud enough to startle the neighbour's cat from its spot under the passionfruit vine. The cool southerly, fragrant with the last of the jasmine, licked over my back and around my calves—a welcome relief from the hot northerlies, which had plagued the capital city for weeks. A quick scan of the distant harbour caught the glint of white caps dotted from shore to shore, the Interislander ferry pressing through a burgeoning swell and those massing clouds.

Nash's arms slid around my waist from behind and I startled. "Mmm, I do love a man wielding a hose." He nuzzled against my neck. "Breakfast is ready, if you're hungry."

I let my head fall back against his shoulder, exposing my neck, and he accepted the invitation to press a trail of kisses down my throat to my shoulder, making me shiver. "Well, I'm certainly hungry for something." I turned and took him in a deep kiss, the hit of coffee and maple syrup on my tongue making me smile.

"You started without m—"

"Dad?"

Shit. I jolted out of Nash's arms and spun to find Abbie staring at me wide-eyed from the open patio doors.

"Nash?" She shook her head, a deep frown cutting across her brow. "Jesus, Dad, really?"

I shot Nash a panicked glance.

He lowered his voice, his eyes steady on mine. "I'll do whatever you want. I'll follow your lead."

"I—shit!" I hissed, dropping my gaze. I had no fucking idea what I wanted.

"Poppy!" Bridie pushed past her mother's legs and hurtled across the grass, her face beaming—because of course things could get a whole lot fucking worse. "Let me do it." Her gaze fixed on the hose. "I can do it. Let me."

She reached me before I had time to think and tugged at my towel . . . and, oh god . . . I was only wearing a towel. *Fuck.* I secured the waist before she could pull the whole thing off and take a bad situation to fucking awful. And then, with shaking hands, I lifted her up for a kiss before putting the hose in her hand and pointing her toward the garden. "Thank you, sweetheart. Make sure they all get a big drink."

"Okay." She squinted up at Nash. "Hello, Mister Collingwood."

Nash's smile was instantaneous. "Well, hello there, Miss Bridie."

And off she went with the blissful ignorance of an innocent child completely unaware of the shitstorm about to break over her family.

I watched her for a couple of seconds, aware of Abbie's hot stare on my back, mostly because I had no fucking idea what to do next. Then Nash's hand landed on my arm, and I looked around to find soft eyes holding mine, solid and reassuring.

"You have nothing to be ashamed of," he said, almost sternly.

And he was right. It was enough for me to take a deep breath and face my daughter . . . and her husband . . . and oh god, Tamsin and Ewan, and even Neil who was standing awkwardly to one side, looking like he wished he was anywhere else in the world.

My son's shaking head and look of incredulity mirrored that of his sister's. And Ewan was the laid-back one. *Lord, help me.* But also —did no one pay any fucking attention when I said I wanted the day to myself? I would've been angry if I wasn't so bloody mortified.

"Oh, Jed, I'm so sorry." Tamsin stepped in front of Abbie. "I only found out about the plan at the last minute." Her gaze flicked to Nash, then back to me. "They wanted to surprise you."

Well, mission fucking accomplished. I squashed a hysterical laugh.

"I did text to warn you about ten minutes ago," Tamsin added.

I opened my arms and looked down as if to emphasise the fact I was only wearing a freaking towel, and where the hell was I supposed to keep a phone? And why should I even bloody need one when I expected to be left alone in my own damn house? But of course, I said none of that.

Tamsin gave a resigned sigh. "If you'd just told me Nash would be here . . ."

And that was it. "I wasn't aware I needed to check in with you, Tamsin." It came out sharper than I intended, and I saw the sting hit in the flush that broke over her cheeks. I waited for the guilt that didn't come.

"No ... I ... " she flustered. "No, of course you don't."

Abbie spun in a slow circle to face her mother, her expression unreadable. "You knew?"

Tamsin huffed and stood straighter. "I've always known. And yes, I knew about Nash as well."

"Mum?" Ewan sent a frown Tamsin's way. "But—"

"Leave your mother alone," I warned. "I asked her not to say anything. I was going to talk to both of you once Christmas was over."

Abbie took a second to digest my words and paled. "Are you . . . Dad, are you gay? Is that why . . . is that why you guys divorced?"

Shit. "No! No, that's not the reason. Jesus, Abbie. No—" I hesitated, hating that everything was coming out in the worst possible way. But then Nash's hand wrapped around mine and I turned and sank into his gentle eyes.

I'm here.

It was enough to steady my breath and the words finally came. "No, I'm not gay. I'm . . . bi. And yes, I've always known and so has your mother."

A wash of obvious relief crossed Abbie's face.

"Why didn't you tell *us*?" Ewan demanded. "Why the big secret?"

"Ewan!" Tamsin's tone carried a warning. "This is your dad's story to tell *if* he wants to."

A spray of water hit my calves and I glanced down to find Bridie grinning up at me. "Sorry, Poppy. Am I doing good?"

I dredged up a smile and nodded. "You're doing great, munchkin. Now Poppy is going inside for a bit. Would it be okay if Nash stays out here with you?" I shot Nash a beseeching look.

He immediately took Bridie's hand. "We'll have fun, won't we, sweetheart?" He knelt beside her. "But you might have to teach me how to do it right."

Bridie nodded enthusiastically. "I can teach you. Poppy showed me."

"No, *I'll* stay with her." Scott cut in front of Nash. "You've done more than enough for one day, don't you think?"

Nash's eyes flashed with anger. "What the hell is that supposed to mean?" He shot me a questioning look and I knew he wanted to say more, but my expression clearly relayed my panicked state because he simply sighed and stepped away, his gaze sliding off mine with something close to resignation.

Oh god, I was screwing this up. I should've told Scott to watch his damn tone around my boyfriend, but I fucking didn't. I should've told them how much I loved Nash, how I saw a future for us together as a family, how damn happy he made me. I should've said so many, many things, but the words jammed on my tongue, frozen by the glare in Scott's eyes and the confused hurt in Abbie's and Ewan's.

"Scott!" Tamsin glared at our son-in-law. "That's totally unnecessary."

It was exactly what *I* should've said if I'd had the balls.

"Stay out of this, Tamsin." Scott's eyes brimmed with anger. "You should've told us about this. It's the kind of thing parents should be warned about, don't you think?"

You could've heard a pin drop and my stomach lurched. *What the hell?*

Tamsin gaped, her gaze narrowing. "And just *what* exactly should they be warned about, Scott? What the hell are you suggesting?"

Scott didn't get time to answer before Abbie stormed off the deck and got up in her husband's face. "Don't you dare talk to Mum like that."

Ewan was hot on his sister's heels. "You better be careful what you say, Scott."

Nash stepped between them, beating me to it . . . again. "How about everyone calms down?"

"How about *you* butt out of what's not your business?" Scott elbowed Nash roughly out of the way. The he glanced my way and shook his head. "And can you put some damn clothes on in front of your granddaughter, Jed? I can't believe this. She's only three. *Three.* She doesn't need to see you and . . ." He flicked Nash another scowl. "Well, *any* of this."

No, she absolutely didn't. We agreed on that much, at least, even if for different reasons. I glared back at him. "Need I remind you, *Scott*, this is *my* house, not yours?"

"Daddy?" Bridie's worried gaze flicked between Scott and me, and my eyes filled without warning.

That was my doing.

"It's okay, honey." I moved toward her, but Scott grabbed my arm none too gently.

"I said *I'll* look after her."

"Scott!" Abbie cried out, horrified.

"Let. Him. Go." Ewan lurched forward but Nash got to me first.

"Take your hands off him." Nash eyeballed Scott, who took one look at the fury on Nash's face and instantly released me.

I put a hand on Nash's chest and gently pushed him back. "I'm okay. It's . . . okay, Nash." It wasn't and we both knew it, but I had no clue how to put things right with Nash without making the situation worse with Scott. Nash took another step back, but not before shooting Scott a glare that needed no interpretation.

"Poppy, you okay?" Bridie stood watching with big worried eyes, the hose forgotten and hanging limp in her hand. "Did you do something bad?"

Out of the mouths of babes. "I—"

"Poppy has to go inside and get dressed, sweetheart. He *forgot*." Scott fired me a blistering look chock-full of anger, and for the first time in my life, shame welled inside me.

"As Jed said, we weren't expecting company," Nash repeated my point in an irritated tone.

Scott rolled his eyes. "Clearly."

Heat raced into my cheeks, half-embarrassment, half-anger, and I saw Nash bristle, his patience obviously shredded. I so fucking got it, but adding fuel to the fire wasn't going to help. I shot him a warning look. He grimaced and snapped his mouth shut, but not before a flash of disappointment crossed behind those beautiful brown eyes, a look I thoroughly deserved.

I shot him an apologetic look, willing him to understand, and then turned back to Scott and spread my hands. "If you'd just come inside, we can talk about this like adults."

But Scott shook his head. "There's nothing to talk about. I won't have Bridie around this."

Abbie confronted her husband, bright spots of anger staining her cheeks. "What the hell do you think you're doing?"

Scott huffed. "So, you're okay with our daughter seeing her grandad and—" He waved a hand between Nash and me. "All this?"

"Keep your voice down in front of Bridie." Abbie grabbed Scott's hand and tried to tug him toward the house, but he pulled free and looked ready to let loose on someone.

"*Both* of you keep it down." Tamsin shot daggers at Abbie and Scott before scooping Bridie into her arms. "Come here, sweetheart. Let's go see if there are any berries left." She walked Bridie to the far side of the lawn where the last strawberry stragglers cascaded over the raised bed Bridie and I had planted only a few months before.

Ewan, always the peacemaker, ignored Scott and took his sister's elbow. "Come on, Abbie. Let's just go inside and hear what Dad has to say."

Like I'd fucking done something wrong.

But Abbie ignored her brother, and after a sideways look to where Bridie, still in Tamsin's arms, was happily munching on strawberries, she leaned toward Scott and whisper-hissed, "What the hell is *wrong* with you?"

"Me?" He rounded on her. "What about you? Why aren't *you* upset?"

Abbie sucked in a deep breath and said nothing for a minute. Then she glanced my way and sighed. "Am I surprised to find out my dad is bi? Yes, I'm surprised, shocked even. But I don't give a damn about the rest. *You* are the problem here, Scott. Not me, not my father or Nash or Mum. *You*."

"Me?"

Abbie's voice rose. "This is *my* family, *my* dad. And whatever you think about what you saw, you keep it to yourself in front of them and in front of *our* daughter. I won't have her raised in the environment you were. We are *not* going to repeat that, do you understand?"

My heart ripped open at the anger and hurt in my daughter's eyes. "Abbie, please. It's *my* fault." Because I hadn't had the balls to do what I should've done weeks ago—talk to my kids or end things with Nash. I'd been too fucking selfish. I'd wanted it all and I didn't want to rock the boat. And I was paying the price.

"Keep out of this, Jed." Scott shot me a warning glance before turning back to Abbie. "That's *my* family you're talking about. I am *not* a homophobe, if that's what you're implying. I just don't think Bridie's old enough to . . ." He flicked another glare our way. "To understand *this* kind of thing."

I caught an epic eye roll from Nash, which I ignored, too busy trying to process the shitshow raining down on my family, and the fact that my daughter was standing up for me against her husband two minutes after finding out I wasn't the straight man she'd thought I was her whole life. I should've told her. I'd been a total idiot.

"*What* kind of thing?" Abbie's voice rose another few decibels and I shushed her.

"Can we please take this inside?" I tried again.

But they ignored me, Abbie continuing, "What are you saying, Scott? That our daughter can't understand two people caring for each other? Holding each other? You and I kiss in front of her. Mum and Neil do. Hell, even Ewan and his girlfriend hug and kiss while Bridie's around. I don't see you telling them to knock it off."

Scott's jaw ticced and he almost spat the words, "It's not the same and you know it."

I flinched, seeing my son-in-law clearly for perhaps the first time and not having a clue what to say to him. Scott was so wrong about so much, and I wanted to tell him that. Just like I wanted to tell him it wasn't okay to rank what I felt for Nash any less than what straight couples felt, but he was Abbie's husband and I'd done enough damage to my family for one day.

Abbie's mouth dropped open at Scott's words. "It *is* the same. Jesus, Scott, you've said some pretty ignorant things in the five years we've been together, but I truly believed you were changing, that you were capable of change. And I never thought you really meant any of them. If I had, I would never have married you."

Oh, Jesus Christ. "Abbie—" I tried but she was past listening and Nash took my hand in quiet support as she continued.

"I just put it down to what you'd heard in your own house when you were a kid."

"What the hell is that supposed to mean?" Scott growled low and angry, his tone matching the distant rumble of thunder over the Strait.

But Abbie's jaw was set, and I knew that stubborn look from her mother. She eyeballed Scott. "You know *exactly* what I mean."

He held her gaze, a flush growing on his cheeks. "I am *not* my father, you know that."

Abbie raised a brow. "Aren't you? I used to think that. But after today, I really don't know."

"Guys, come on. How about you bring it inside?" Neil again tried to herd everyone into the house, but I took one look at the body language of my daughter and son-in-law and saw that was never gonna happen.

Still, I tried. "Neil's right. Let's go inside."

But Scott was on a roll. His gaze swept the backyard—glaring at me, at Nash, blinking hard as he took in his daughter in Tamsin's arms, landing anywhere but on his wife's face as he ignored me and answered her. "You know very well I *never* agreed with Dad on a lot of that stuff. I don't care what people do with their own lives. But this is our daughter, Abbie. We have an obligation to consider what we're exposing her to."

"*Exposing* her to?" Abbie looked flabbergasted.

"Yes," he flustered. "I'm not against—" More hand waving. "—*this* per se."

"*This?*" It appeared Nash had finally reached his limit and I didn't blame him. "I take it you mean the fact I care deeply for Jed?"

Abbie shot Nash a surprised glance, but Scott avoided any direct eye contact as he answered. "Yes, I suppose. But I don't want Bridie—"

"Surely, it's something we can talk about, please?" I'd do fucking anything to finish the shitshow that was happening around me.

Neil tried once again to get us inside, but this time it was Nash who pulled away, turning to me in total disbelief. "Scott wants a behaviour contract from us regarding Bridie, and you'd be okay with that?" He looked understandably horrified and I had no answer for him. At least none that made any goddamn sense.

"I don't think it's too much to ask." Scott threw me an aggrieved look, then glanced at his daughter with such obvious love and concern, I almost felt sorry for him.

"Jed?" Nash pressed.

All three of them stared at me, but I didn't know what the fuck to do or say, and Nash took one look at the panic in my eyes and his expression immediately softened. He stepped in, cupped my face, and whispered, "I'm sorry. That was wrong of me."

"This is all my fault." I stared back at him, shaking my head.

"Scott, please?" Abbie begged.

"No." Scott rounded on his wife. "I'm taking Bridie home. I'm sure *you'll* tell me what I should be thinking and feeling about *everything* once you're done *discussing* it. It's what you usually do. Until then, I'm looking after our daughter. Somebody has to. I'm sure your family will drop you home." He flicked me an unhappy look and walked over to collect Bridie.

Tamsin handed Bridie over without a word, although I could tell she was struggling to hold her anger in check.

"Scott, wait." Abbie ran after them. She kissed Bridie on the cheek, said something to Scott that made his shoulders stiffen, and then watched the two of them leave with tears brimming in her eyes to match the ones in mine. Before they turned the corner, Bridie peeked over her daddy's shoulder and gave a hesitant wave, her expression full of confusion.

Jesus Christ, what have I done?

I raised my hand in reply, choking back the tears and wondering how long I'd have to wait to see my granddaughter again.

A warm hand slid around my waist and squeezed me close. *I'm here. I'm here.* And I leaned into Nash's hold, the only thing keeping my knees from buckling.

Tamsin raced over to Abbie and immediately steered her toward the house. Ewan glanced my way with a shake of his head, like I'd disappointed him in some way, and then followed his mother and sister inside. And from the shadows of the deck, Neil grimaced in sympathy and indicated he'd wait outside until we were done.

Oh god. A wave of guilt and panic flooded my chest. My daughter, her marriage, my son, my granddaughter. I'd screwed things up for everyone.

Merry fucking Christmas.

Nash tugged me around to face him, his eyes brimming, for me, for us, for everything that had just happened. But there was something else peeking out from those brown depths as well, and it looked a lot like fear and resignation. Like he knew we might be done.

Like it was killing him.

And oh god, I'd hurt Nash too. I'd let Scott say all those things. I'd let it happen and not said a word. I swallowed around the ball of heartache growing in my throat and tried to find the words to reassure Nash that we were okay, that we'd get through this. But who the fuck knew? I couldn't hold his gaze, too scared he'd recognise the uncertainty in mine.

"This is *not* your fault." Nash tipped my chin up, forcing me to look at him.

"Then whose fault is it?" I asked in a ragged voice. "Whose

fucking fault is it, Nash?" I gave up trying to hold back the tears and Nash crushed me to his chest. I let him. If this was the last time I got to be in his arms, I was going to have this moment.

"There's nothing you can do except talk to them," he whispered into my hair. "Don't assume the worst." The soft, sure sound of his voice did little to soothe the tide of emotions circling my brain. "You have a right to be happy, Jed."

But at what cost? My daughter's marriage? My granddaughter's loving home? And me having Bridie in my life? I'd risked everything.

"That sounds good, in theory." I blew a sigh against the soft cotton of his T-shirt, his warm chest swelling against my cheek. Not two hours before, I'd revelled in the intoxicating feel of my skin sliding over his, slick with sweat—inside a man for the first time in my life. But not just any man. Nash. And not just sex. We'd made love. Whether we admitted it or not.

Tears filled my eyes, and I clutched him tighter. "You need to go," I murmured softly.

"What?" Nash pushed me back, his eyes searching mine. "I can wait in the bedroom—"

"No." I cupped his cheek and silenced him with a brief kiss, drawing every thread of strength I could from his solid presence while I had it. "Go home, Nash. Let me talk to them. Give me some time. I'll call you later."

"But—"

"Please, Nash. My family needs me. And I need to . . . think."

He looked about to say something, but the words never came. A part of me hoped against hope that it was to say that he needed me too. Not that I deserved it. But none of it changed how I felt as a father, as a grandfather. I could wait. What I wanted, needed, could wait.

"You've waited your whole life," that needling voice in my brain reminded, but I ignored it, the strongest image in my head remaining that of Bridie's puzzled eyes as she watched her father argue with her mother and me. Because of me. Because of us.

"I need to try and fix what's happened with Scott and Abbie," I told Nash, stepping back.

"That's not your job."

I knew he was right, but that didn't change anything.

"And what if you can't?" Nash's gaze fixed on mine, but I had no answer for him so I looked away, far off to the towering black thunderclouds. He sighed and ran the back of his knuckles down my cheek but still I couldn't look at him. "Scott loves Abbie. He'll come around."

I wasn't so sure. A flash of silver lit up the sky and a few seconds later, thunder rattled the old sash windows.

"I knew there was a chance Scott wasn't going to like it, and that's part of why I put off telling them," I admitted, finally turning back to Nash. "You must've felt it from him?"

Nash hesitated, then nodded. "Nothing overt, but yeah, he had a vibe."

I took a deep breath and sighed. "Scott's father is a piece of work. Tamsin and I never really took to him, even though his wife seems nice enough. And like his dad, Scott's always been quick to judge, although he rarely pushes it with Abbie there to shut him up pretty quickly. But there are plenty of people like Scott in the world when you scratch just below the surface. If I'd had the balls to tell Abbie sooner, she might've been able to manage things with him better, and maybe none of this would've happened."

"You don't know that." Nash glanced to the window where Tamsin was standing, watching us. "You never know what's going on in people's heads. Abbie and Scott have to work this out for themselves."

"But it was my fau—"

"You can't solve their problems for them, Jed," Nash pressed. "Are you going to put your life on hold because your son-in-law doesn't like your sexuality?"

I bristled and pulled away, the words out before I could stop them. "Do you think I can stand back and have access to my granddaughter threatened because of *us*? Or watch my daughter's marriage struggle because I want *you*? Do you think I'm that selfish?"

"I didn't mean—"

"What if Scott won't let Bridie be with me unless—"

"Abbie wouldn't let that hap—"

"But that's forcing Abbie to stand against her husband, for me. For what *I* want," I insisted, desperate to make him understand. "Do you get how watching her do that rips me apart? I'm her dad, Nash. *I'm* supposed to be the one who makes everything okay, who protects *her*. Someone she can rely on when everything else goes to shit. And today I didn't do that. I did exactly the opposite. I brought chaos into her life and her relationship. What father fucking worth his salt does that?"

Nash gripped my shoulders. "Jed, listen. I know how you feel—"

"No." I stepped free of his grasp, my voice rising. "If anything happened to my relationship with my kids and granddaughter, we, *you and I*, we wouldn't survive that. Do you understand, Nash? You don't have kids or grandkids. You can't possibly know how I feel"—I ignored the way he flinched—"how this is tearing me apart. Parents don't get the luxury of putting themselves first—"

"Abbie is thirty-one—"

"And I haven't been there enough over the years when it counted. *Now,* I can be. And I refuse to turn her life upside down just because I've got a crush on someone that might go nowhere."

Nash froze, his eyes wide and genuinely shocked. "A *crush*?"

Fuck. "I'm sorry." I reached for his arm. "I didn't mean it that way. You know how much I care. But I can't do this, Nash. Don't make me choose between you and my family's happiness." I finished on a gasp and a trail of tears, my gaze sliding from the sting of hurt that flashed in Nash's eyes in case I caved and changed my mind. I couldn't face what I'd done, what I'd had to do.

Nash took a deep breath, and for a few long silent seconds, I thought he would simply turn and leave. I wouldn't have blamed him.

But then he spoke.

"You know, Jed, I might not know what it's like to have children of my own or grandchildren, but I would *never* ask you to choose between me and your family. I might not know the type of love and self-sacrifice you're describing—" His hoarse voice was cut with emotion, drawing me back to the raw misery hanging in his eyes. "But I can tell you this much. I felt every gut-wrenching stab of guilt and pain that crossed your face today, because I *do* know what it's like to love *you*, to care for *you*, to want to take *your* pain away. And I also know how it feels to walk away from something in order to do what's right for another person, because I'm doing that today. I'm doing it now." He stepped in and pressed the briefest of kisses to my cheek. "I love you, Jed. I hope this all works out like you want. You deserve the very best life. And so, I'm going to do what you want and leave. You know where to find me if you ever change your mind." He stared at me for a long minute, his eyes brimming with tears, and then he turned away.

"Nash, wait." I reached out a hand and he turned, his expression hopeful. I wanted to tell him to stay, that I hadn't meant what I said, but then I saw Abbie's face in the kitchen window behind Nash and no words came.

Nash followed my gaze and his eyes filled with sorrow. "Take care of your family, Jed. They need you." And he disappeared into the house, and the bone-deep ache of knowing he'd taken my heart with him flooded the gaping hole he left behind.

I lifted my face to the dark sky and blinked as the first fat raindrops mingled with my tears.

CHAPTER TWENTY

Nash

I GOT A KILOMETRE DOWN THE HILL FROM JED'S PLACE WITH MY duffel in my hand before the quickening rain brought me to a stop. What the hell was I doing? Walking home? I ran under the eaves of a nearby garage and called an Uber. And while I waited for it to arrive, I racked my brains about what the fuck had just happened.

Not three hours earlier, I'd woken in Jed's bed to his voice in my ear, asking to fuck me, telling me how much he cared, telling me he loved me. And I'd taken a chance and handed it all back to him in spades, just the second time in my life I'd ever told another man I loved him.

It had been reckless, on both our parts, especially with so much not settled in Jed's life. I was paying the price. And it hurt. It hurt so fucking much.

I stared back up the way I'd come and worried about what was happening in that house. I had no doubt Abbie and Ewan would be okay about Jed's sexuality—they were mostly just pissed he hadn't told them sooner. But what would happen to Abbie and Scott's relationship was a whole different story. Abbie was a naturally inclusive soul. She'd shown that at school in so many ways. The situation with Scott would likely have raised its head at some point, regardless, not that Jed would see it that way. He'd be blaming himself.

Jed.

Walking away had been the hardest thing I'd ever done. We'd barely known each other a couple of months and dated for just one of those, but I'd lived too fucking long not to recognise something special when it came along. And Jed *was* special. I'd known that the first time I'd laid eyes on him. He was so much himself in ways I had never been, not that Jed saw it that way, but he was wrong. It was so refreshing, it still made my head spin. And being around him had forced me to take a long, hard look at myself, and for the first time I was *almost* okay about getting older myself, no small miracle there. Jed undid me in ways no one had even come close to. In ways I hadn't been prepared for. And I'd lost my heart to him with my eyes wide fucking open.

But he hadn't been out, and I'd known the risk of that. His family meant everything and would always be his first priority, and I'd known that too. He'd never promised me anything and had even warned me, "I hope I don't disappoint you." So yeah, I'd known that as well.

And the crazy thing was, Jed still hadn't disappointed me. He'd done exactly what I'd have expected him to do, maybe even what I'd have done in his place. He was loyal to a fault, and when he loved, Jed loved with everything he had, balls to the wall. You only had to watch him with Bridie to know the truth of that. He'd give anything to see his family happy, and he'd just proved that. He'd given *me* up, after all.

How the hell could you be disappointed in someone who loved like that? The fact that it left my own heart shredded was something I would have to live with. Because Jed was right. If he forced the issue just for me and it didn't work out with his family, we *wouldn't* survive. And that would hurt both of us a whole lot more.

I'd done the right thing by leaving. I *had*. And yet no matter how many times I kept telling myself that, something niggled in the back of my brain, like I'd just made the biggest fucking mistake of my life.

I pulled out my phone and texted Devon.

Mayday.

He texted back almost straight away. ***Fuck. Where are you?***

When I was finally back at my apartment, soaked to the bone and trembling, I walked straight past Jed's spare jacket hanging by the front door, not daring to look in case the sight of it fucking broke me. Past the kitchen where his bananas mocked me from the fruit bowl. I hated the damn things. And down the hall and into my bedroom where his black merino jersey stared at me from the chair.

I picked it up and threw it in the wardrobe under his shirts and shut the door. Then I closed the partly open drawer where he kept his spare briefs and headed straight for the bathroom and glared at the mirror, my fists clenching and unclenching at my sides.

Jed was everywhere. We'd fucked in the shower, kissed in front of the mirror, shaved alongside each other, laughed, and chatted about our day. His toothbrush sat on its charger by the second basin. The bottle of Calvin Klein I'd bought him for Christmas after we'd spent an hour in a department store, testing a million options, still sat in its bright red Christmas paper under the mirror, waiting for him to find.

We'd been building something together, Jed and I. Something I never thought I wanted. Something that made my heart sing for the first time in forever. And at the first sign of trouble, I'd behaved like a fucking child with my feelings hurt.

I should've stayed. I should've fucking stayed. Not listened to him. Waited in the workshop, even at the risk of being rejected again. *Anything* except leave him there alone to tell his family.

Who was going to look after Jed when all the talking was done?

Abbie would go home to fix things with her husband. Tamsin would go home to be with Neil.

Who in the hell was going to have Jed's back? To listen to his feelings, to his pain. To hold him when the day finally knocked the breath from his lungs.

No one. Because I'd been a total selfish idiot and left him to handle things on his own. I deserved to lose him.

"Dammit!" I cleared the vanity in a single sweep of my arm, bottles and tubes clattering to the floor. Broken glass skittering across the tiles to bounce off the walls. The cloying scent of aftershave rising from the shattered mess to send bile up the back of my throat.

"Fuck." I threw a towel over the whole disaster and then slammed the door shut on the whole mess. Then I headed for the second bathroom and collapsed onto the floor in the shower, my back against the wall as I drowned under the steaming spray of hot needles that almost took the flesh from my bones. Nothing less than I deserved. And when Colin and Devon arrived twenty minutes later, I was still there, wallowing in the comforting arms of self-pity.

"Jesus, Mary, and Joseph." Colin took one look at my sorry state, flicked the water off, and threw a towel at my face. "Dry yourself." He muttered something about kicking Jed's arse, senseless best friends, and this being the last thing he needed the day after Christmas. After that, he dragged me bodily out of the shower and threatened to kick my arse if I didn't at least clean my teeth and brush my hair, for fuck's sake.

I obliged, if only to save myself the embarrassment of having it done by my brother and my best friend.

While Colin had been dealing with me in the shower, Devon had apparently been rustling up some clothes and toiletries, and they both supervised me dressing like I was eight frickin' years old. After that, I was hustled into the living room and dumped into a chair at the dining table where they made me spill the whole sorry story.

"So, you just walked away?" Colin cuffed me up the back of my head as he walked behind into the kitchen. "Idiot."

"Ow." I rubbed the spot where he'd got me. "I know. I know. I got to that conclusion all on my own, okay? I fucked up. I get it. But Jed asked me to leave. What was I supposed to do? This is his family we're talking about, and you weren't there. It was . . . not good." I slumped in my chair with a long-suffering groan.

"But you'd already said that you loved each other, right?" Devon pushed my water glass across the table and pointed at it. "Drink."

I glared at the glass. "Why can't I have a damn beer? It's *my* bloody apartment in case you've forgotten?"

Colin patted my hand. "Because you're emotionally distressed and it's not good for you. And because we're your friends and don't want to see you make a bad situation into a colossal disaster. Now drink your water like an adult and answer your brother's question."

"I clearly need to get me some new friends," I groused, but did as he said and took a few sips of water.

He chuckled. "Yeah, good luck with that. You're way too high-maintenance. And you still haven't answered the question."

I gave a grumbling sigh. "Yes, we said we loved each other." I remembered the exchange with a sharp sting to my heart. "But that doesn't change the fact his son-in-law is being a difficult ignorant prick, which has put Jed in an impossible position."

"Of course it changes things." Devon followed Colin in cuffing me up the back of the head, and I growled.

"Jesus, will you stop doing that?"

The two exchanged a smile and answered together, "No."

I flicked water at them and they sprang backward in their chairs. "And you wonder why I didn't come to you last time?" I dropped my forehead to the table with a groan of misery.

Devon pulled his chair closer and a warm hand landed on my back. "You really love him?"

I mumbled something that sounded like a yes and banged my forehead against the table once again like I could drum some sense into it.

"You don't know how happy that makes me." Devon rubbed my back. "We'd almost given up hope."

"I'm glad one of us is happy."

Devon snorted. "Stop whining. It could be worse. At least he loves you back."

I lifted my head enough so he could see the roll of my eyes. "Did you miss the part where we're done?"

"Pfft." Devon waved my comment aside. "You and Colin here might not have much experience in matters of the heart, but I do, so listen up, bozos."

I dragged myself vertical and scowled at my baby brother. "I am so close to fucking with you right now."

"But you won't because you need to hear what I have to say. You and your newly engaged friend here—"

"Oh god." I shot Colin a look full of apology. "I've got my head so far up my arse, I never even asked. She said yes, right?"

Colin's grin could've lit the room on fire. "Hell yeah, she said yes. Next winter. You better be ready to stand up for me, fucker."

I clamped my hand over his. "I promise."

Devon rolled his eyes. "I can't believe you finally did it. You could've knocked me over with a feather."

Colin flicked Devon between the eyes. "This advice of yours better be good after that."

Colin turned back to me. "You're not competing for Jed's love with his family, Nash."

For fuck's sake. "Really? That's all you've got? Cause do you think I don't know that already?" It came out a little more petulantly than I'd intended, but all Devon did was throw me an overly patient look.

"No, I don't think you do," he said evenly. "Because it sounds very much like you're playing martyr for the cause."

"What—"

Devon cut me off with a hand over my mouth. "Just listen."

I scowled but nodded, and his hand fell away. "Jed's right when he says the love a parent has for their kids is different from that for their partner. I'd take a bullet for my kids. But Fiona? Yeah, I might have to think about that one."

I gave him a playful shove. "You're damn lucky she can't hear you."

Devon laughed. "Right? But the fact I carry around this insane protectiveness for my kids doesn't mean I don't love her with all my heart, or that she's not as important to me as they are. She's *everything* to me. They're out in the world with their own lives. *She's* the one at my side. Jed will be feeling the same. What I'm trying to say is *don't* make him feel like he has to choose, and *don't* walk away. Show up, Nash. That's what adults do."

"You think I don't know that?" I narrowed my gaze. "He *pushed* me away."

"And you *let* him. He was messed up. Maybe he thought he had to choose," Colin chimed in.

"But I never asked him to," I protested. "I wouldn't."

Colin shrugged. "But you walked away at the first opportunity, didn't you? Which kind of sealed his choice and probably told him he was right to make it." He sighed and his hand landed on my arm, squeezing gently. "You're his first experience with a man, Nash. He's fifty-five years old and you've been together what, a month?"

"Yes, and yes." I groaned, seeing where this was going.

"Which means there's a fuckton of stuff going through his head about *that* teeny tiny development in his life, let alone anything else." Devon leaned forward on the table. "Jed was planning to come out for you. He was going to change his life. He was risking a whole lot, not just his heart. Scary stuff. And what were you risking?"

Oh god. "Jesus, why didn't I see this earlier?"

Devon folded his arms and leaned back in his chair. "'Cause you're not as smart as I am, a fact I've known for a long time."

I ignored him, too busy replaying the day again and coming up with the same goddamned answers about what I could've done differently. "I should've told Jed to wait before making any hasty decisions." I groaned and fell back in my chair. "Told him I'd be there for him, and that I'd work with whatever he needed to help his family. That I'd go at his pace. Even keep my distance from Bridie until things settled. We could've worked on a plan. I could've at least tried. And I didn't do any of that. Fuck!"

Devon pushed my water glass closer. "And my work here is done," he said with a smirk.

Colin raised his glass in salute. "You know, that was actually pretty good."

"Why thank you." Devon clinked their glasses together and they both took a long swallow.

"So, what should I do?"

Devon shrugged. "The meter just ran out on your five cents' worth of advice. The rest is up to you."

I threw him a scowl. "Gee, thanks."

Devon's gaze softened and he covered my hand with his. "Is he worth it?"

The smile was there before I knew it. "Yeah, he's absolutely worth it."

Devon all but beamed, so I quickly added, "But that doesn't mean he wants me turning up so quickly again, not while he's still talking with his family."

He nodded. "Then I'm taking you back to ours for a bit. Colin too, for moral support. Mine, not yours. I can't handle your mopey arse all on my own."

I turned to Colin with a beseeching look. "Oh god, do I have to?"

Colin handed me my jacket from the back of the chair. "You heard him. Let's go."

CHAPTER TWENTY-ONE

Jed

ONCE I WAS SURE NASH WAS GONE, I BYPASSED MY FAMILY silently waiting in the family room and headed straight for the bedroom to dry off, put on some damn clothes, and get my head into order before anyone registered just how completely fucked up I was. Then I took a few deep breaths and headed back out to face the music. The lashing rain and thundering overhead clouds seemed kind of apt.

Tamsin pushed up from the couch to confront me the minute I reappeared. "Why did Nash go? What did you say to him?"

"I...I..." *Shit.* So much for keeping a grip on my heart. My eyes brimmed and I couldn't catch my breath.

"Dad?" Ewan was at my side in a flash. "What the hell?" He peered at me. "Are you...crying? Holy shit."

"Jed, what did you say to Nash?" Tamsin pressed.

Abbie's head jerked up and she shot to her feet from the armchair she'd curled up in, her tear-stained face wrenching at my heart.

"Dad? Oh, fuck, Dad, I'm so sorry about Scott. I don't know what to say. I don't know what the hell he was thinking." She threw her arms around me, and Ewan did the same, while Tamsin watched with an angry glint to her eye, aimed solely at me.

"Why didn't you tell us?" Ewan pulled back, shaking his head. "Didn't you trust us? Jesus, Dad, you've known you were bi our entire lives and you never said a word?"

"Ewan, I—"

"Stop." Tamsin nailed Abbie and Ewan with her patented take-no-prisoners glare. "This isn't an interrogation. Let your father talk. And no questions till he's done." She herded everyone toward the sofa and chairs. "Now sit."

I shot her a grateful look, collapsed into the nearest armchair, and told them what I should've done weeks ago. I told them everything . . . well, almost everything. All except the part about falling head over heels in love with the man I'd just sent packing. Yeah, *that* part.

"I still don't get why you didn't say anything?" Ewan pressed.

"Because I thought that was the best option. It was *my* choice." I held my son's gaze, wanting to make a point. "And as much as it might surprise both of you, my sexuality is actually none of your business, not unless I choose to make it so. I was married to your mother for a long time, and after we divorced, I wasn't looking for another serious relationship. Hell, *any* relationship. And I certainly had no intention of looking for a man."

God, was that only a month ago? I very nearly smiled. Almost.

"And then Nash came out of nowhere and flipped everything on its head. I was almost as surprised as you. I've barely gotten my own head around what's happening, let alone been ready to come out to everyone else. I fully intended to, but then there was Christmas, and yes—" I looked to Abbie. "—I *was* concerned about Scott."

She gave a sharp nod but said nothing, and again I wondered what today would mean for them.

"You didn't worry we'd find out?" Ewan was relentless.

I blew out a long sigh. "Of course I worried. We've been careful, and we mostly stayed at Nash's apartment rather than him coming here."

Ewan's cheeks flushed a deep red. "TMI, Dad. TMI."

"You asked," I reminded him. "And while we're on the matter of expectations, the only reason we were even here today was because I wanted to spend at least some of Christmas Day with a man who's become hugely important in my life." *And damn, that felt good to say out loud.* "I wanted Nash *here*, in *my* space for once, in *my* home, and you guys weren't supposed to be here. We'd agreed that I'd have today to myself, or I thought we had."

Abbie couldn't hold my gaze. Ewan's jaw dropped open. And even Tamsin wriggled uneasily in her chair. But I left the point hanging like a knife blade between us because it had to be said. I rarely said no, and almost never prioritised myself, and the wide-eyed looks I was getting told me they knew.

The conversation was well overdue, and it was just beginning to hit me that maybe I'd done something really, really stupid. I'd convinced myself that sending Nash away was for my family when it was more about me being too damn scared to stand up for my own life. The more I thought about it, the faster that overdue clock ticked, and those glowing embers of anger began to kindle bright.

I studied my family, who were eyeing me like an unexploded grenade, and I suddenly remembered something Nash said about if it was too easy to fuck up, then maybe what we had wasn't real. He'd meant it about us, but I was pretty sure it applied to families as well. I had to trust my family, trust Abbie. And I needed to show them that I trusted them a whole lot more than I'd shown Nash. He'd wanted to stay. What the fuck had I been thinking?

And so, as a flash of lightning lit up the room and the rain hit like shotgun pellets on the glass, I took a deep breath and steeled myself. It was now or never.

"You guys have been at me to date for years. *Years.* But the truth is, in order for me to be able to do that, with a woman *or* a man, things have to change—*I* have to change. This is not about you. I've done this to myself. I've let it happen. I know that, and now I have to undo it. I love you guys so much. You mean everything to me. But as you've all been quick to tell me, I need a life. Something separate from work and the time I spend with all of you. Something you don't necessarily get to know all the details about." I flicked my gaze to Tamsin who looked away, cheeks pinking nicely. "Just like I don't know everything about your lives, right?"

Tamsin sighed and raised her hand. "Mea culpa. Message received."

Ewan winced. "Yeah, okay. No more setting you up on dates."

I snorted. "Please. But it also means I might not be quite so *available* as I've been. I might actually say no now and then." I glanced to Abbie.

She followed her mother in sticking up her hand. "That's on me. I know we've been taking advantage of you. And I'm sorry that I ignored what you said about today."

I shot her a quick smile. "Thank you. But really, I'm the one who let it happen. I wasn't there for you kids enough when you were growing up, and since the divorce, I've tried to make up for that. I built a new life around the idea of being the perfect dad and grandad."

"Shit." Tamsin blinked hard and eyeballed me. "I know some of that's on me, making you feel like you weren't good enough before the divorce. I was angry, but looking back, maybe it wasn't so much with you, as with the way things didn't work out like I thought they should. Yeah, maybe you could've been home for dinner more often, but the business took a lot to get on its feet. I knew that. But you were there when it mattered, Jed, and you were, *are* always a great dad." She winced. "I should've told you that sooner and I'm sorry."

Abbie and Ewan stared at their mother and then back to me.

Abbie spoke first. "Jesus, Dad. You might have been away a bit when we were growing up, but when you were home, you were there a hundred percent for us. I always knew I was important to you. That you loved me."

"What she said." Ewan looked aghast and threw up his hands. "And just when you think your parents have their shit together."

Tamsin snorted and we shared an amused look. Then her expression grew serious once more. "So, what happened with Nash?"

My face must've said everything because she was out of her chair and sitting on the stool at my side in a second. "You sent him away, didn't you? Oh, Jed."

"Because of Scott?" Abbie paled. "No, Dad. Why would you do that? Let *me* handle Scott."

"But . . . Bridie—" My voice broke and my eyes closed for a second. "If I thought for one minute that I screwed things up for your family or that I couldn't see her—"

"Fuck that." Abbie joined her mother at my side. "Scott doesn't get to decide what's best for our daughter based on whatever messed-up ideas he grew up with. And if he pushes it, he'll cross a line that I'm not prepared to give way on, and he'll find he has to make a decision."

I cupped her face. "That's exactly what I was afraid of. You love Scott."

Her jaw set. "I do, but what I can and can't live with isn't *your* decision to make, Dad. I think I always knew this day would come in some form. But what if Bridie questions her sexuality or her gender later in life? If I don't clear this up with Scott now, what happens then, Dad?"

Jesus. I hadn't even really got that far in my thinking.

Abbie continued. "Maybe this is Scott's turning point. Maybe it's mine. But if he can't see what's right in this, then he's not the man I thought he was under all that family baggage. I'm going to hope I was right about him, but if I'm not, then I'm better knowing now." She stared at me with fire in her eyes, and I couldn't have been prouder, or more worried.

"Well, damn. Go sis." Ewan regarded his sister with something like awe and she elbowed him in the ribs.

"Watch it. I might end up living with you."

His smile dropped in horror. "I've heard couples' therapy can be beneficial."

Abbie sighed, her smile fading. "I sure hope so. Because that's gonna be high on my list of suggestions."

Oh god. "Abbie, I—"

"It needs to happen, Dad. Either Scott starts talking about this shit with me or he does it with someone else, or we both go."

I pulled her into a hug. "I'll do anything you need."

She pulled away and side-eyed me. "You can start by making up with Nash. Which reminds me." She rolled her eyes. "My boss, Dad? Really? Man, this better get me a better teaching timetable." She winked. "I still can't believe it."

Heat burst across my cheeks. "Yeah, he's way too good for me."

"What?" Abbie frowned and kicked me in the shin. "He is not. He's bloody lucky to have you. But I have to say the rumour mill had him down as a bit of a player, so it's kind of surprising. The fact that it's been you to tame him is blowing my mind. Didn't know you had it in you."

I had to smile. "I think he'd say the same about his previous history. And I'm gonna pretend I didn't hear the rest, oh ye of little faith."

Ewan's eyebrows drew together. "Maybe I need to have a word with him. Lay down the rules."

I laughed, and the sound of it shocked me. "Much as I appreciate your concern for my virtue, I think I've got this." That was, if Nash agreed to give me a second chance, and there was zero guarantee that would happen regardless of his open invitation at the end. I'd hurt him just hours after saying I loved him. Hardly the best start to a relationship.

But I wanted him back. That much was sure. I wanted him in this house, in my bed, and in my life.

"You deserve the best," he'd said.

And for once in my life, I agreed.

But the best for me was very definitely Nash Collingwood, by a fucking country mile.

It was late afternoon by the time we'd reheated breakfast and patched up our family enough for Neil to drive everyone home. Abbie had texted to check on Bridie, and Scott had answered civilly, so that was a promising start, and I left Abbie and Tamsin to discuss Abbie's options if things didn't go well when she got home—Tamsin making sure Abbie knew that she and Bridie had a bed if they needed it.

I wanted to shake some sense and a whole lot more into my son-in-law, but I was increasingly being made to realise that wasn't my place, even if the father in me found it almost impossible to take a back seat. I guessed we were all learning to do things differently. But a text from Abbie forty minutes after they left to tell me she was home and that she and Scott were at least talking gave me the smallest glimmer of hope.

That done, it was my turn to set things right with Nash and I wasted no time in getting in the Merc and heading out into the storm. After an irritatingly slow drive through pelting rain, I finally pulled into the visitors' car park in front of Nash's apartment, my hands shaking on the wheel, my heart jumping in my chest.

I unbuckled my seatbelt and peered up at the third-floor apartment, the wiper blades offering interrupted moments of clarity. But it was impossible to tell if Nash was home simply by staring at the front door. Go figure. His car wasn't in the outdoor car park, but I knew there was also covered residents' parking around the back, under the building, so that didn't help either.

Maybe he'd gone out? The idea unnerved me. After all, that's what he'd done to cope with bad days before I came along. He went out and got laid. The thought curled sourly in my stomach, but I let it go. I had to, or I wouldn't be able to leave the damn car.

Black thunderclouds sat heavy over the apartment's roofline, and huge puddles of water jumped and popped with the splattering rain. It was hard not to take it as an omen, but I swallowed down my nerves.

I took a long, deep breath and blew it out slowly. *Showtime.*

I clambered out of the car, a blast of icy rain-needled wind slicing across my face like razor blades, a loud rumbling crack of thunder making me duck. *Jesus Christ, what the fuck was up with this weather?*

I made it through the torrent to the stairwell without hurling, so that was a plus, but as I climbed, I was hit by memories of the first time I'd followed Nash up those stairs, eyeing his arse and wondering what the hell I was doing. In contrast, I knew exactly what I was doing right then, and I made it to Nash's door more determined than ever.

This couldn't go wrong. I wouldn't let it.

Which would've all been nice and dandy if he'd been home. But when my third press of the doorbell went unanswered, I figured I was wasting my time. Deflated didn't even begin to cover the defeat I felt, the opportunity missed, and I stared at the door like I could will it to open.

"You know where to find me if you change your mind." His last words to me.

I played with my car keys in my pocket and then pulled them out to stare at the most recent addition. I looked at the door, then back to the key.

Fuck it. I was going to take his words for the open invitation I hoped they were. I used the key he'd given me and let myself in. After all, he had to come home sometime. And if he brought someone with him, I had no one to blame but myself.

I did a quick sweep of the apartment just to make sure, the last room I checked being Nash's bedroom. I hesitated before stepping over the threshold, the memories hitting like a punch to my chest as my gaze swept his unmade bed and landed on my black merino flung in the bottom of his wardrobe.

I stared, knowing it hadn't been there when I'd left. Nash's wardrobe was practically colour coded. I was always apologising for messing up his impossibly tidy apartment, and he was always telling me not to be concerned—that I was loosening him up, that he liked seeing my stuff in his space. But the other night after we'd burned up the sheets, he'd picked my jersey up from the floor where I'd dropped it and draped it over the chair.

Seeing it sitting in the bottom of the wardrobe said far more than I was ready to hear. My heart squeezed and I slumped on the mattress, running my hand over the cold sheets that reeked of Nash's clean scent. Three nights ago, we'd shared this bed, and just the thought of it tore at my heart. I blinked back the tears and blew out a sigh.

This was getting me nowhere.

I stood and headed to Nash's bathroom for something to take the edge off the thumping headache behind my eyes. The door was closed, and I hesitated, like something in me knew. I finally pushed it open and . . . froze.

The room stank of cologne, the floor awash in glass and so much misery, I could barely breathe. My hand went to my mouth, and I fell back against the jamb, trying to take it in. *This was my fault.* My gaze tracked the room, the towels strewn on the tiles, my toothbrush by the wall, Nash's alongside.

And that's when I saw it—the small Christmas present with my name on it. The only thing left in place on the vanity.

I stretched out a hand and turned it to read the tag.

For Jed.

Although nothing will ever smell as good as simply you in my arms.

Nash.

Oh god. I slid down the door until I was sitting on the floor and let the tears come again.

How long I sat there railing at myself for the idiot I was, I had no idea, but I eventually dragged my sorry arse back up the hall and onto the couch in the lounge.

But when Nash still hadn't appeared a few hours later, and with the rain no more than a wet kiss on the pavement and the city lights blurred and dancing on the other side of those enormous glass doors, my confidence in his return had taken a hit. I sat in the dark, a half-drunk beer in my hand, staring at a night sky curtained in cloud and devoid of stars.

I thought about calling him, but it didn't feel right talking on the phone. I settled for a text. **I miss you.** It was all I could risk until I laid eyes on him. Until I knew. I didn't tell him where I was in case he decided not to come home.

He never replied.

Outside the glass, the wind kicked up again, a cool wash sneaking through the tiny gap in the sliders I'd opened to freshen the room once the rain eased. Goosebumps popped on my skin as I lay on the couch waiting for Nash, but I didn't have the energy to get up and close it. Instead, I drew Nash's blanket around my shoulders and kept my eyes glued to the front door, willing Nash to walk through it. Willing him to give me a second chance.

He didn't, and it wasn't long before my eyelids drooped with the weight of the watch and the excruciatingly long and arduous day. Abbie woke me briefly at ten with a text to say that she and Ewan and Bridie were bunking with Tamsin and Neil for the night. That she and Scott were taking a couple of days apart to think. My heart clenched, but as Abbie had so clearly pointed out more than once, it wasn't my problem to solve, so I set it aside to worry about later.

I needed Nash to walk through that door.

Then I could worry.

Then we could both worry *together*.

I hunkered down on the sofa and pulled a cushion under my head to wait.

But he never came home.

CHAPTER TWENTY-TWO

Nash

I MISS YOU.

I stared at Jed's text and tried desperately to wring something more from it. Did he mean he missed me but nothing had changed? Or did he miss me and realise we'd made a mistake? Or did he miss me and want to talk? Jesus Christ, it was driving me nuts. If he wanted to talk, he'd be lucky if I didn't wring his bloody neck first for putting me through hell.

Of course, the fact that I was so late in finding the damn thing didn't help. Jed had sent it hours before, but I'd been in such a state by the time we got to Devon's that I'd left my phone in Devon's car and then thought I'd forgotten it back at the apartment. A few beers didn't help, although Devon had cut those off way too early for my liking, and I was annoyingly sober. I only discovered I actually hadn't left my phone behind at all while Devon was driving me home. I'd replied immediately to Jed that I missed him too and asked if we could talk.

No reply.

"Will you stop staring at that thing?" Devon growled. "He's probably asleep. It's been a wreck of a day for both of you. He'll still be there in the morning."

I was pretty sure I'd have exploded from frustration by then. "He wouldn't text if it wasn't hopeful, right? That has to be a good sign."

Devon shot me a sympathetic look but didn't answer.

I groaned. "Wow, thanks for nothing."

He sighed. "He might just want to tell you how things went with his family. He cares about you. He knows you'll be worried. I just don't want you to get your hopes up. The good news is he's keeping the lines of communication open, so at least you'll get to say what you want to, just not over the bloody phone, please. Don't be like those idiot students of yours."

"Have a little faith," I said loftily, as if I hadn't considered that very thing just minutes before. A little distance was a whole lot safer for my heart.

Devon's expression didn't need interpretation. *Do you think I'm an idiot?*

Enough said. And I was still staring at my phone when Devon drove through the car park and pulled up right outside the main entrance of my apartment building. At almost midnight on Boxing Day night, other than the foyer, the building was almost in darkness. At least it wasn't raining.

"Get some sleep, Nash." Devon patted my knee. "You need to be fresh if you're going to talk to Jed in the morning. And okay, yes, I think his texting you is probably a good sign."

A ridiculous smile burst over my face. "It is, isn't it?" I gave him a one-armed hug. "Thanks for everything. And I'm sorry I didn't come to you when all that shit went down with Jeremy back in the day. I think I was just embarrassed by the whole getting-dumped-by-a-younger-man thing. And maybe a bit of older-brother arrogance. But you're actually all grown up and shit, go figure."

That made him smile. "Get out before I'm forced to tell you I love you too." He shuddered. "And I'm still younger and way better-looking than you are. You forgot that part."

I snorted and wagged my finger at him. "Pushing fifty, bro. Catching up fast."

He winked. "But I'll *always* be younger. Now go get some sleep."

I got out, skirted a huge puddle shimmering in the dim foyer lights, and watched Devon drive off into the dark. Then I made my way up to my apartment, the weight of the day finally sinking into my bones.

My brother was right. I desperately needed sleep. I needed to get my thoughts together. To plan what I wanted to say to Jed. I might only get the one chance to state my case, and I was damn well going to make the most of it. I wanted Jed in my life, and I wasn't giving him up without a fight.

I dropped my jacket on the hall table, squinting in the dimmed light, which I'd clearly left on. I made it halfway to the kitchen before I caught sight of the large shape sprawled on my sofa, a blanket pulled up to the thick silver scruff on his beautiful chin.

Jed.

Oh god. My knees almost buckled. Jed. Thank Christ.

My heart leaped in my throat, but I didn't move. I needed a minute to drink him in as he slept, rejoicing in the sight of him back in my apartment when I thought maybe I'd never have that again. He looked . . . exhausted and deeply asleep—a slow rhythmic rise and fall of his chest, his mouth slack, his eyes quiet behind heavy lids.

He looked . . . so fucking beautiful.

I found my legs and quietly made my way across to where he lay unmoving, every step closer a soothing balm to the gut-wrenching emotion of the day. None of it mattered because Jed was here. In my apartment. Asleep on my couch. Waiting . . . for me. It meant something.

I miss you.

"I missed you too," I whispered, smiling down at him. "Look at you. It's like Goldilocks all over again." I gently touched his hair and smiled. "Or maybe that should be Silverlocks?" I was almost too scared to wake him. Asleep like this, we still had a chance. Awake, I would have to hear whatever it was he'd come to say, and there were no guarantees.

A lick of cold southerly air curled around my ankles, and I turned to find the patio doors cracked open. I laid the back of my hand on Jed's cheek and frowned. He was cold. "What were you thinking, baby?" I tiptoed over to close the doors and then returned to take a seat on the coffee table in front of the sofa, intending to gently wake him.

Jed beat me to it, croaking, "I was *thinking* that I might've made the biggest fucking mistake of my life." His eyelids fluttered open, and those blue-grey bombshells scanned my face, nervous, maybe even hopeful. "And I was kind of hoping it wasn't too late to change my mind . . . if that's something you think you'd be interested in?"

Interested in? Had he lost his damn mind?

Before I could answer, Jed groaned and pushed himself up on one elbow, bringing our faces almost within kissing distance. "And FYI, this couch isn't great for my hips." He winced. "We're gonna need to do something about that if I'm going to be staying here more often." His eyes landed on mine and he waited.

More often. My heart thumped against my ribs, but I couldn't seem to get any words to work on my tongue and Jed's hopeful smile faded.

"I'm so sorry, Nash." His eyes clouded. "What I said to you, especially after everything we'd said to each other before they arrived, I . . . I don't have any excuse for—"

"What the hell are you talking about?" I slid to my knees and cupped his face. "It was me who fucked up. You were in shock, and I was trying to logic our way out of it, which was never going to work. They're your kids, Jed. Of course you were upset and angry and scared, and I shouldn't have pressed. I should've simply told you that I loved you and that I wasn't about to be pushed away no matter how hard you tried. I *want* this, Jed. I want *you*. I want it more than I've wanted anything, maybe ever. And I'll do whatever it takes to give us a chance."

"It wasn't just you." Jed rested a hand over mine still cupping his cheek. "I should never have allowed Scott to talk to you the way he did, and in my house. I let you down and I'm so ashamed—"

"Shhh. It's okay." I brushed my lips across his, just the barest touch, just to reassure myself he was really there. Then I rested my forehead against his. "I'm fifty-three years old, Jed, and I'm in love for the first time in my life. So if you need to cool things between us for a while until Abbie and Scott can sort their stuff out, then that's what we'll do. I can wait. If you need me to keep my distance when Bridie is around or hold back on the PDA stuff, I'll do that too. We'll do what needs to be done. I want *all* of what's important to you in my life, and that includes your family. I want to sit with you on that front deck of yours when we're older and greyer and neither of us gives a shit if we can get it up anymore."

He snorted.

"We'll sit with great-grandkids on our knees and watch the white horses race across Wellington Harbour. I'm in this, Jed. One hundred percent, and we'll cope with whatever compromises it takes to get us there, because we'll do it together. And also, you're not going to be sleeping on the couch, sweetheart. Just saying. You'll be with me, as close as I can get you. If that's something you think *you'd* be interested in?"

Jed's eyes danced over my face and then he bridged that distance between us and softly pressed his lips to mine, just the faint slide of his tongue along the seam of my mouth. No pressure, no need, just . . . there. Letting me know. Promising things I'd thought I'd lost. And when he pulled back, he cradled my face, his lips hovering just in front of mine as our eyes met.

"I want that too, Nash. So fucking much. I've been thinking a lot about a future with you. Not so much the not-being-able-to-get-it-up part of it—I can wait a lot longer for that. But having someone to share my life with. Someone to laugh and complain with about how our kids are raising our grandkids. Having the time to encourage you in the value of insect repellent so we can explore much more of this big brave outdoor world you avoid. Maybe even travel some. I'll even net in that front porch just for you. Although I'm still working on the idea of parking a BMW in view of my workshop."

I chuckled and kissed him.

"But—" He chased another kiss, more lingering this time. "God, you taste so good. Come here, I need more of that." His tongue swept through my mouth. "Mmm, better. Now where was I? Oh yes. The BMW." He sighed. "How about I do up a car for you?" He snorted as my eyes blew wide.

"Really?"

"Really. But you have to help, to learn, and there'll only be a select few options to choose from." He side-eyed me. "I won't have my man driving just any old thing."

My man. The words did silly things to my heart, and I felt fifteen all over again, hearing someone tell me they liked me in that more-than-friends way for the very first time. Knowing I mattered.

Maybe firsts felt the same no matter when they happened in life.

Jed shook his head and brushed his thumb over my lips. "Are you even listening to me?"

I nodded soberly. "Absolutely. No piece-of-shit cars. Got it. Heaven forbid." I took his hands and threaded our fingers together. "But I want to revisit that *our*-grandkids thing, because I definitely like the sound of that. Jamie and Brian might even grace us with a few more, you never know."

Jed's eyes sparkled sapphire in the light from the hall. "The more the merrier. Now . . ." He put a finger to my lips. "You need to let me say what I came to say tonight. Sorry for just walking in uninvited, by the way." He flushed pink to his ears.

"I told you to come if you needed, and you came. And I found you all curled up on my couch like my own silver-fox Goldilocks. The cuteness overload was real." I pressed his hand to my heart and looked him in the eye. "It was the best Christmas present ever. No apology needed."

"Thank you." His eyes crinkled and his mouth tipped up in a beautiful smile. Then he sobered and took my hands in his. "But I still haven't finished what I came here to say."

"Okay." I took a breath. "I'm listening."

"This morning, I got scared. I think I just fell back into that familiar way of thinking I had before I met you. Be reliable. Be safe. Be there when they want you, even if you're not really needed. Don't want too much. Be happy with a less-than-fully-lived life. Make up for how you failed. Be the support act, not the main event."

"Oh Jesus, Jed." I cradled his face. "You are so much more than any of that."

"Tamsin and the kids were furious when they found out I'd sent you away."

I sent him a wry grin. "I always knew your family was smart."

He huffed and went quiet for a moment, and I waited, sensing . . . something. Eventually, he drew breath and spoke again. "But I've learned something this last month. I don't want to be just the support act anymore. I've found out I can do that with my eyes closed. And I'm not that selfish younger guy I used to be. I deserve to be a main event in my own life, and hopefully one in yours as well, if you're interested."

I kissed him softly. "You already are. You and me. Side-by-side headline acts."

"Yeah?" He smiled brightly and my heart filled. "I can't guarantee the audience reception."

I kissed him softly. "Fuck the audience."

He laughed and slid his arms around my neck. "Silver-fox Goldilocks, huh? There might be an X-rated rewrite in there somewhere."

I got to my feet and pulled him up and into my arms, burying my face in his neck to breathe in that sharp, sweet mix of machine oil and engines and soap and everything Jed. He groaned and arched against me, his cock filling alongside my own.

"You know—" I nipped along his jaw to the soft lobe of his ear. "—in the original story, the bear finds Goldilocks in his bed, not on his sofa, so you went a bit off-script there. I think we should redo that part for the sake of accuracy."

Jed chuckled, then took my mouth in a hard kiss, almost pulling me off my feet as he backed me against the patio door and fucked his tongue so deep into my throat he left me gasping for air. "Well, if accuracy is an issue—" He groaned against my shoulder as he pulled the neck of my T-shirt down so he could suck a mark. "—then need I remind you—" He ground against me as he sucked, and oh yeah, I wasn't going to make it to the bedroom if he kept that up. "—that Goldilocks—" He licked back up to my nose where he placed a kiss on the end. "—was a girl with golden hair and a woeful disrespect for private property." He drew my lower lip between his teeth then let it pop free. "Not a fifty-five-year-old man with grey hair, a dodgy prostate, and the worrying development of singularly long hairs sprouting on his back."

I jolted back and stared at him. "Really? Since when?"

He flushed a deep crimson. "Well, it's not like I study my back on a regular basis, but today, seeing me in my . . . *towel*—" Jed rolled his eyes. "Abbie and Ewan took great delight in enlightening me of the development. Abbie even offered to pluck them."

I choked out a laugh and he scowled.

"Thank you so much for your support. Anyway, on the basis of that, you may want to rethink the whole boyfriend thing."

I laughed and spun him around. "Oh. My. God. I have to see." I ripped his shirt up his back and stifled a chuckle, because yes, there were indeed a few rogue silver tresses.

"Okay, so how bad is it really?" Jed glanced over his shoulder with a hopeful look.

"Well," I said, keeping my tone deadly serious. "I'm sorry to inform you that we're definitely looking at silverback gorilla potential.

And there's possibly decent sweater material to be had as well. If you pass me a set of needles, I can get right on that."

"Fuck off." He tried to jam his shirt back down. "Just because you have a back as smooth as a fucking ice rink. No one warns you about this shit."

I wrapped my arms around his waist and pulled him close. "Honestly, there's no more than three . . . okay, maybe six . . ." I grinned. "Ten, absolute tops."

His lips flattened in a thin line. "I hate you."

"No, you don't. And I fucking love them. They're you, Jed, and they're sexy."

He stilled. "Really?"

"Really." And I meant every word. "I love your body. Every grey hair, every glorious wrinkle, all those bumps and bangs and scars you carry from the cars you've worked on. And I love how you're teaching me to be okay about mine as well. But if you really want them gone, I'm sure we can make that a fun game." I dropped my hand from his waist down to cup his solid dick. "I'll pluck one for every orgasm I give you this week." I stroked him firmly through his shorts. "Now let's rewrite Goldilocks in a way Robert Southey never imagined in his wildest dreams. And I think we both know who's going to be the bear."

"You're such a little shit."

"And you love it." I grabbed his hand and went to tug him down the hall, but he resisted, pulling me back around to face him.

"You know, I learned something else today."

"Mmm?" I brushed my nose against his. "Do tell."

He leaned back just enough for me to see his face, and my heart stuttered at the glisten in his eyes. "I learned that the best version of me is the one that's loved by you. And I'm so fucking sorry it took almost losing you to realise it."

"What a coincidence." I pulled him close and brushed my cheek over all that gorgeous silver scruff. "The best version of me is the one that's loved by you as well. Maybe we both had a lot to learn before we were ready for each other."

He pulled back and stared at me. "I think you're right. It's taken me fifty-five years to be ready for you. I'm a slow learner."

I chuckled and ran my finger down his nose. "Then it's just as well I'm an excellent teacher."

"Promises, promises."

I nipped his nose. "Get into that bed, Goldilocks, and you'll find out."

EPILOGUE

Jed

IT FELT STRANGE.

A New Year's party without the usual family celebrations hosted by Abbie and Scott. But I was trying to look on the bright side. One of which was definitely the shirtless silver-fox hottie currently stringing fairy lights across my backyard. Nash wore a wide-brimmed hat, a pair of Abbie's oversized pink sunglasses, which she kept at my place, and enough insect repellent for an expedition up the Amazon. He also had the sexiest fucking smile whenever he looked my way, so there was that . . . and the shirtless thing . . . Had I mentioned that?

Another bright side was that Nash and I had accepted the temporary hosting rights for the New Year's party instead . . . as a couple. Something I was still getting my head around. It had been a last-minute decision that felt oddly monumental. Like we were making a stand, staking our claim on each other.

Our two friendship groups and families—minus Scott and Bridie —were coming together for the very first time and many people had changed their plans to make sure it happened. The support was both humbling and reassuring, especially in the wake of recent less-than-positive reactions.

I'd had my own batch of freshly unearthed bigots to deal with.

I'd worked overtime to get Tom's Oldsmobile ready in time for his daughter's wedding, only to have the arsehole arrive to pick it up and walk in on Nash and me with our arms around each other, laughing at Rollo trying to convince us that he'd known about the two of us ever since that first day in the workshop.

Tom had taken one look at Nash and me all cosied up and proceeded to treat us like we were last week's trash left out in the sun, harrumphing around the workshop with a half-sneer nailed in place. He refused to shake Nash's hand and was barely able to meet my eyes. He took the keys to his Olds and drove off with barely a fucking thank you for the effort I'd put in to get it ready in time. And a day later, two of our mutual friends pulled their cars from my books.

Fuckers.

I tried not to care, but there was no denying it hurt. I'd known those guys for twenty-five years and had rebuilt engines for each of them at mates' rates. In response to Tom's fuckery, Nash had run me a bath in my huge clawfoot tub and climbed in behind me, wrapping his legs around my waist and washing me head to toe while he shared a few of his own war stories. It helped smooth the edges of a rejection I doubted I'd seen the last of. But as much as the week had confirmed some of my deepest fears about coming out, I couldn't find too many fucks to give, not with Nash curled around my body every night as we slept.

Rollo, bless him, furious on my behalf, had added a five-percent arsehole tax to Tom's final bill before emailing it out. It was too late by the time I found out, and although I tried to be mad, I burst out laughing instead.

Nash and I had been pretty much inseparable since Boxing Day, something my arse could definitely testify to. Calvin Klein might've been an excellent Christmas gift from Nash to me, but the dildo I'd bought him to use on me with the aim of building up to bottoming for the first time had put me way ahead on the boyfriend leaderboard pinned on my fridge . . . Don't ask. I wasn't quite ready to take him yet, but I was getting close.

And as for the rest of my family, Abbie and Bridie had yet to move back into their home, so Bridie was flitting between her parents —a little confused as to what was happening but happy enough. And Abbie and Scott were still talking, a fact which buoyed my hope for their relationship. Scott also hadn't dismissed the idea of talking to someone professionally.

But when news of the events had trickled through to Scott's family, his father had weighed in on the matter with some less-than-savoury comments to Abbie about Nash's and my relationship, which created a teensy bit of a setback. I wasn't sure how I felt about being the subject of ignorant speculation and bigotry, but there wasn't much I could do about it.

Abbie visited me most days, bringing Bridie with her if I was on my own. Keeping Nash out of the picture if Bridie was there wasn't something that had come from Abbie *or* Scott, but instead, it had been Nash who'd suggested it. He wanted to keep things as clean as possible, at least in the short-term, so that the focus stayed on Scott and Abbie and our relationship didn't aggravate things unnecessarily.

To say I was less than happy was an understatement, but I could see his point . . . for now. But my patience was coming to an end, and I was determined the new year wasn't going to start with any more homophobic bullshit. I wanted Nash front and centre in my life and that included with Bridie. I was done catering to my son-in-law's bigotry.

Ewan and Nash were also slowly getting to know each other. The day after Boxing Day, Ewan had given Nash *the talk*, wanting to make sure Nash looked after me properly and kept it in his pants. I wanted to throttle my son, even if Nash thought the whole thing was hilarious.

And in between all the goings-on, I was doing my best to get my head around the fact of being out and having an actual fucking boyfriend for the first time in my life.

At fifty-five.

"All done." Nash's hot arms slid around my waist as I stood at the kitchen sink finishing the last of the salads.

I wasn't sure I'd ever get used to the way my heart tumbled every time he did that. "Mmm, you're boiling hot." I spun in his arms to run my fingers through the growing nest of silver-threaded curls sprouting on his chest and then immediately recoiled when a waft of insecticide hit me full in the face. "Good God," I choked. "Agent Orange has nothing on you."

He snorted and displayed his arms with relish. "But not a single bite."

"I'm not surprised." I cleared my throat in an attempt to breathe again.

He winced. "Point taken. I'll go shower."

"Wait." I grabbed his hand and glanced at the clock. An hour until the guests arrived. Time enough. I could handle a little insecticide. "Come with me." I pulled him roughly from the kitchen and down the hallway.

He laughed, jogging to keep up. "Where are we going? We passed the bedroom, by the way."

I shot him a less-than-amused look, which he shrugged off with a smile. "Just saying."

"Hurry up." I tugged him through the front door and along the path toward the workshop.

"Jesus, what's the rush?" He laughed and goosed my bum and I jumped.

"Quit that," I grouched, grinning like an idiot as I dropped his hand to key in the code of the workshop door. It swung open and I yanked Nash inside, locking the door behind us.

Nash glanced back at the door and then at me. Whatever he saw in my eyes brought a slow, sexy smile to his face and he stepped in close, putting his lips next to my ear. "Oh, I think I like where this is going. You've been scheming, you devious man." He pressed a trail of kisses down my throat. "I'm all hot and bothered just imagining what you've got planned."

I couldn't help but smile. "Turn around."

He pulled back to look at me. "Okaaaaay." He spun slowly in place, a soft gasp of delight breaking his lips as he laid eyes on the Mustang, which I'd parked inside the workshop just that morning. "Jed?" He looked over his shoulder. "This had better mean what I think it does or my dick is gonna hate you forever."

I chuckled and made my way past him to where the Mustang sat with a plush rug thrown over its hood, lube and condoms just to one side. I patted her gently. "Forgive me, baby."

Then I started to strip.

I'd made it as far as dropping my jeans to the floor when Nash grabbed my hand.

"Oh no you don't." And then he took over, slowly peeling me out of my briefs and T-shirt with care, and a wonder in his eyes that sent my legs to jelly. He peppered my body with kisses from neck to hip to thighs.

And then he got down on his knees and pulled me close, swallowing my half-hard cock down his throat in a single long, slow slide. He was so fucking good at that, and I barely recognised the groan that rumbled up my throat as my dick filled and pulsed under his skilful ministrations. But the minute my gasps of pleasure got hot and heavy, Nash pulled off, grabbed me around the arse, and hoisted me up onto the hood of the car, laying me flat with a hand to my chest before taking my cock in his mouth once again, sucking and licking until I was writhing and panting and desperately trying to hold off flying over the edge. Then he slowed and I caught the snick of the lube cap just seconds before a slick finger made its way up my crease and slid unceremoniously into my hole.

"Oh fuck."

He chuckled around my cock and then pulled off to nip along the underside—a personal favourite of mine—while a second finger found its way into my arse. I groaned and fisted the rug, trying not to think of the paintwork as Nash continued to masterfully work my dick. But this wasn't how I planned coming, for either of us, and the minute I felt that tingle in the base of my spine, I shoved at his shoulder.

He groaned and lifted his head, and a pair of unfocused beautiful brown eyes landed on mine, his lips thick and swollen. His fingers slid free, and Nash kissed his way up my body to my mouth where I sucked his tongue greedily inside and feasted on the taste of me filling his mouth.

"You gonna finally fuck me over this machine, baby?" He licked a stripe up the side of my face, and good lord, I prayed we had time for a shower before people started landing on us.

"You better believe it," I whispered against his hair. "That is, if I can get my hips to work. This isn't exactly Posturepedic material."

He laughed and helped me stand. It wasn't until then that I realised he still had his board shorts on while I'd been buck naked in the middle of my workshop, sprawled over my Mustang. And okay, that was a hell of a lot sexier than I'd given it credit for. I pulled at the ties on his shorts, ripped the Velcro open, and in two seconds, they tumbled off his slim hips to the floor, leaving nothing but skin.

"You never said you were naked under those." I stepped forward and cupped his hard cock, giving him a couple of solid tugs, which earned me a filthy groan in reply.

"God, yes." His forehead dropped to my shoulder at the same time as his hands found my arse and tugged me close. "Fuck, that feels good."

I tightened my grip, making sure to give a decent twist on the upstroke while sweeping my thumb over his slit, which I knew he loved.

"Too close," he muttered. "Fuck, I'm too damn close."

"Good." I flipped him around and pushed him face-first over the

Mustang. "You're driving me crazy and there's no way my tongue is touching an inch of that toxic shit on your skin."

"Charming." He chuckled and leaned forward, his arms spread wide across the hood, his feet on the ground, his beautiful arse there for the taking. He looked over his shoulder and winked. "Ready?"

"Like you wouldn't believe." I slicked my fingers and draped myself over his back, finding his hole by feel alone to slide one finger inside.

"Oh fuck, yes." He pushed back, then forward, as I added a second finger for good measure.

"I have a condom if you want," I offered, watching him fuck himself on my fingers. "But if you don't, I'm more than okay with that."

He stilled for a second and looked over his shoulder. "Are you sure?"

"If you are."

His grin widened. "You'd be the first, and that's exactly how I want it."

I was pretty sure my heart exploded in my chest.

"Come on. Don't make me wait." He turned and widened his stance, rubbing himself against the side panel of my baby to a soundtrack of filthy fucking groans. I'd never be able to wax that spot again without blushing.

I slicked my dick and stood between his legs, finding his hole and following the gasps of his stretch as I pushed in slowly, advancing every time he bore down until I was fully seated, and he was moving his hips in tiny circles while I struggled for control.

"Jesus Christ, if you don't quit that, this is all going to be over far too soon," I warned. "You feel too fucking good. Hot as a furnace and so slick. No resistance. All you. Nothing but you. Damn, Nash, I want you to feel this too. Soon. I'm gonna give you this soon. Fuck, this is amazing."

"Quit talking and just move, will you, before my stiff cock puts a dent in your girl." Nash butted his arse back into my groin to make his point, and I laughed.

"Don't you fucking dare." I pulled almost all the way out before slamming into him just as he liked. It did the job of shutting him up, although I almost came on the spot. Being bare inside him made everything . . . more . . . just . . . more and had me so close that I wasn't going to last. Him either, by the strangled groans and expletives falling from his mouth.

"Harder." He moaned into the blanket, edging back off the car just enough for me to get my hand around his cock. I stroked him hard and his arse clenched on my dick, ratcheting up the pleasure for both of us.

"Oh fuck!" He tensed and threw back his head, grunting and spilling into my hand, through my fingers, and down the alloy wheel. I might've groaned at the sacrilege if I weren't too busy following him over, pumping deep inside while my body shook and heaved, pleasure flooding my veins along with a bone-deep gratitude for the man beneath me.

The man who filled my heart.

"Oh. My. God." I collapsed over Nash's back, pressing baby kisses to his hot, sweaty skin, anywhere I could reach. "Fucking cat's pyjamas. Happy New Year, baby." I drew my hips clear, just enough for my cock to slide free, and then stood to stretch the kinks out of my back.

He winced and froze, still spreadeagled over the hood of the Mustang. "Man, I hate that part," he grizzled.

I trailed both hands down his back and over that beautiful arse, then slid fingers into his still-wet crease. I eased his butt cheeks apart and marvelled at the sight of me trickling from his body. It stirred something deep in my soul, something powerful. I stroked him gently from hip to thigh. "You are so beautiful like this."

He groaned and looked over his shoulder. "I love that I'll carry something of you inside me tonight."

"Me too." I patted his arse and moved back so he could stand. "I may need to check on the state of things again later."

He chuckled and levered himself up off the hood. Then he turned and cradled my face, his legs noticeably wobbly. "All those people around, and only you and I will know what we did here. It'll be our secret." He kissed me, sliding his tongue into my mouth and his arms around my waist. "And when they all leave, I want you to open me up and take me again, just like you did now. Fill me until I'm fucking stuffed with you."

Goddamn. I gripped his dark grey waves in my hands and took his mouth in a blistering kiss, shoving him back against the car door until he groaned and melted against me, slowing the pace to a tender skirmish, a gentle meeting of lovers, a promise of a life to come.

"As hot as that sounds," I whispered into his open mouth, "by midnight and after a few beers, I'm not at all sure I'll be able to live up to those expectations of yours."

"Good point." He nibbled at my lower lip. "Let's take a rain check, or—" He waggled his eyebrows. "—we could make use of a bit of blue help."

I snort-laughed and tucked a few locks of hair behind his ears. "We're pathetic, you do realise that?"

"No. We're practical."

I stared at him, lost in the way his brown eyes caught the harsh light of the workshop and seemed to dance just for me.

"Move in with me." I startled myself, and certainly Nash whose eyes flew wide in response, but the shock didn't last long, the rightness of the idea nestling into my soul in a heartbeat. "Okay, so maybe not tomorrow or even next week, and keep the apartment, of course, if you want." I searched his blinking eyes. "But let's do it before the new school year starts in February. We've barely been apart in three weeks and I know it's fast, but we're not exactly kids and—"

"Yes."

I froze, staring at him. "Yes?"

A smile burst over his face. "Yes. Before the school year starts in February. Yes."

I sucked in a shaky breath. "Well, okay then. So that was easier than I thought."

He shook his head, chuckling. "You mean you actually planned that?"

"Yes. No. Kind of." I shrugged, feeling the blush rise in my cheeks. "It just feels right, doesn't it?"

"Yes. So very right." He reached down for my clothes and handed them to me. "And the answer was easy because it's you. I want this. I want us."

"I want us too." I straightened my shirt and leaned in to kiss him. "I love you, Nash Collingwood."

He cupped my face and kissed me a second time. "I love you too, Jed Marshall."

The smile in his eyes made my heart soar, but the state of the rest of him was dubious at best. Me too, for that matter, and as I looked down between us and took full stock of the situation, I flinched. "But I'm not sure if the fact we love each other will save us if we get spotted looking or smelling like this. You take the shower first. Beauty here needs a bit of TLC before I leave her."

Nash rolled his eyes. "The other woman. It could be worse, I suppose. But if I catch you jacking off on her, we're gonna have words."

I laughed and shoved him out the door before turning to my girl. "Yeah, I know, but he grows on you." I patted her hood, took a look at my less-than-pristine alloy, and grinned like a fool.

An hour later and our back lawn was flooded with guests happily chatting under Nash's fairy lights and enjoying a fresh summer breeze, fragrant with ocean salt and the last of the jasmine. Standing at the kitchen window, I watched as Nash handed around plates of food, laughing and talking with my family and friends like we'd been together for years.

"He fits you like a glove." Tamsin joined me at the sink and followed my gaze.

"He does, doesn't he?" I turned and kissed her on the cheek. "Thanks for your support, and for encouraging me to take a chance with him."

She smiled fondly. "You're welcome. You deserve to be happy."

"I think I do too." My gaze slid to Abbie and Ewan, talking quietly beside the vegetable garden. "I worry about Abbie and Scott though."

Tamsin watched Abbie and sighed. "Me too. He's a stubborn man."

I shrugged. "Well, if nothing else, New Year is a reminder that every day is an opportunity to do something over, to make a different choice. And it's not just for that one day in the year. Every. Single. Day. is an opportunity to change direction. Let's hope Scott recognises that before it's too late."

Tamsin snorted in amusement. "How very profound of you. How many beers did you say you've had?"

I zipped my lips and she laughed. Nash turned his head at the sound and his mouth curved up in a huge smile. Then he winked and ran his hand suggestively down his hip, and heat rushed into my cheeks.

Tamsin looked between us and rolled her eyes. "Do I even want to know?"

"I wouldn't advise it," I warned, turning my head at the sound of the doorbell. "Take this out, will you?" I handed her the plate of sushi I'd been getting ready. "It'll be Rollo. That man is never on time."

Tamsin took the plate while I headed up the hall and opened the front door with a flourish and a very loud, "Happy New Ye—"

The sight of Scott with Bridie in her best party dress at his side cut me short.

"Poppy!" Bridie launched herself into my arms. "Happy New Year. Daddy said it's a party. Can I come?"

Holy shit. I blinked. Looked at Scott. Looked at Bridie. Blinked again, then looked back to Scott. "I, um . . . y-yes. Of course, sweet-heart. Absolutely." I put a big smacking kiss on her forehead and set her down. "You're the best New Year's surprise ever. Mummy is in the backyard. We have fairy lights and lots of food. Why don't you go find her?"

"Okay." Bridie raced up the hall, leaving Scott and me facing each other, the veil of tension between us thick enough to slice with a knife.

"Wow. Thanks for bringing her." I studied him warily, not sure what to expect. He looked about as uncomfortable as I'd ever seen him and twice as nervous.

"Scott?" Nash's voice startled me, and when I turned, I saw him waiting cautiously at the far end of the hall. "Are you okay, Jed?"

I nodded. "I'm fine . . . so far." I turned back to find Scott studying Nash with a lot less hostility than the last time they'd been in the same space, and the breath I'd been holding shuddered free, and the fact he hadn't said anything yet seemed oddly encouraging. "Would you like to come in?"

Scott's gaze darted past my shoulder and up the hall to where Nash stood watching. He shook his head. "I'm not sure if . . . I just thought I'd drop Bridie off. I, um . . . To be honest, I didn't think I'd be welcome." His gaze shot again to Nash, who said nothing, although I could sense him moving closer.

I took a few seconds to digest Scott's words and what they might mean, because he was right. It was very, very tempting to simply accept his no and close the door. But I didn't, of course.

"Well, that depends," I began. "I'm assuming by the simple fact you're here at all that we won't be having a replay of last week. This is my home, Scott. And Nash is a part of my life. He's not going anywhere, and I won't have you talking to him or anybody else the way you did last week. I love my family, *all* my family, including you. And I love Nash. I won't let you come between us."

Scott's eyes widened at my declaration and his gaze darted again to Nash, although more considering this time. And then Nash was there right at my shoulder, his warm hand resting on the small of my back. A show of solidarity. I wasn't alone.

A peace settled in my heart.

"Scott?" Abbie's voice came from the end of the hall, and I turned and held up a hand, asking her to wait. She gave a quick nod and stayed where she was.

Scott's gaze flicked to his wife, the colour on his cheeks darkening to a burnt blush, and when he turned back to me, there was a determination there I hadn't seen before. He took a deep breath, his eyes steady on mine.

"I know you'd never do anything to hurt Bridie, Jed. I know that you love her just as much as we do, and I'm sorry for what I said. Contrary to popular opinion, I'm not a total arsehole." He glanced over my shoulder to Abbie. "Well, at least most of the time." His lips twitched and I looked back in time to see Abbie smile.

"Thank you for that." But I needed more, and so I waited, letting the silence grow between us.

Scott's gaze dropped to his feet like he was trying to find the right words. I didn't press, secure in the knowledge that Nash was right there at my back. Regardless of what Scott said, Nash and I would be okay. We'd get through it. My family would get through it.

Finally, Scott looked up. "I—" He swallowed hard. "I'm not going to pretend that I understand . . . this . . . thing . . . between you." He looked between Nash and me and then sighed. "But I get that I might've . . . *did* overreact and that I haven't exactly been open to the idea of different . . . relationships . . . over the years. And it's been pointed out to me that with Bridie getting older—" He glanced again to Abbie who gave him a sharp nod to continue . . . "Well . . . maybe it's time. I'm not sure if I can ever be what Abbie seems to think I can . . . but I'm willing to try . . . and to be open and . . . respectful. That's all I can promise."

It was enough and the squeeze of Nash's hand on my waist let me know he thought so too. The breath whooshed out of my lungs like I'd been holding it all fucking week, and maybe I had.

Scott heard and gave a half-smile. "I'm sorry, Jed. Nash."

"Apology accepted," I replied and turned to find Nash nodding as well. "So, maybe you'd like to come in and get yourself a beer?" I waved Scott into the house and he walked straight past and into Abbie's arms at the end of the hall. She held him tight and stared at me over his shoulder, her eyes glistening with tears as she mouthed the words, "Thank you."

"Mummy, Daddy, they've got marshmallows . . . and a fire . . . and everything." Bridie ran up and slung her arms around her parents' legs. "Come on." She tugged on her father's jeans and Abbie steered them all out into the backyard.

I closed the front door, hearing the reassuring snick of the lock like a welcome full stop on the best and worst week of my life. Then I turned and slumped against it, my legs shaking as I thanked every deity I could think of for the gift of a little common sense.

Safe hands caged me against the old oak as the shadow of Nash's warm, familiar body, redolent with soap and fresh hope, fell over me like a shield. Brown eyes glinted gold in the setting sun that pierced the bevelled glass, and dimples as deep as the heart that owned them smiled down at me.

"That was a good thing you did." Nash's mouth found mine in the sweetest of kisses, but it wasn't enough. I chased his lips when he pulled away, needing more, circling my hands around his neck until he gave it to me, wanting his courage, his steadfastness, holding tight as he pushed me up against the door and held me in place, letting me know I was his.

And when my tears were done, he set me on my feet and kissed my cheeks dry. Then he cupped my face. "Are you ready to do this thing, sweetheart?"

I grinned and patted his cheek. "Abso-fucking-lutely. Start your engine, baby."

The End.

**Want a glimpse of Nash and Jed down the track?
Sign up to my newsletter and download a
BONUS SECOND EPILOGUE**

To sign up to my newsletter and download the bonus second epilogue
click HERE.
or copy this link https://bookhip.com/MQFTJBV

If you are already signed up, you can download your bonus epilogue
via the same link and you will not receive a second newsletter.

Join Jay's reader's group Hogan's Hangout for updates, promotions,
her current writing projects and special releases.

Thank you for taking the time to read

FOXED

If you enjoyed Jed and Nash's story please consider taking the time to
do a review in Amazon or your favourite review spot. Reviews are
hugely important for spreading the word. Thank you in advance.

Have you read Jay's Southern Light's Series yet?

**POWDER AND PAVLOVA
by Jay Hogan**

Southern Lights 1

ETHAN SHARPE is living every young Kiwi's dream—seeing the world for a couple of years while deciding what to do with his life. Then he gets a call.

Two days later he's back in New Zealand. Six months later his mother is dead, his fifteen-year-old brother is going off the rails and the café he's inherited is failing. His life is a hot mess and the last thing he needs is another complication—like the man who just walked into his café,
a much older...
sinfully hot...
EPIC complication.

TANNER CARPENTER's time in Queenstown has an expiration date. He has a new branch of his business to get up and running, exorcise a few personal demons while he's at it, and then head back to Auckland to get on with his life. He isn't looking for a relationship especially with someone fifteen years his junior, but Ethan is gorgeous, troubled and in need of a friend. Tanner could be that for Ethan, right? He could brighten Ethan's day for a while, help him out, maybe even offer some... stress relief, no strings attached.

It was a good plan, until it wasn't.

REVIEWS OF POWDER AND PAVLOVA

"... (Ethan and Tanner's) romance is a gorgeous slow-burn, full of chemistry that fizzes and pops every time they're together on the page. Powder & Pavlova is charming, sexy and poignant; funny at one moment, heart-breaking the next, and I loved every minute of it."

—All About Romance Reviews

"A love story evolves that will make you swoon and just fall in love again!"

—Love Bytes Reviews

MORE BY JAY HOGAN

AUCKLAND MED SERIES

First Impressions

Crossing the Touchline

Up Close and Personal

Against the Grain

You Are Cordially Invited

SOUTHERN LIGHTS SERIES

Powder and Pavlova

Tamarillo Tart

Flat Whites and Chocolate Fish

Pinot and Pineapple Lumps

STYLE SERIES

Flare

Strut

Sass

PAINTED BAY SERIES

Off Balance

(Romance Writers New Zealand 2021 Romance Book of the Year Award)

On Board

In Step

STANDALONE

Unguarded

(Written as part of Sarina Bowen's
True North—Vino & Veritas Series and published by Heart Eyes Press)

Digging Deep

(2020 Lambda Literary Finalist)

Foxed

AUDIOBOOKS

The following are available in audiobook format from most audiobook retailers

Auckland Med Series

First Impressions

Crossing the Touchline

Up Close and Personal

Against the Grain

You Are Cordially Invited

Painted Bay Series

Off Balance

On Board

In Step

Buy direct from the author here on Authors Direct.

Audible

Apple Books

Barnes & Noble

Chirp

ABOUT THE AUTHOR

Jay is a 2020 Lambda Literary Award Finalist and the winner of Romance Writers New Zealand 2021 Romance Book Of The Year Award for her book, Off Balance.

Jay is a New Zealand author writing MM romance and romantic suspense primarily set in New Zealand. She writes character driven romances with lots of humour, a good dose of reality and a splash of angst. Jay has travelled extensively, lived in many countries, and in a past life she was a critical care nurse and counsellor. She is owned by a huge Maine Coon cat and a gorgeous Cocker Spaniel.

Join Jay's reader's group Hogan's Hangout for updates, promotions, her current writing projects and special releases.

Sign up to her newsletter HERE.

Or visit her website HERE.

CPSIA information can be obtained
at www.ICGtesting.com
Printed in the USA
BVHW050317140123
656266BV00008B/500

9 781991 104045